AN OLD WOMAN'S LIES

by

Belinda E. Perry

AN OLD WOMAN'S LIES

Belinda E. Perry

Published in 2012. The author may be reached at sajaluckey@gmail.com The website is waluckey-west.com

Author's photo by Karen Nord

to all my friends, young and old, who have enriched my life; thank you

Belinda E. Perry

ONE

Life begins the process of dying. This is not morbid but fact. Not a lie but a sturdy, indomitable truth we hide from, invariably try to dodge it, blithely live our days until the first dying. For some it comes too early, often so early we never are aware of its course through our lives, only stories about 'when your late…' added to a tale of a stranger we might remember from a picture but nowhere else. For others it comes at the fragile time of life, when we are thinking outside our own needs and notice the lives and the pain that others experience. Then the lie is to ourselves, born in that first comprehension of the distant end of life; death.

Seventy years is long enough. And having lived those years after seventy, they uphold my initial statement. But then according to everything we're told, it isn't up to me or you how long we have to endure. Sad when you think on it, the last years can be unforgiving of how you spent the first. A doctor told me recently that the almost literal starvation of my childhood has affected my entire life – I could have told him that. But what he meant was that poor nutrition early in life leaves the physical self open to more serious problems later on. And I am now living my 'later on' years.

What I have after all these years are stiff joints, a cranky mind and lots of unendurable memories. These might be considered an odd choice of words but for the truth of the matter, which is that most of life is unendurable and yet we endure. Too well if you ask me; we're overrunning the planet, a species that doesn't know when to quit. I told you I am cranky. I will tell you exactly what and how I feel if you're interested, and if you aren't, then don't bother with the next several hundred pages.

We can't help most of what happens to us, starting with our birth. If I'd had a say-so, I would have asked not to be born at all, or certainly not at the era when I was born. In the Dust Bowl and the Depression – now tell me would any sane being choose such a place and time for entering the world and beginning this life. Dust all over me, I can remember it,

5

don't you laugh, but that sense of being covered with birth matter and blowing dust went right to me, made me itchy and got me crying. My early fussing of course had my poor mother thinking I was going to be a colicky baby from the start when all I wanted was to scratch at that damnable dust and be clean, warm, dry, and fed. I still have those dreams and wake up scratching and wheezing and the nurses here think I'm having a fear or panic attack as they call it when all I'm doing is remembering far back to more than I want to remember. We were more fortunate than most born or living to that time; the winds and most of the dirt went east of us, tearing up Texas something terrible. We suffered without water, and damn but I remember that dust. Until I learned too many years later how awful it was for most other folk.

Now do you want to guess at the lie in the above statement, or is there a lie. A fact of life I want you to accept from the beginning is that no matter how hard we struggle with our base selves, we lie. Every one of us, even those sworn to tell the truth. I'm not talking little white lies like 'yes dear, that was so wonderful last night' version, although such a statement must be said thousands of times each and every day throughout the world. It is a lie, no doubt, but not a damaging lie except for the woman or other lover, who must abide by their spoken falsehood instead of asking for what they would like in bed, here, there, a different touch, a new angle. Ah yes, right from the beginning sex is involved. How could it not be, it's what brought us all here together.

Did you determine the lie this time? It is so obvious I would be embarrassed for you if you didn't see it. And I won't continue to ask, you must read these words knowing some are true, some are obvious lies, some are designed to confuse you. Sort of like living.

My family was already so poor we hardly noticed when the Great Depression hit. Food was scarce, blown out of the county by the dusty winds, so a drop of millions in a city market wasn't much by our standards. We couldn't eat those dollars, they were all hot air if you ask me. I barely remember the blowing dust, excepting when I was first born. Later, when that huge black cloud like no one'd ever seen before came over the land, we were at the edge and that was bad enough. I heard the stories and don't want to tell them since there's enough folks written down what happened, and even a book or two of history that told all our miseries, making us humans instead of stick figures that East Coast folks called foolish for wanting to stay on our land.

No lies there and no lies intended.

There were two older sisters in my life, the youngest born twelve years before me, the older one thirteen years ahead. As if I had two aunts taking care of me, not sisters. Mama always told me I was her gift, her special surprise. As I got older I learned a bitter truth about such babies. We were surprises all right, Mama was forty when I was born and certainly neither she nor my papa expected another child. It was her old woman's lie, about me and my birth, that started me thinking this way as I aged and had too much empty time.

My birth name is Roberta Ellen McClary or Runt as my sisters called me. I was born in the small eastern New Mexico town of Coolidge, which isn't there any more. Not even a dot on a map or a sign on a road, 'Coolidge, pop 3' or some such notation of the lives of those few who managed a sort-of living. We were at the mercy of a wind came all the way from eastern Kansas and eventually blew us the hell off the map.

You look on a map, you'll see where we were. It's labeled 'Kiowa National Grasslands' now, but it was home to us for a few important years.

Coolidge was a raw farming community, based around a spring that kept flowing no matter how dry the summers were. Not enough water for irrigation though, we dry-farmed, which was the reason we didn't survive. But there was always water to drink, to wash your face, to take that Saturday night bath. Of course the relentless wind eventually filled up the spring and it's not there, except for way underneath a huge sand mound, covered under the dry grasses that exist in such deprivation.

Eventually friends called me Remi, from of course Roberta Ellen McClary. Not a pretty name but better than Runt, and I certainly wasn't going to be called Roberta. Ellen, no, far too plain and I was a wild and adventurous child.

See the lie there, bet it surprises you. I promise I won't do this again, prompting you to seek an underlying, different message in the words I wrote.

Life terrified me, for no particular reason except I believe it was being birthed in the wind and always lived with the ghost of a newborn, of that terrible sense of suffocation. No air, nothing to breathe and I struggled with this the rest of my life. Mama told me that before my first year was up I was in the local hospital to Clayton, a small ten-bed affair where they studied me and watched me but there sure wasn't much to be done. There were no machines yet that could help me, no incubators for a deprived child.

I remember a nurse sitting next to me, patting my hand and murmuring funny sounds, a clear memory of her face with its crooked nose and hairs around her mouth. By all standards this was not a pretty woman, but she remains a face and manner I seek out in acquaintances and lovers. Which isn't too bad since those features would serve fine on a man.

Mama's face is always pale in the early memories; I have little recollection of Papa at all those years on the small farm. Which as sister Rosie tells me is reasonable since he was out working the fields. I didn't know better then so I came to hate him as a young woman; now, thankfully, I have compassion for what he must have endured to keep his family alive.

I also learned that Papa fought in the Spanish-American War, a horrible affair too far south where men struggled through absurd foliage to recover an honor we had given up; an excuse for war, self-congratulation, and territory. You realize of course that all this editorializing comes from studying history at a much later date. At the time of my early schooling, such an attitude toward that war and dear old Teddy would be considered treason.

Belinda E. Perry

You figure out where I lied, don't matter to me, I know what I know.

Papa was a McClary from Texas, he told us there's a town named after him in that state some place. Now I ain't never been there but it is on the map and who knows, our family might have been fancy enough at one time to name a town, or have it named for them. I won't quarrel with Papa's memory on this one, I used to nod and smile for him and he'd shake his head as he told me it was the god's truth.

Now god is another matter where lies come in handy. I came to the decision when I was maybe five that god doesn't exist except in books and people's need. You might think that heavy for a child, for me it was simple logic as I got forced every Sunday to attend a small church about two miles from home. We walked, of course, the mule too precious to waste on a journey our feet could manage. Took our shoes off and carried them so the soles wouldn't wear out any sooner than necessary. I got Rosie's hand-me-downs and took extra care warning her not to wear out my shoes. She'd hit me, on the way to church mind you, and Mama would hush us in god's name and we'd glare at each other behind her back.

Betsy was long gone by then. If I was five, she would be eighteen and when she was sixteen she married a neighbor boy, Fred Wiggin. Mama told us they was in love; Betsy had her a baby eight months later – an old lie don't no one bother about anymore, which is why I'm telling it to you. See how easy it is, to lie and smile about the lie and base your life around it. Mama brought Betsy and the baby home to us when Fred went north on the threshing crew.

I smiled and cooed, now that's a horrible word, and patted that baby, my nephew it was, and told my family how beautiful he was and hated him every minute since I wasn't the youngest no more.

I won't bother asking but you get the idea.

9

AN OLD WOMAN'S LIES

Back to god - I didn't see this as a child when I made my decision but what I learned later, some of it the hard way, was that mankind needed a god even if there wasn't one. No matter the beliefs, some of them so complicated and laughable that it would have been near impossible to worship in that particular church, humans needed to know the why and whereof and most of what we are isn't knowable so they invented god.

Science thinks it has the answers but only to a few of the unanswerable questions, and even those answers are constantly changing. What we know can only be defined by what we know, which is absurd if you think on it. I take the stand that we don't need to know everything, what's the point since the knowledge can change and then we're stuck with beliefs that don't make sense. I studied on all this as a child, and I've talked and listened and read as an adult and nothing's shifted for me.

We need answers, we need to know who we are – says who. 'Find myself' is one of the excuses too many use to walk away from their responsibilities. Hell, lady, grab your own ass and pinch down and you'll find yourself all right. You'll know exactly who you are and where you stand. On the floor or level ground if you have any sense to you.

I got all the way through two months of first grade, a few years of home-learning on a ranch, and much later talked my way into a year of college and finally some highbrow professor said I was a rarity, a practicing existentialist. I had to ask, he expected me to, and the answer is still pleasing. I believe in what is, here, now, not yesterday or tomorrow, not no big-time religion or possibility but what I can do and fix and taste and spit out.

 If I don't need a reason or explanation for why the stars hang in the sky then I don't fret on why they don't fall. They're there, any fool can see them, so who put them there, well it can be your star god or a universal god or a stick of cinnamon or who the hell cares.

Hell is a different discussion.

Belinda E. Perry

One thing about believing such matters, it gives me more time to work on what is rather than fretting about what might be or can't be or is coming or isn't here yet, or already went by and I didn't notice.

A man I knew in a college English course told me not to look at anything about the history surrounding a story but to simply read the assignment based on the words inside the printed page. I told him he was plumb full of it. Nothing can be discussed, digested, dissected without knowing the history, the time and place. My whole life was blown to hell by wind; do you think ignoring the Dust Bowl or the Depression would change what happened. And a whole lot happened because of those evil twins; don't go thinking my date of birth and the closeness of my death would be the same without them.

No lies in that paragraph except for the dumb fool man who tried to convince me history wasn't worth the effort.

It's a scientific fact, for once I agree with them, that nothing lives in a vacuum. And for certain sure folks don't get born, live and die without what swirls around their lives and distracts them from their own wants and possibilities. I once almost married a man who was trained as a pianist, and had to give up that training because his family fell on hard times during the Depression. You think his changed plans weren't based on history? Then you don't understand how the world revolves.

You getting the idea that I have an opinion about everything, you're right, except maybe reality television and shopping malls. Some things in this world don't need an opinion, they're there, like an outhouse, used but not discussed. You want to try something unique, use a shithouse in a high wind.

It may be occurring to you about now that I have a foul mouth. Not really, at least not all the time, and I can behave in public, mind my manners as Mama taught me, use the right fork and the correct adjective, but there are times and places which deserve the flat end of a shovel. Do you remember I spoke on shopping malls and reality television?

Probably at this point I could tell you about me, not my mind, you've been getting pieces of it, but give you a physical glimpse of this old lady, what she started out being, then the progression to sainthood as an old crone. Mama had shiny red hair, Papa was mostly bald with a black fringe, and he had the lightest blue eyes I ever seen. From a distance you could think he had holes where eyes were meant to be, black lashes and then a pale shine. Eerie, weird, my friends were scared of him when he got in a mood. Which meant when he was quiet and not out to the land picking up rocks or sighting down what was left of his fence.

Papa grew corn and beans enough we could eat, and he worked a trade with a local rancher for a cow, milk and beef if she calved out. He was a smithy too, had a shop to the back of the barn and folks brought him busted wheel rims and bent plows and he pounded them back into shape or built a whole new rim, an extravagant activity I watched with awe. Pulling shape out of lumps, flattening hard immoveable metal to go where he wanted. He could judge the rightness of his work by lifting the new strap or hinge and eyeing it, smiling as he put it down or frowning as it needed a few more hits to bend the offending item into final perfection.

He worked enough as a smith to pay our taxes and keep us fed. Folks from fifty miles came to bring him work; without his skill we would have been part of that long line on its way to California.

I know, I been digressing but you have to see Papa first, then Mama, before I make any sense at all

Mama's name was Didia and her family had come from northern New Mexico. She was descended from a man named Maxwell and there had been a whole lot of land in his name that no one owned any more. She tried to tell us about her family, she made up little stories when I was a baby to let me know how important her great-great I forget grandfather was, but I didn't listen. It didn't matter for we were literally dirt poor and what had been lost way in the past had no value in our daily lives.

Belinda E. Perry

Papa was Eben McClary, like I told you or weren't you listening. A McClary from Texas. He met Mama and my oldest sister was born pretty close after the wedding so obviously marriage was the only honorable thing for them to do. Papa was a farm boy with big ideas and good skills as I already told you, and an honorable service in that Spanish War. He missed the WWI engagement, being a new father, and having served previously. He was lamed from some encounter he never explained, and already too old at thirty.

Of course I looked at my parents and learned about sex and thought oh no they never did that and then I grew up a bit and watched Papa, saw him pull Mama to him when we weren't meant to be looking. I knew though, I'd come in their curtained-off room one night scared out of my mind 'cause Mama was making noises and I got to see the act and knew before I was ready just how damned foolish it looked.

Now I ain't saying nothing about how it felt, just how it looked.

Here's another time you might be squeamish or delicate and don't want to hear what I have to say. Good time to close the book, or maybe take a risk and see what life's about. If you're still fussy about sex, you sure ain't had much of a life. Now I don't know and can't imagine and refuse to speculate about why women don't like sex. That don't say I don't understand if you've had a brother come at you or your own pa, it ain't right, and those men know it. They cover their tracks with promises and talk about you being special and you asked for it you slut, words I wouldn't hear from my own pa 'cause he was so taken with Mama and she with him that the rest of us were the result, and not of any interest except as being their children.

And there is a knowing about such relations, an instinct from our distant past, that such breeding cuts into a species' survival. We know, man or boy, child or woman, that related sex is wrong. Which is why children from such houses are troubled; they know through the past and it goes against what they are being told. 'Collective Unconscious' it's called in the books, a fancy term for knowing certain absolutes. Killing, eating your own kind, sex with your baby – we know these are wrong.

Hell even animals don't practice such behaviors, 'cepting a few species where the males eat the offspring of another male to bring the female into season. Makes sense if you think on it but it sure isn't nice.

I knew from the beginning that we were additions to the family and not the core. We weren't why they married even though the two older girls were the cause. They wanted each other, often as possible in the beginning I suspect, then later when the wind and the poor wore us all down, they were safety and sanity for each other in that bed, which was nothing more than a filled sack of hay and straw. It was their bed, with a curtain to keep us out, a place for them to have one moment of love in a loveless world.

That night I crept in from fear and fretting and saw my mama's legs wide apart on that rustling bed. Her eyes were closed, her mouth huge and she was moaning, soft as she could but that sound jumped out of her each time Papa moved into her and I mean into her. From a ways back, he would glide forward and jerk upward and Mama moaned and I hadn't ever seen nothing like it.

I stayed to watch knowing it was wrong; again instinct tells us things and we ought to listen. Papa moved quicker and quicker and finally Mama bit down on her own hand to stop the moans and he grunted, face against hers, mouth to her neck, at her ear, licking sometimes, then his backside hunched and he bucked like a bee-stung billy goat and Mama she lifted him with her own hips and he collapsed on her and I thought he'd hurt her somehow but she let go biting her hand and kissed the side of his face, sucked on his neck till I thought she'd gone mad.

It was one hell of an education that night. I was maybe four, Betsy and Fred and little Hammie had moved to Oregon, looking for work in the lumber mills, Fred being from there originally. He had an uncle told the two of them, with the baby, that Fred could make a decent living to a CCC camp cutting down trees and the missus and baby, they could stay to the uncle's back room. I wondered about that when I got older, the uncle was a bachelor, wonder how he coped with a woman and a

14

squalling child in his house. Don't like to think on it, and I never got the courage to ask my oldest sister those few times we met up later.

You notice I haven't told a lie for a while or weren't you watching? And I won't tell one now. What I saw my parents doing made me feel strange and achy, you all know the feeling whether you like sex or not. It's a common human response, nothing to be shamed by, a big part of who and what we are. It's how each and every one of us got here, no other way no matter which fable you were told.

We never had pets, couldn't feed them, so I never saw sex before, not like so many farm kids. No dog or cat to educate me and even the cow got led to the neighbor's ranch and Papa wouldn't let us go with him. Said we had chores, and we always did. See, no lies from Papa. He never talked about what got done to the cow and we never asked and wouldn't of believed the answer if he had told the truth.

Rosie now, I suspected she'd known all about sex but she wouldn't tell me. Too young, she said, and I bribed her for more with promising to tell what I'd seen with Mama and Papa.

It surprises me still that she wouldn't take the gossip, wasn't interested. I asked her once when I was sixty-three and she was seventy-five, by then I figured we could talk about such things. I asked why she didn't want to know way back then and she blushed if you can imagine. Told me and I still don't know if I believe her. Lies from your family are the toughest to root out, except when it's from a child and you know the truth from a lie by their expression.

Rosie said she was afraid of sex and thinking that her mama and papa did such a thing horrified her. I got up from my chair and went over to Rosie and put my hands on her shoulders. She looked up at me, tears in her eyes and I had to ask again, and this time maybe she told me the truth.

Seventy-five and my older sister finally tells me the truth.

TWO

The house was near railroad tracks and the truth of that changed her life. Mama named her Rosie, not Rose or Rosalind but Rosie because when she was born her hair was pink. Later on it turned a fine red, but when she was born her hair was pink like little roses.

After Runt was born, Rosie would go down to the tracks and sit there, on the small ridge which ran parallel to the tracks, listening for the trains and not hearing her mama call. That squirmy yelling smelly little thing back at the house was ruining her life. Despite the blowing dirt and the shattering noise, Rosie liked sitting to watch the trains. They gave her a sense of maybe going someplace.

She was tall for her age, everyone told her that. Gawky was a word she heard one teacher use and she looked it up. They had a dictionary at school; Mama and Papa didn't have a book to the house excepting the bible. The summer she was twelve, Rose grew two inches and sprouted nubs for breasts and a few twigs of reddish hair at her joined legs and under her arms.

She waved at the men on the trains, the engineer and the brakeman, she knew what they were called and what their jobs were, for her best friend at school Minnie's father was a brakeman, and sometimes he got the engineer to pull the horn when they passed and Rosie knew it was just for her.

She was often the only living thing in sight, a thin child hunched up, legs curled, short dress unable to cover her underpants and bare feet but she never knew that. The men who waved back were the hobos seated in an empty freight car. With the door slid back, three or four of the men would sit at the opening, legs hanging over the fast rails. They would wave, and sometimes hoot and cheer, and she would wave again shyly. Unable to distinguish the exact words, she thought they were being kind.

The land wasn't much, only miles of yellowed grasses, tall as Rosie when she was a baby. Now that she was taller, she could always see where she was going. Literally as she sat and watched the trains, she could see their farm disappear; loose dirt blowing since Papa had plowed and dug up and smoothed it for crops.

Mama watched her during the summer months and kept reminding her she needed to wear a bra but there were no bras her size in the house and no money to buy one. This seemed to be the biggest sorrow Mama had, and it made her cry sometimes, at least Rosie would find her crying with the runt held to her tittie and it got Rosie mad enough she wanted to hurt her little sister, which was what drove her to the trains in the first place.

It all came back to Runt and her appearance in their lives. Betsy was all broody and mother hen with the baby so when Rosie made her opinion known, Betsy threatened to tell Mama and Rosie tried to pretend what she'd said wasn't what she felt at all.

Rosie'd told lies before but Mama always knew; Betsy thought she was Mama sometimes but she didn't know, and Rosie saying it was just a joke seemed to let her older sister forget what'd been said. It was a way to approach the outside world, to tell a real truth and then pass it off as silly. This behavior seemed to be expected from a girl.

The train was Rosie's dream; sounds of distance and going, a motion she rarely experienced. A mule pulling a buckboard didn't take a person too far, certainly not at speed. She'd seen a few automobiles, they came along the dusty rutted paths and the driver would sometimes wave. Their village didn't own a car among them, over fifty souls wrote Coolidge as their hometown and none of them ventured much past Clayton and perhaps to Raton if they took the train and not many folks could afford such luxury. Not in these times, as Papa constantly told them.

Rosie wanted to be gone; her private music was in the power and flashing lights of the train beast. Her heart quickened with the distant rumble, her belly opened, her legs went weak and forced her to sit curled into herself, sometimes she wet her pants and she would cry from humiliation and a wild unexpected loss.

Still each time she could get away, she came to the trains.

SHE EVENTUALLY LEARNED that there was a crossing maybe a half mile down from her favored perch, and on occasion the train would grind to a halt and she could venture near enough to touch the hot metal slats, the splintered wood siding, and even once the brakeman spoke to her, warning of the men who rode the trains. It came naturally to stand close to him as he told her, and eventually his hand rested on her arm and the tingling warmth of touch was what she'd been missing. He said his speech all over again, then shook himself like a dog and took his hand away and asked her how old she was. She lied and said fourteen and he answered in that case she should know better than to flirt with a stranger. She wasn't quite sure what he meant, but it was fun to smile and see his face turn red.

He carried a peculiar smell, of grease and something raw that made her want to lick her mouth, touch each corner with her tongue and taste whatever it was.

At home, Runt cried a lot and kept everyone awake. Mama took the baby into bed with her to keep her quiet but still her thin wailing cut through sleep and the night. Rosie wanted to take the little thing outside and leave her in the barn with the roosters and chickens and the mule but even she knew the suggestion would get her in trouble.

It wasn't that she didn't love the baby she wanted to tell them. It was that the crying hurt, way deep inside. It couldn't be good for the baby to want so much and not be able to point or grab or reach for what it was.

Mama's tittie couldn't offer enough of what Runt needed, not with too little food and all the dirt. Rosie feared for bearing children since she knew she'd marry of course, and have a brood of her own. No other life was imaginable out here; she would be a farmer's wife, a dutiful helpmate in the kitchen and in bed. She was terrified by this future; there was only thin joy in a man and a farm, children, wind, tall grasses and the echo of the train. She knew that from watching her Pa work too hard for so little, and the worry that made her mother thin down to nothing, deep lines changing her beautiful smile.

There had to be bigger places and that's where the train would take her.

BRANSON HEMMINGS CAUGHT her at the tracks once; he was a boy from school, a year older but in her grade; a big boy with fat hands and muscled legs and a head overflowing with white-blond hair. Rosie despised him. He trailed her to the ridge, to her private spot on the banking near the tracks, and sat behind her only a short distance away. Bran said nothing but he was there. Mute and solemn and a pain in the behind and she wanted to turn on him and yell at him to go away. Common sense told her the boy would like that so she hugged her legs to her chest and when the train went by, this one slow, long, not stopping but the creak and whistle and moan was enough, she heard the calls from the hobos in their open cars and she smiled to them, took one arm away from her knee and waved.

"Don't you know what they're yelling at you, girl?" Branson's squeaky voice inserted itself into her mind, tearing apart her world. "You don't know nothing." He laughed at her; "They're looking at your skinny legs and bony ass and calling you names." He was standing next to her now, to her shoulder and if she looked up it would be his knees and legs in raggedy pants cut down from his own pa's castoffs she'd see. Nothing decent a girl would want to notice.

She made the mistake of talking back to him; "They're more my friends than you'll ever be."

He bent his knee and pushed her shoulder and she spilled over onto her side. Her first thought was to rise up and screech at him but instead she rolled onto her back and let herself lie there, on the spiky ground, looking up to his face against the sky, his chest wide, head bent to look down at her.

Then he stepped over her, a leg on either side of her skinny legs and his pants were bunched out where his legs joined. She'd seen that before, in the boys running after her sister.

She bent one knee and kicked up between his thighs; he jerked back and coughed and stood off her like she wanted. It pleased her to stay on her back, legs apart now, hands pulling at the grasses. Another train would come along soon, the 7:15 from down to Roswell on its way north and west to where she'd never been.

There was no hooting and calling when the train passed her going too fast, a rush and roar, the kind she liked, going to get there sooner, faster, a long high whistle to let her know she'd been seen and the train was gone.

So was Branson, he didn't come back to punish her again. She almost missed him.

ONE NIGHT WHEN RUNT was a year old and Rosie was thirteen and still going to the tracks, to watch and wave, bolder now, tall and pretty her mama told her, that night the train stopped. It wasn't the usual stop and there was a car loaded with those casual drifters sitting right in front of her.

Two of the men slipped off the car, another stayed seated but yelled something at them. They shook their heads and crawled up the slope to where Rosie sat. She didn't move, held her legs to her chest and felt the night air on her private skin as she smiled at the men so eager to greet her.

One of them was young and he held back, the older man was skinny and had a fuzzy beard and wore patches and tape-bound shoes, a shirt might have been white when it was made. Even downwind she could smell them. The boy was scrawny too, figured it would be so from traveling like they did.

"Missy you make this trip a pleasure. Mind we sit with you?" She wanted to say no but he'd sat down, not too close, and the boy hung around to his back, away from her, not looking at her like the man did. "May I ask your name?" He had manners and she felt safe enough so she finally twisted her neck to see his face clearly.

There was a sore at the edge of his mouth, and a knot of hair pulled back over his collar, held tight under a flat-roofed cap like she'd seen in a magazine. It wouldn't do no good out here in that cap, the sun'd bake your neck and ears crispy.

"Rosie", she said after a minute's deliberation. He flinched; "Huh?" "Rosie's my name." He pulled off the cap and she wished he hadn't for he was bald and freckled, not smooth and clean and a place to kiss like Pa but with open sores. "Ma'am. It's a pleasure." And when he put the cap back on she let herself take a breath again. He sure wasn't much to look at but he was polite. "You born here, Miss Rosie?" "No place else." "Sure is pretty. Like you."

There was nothing pretty about old grass and blue skies she could see, it was all she'd ever seen. There had to be more in the world, like lots of trees and rivers and big towns and dresses in store windows that she knew about only from pictures in books from school.

She glanced at the man, who seemed to be sitting closer to her. The boy behind him grunted, "Yeah" and the man placed a hand on her exposed knee. She shivered; "You like that huh?" He rubbed his hand up and down the inside of her thigh, close to her panties and she closed

20

her legs and he grunted but his hand stayed with his fingers tucked into the edge of her panties.

"You like that?" She did and told him so and told him too her mama warned her about men like him and he best take his hand away. "Or what, pretty missy? Who you gonna call for help?" The boy grunted several times and his hands were busy at the front of his britches.

A voice called, the man removed his fingers and for the briefest of moments she wanted him to keep touching her. One of the hobos called up to her hilltop; "Eddie, train's going, you get down here quick you two or I'll tell the law to the next stop." The man stood, straightened his pants and the boy was grunting too quickly, a series of short gasps till the man shoved him down the hill toward the rolling wagon.

The train was gone in that slow puffing which gathered speed and echoed her breathing. Her legs twitched and she rubbed her thighs together until the warmed bright light let her melt and she rested against the ground, didn't mind the prickly grass heads or a small bug trying to climb her ankle like a fabled mountain.

It was wrong when the man did it to her with his fingers, it was wrong when she did it to herself, and right when Mama and Papa shoved against each other in the room and told her to go away, go to sleep, leave them alone. She had to get married.

Betsy wouldn't talk about it, even when Rosie got enough courage to tell her what she'd discovered, what she could do in church while setting right next to Mama and Papa. Squeezing and rubbing her legs and getting small bursts of light even as she listened to the preacher talk about the fires of hell and the angels of the Lord. Made the light sweeter sometimes, and in the winter when she was extra restless and couldn't go sit at the trains, she could find the light on her own twice during a long sermon.

Betsy got caught kissing with Fred Wiggin by Papa that spring. Betsy was sixteen and too old to talk with her younger sister. Runt wasn't a part of life yet; barely two she staggered around the house and sometimes escaped outdoors even in the cold or the few spring rains. The damned dust as Papa called it blew endlessly and Runt had a hard time breathing. Mama told the older girls to take extra care of their baby sister.

When Betsy ran away and married, Mama had a sad sort of look. Betsy brought Fred to the house to announce what they'd done, and Papa sort of slapped Fred on the back and offered him a drink of old coffee, which was all they had to celebrate with. And it wasn't really coffee, mostly herbs and leaves with a few beans for flavor. Coffee was one of the things Papa normally took in trade for his smithing, and he'd had no customers lately.

The men vanished, blown out the door by Mama's disapproval and the wind, and Rosie immediately asked Betsy what it was like being married. Betsy patted her on the head and smiled and immediately Rosie knew she would not be told the truth.

"It's wonderful, Fred's sweet, it didn't hurt at all." Rosie looked at her sister, wondering if they were thinking of the same thing. How could it hurt, just rubbing like the boys always wanted to do with her.

BY NOW YOU might be thinking our family was besotted by sex. It's no more true for us than any folks. Think on it, three girls living nowhere, with a hard-working papa and a mama barely keeping her brood fed. Her milk went dry and I didn't like what food got shoved in my mouth. There was a time that third winter they thought I would die.

Yes it's me back on you, speaking my mind and letting you know. The truth, or the lie, always your choice. I came to think Rosie never quite knew what she was looking for down to those tracks, and it seems to me she never found it in her three marriages neither.

That first time hurts unless you and the cross bar of a bicycle or some such protrusion have already made contact. There is a membrane across our opening, piercing it and shoving it aside has to hurt, think about it. Oh the lies we tell. A woman's first big lie, to herself and her daughters or friends is about pain; what women experience as they have their first sexual encounter.

The second big lie is that childbirth don't hurt, at least you don't remember the pain with the miracle of holding your own baby. Now you city and suburban people might take to the lie as a way to get your own daughters fooled into reproducing, but your country cousins have seen the truth.

Even a man can think through the process and recognize that giving birth hurts. Now they might not always be tuned in to what a woman wants, but they're bright enough, most of them, to understand pushing something large and firm through a small space has to be painful.

It was our cow who taught me when I was maybe three and a half. It's for you to remember being that young, when each month was a step to getting older and not being the baby anymore.

Our cow that year lay down hard, with a grunt, not her usual folded legs and careful lowering but a thump that hurt just to hear it. Her tail came up over her back and liquid squirted out her hind end, not urine or that runny slop passes for cow manure but a thick stinking mush even us kids could smell that it was soured.

She grunted, head thrown out, ears flapping, and Papa showed us the muscle twitching across her back and hind legs and then something poked out through her slit and she groaned. Just like Mama did sometimes when Papa was humping on her but this groan got stronger and sadder and more of whatever it was showed in the slit and the cow's neck was all sweaty.

Hooves it was, and a nose, a whole head, and there's no one can tell me pushing pointy hooves and a skull through that part of your body don't hurt. This time it was really bad, the baby got stuck and Papa shucked out of his shirt and told us to go to the house but I stayed by the door and watched him. Rosie was the coward this time, not wanting to see and learn and know the truth. She was still searching for a man to give it to her. Her words, not mine.

Papa put grease on his arms and stuck one inside the cow. She bellowed and tried to get up but he kicked her front leg out from under her and did his own grunting. She moaned, screamed too, and his face got white until finally he pulled his arm free and it came out slick with blood and a pink mess, strings and snot and I don't know what.

The pink hooves and the tiny nose were poking out of her. Papa used both hands this time to pull on them and our cow let out a long moaning bellow like I never heard before. Then she stiffened and coughed. Her head went to the straw on a thump and Papa pulled the calf out, slick like his arms and hands, soaking the straw. He pulled it free and dropped it where it lay flat and motionless.

The mama cow died, the calf lived two days. We ate it, fried in the pan with wild onions and the meat was tender and tasted the worst I'd ever had. Death that way doesn't make for a delicious steak. The mind grabs that picture and scalds each bite. We got us another cow after Papa traded labor for the need.

See I told you about lies. I birthed out two children, and by God it hurt. No I don't remember the pain exactly, we don't remember pain intellectually but with our core. You look at your own blood, tissue separated, wounded to the bone, and you know it hurts.

This is the lie I hate most. Deception of an evil sort, meant to confuse us so we are willing, even eager, to carry on our genetics and our lines. We'd do it anyway; why bother with a lie, none of us don't drive 'cause a car accident hurts; don't you demean women with this foolishness.

By the time I was seven Rosie too was married, although her lover wasn't of the character and quality of Fred. Fred done us all proud with his work, he eventually started his own contracting company with what he learned to the CCC and was important during the second damned war, bringing home enough for Betsy and their five kids none of them went shoeless or had to eat cornbread and fatback for supper five days in a row like we did.

You might take it I ain't none too fond of Rosie's choice. But first you got to meet him the way we all did. It was a hell of a night we first was introduced to Jay Voorhes, my goodness he was a handsome boy.

24

THREE

At seventeen Rosie'd almost stopped going down to watch the trains. Runt was five now and would follow her so the men quit waving and the train rarely slowed down any more. Papa said the economy was better and the line of bums on the boxcars was whittled down to maybe two at an open door, never four or five.

Once in a while when it was hot and Mama let Runt sleep outside under netting, then Rosie could slip free and make her way down the well-defined path to her dreaming place. Out of school now, tall, angular, long red hair and too many freckles, Mama said she would soon enough be pretty, for now she was a witch, long fingers pointed at the ends, legs and knees sticking out below short dresses and elbows banging into doorways, school desks, even the kitchen table.

She'd done it at fifteen with Branson Hemmings and his little thing got hard all right but she barely knew it was inside her and it didn't hurt at all. Branson got into trouble during the last day of school and no one saw him again.

She didn't get in trouble, she wasn't even sure they'd done it, for he slid out of her and there weren't nothing but a tiny dribble of blood and that happened to her every month. There was no one around for her to try again, so she went back to the tracks for a month or two but none of the passing men stopped and came to her.

It wasn't dark yet when she sat down this time, but the distant train had a clear whistle and a loud hum already shook the rails. Fast, she thought, no one to wave at her or slow down to maybe talk. There were lights at the new crossing, a car going to a distant place. She thought about walking the tracks to find out who they were and would they take her along.

The train didn't slow, and the curve here was sharp, the new crossing a blunt set of rails with raw markings. The lights there wavered, started across, she felt the wind ahead of the engine and moved back, frightened, already knowing she was going to witness horror. The train blasted by her, then it screamed and sparks skidded from its wheels and she didn't imagine but knew she heard the train hitting that unseen car going someplace in her dreams.

She ran along the tracks, feeling the lifting heat from the wheels' recent passage, smelling grease, oil, her own sweat, tears on her face. Running. The train had gone on, unable to stop and the car was crumpled to one side; at least it hadn't been caught and dragged. Rosie stopped, put both hands to her mouth and wailed. Nothing could be alive inside there; fenders twisted, the roof flat, a tire resting on the hood, attached to a long metal bar. One tire was exploded; a door lay on its top edge maybe ten feet from the wreck.

He crawled out of the wreck and Rosie was still crying. She watched through spread fingers as he stood, pushing himself up from the ground, then slowly straightening until she realized he was that tall. And unhurt which had to be impossible; he looked straight at her and she finally took a step, another. Until he was close enough she could see the small cuts and scratches that marred his face.

"You come to my rescue pretty lady?" He had a soft voice with the lightest of drawls, and he used a hand to wipe at his eyes, then his mouth. Then he looked to one side where a mound stretched the imagination and became a body. "Damn," was all he said. He took a step and crumpled at her feet and Rosie knelt beside him. If she'd seen his face then, she would have kicked the boy for his playacting but she thought his pain was real.

It didn't occur to Rosie that the mound might be alive, nor did the boy say anything except, "Help me." She responded perfectly, putting her hands under his arms and trying to drag him until his eyes opened and he asked her to wait. He had clear light eyes like her papa, and his hair was curly; her fingers slipped through that hair and she felt the curls loosen then tighten again and she knew she would do it with this man.

He stood leaning on her and they limped and struggled the mile to her family's home. The entry was dramatic, Rosie enjoyed their plunge into the house, her parents' faces upturned and startled. This time it wasn't play-acting, the boy sat heavily in a chair and Mama went for water to boil on the stove and torn cloths, ointment from the barn. "Hurry, Eben, he might bleed out."

Rosie comforted Runt, who'd come in from her nest near the trees and was frightened by the boy's face, all little cuts and quickening bruises. His shirt was torn, hanging off his back and there were more cuts yet nothing was fatal or even serious.

Papa sat and talked while his wife did the mending. "Where you from, boy?" The answer was slow to emerge; "We were coming from California." The boy raised a hand; "I know it's usually the other way but my father and me, we didn't like the living there, we wanted to be back home." The next question came naturally and the answer was just as simple. "Where's home?" "We started out in Arkansas, went west when…all that dust." The boy closed his eyes as a stitch was taken in his shoulder and Rosie's father took that for pain and not deceit.

The boy spoke through closed eyes; "My pa was a smith, if he could get work he was the best. Papa…" That pause again, a studied despair. "He's back there, oh god I left him." The boy's voice rose into that bereaved wail of anguish and heartbreak. "I need to go back." He stood, shoving Mama's hand off his arm, eyes suddenly wild and my, he was tall, Rosie thought. Then she too jumped up; "I'll go back, I'll find him."

Papa's voice settled them both. "Girl you sit." Rosie sat down. He turned to the injured boy; "What's your name?" The boy's head dropped, he mumbled into his chest. "Jay, sir. Jay Voorhes." "Well Jay Voorhes, you set here and let my wife finish her job. I'll harness the mule and go find your pa."

The task was unpleasant but Eben McClary had been in that Spanish war and he knew too well the effect of metal and might against human flesh. That the boy escaped pretty clean also didn't surprise him. He'd seen it all, a horse blown into pieces by cannon shot, a man thrown into the air and come down looking like he was sleeping but deader'n a trapped coyote.

The mule didn't take much to being harnessed this late and tried kicking in protest. Eben only went to the mule's head and took hold of the bit, looked into that narrowed, glaring eye. "Don't blame me, son. Folks' lives are peculiar and sometimes we got to work 'round that." The mule settled, Eben nodded and went back to his fitting the collar over the prickly mane.

The buckboard traveled rough to the tracks. Their house wasn't close enough to the new crossing to bother with the road. It went from Coolidge Center to a big ranch owned by some movie star from

Hollywood who thought horses and cattle and too many acres made him a real-life cowboy. Man couldn't ride...ah hell, Eben chided himself. It wasn't his place to pick on another for being able to buy his dream.

Eben's dream, so much smaller and simpler than the movie star's, was to feed his wife and kids, and maybe one day own a truck that could take them all into town. Not much of a dream, not beyond hope but still out of reach. Occasionally there was some rain but not ever enough, the furrows dried out so a man sneezed and an acre blew west. Eben had planted winter wheat and that fancy soy bean and at least now the land mostly stayed home.

It was pitch black and Eben allowed the mule had good sense to complain on their errand. But after a while the night sky held depth and light enough they could find the way. Eben chose to cut across the back pasture at an angle, where he could almost see direct to the new crossing. Mule kind of fitted into a trot and the buckboard beat against Eben's skinny behind and he found himself laughing with the stars, the clean night air. At one point the land dropped from a ridge and the buckboard came up too close on the mule's heels with a too-loose breeching and a wreck was moments off when Eben got after the mule with a cracking whip and the mule pulled harder, clipped into a lope and straightened out the whole mess. Eben was smiling when they crossed the next ridge

Once in a while a thing got done right and it made a man feel proud. He'd have to remember to shorten the breeching tomorrow, so his family didn't come that close to an accident even though they traveled mostly on flat roads which is why he'd not seen the problem before.

The crossing's simplicity was spoiled by the wreck. He tethered the mule away from the metal and stench, knowing a spooked animal made for a bad trip home. Most of the messed-up car was on the east side of the tracks, wadded together in a form he wouldn't recognize at night. Tires in the wrong places, a broke axle, windshield smashed and glittering. He walked careful, picking through large shapes of broke glass and small bent metal puzzles.

How in hell the kid lived through this was his first thought, then of course the boy's pa died in the crash. A horrible way to die, seeing that white round light coming, hearing the wail, knowing the final truth and unable to do nothing but accept.

Off to the side was a dark mound he guessed would be the driver. It got hard to swallow; he wiped his mouth dry, a remembrance of his own mortal flesh. Fear soured in his mouth. Then he heard it, the slightest sound out of place in the grass and stars. A moan, low, fluttering like a kitten's heart beat. His foot froze mid-air and he almost fell. Again, a long wavering cry too often heard in Eben's fading dreams about war. His first thought was to run; then he talked to the moan like it had a soul and a need and that made him brave enough to get in close.

"Mister I'm coming and I know it hurts but goddamn you scared me some." He wasn't a swearing man normally but Eben felt like this time he'd earned the right. He found the mass, couldn't guess where to touch, what to turn over, how to ask. He knelt down, put a hand on something, wet, sticky, a sharp splinter poking his palm. He said 'ouch' and drew the hand to his mouth but the mess smeared on his own skin stopped him.

Ouch wasn't much use when he finally could see the man. Mangled, arm torn, legs bent back, head flayed open, features run to gore and skin. And impossibly alive. A small moan escaped again from that tangled mouth and Eben felt the pull of his own mouth in echo. He bent down; broken fingers reached for him, caught his shirt, barely tugged then fell away.

He knew, he put his head down to where a mouth might be and felt wetness, cool air, pushed then withdrawn, seeping into his own mouth. "Did the boy...?" He knew; "He's to our house, my wife's taking care of him." "Watch..." Then nothing and the time was gone. Death invaded, the night went blacker, Eben settled on his heels, studying the stilled mound. Knowing he had a choice.

The boy'd lost everything; there wasn't nothing to the car could be used or made useful. Except for selling metal for pennies to a scrap dealer, what had been a car was done. He'd come back in the morning and bury the flesh. No sense hauling it to the house, staining the buckboard where his family had to travel, hurting that boy all over again with the knowing he'd left his pa to die alone. Nasty business losing your kin this way, worse if you grow knowing you abandoned what couldn't live but managed an hour or more in terrible pain.

AN OLD WOMAN'S LIES

It was the knowing 'bout that pain which kept Eben silent. No boy needed to live with doing such a terrible thing to his own pa.

SEE, HERE'S THAT lie coming toward you. It ain't only old women who've made that choice and offered the word. This one's clear though; if Papa had spoke up and told us what Jay did, maybe then he wouldn't have come into our family so hard and fast and took from us our beloved Rosie.

We knew she was different, her tall body, long legs, that creamy skin and thick red hair. Why all the boys and some of the fathers and husbands to the surrounding country were in awe of her. What we didn't know was her own inner heart, her need, and this boy we took in, he was more than willing to give Rosie what she craved.

I do think if Papa had told the truth, Rosie would have made a better choice. But that's what hindsight and reflection are good for, fixing up the supposes and might-ifs in our lives.

Some of us never clear our minds; we look to others for the mistakes we make. Our poor judgment, our taking a risk that proved damaging, for many it's preferable to blame these incidents on anyone but ourselves.

Then there are those who never see, never realize their own weakness but dismiss the rest of their company as flawed beyond redemption. Here again is where, in my estimation only, you realize, the written word does terrible damage. We carry our own trouble, we are fed a line which tells us others are flawed in these many ways and their salvation depends on following a rule written by a man too many years ago. Then perhaps we don't follow this rule even as we expect our perfection will redeem us, but not those other people, those who wear long hair or have a small earring or drive a foreign car.

I've sat in classrooms and listened to professors and students spellbind each other with their knowledge. Listing the point of each worldly philosopher, deeming it important to know who thought what, when, not why particularly, and then to follow these thoughts and their redeemers, expecting salvation because a path was chosen, a way was lived.

How about thinking on your own, using sense and not regulation, how about giving your word and keeping it, small human notions to create an honest life.

Ah yes you say, the title of this polemic is …Lies. Yes and they are the lies we live with. The hurt of truth managed daily; have you ever had a drink or two with a person who insists they 'tell it like it is.' And just who are 'they' and how have 'they' been designated to do the judging, who are they to 'know' what only they can see. But, consider, they see from their eyes and no one else's. Don't ever trust a person who brags about their uncanny ability to speak the truth others will not find. They are liars to themselves, and leaders of revolutions, gurus of holy ground who disdain the non-believers.

Had enough of today's lecture, me too. But I told you I was cranky and am spelling out the reasons why. I don't know the truth; I don't tell it like it is for all those around me, I don't ask that anyone study my thoughts and parables. I know only that within me, and I suspect within most of you, there is the ability to think and sort through and make up my own mind.

Do you honestly think that anyone driving a car on a main street in any town would not understand the need for rules and regulations? Do you know why we have invented manners - a friend's son went to a school one summer and he called home to tell his mother that sitting across the table from six teen age boys eating with their mouths open was enough to convince him that table manners were important after all. Now that is a young male coming to understand a basic tenet of world survival.

See, sometimes words and lessons make ultimate sense.

If Papa had told us the truth about Jay, do you think what occurred would have happened at all? This is your question to answer after today's lesson. This one I don't speculate on too often, it hurts still, and it changed Rosie forever.

JAY WAS GIVEN a pallet near the fireplace; it was summer and only the outdoor oven was used. That's where water got heated and the cornbread baked, a chicken stewed in a pot. Inside, close to the fireplace was away from the room's center, and not too near the girls' shared room.

It wasn't too difficult to see that Rosie had an interest in the boy. And Didia McClary could understand her daughter's fascination. The boy was a pretty child, long in the belly and chest, strong legs, good muscles. She could tell wherever he and his pa'd been living, they worked hard, for the boy was more iron and steel than anything soft. And such lovely hair, the temptation was to pull out the copper curls and watch them spring against his head. He was a boy, maybe not yet twenty, and life hadn't been easy for him; now with the loss of his father he would be all alone.

Eben agreed with her that they would offer the boy a home, to work alongside Eben and get back his strength, make a life here with them. It was more practical than generous; Eben was looking at fifty in a few years and had slowed down enough a strong young boy like this one could be a big help.

Eben in turn could teach him farming skills, and maybe pick up some new smithing skills the boy's pa might of taught him. With the two of them, the boy being strong and young, maybe they could get the axle righted to the surrey and Eben could drive the family someplace without the bounce and rattle from the old buckboard.

The boy, Jay, only looked blank when Eben put forth his notion of learning. He did offer up any tools could be found to the wreck and Eben took them, but that wasn't what Eben wanted. He didn't seem too surprised though, and Didia almost asked him what bothered him about the boy but then Runt, little Roberta, took with another bad breathing spell and Didia sat up with her two nights in a row.

She was pleased when on the third night Jay said he'd take the watch. The offer gave Didia a chance to sleep and she forgot asking her husband why he was slow to like the Voorhes boy.

Belinda E. Perry

Rosie came out of her room about midnight; her folks were sleeping, Runt hadn't cried much, and she figured Jay would be bored, a full-growed man like him watching a child barely able to carry a thought. Jay was snoring; baby Runt rocking in her chair, head on a layer of pillows to help her breathe setting up. Then Rosie saw it was Jay's foot doing the rocking against the chair's motion and Runt was making the noise.

Jay's hand came out and snagged Rosie by the hip. He let his fingers grip her haunch and she got pulled toward him. The chair kept rocking; Rosie knew to lean over, conscious how her breasts swung in Jay's face under her loose gown. His hand pulled up the gown and the sense of his fingers against skin was better'n any ole poking time with Branson. Rosie let herself be shoved from the backside so that her belly was in his face and oh the kisses were liquid gold, hot and wet and she didn't know fingers could feel like that on her skin, inside her better than whatever foolish Branson had done to her.

Jay raised himself up and put a hand over her mouth and told her with a whisper to be quiet but oh it felt like nothing she'd known. When he slid those fingers out she saw the chair still rocking and heard Runt's noises and knew Mama and Papa would be sleeping through all this.

They'd never know what Jay'd been doing to their precious ugly daughter. She had something to tell Betsy now, about no hurting and what a man could do. Betsy kept insisting it weren't much fun and Rosie knew more now than her older sister.

Jay raised himself up and put his mouth against her ear and she wasn't sure what he was talking about. "Now it's your turn, give me your hand." He let go of her, sat down, that rocker still going back and forth and he put her hand to his pants and my god it was a big 'un in there, poking out through stained under-drawers and he fumbled a bit to release it, then splayed her hand on him and made her rub back and forth, kind of like the rocker itself.

It was hard and slick and slippery even though it was dry, till he forced her hand to the very tip and he moaned, so quiet she barely heard him and his body jerked. Her hand was wet and gooey when she pulled away and put it to her mouth, licked her fingers and he moaned again even though she'd quit stroking him.

FOUR

All this about sex is purely speculation of course, I can only guess what Rosie was thinking, and feeling, that first time with Jay. She told me later, way too late it seems. Me, I slept through the digit deflowering, lost in my own dream world of fresh air and sunshine and good food.

I have a pet peeve needs speaking to. You ever go somewhere in a group, like waiting in line for a ticket, yes I go to concerts, I've seen Joan Baez and Itzak Perlman and even the Blind Boys of Alabama but none of that swing music for me. I liked the blues from the forties, their harsh lyrics and thick voices telling me how I already felt.

Anyway, you've done this too, stood in line for something you wanted, pushed into a crowd where no one's comfortable but each stands his ground for what he wants. Space is precious and the air close, and some joker is standing there with arms to his hips, elbows out, taking his space and more besides, talking loud usually, pushing against the world and using up room belonging to the rest of us. Protection, arrogance; me I like to slam into these dense idiots and turn and say how sorry I am but they was taking up my place.

Now that I'm grey-haired and bent, those boys don't fight back but give me my room. There are a few things that better with age.

I believe these folks are kin to those who 'tell it like it is'; their own sense of importance and value comes up rank against the rest of the miserable world.

This is just my opinion mind you. I see an elbow stuck out in a crowd and I head straight at it, cane out in front, planned and aimed so that the arrogant so and so gets wacked by this little old lady and he don't dare complain or refuse my less-than-sincere apology. You notice I keep saying 'he' don't you, you're right, it may be sexist but it's the truth. As I see it.

Belinda E. Perry

Answer me a question, no lies, no hiding the truth for after all I'll be dead soon.

Why does a reasonable, well-mannered and brought-up child face the world by taking drugs? In and out of jail, trouble, irrational hurt, vivid scars to their family; how do they look anyone in the eyes and smile and be pleasant knowing their whole life is a lie. 'It feels good/great' is about as valid as that old saw 'I tell it like it is'. Wrong, both counts, lots of things feel good but that don't mean we indulge in them to the defeat of everything else. Such moral idiocy confounds me.

I said I'd ask but I don't know if I want your answer. 'Specially if it moans about obsession and addiction. Don't get me going on alcohol being a disease, nothing's a disease if you have the choice to not do it. Saying so demeans all those who struggle with cerebral palsy or cancer or the more exotic illness like Friedreich's Ataxia. These people have no choice and yet they fight like hell and you can't tell me it's a decision they've made to have a disease that robs their life.

That's where you get into past life and karma and other dogmas, (yes I've seen the bumper sticker). Paying in this life for what you did in a past life is a simple and poetic way of avoiding the philosophical question of why such terrible things happen to people. No answer is easy because if you believe in a god or godhead, you are faced with terrible cruelty, if you don't believe, you have nothing. Unless of course you're like me and don't care, relying on the here and practical to get you through.

We do have choices and not to drink is one of them. Or to smoke; although I know my own nature is obsessive (I try to control it on my own thank you) having to quit smoking would be awful.

But it would be a choice for me to make and carry out. Look at your hand as you raise a glass or a cigarette to your mouth. It is your will bringing the poison to your face, it is that same will capable of putting it out of the way, gone from your life. Down the drain.

A woman crippled with MS has no choice except to live her life in misery or remaining joy. Taking a drink is not equivalent to what any physical sufferer deals with on a daily basis, their body betraying them, their family life in shreds, their desires lost to wasting flesh and shriveling bone.

This is not the same as taking a drink or smoking a cigarette, or even overeating – we do a terrible disservice to those truly afflicted by allowing the drinkers and smokers and the druggers the same pity.

And it is pity, seeing and being relieved that their suffering is not our own. I know, enough; but all this is a part of the story. Rosie's obsession with Jay Voorhes could have been contained or ended, if any of our family had been able to tell the truth from the lie they each chose to believe.

RUNT IMPROVED QUICKLY, which Didia put to Jay's taking care of her each night. It was a blessing to sleep, and the boy worked reasonable alongside Eben but wasn't much help with the smithing. Eben went out and dug through the tormented car, after he buried the remains of the boy's pa. The man was scooped into a shallow hole under a tree, stunted from poor water and soil but still a tree in a treeless land. Jay said he guessed his pa'd like that, being from Arkansas and living on a river bottom.

They all went on the second trip to speak a few words over the gravesite for the resting of the man's soul and the easement of the boy's heart. He seemed distant, standing to his lonesome and hanging his head. Eyes quiet, my those eyes could flash when he was laughing, Didia could see her Eben in them, like they'd been kin in some distant past. But the day Eben brought out the Bible, which he couldn't rightly read but knew to heart, the boy stood off and hung his head, hardly saying an 'Amen' with the others. Not even Rosie ventured close, out of respect for Jay's feelings she later told her ma.

Looking at the wreck set off terrible thoughts and pictures; Didia held her hands to her throat, holding back the wail threatening her soul and heart. Instinctively she knew it wasn't right to throw yourself down and cry out to the Lord for a man no one knew, while his only child stood grieving by, face all white, eyes red and teary.

They got through the summer with that boy lying to the fireplace each night, and the girls behind their curtain, door left open and nothing major came in but a spider or two. It was too damned dry for nothing else Eben said. Once in a while Rosie went out to her trains but that'd been going on so long they would have thought something was wrong with their child if she didn't go visit her beloved engines. Queer love for a girl to have, but Rosie was always herself and no one else.

Runt grew a whole lot that summer and finally came to look like a McClary instead of some creature brought home with the cat. 'Course they didn't have a cat but Didia knew what they could drag in, mouse guts and play toys and a chipmunk or two. Runt was pale still, had sort of blond hair with red streaks in it and the greenest eyes you'd ever see. Born that way and never changed; Eben was proud of his daughter's eyes, not like the twin ghosts in his head, he told Didia, not enough to spook no one. Like she was staring at you already knowing everything and not telling. Runt was a strange child coming into her own, in a time no child would chose for living. That's what Eben told his wife, to try and explain what made their youngest child unusual.

It was a while still before her classmates would call her Remi so even her own ma said Runt and never Roberta.

Rosie was different that summer too, dreamy and biddable, Didia telling her what chores needed doing and they got done, in slow motion maybe but the chickens were clucking happy, the winter pig cleaned out and the pen dry. Jay was a big part of this peculiar behavior. Didia watched her middle daughter and the boy leaning into each other as they moved a log or took the bucket of pig manure to the garden, pulled weeds with entwined hands. Young love, she thought, remembering Eben's hands on her for the first time. She studied the boy, and decided he seemed respectful enough, and Rosie wasn't all over him but she had her doubts and questions. She remembered the first shock of unwedded sex that they hadn't meant to happen, which forced them into marriage. Didia could remember having no regret, not really, except she'd been so young.

Eben was older, he knew about wanting and he'd gotten her to a point where she couldn't stop. He'd known about sex and she didn't, she'd been told what 'it' was and how it made you do the wrong things and it sounded foolish to her. But the truth was, Eben still did that to her; her skin trembled, her legs went weak; exhaustion tumbled them both into bed against each other and the relief of the other's caress brought joy.

Didia was fearful her daughter would know this joy too soon with the stray boy.

One afternoon Rosie came in while Didia was shucking beans for supper. The girl had that look so her ma told her to sit down. There, in the straight chair, no fussing mind you. She put the beans aside and took a long steady look to her child's face and saw that her baby had grown up. She was a beauty; loose breasts under a thin cotton dress, good hips, that narrow youthful waist ain't seen childbirth or gluttony. A real pretty girl, except for narrowed eyes and a pinched look to her face, nothing a boy would notice once he'd seen that body.

Didia blushed for a mama wasn't meant to see her child in such a light, but she wanted so badly to tell Rosie about love, and sex, and how good it could be with the right man.

"Rosie child, you keeping yourself clean?" The girl grunted, sort of smiled at her ma. "Yes, ma'am. I know about the monthlies." That wasn't quite what Didia wanted; "No girl, you keepin' yourself clean from that boy?"

Rosie determined she'd best not squirm in the chair, though her mama's questions brought an itch to between her legs all right, where Jay had been last night, night before that too. He was hard there, rough against her belly, smelling of rut and sweat and tasting like the sweetest cream, the best cake.

It was easy to look at her ma confused, as if the question didn't make any sense. She told her lie, it wasn't her first, and the words came out easy because what she and Jay were doing wasn't nothing like her parents…couldn't be, they were young together and fresh, and his hands were hot on her skin and she was ready between her legs. She'd learned that need quick enough, was used to doing for herself and it was so much better when Jay done it to her.

"He's a nice boy, Mama, and he ain't shown me nothing but respect." Rosie almost smiled at the word, knowing respect could mean what they'd been doing. It wasn't wrong since he loved her, told her so sometimes with each stroke; god he was good down there.

Her mama was staring; Rosie lowered her eyes and looked at her hands clenched in her lap. All the sweetness Jay gave to her came into Rosie's voice; "Mama, I'm being the best daughter I can."

That was lying, then again Rosie saw a bit of truth. She was being the best…well it sure wasn't being a daughter but she was real good at what she was learning.

And Jay was teaching her how to be even better.

THERE'S NOTHING NEW to be said about our folks in their marriage bed, no image any of us want to share or even keep. Look at any old woman, and then place the thought of sexual bliss up against her withered flesh and old dreams. Now an old man, he's called dirty or a goat since we don't discount the possibility of his sexual prowess but admire him for his ability. An old woman - never. Couldn't be possible her flesh would still hold to sex and fornicating, or love-making or whatever euphemism you choose for our human procreation. Wrinkled skin, flat dugs, belly roll, wattled thighs; how could that shell still hold desire.

Ask one of us old women, we'll tell you, which is why I started this whole lecture and story. I dream still, I notice, I remember with clarity but the act is withdrawn. Those who stay married and love each other, they can fumble with bent fingers into familiar places, roll onto each other, sag and move as best they can and the feeling is there, hallowed for them, an energy and hope built from years of loving.

Those of us who are alone, by choice or ill-luck, we are anxious to find a lover if we have loved well, we are relieved to remain alone if the act has been a minor irritation or even a tribulation.

Me, well you know already, I watch young men, by young I mean those under sixty, I see their bodies ill-defined by clothing, I sometimes can taste them as they stand too near, yelling into my ears as if I am of course quite deaf. I don't mind, I don't chastise them for their assumption, I feel my pulse and know the contentment of one moment next to a viable male.

There has to be some good in being old, and one benefit is the presumption of deafness and people standing close by to speak directly into your ear

If we believed in how the world perceives us, we would all quit our dreams and our living. Once young flesh had served its apprenticeship, we are thickened, mutilated, too much of us is extra padding, gut, or protruding bone.

What I don't understand, never have and don't want to know, is why women allow the concept of a husband or lover to dictate the extremes of their fashions. Growing up mostly barefoot and half-wild, I have only once worn heels. They are an abomination and does anyone truly believe, in their hearts and between their legs, that men would never have sex again if women didn't go through this erroneous self-mutilation of wearing a tiny prick of a heel raising them three or four inches off the ground? (And I won't ask your pardon for the terrible pun.)

If none of us wore heels, and 'uplift' bras, would men simply stay home and play with themselves instead of us.

Don't bet on it...

Men have been burying themselves between our legs since one of them figured out open slot A and insert pole B; stand in front of a man, bend over, let your skirt rise a few too many inches and he'll be all over and inside you in a minute and it don't matter that you're wearing comfortable shoes or bare feet or the latest in running shoes. Talk about ugly – but there the men are, ready at any moment. It's part of their genetic matter.

So you think you have to wear five-inch spikes on your feet to get a man or to be a real woman? You actually call this distortion sophisticated and dressed to the height of fashion – why are we so vulnerable that we

40

believe this…I can't even begin to find the words of contempt and shame I feel for our duplicity. We as half the species are more guilty than the advertising geniuses who dream up the campaigns to sell their beer and cars and we see a man drooling over the half-clad girl thing sprawled across the car hood, legs slightly parted, breasts squeezed together and he can't help his instant erection. So we go with him, we accept this misplaced version of our sexuality as the real, the desired.

How did we forget that we happen to own slot A and pole B needs to find itself in there? Not in a picture, although some men only relate to those plastic females, they're afraid of real flesh. No, if we are willing, there is a man who wants us. You don't need to wear those heels and a tight dress, hobbling yourself, removing yourself from real life to become a parody of your true selves.

Life to me has been a series of men, conflicts, disappointments, deaths, and losses which are now faded but still painful, and still I have carried one banner throughout my history. If I am told this is how it must be, I take a long look. I don't parade or protest, I sit down and figure through what is to be gained by those making the particular pronouncement, and I resist at all costs their attempt to change me and my life. What idiocy would prompt me to accept the pain of a push-up bra and heels when I know if I put my hand on a man's penis and squeeze, he'll forget about the heels and the inflated breasts and dive right in.

You say I'm old and without a lover, and do you really think that the sight of me at this point shoved into any such garb would attract a male willing to mount me? Think on it, envision such a picture and tell me the truth. Or don't you want to accept the ultimate test of such barbaric techniques?

Personally the thought of me shoved into a lacey bra and high heels is enough to bring on a giggling fit which might be bad for my health right now, but something has to kill me as the old drunk once said.

Other questions tickle my mind, like why do some of you pay to wear some fool's name on your clothes and call it sophisticated, in style –

that's plain silly. And quite expensive, all done to show someone else you have the bucks to buy. When you throw in discount stores and entire malls, who knows what your opponent paid for the same item, is it worth that label or signature? As I said; silly.

In its own reversed way, the 'designer label' craze is a form of omitted lying; 'if you wear this, you will be…' fill in the dots. The sad part of this diatribe is that some of us believe what we're being sold without ever taking a closer look. Shame on us for being so gullible, and that has nothing to do with being sophisticated.

Back to sex; like I said, it's all about sex.

HIS FACE WAS healed and yet they kept feeding him and letting him stay. He didn't mind, the girl made up for the farmer's insistence he work for the luxury of food. It beat his previous job, blowing on that old man while he drove too fast. It was being face down in the front seat mouth working away that got the fag killed and Jay thrown clear. He didn't see it coming, never braced or turned to jelly, just kept working and thought the stiffened body and low moan was the result of his clever tongue and lips.

Boy had he been wrong. The girl made up for that too, learning as she went, doing what he told her. It ain't a bad life, he thought, even now when she was beginning that old chestnut of marrying. He thought about it when she had her mouth on him and looked up, smiled with those plump and busy lips of hers and said something about them married and how much more they could do when no one could stop them.

Sometimes when she was pounding away on him he saw her, face buried in his hair, that plumped mouth going up and down fast as she could, he had visions of those old men and their flabby thighs and fast cars and how he'd grown into sex, learned to accept sex as a commodity to broker daily for his existence, and this child was different. Marrying up might not be a bad idea; living here was the easiest life he'd known; the old man needed him, the woman cooked, the little girl stayed out of his way. She was a strange duck to be sure, all eyes and knees and watching without a word.

The old man got him once; blunt and to his face. Male statement of protection, Jay kept his grin to himself. "You keep your eyes off my daughter." Jay stood at attention, right smart, looked Mr. McClary in the eye; "Yes sir." And it weren't no lie, he kept his eyes shut most of the time 'cept when she was sucking and he liked to watch.

September second was the day they got caught. By the wife who needed the outhouse and they were up against the barn, the girl sliding up and down his pole like she was playing on the swings and it felt good enough he didn't see the old woman, didn't hear her, could feel nothing but that child gliding on him until the scream stopped him cold.

"You horrible boy get off my daughter." He wondered what she was seeing, since it was the girl on him. But he knew her meaning and had to quit and of course the old man came out with a shotgun and damn he could feel those pellets going in him sure enough even as the child stood by him, with his pants down, his thing out all shrinking and cold.

They were shouting at each other and the woman cried and even the kid came out, in a flimsy gown crying for her ma and wrapping herself around the woman, which Jay believed kept the mama from killing him.

They took Rosie to the house, the pa staying with him while he hiked up his pants and tucked himself in safe. Eben McClary kept that shotgun nestled to his arm and his eyes on Jay and there wasn't no escape.

It was settled real quick, the shotgun never left the old man's arms. They would marry soon as they got a license and Jay figured it wasn't a bad deal. The old man wasn't Bible-strict and the wife cooked a good meal. Now he'd own the daughter, could make her do whatever he needed and it was all right and legal.

It was fine by him; into Coolidge for the preacher and then home to his own bed and the right to do what they'd been doing all along. He didn't count on Rosie who married him all right but hauled out her few bucks saved and bought them a bus ticket north and east. Jay went along for the ride, he still owned the rights to her and it didn't matter where they did it, all nice and legal. It was a first in Jay's life and he couldn't help but wonder if the sex would be better now that she belonged only to him.

43

ONE UP, ONE-UPMANSHIP, now that's a lovely and highly descriptive term for what we humans indulge in daily. But it is the truth; "I fell and hurt my elbow yesterday" gets "I broke my elbow tomorrow." Pure nonsense but we can't seem to help it. I know it is one of my most grievous flaws and only lately have I run out of things to top anything anyone's ever done. That has more to do with the death of my friends, and the absent ears of my acquaintances who take me out for lunch, yell at me without listening to what I want to say and consider it a good deed done for the month.

Let me give you an example; the night Mama and Papa found Jay Voorhes assaulting my sister Rosie, I came screaming out of the house and immediately clung to my mother, crying that I wanted her to pick me up. I wasn't hurt, I hadn't had a bad dream or cut my finger. I had seen my father running from the house, heard my mother's racket and decided since no one was paying much attention to me that I needed to be in her arms immediately. It had been maybe two years since Mama had carried me, I prided myself on not being a baby any more, yet there I was, wailing and howling to be held.

I knew exactly what was going on; I'd already seen the two of them at each other like Mama and Papa. I figured it was what grown-ups did, since Rosie was so much older than me. The sin of fornication hadn't been discussed yet in the church, no one wanted to put notions in a child's head. Well they should watch out my window to where my sister was kneeling in front of our hired man sucking on him like he was the grand tittie of all time, or rocking on his body. What my parents thought they saw was their child being mauled; what she was doing to the boy was for her pleasure as much as for his enjoyment. But loving parents cannot believe such a thing 'bout their own child. The great lie of all times.

My goodness my mouth and mind can get lost real quick in any kind of sexual oration. I have been married three times and it was so constant in my life, so much a pleasure except for a few minor incidents, that I miss sex, I think about sex. I preach sex to my youngest friends and they look at me in shock. There are dirty old ladies you know.

I've read a book or two, studied them in a class I took, all about sex and how it was male domination and not pleasure. I guess the writer didn't think much of men, or sex either, for she wasn't too pleased with females. She believed that the penetration was the male world's attempt to violate and control a woman, to penetrate was to punish, make us less than what we are.

Now me, and you might already have guessed I'd feel this way, I see the need for penetration as strength for women; we can take them inside and they need to be there, beg to enter there. Sometimes it is done by force, but that is about power and hatred, and not about sex. To have a man inside you, to hold him with your own body, is a power above and beyond words. At that moment the woman literally owns the man's being.

And we love it, those of us who love men. I don't know about others who love their own sex, the parts don't fit right, either there is two that don't fit together or two empty places needing and wanting what is not there. It's all right with me if that is how you love, but oh how much I miss holding my man in that way, special between us for that moment, no other moment like it. It's good we have private choices, only fair after all.

AT FIVE YEARS of age Runt had lost both her sisters to marriage, or at least to sexual activities associated with the marriage bed. She never believed that Rosie loved that awful boy, but they were gone, both of them married, her papa said and Runt had no evidence otherwise. Mama sighed a lot the first month, then seemed to quiet down, watching Runt, working alongside Papa since they was now missing two sets of hands to work the crops.

Runt got brought in to the work, pulling weeds, using a broke hoe to yank out those pesky greens they couldn't eat. She was always reminded; do her chores and there'd be supper on the table. At five and then five and a half, she tired easy, and sometimes she crept away to nap under the off side of a ridge, where the sun got blocked by high rocks and packed sand. On those nights, there'd only be corn bread and syrup and a glass of muddy water from the spring in town. Runt began to suspect Mama of torturing her but in case the connection was real, she tried to finish the weeding each day before she found a cool place to sleep.

Sometimes she cried and came in for supper with reddened eyes and sand stuck to her chin. Mama brushed her clean, sat her down, once she even offered up a treat of biscuits and clover honey. There wasn't a sweet better'n honey on a hot biscuit, she loved the flavors, salt and tart against the sugary sweetness of honey from those bees the other side of Coolidge.

Papa came to her only once when she was huddled up to the ridge. He sat a few feet away, took out a pipe he liked to chew on, didn't smoke it, wouldn't waste the few pennies needed to buy the rough tobacco he favored.

"Runt, I don't take to seeing you so filled with misery." He didn't look at her but stared to an unknown distance. "Rosie didn't know better, I guess your ma and me, we forgot to teach her." Runt looked at her pa and thought his face had lines and wrinkles she hadn't seen before. She slid herself sideways, across a patch of prickly weed grass, and it felt safe to be next to him. He smelled of sweat and papa, with his big hands cupped around the pipe stem, making it small and fragile against the enlarged knuckles and scars. Of course her child's mind didn't take in these details as comfort or curiosity; they were lodged inside the brain without permission, proof of her daddy to be treasured when he died.

"Rosie took what she wanted, child. Or what she thought she wanted. I ain't sure 'bout that boy." Papa drew in a deep breath and Runt pushed herself in closer. The rumble of his words could be felt through his arm, his side, she wanted to crawl in deeper. "There's times when taking what you want hurts those around you. If it ain't real you give up love purely for loving." His voice got softer, words coming slow as if he was sorting through them before he spoke.

"You're young for all this, Runt. But I know you saw them…it was wrong of that…boy to do such things outside the window where you could see them. Relations between a man and a woman, they're meant to be private." He was struggling and Runt felt she had to comfort him. Her hand went into his lap; it was how Rosie comforted that boy Jay even before they were married. Her pa jumped, yanked himself away and turned a red and scary face toward her. "Don't you go touching me like that, child. It's wrong; you know some better than to touch any man that way. Your ma needs talking to you." He got up, turned away from her, left Runt huddled into herself; knowing she'd done wrong but not quite knowing what or why.

Mama never did talk to her why Papa got so mad. She tried to ask but Mama seemed to not hear her, and then a week later Mama and Papa came to Runt and told her there would be a new baby brother or sister soon enough. Runt wanted a boy, she said. She was tired of older sisters and she told her parents her exact feelings on the subject. Her papa looked at Mama and they shared a thin smile for the notion of choosing. Mama sat down and drew Runt to her. When she got held close to her mother, she smelled a difference, not that air of chilled work from Papa's skin but a salty heat, a foreign sourness Runt didn't much like.

Mama's belly was high and hard, Runt instinctively laid her head there and could feel her mama's smile, saw that pleasure reflected in her papa's tired gaze. Mama's hand lay in her hair, gentle through the snarls and ribbons. "Child we don't get to choose these things. Whoever it is, they'll be welcomed and loved."

Four months later Mama died.

NOW YOU THINK you know what I'm going to say and more'n likely you're wrong. I don't remember the why of her death, but I got Papa to tell me when I was fifteen. She and the baby, it was a boy, died when the child started coming and then turned around, Papa said, looked like he was going back, as if his one glimpse of the world didn't agree with him. There wasn't a hospital, not even a mid-wife to stop the bleeding. Papa tried, I helped, I pushed clothes into Mama's opened legs and couldn't bear what I seeing, what I smelled. But I can remember; sweet blood and death flushing out of her. I remember that smell, and I remember Papa crying.

EBEN'S HANDS WERE greasy; he made the mistake of wiping his nose and could squint and see the bloody streak. Her eyes watched him, calm and knowing, no sadness or anger. She was the woman he loved and even as he tried to stop the bleeding, she smiled to let him know she understood.

Eben yelled at Runt to bring up more towels, it didn't matter if they were dirty, it didn't matter if it was the quilt Didia had spent two years working, what mattered was the rich dark fluid that quickly stained, then drenched whatever they used to dam it.

It wasn't right yelling at Runt, he felt it beneath his heart, in his hands, soft and quickening in his mouth, the wrongness that could never be right. But he needed those towels to stop death. Eventually, out of desperation at the end, they pushed a wool blanket there, and watched in horror, his hands on the child's shoulders, while the blood simply flowed around the scratchy wool, not bothering to slow but pushing relentlessly until nothing was left. Eben sat with his wife, took her hand and they waited.

Didia didn't open her eyes again, not after they closed when her husband held her. He watched her breathing, recognizing that the slow rise and lesser fall were becoming the last. Her hand was weightless, each finger a length of string, a nothing in his own hand, fragile enough he barely knew when she left him.

Runt had crawled under the bed and wet her pants. He didn't tell her that when they talked years later. There was no reason she should know. The truth of her mother's dying was hardship enough; Eben sat in the chair, still attached to his wife through an empty body. The blood flow eventually stopped, he grunted and stood up, her hand came with him, curled around his blooded fingers. He rested that hand on her breast, pulled her other hand and arm into the same pious position. It was fitting despite her refusal to attend church these past few months.

She wouldn't tell him what had changed so he never knew. He figured it had to do with the girls, Betsy and Rosie.

THE BOY'S HEAD was exposed when he took away the sopping blanket. The boy, Eben's only son, came into the world ass to the air, knees drawn up to his tiny belly, the cord tight around his neck, skin ice blue; the small child never drew a breath. Eben handled the carcass gently; this bloody skin and bone was meant to become his immortality. He checked the boy, fingers and toes like he'd done with the three girls at their mama's request. But this inspection included testicles and penis, wide between the bowed legs, flaccid now, but enormous in size compared to the tiny fingers, the membranous toes.

His son would have grown to be a man, and now he was nothing but tissue and drying fluids, no mama to grieve him, only Runt and an old man there to tend his burying. Eben looked around the small cabin, never more than shelter, not really a home despite the curtains she patterned and sewed, the braids of old clothes made into circular rugs; these simple things surely brightened the room and felt good come the cold mornings. She had tried to make it a home, he'd never given her much and now there was so much less. Eben set the baby in the center of that blanket, blood red against his blue skin. Then he wrapped the tender flesh, the unfilled bone, and set the bundle aside.

Kneeling on the punched floor, he swept his hands under the dusty bed and saw the blood had dripped through here, staining Runt's back, drenching her hair. He touched her, she shivered and withdrew. He tried to make his arm longer but his shoulder caught, his knees hurt and he had to bite the inside of his mouth to keep from yelling. "Girl you come out, we got chores still."

He straightened, wiped his hands together, angry at the blood staining them. Then Runt appeared, thin blood dried on her face, her eyes wide, not tear-filled but dry and shining like he'd never thought to see. He spoke careful, yet the words were harsh on a child.

"We ought to clean her, and the baby…I need wood from behind the barn, got to make up a coffin right. You drag in the lumber to where the saw is. I'll finish here."

The little girl's eyes almost spun in her skull, too large, too intent on his words as if any sound could be salvation. She turned quickly, one look to her ma and then went flying around the room, skipping over the bundled wool and blood. Eben spoke without thinking; "He was a boy, and he don't have a name. You want to name him before he gets buried with his ma?" Eben wasn't sure if this was the right thing but he couldn't bear his son dying with no proper given name.

She was just six years old and tiny but she looked at him steady and clear. "His name is Thomas." Eben nodded; it was a good name.

He pulled out the mattress and the quilting and put them behind the barn to set on fire later. He could see Runt's shadow pulling out lumber. It was late, full dark, and the little girl was tireless. He knew the same sensation; sleep was the last thing possible, he would scrub out the floor with kerosene and pull the mattress from where Rosie had slept. He'd make a pallet for Runt and then maybe they both could sleep.

He lifted Didia's empty flesh, the soiled bedding wrapped around her as a shroud. It wasn't far to the barn yet she seemed to weigh more with each step. He was careful to lay her out away from the saw and the scattered lumber. It had been a cruel task for Runt but it would make building a coffin happen sooner. When his daughter, his one remaining family member, struggled into the barn with a six by two, he picked up the long unbalanced weight and thanked her, his voice carefully sincere. Then he kissed the top of her head and tasted the dry copper of his wife's blood. He could not stop a shudder. Finally he spat and Runt cried.

Eben carried his daughter back to the small house, which smelled now of burned oil, soured wood, heated remnants of their loss. He laid her on the clean, barren mattress and covered her with his coat. Patted her head, felt that dried blood again and knew he needed to wash her. It would have to wait until tomorrow, before the ceremony.

Where he intended to build a coffin, large enough to lay the baby across his mother's breast, Eben stood mute, searching for the ultimate push to begin his final task. The wood turned in his hand, splinters creased his palm, he hammered a nail through the web between his fingers and pulled it out, drawing blood that was his, belonging to no one else. Eben almost cried.

Each crosscut, each draw, was a reminder. He persevered beyond exhaustion, unwilling to leave that last vision of his wife and the baby's shared death exposed, for Runt had suffered enough. By dawn the coffin was finished and Eben as the father laid the blanket-wrapped child across his mother's belly and hips. Eben cried as he nailed the top boards over her face. He purposely focused on Didia's beloved features and refused to remember the stale flesh of his son.

When he got to the house he was hearing a solid pound, a strange rattling noise in short rhythm. He ran the last steps, fearful of Runt, and found her crawled onto the stovetop, smashing with a rock on a mound wrapped in white cloth. He stopped, bellowed her name, then smelled what she had been doing.

His daughter was making coffee. The cold pot was next to her, the lid upside down on the stovetop. He could see the water shimmer between blows as she kept pounding, not hearing him, not wanting to know he was there. This was a chore her mama did every morning, making coffee for them both to help face the long day. He walked to Runt and put his hand on her back – she jumped, the rock flew from her hand, he caught it easily. "I use this here grinder, child."

It was a reach overhead to the shelf, to pull down the waxed wooden box with the black metal handle. He wanted to yell at the child for making noise and a mess, but his wife's voice sat behind his ear, telling him the child needed praise not anger.

Eben showed their daughter how to fill the grinder with the right amount of beans, already he had to change the proportions, coffee for one now, not two. While she worked the stiff handle for cranking, he lit a fire in the stove box, feeling his fingers tremble; these were Didia's jobs, what she did unless he was up earlier tending a sick animal or child.

And it was his wife who'd taken care of the children. Child. Eben shook his head. Her not being with them would take time to accept but he'd never understand, and he looked at his one daughter's head bent over the unfamiliar task. Her tongue was to the corner of her mouth, like her ma, and Eben rested his hand on the bright red-blond hair, feeling its bristly electricity, noting tangles and snarls and that was something else Didia took care of and he would have to learn.

FIVE

I want to tell you now, no shading the truth, that it's not only women who lie to preserve and salvage – my papa lied to me that horrible morning and said the coffee which eventually came to boil on the stove tasted good, just like Mama made for him. I saw his face when he drank that first cup; I knew the truth despite the praise he gave me. It was my lesson in going on, surviving…it took me a few years but I began to understand.

The lesson from this is that men lie for the same reason women do. Papa's first lie brought on the rest, a lie of not telling, about Jay Voorhes and the death of the man with him. You can add the possibility of sex to their lying, but not with my Papa, not as I grew up and he tried to make life easier for me.

I never did learn to make decent coffee, boiled on the stove, stick in another piece of wood, keep the pot boiling. I either burned it or it was too weak. It wasn't until I got to an electric perk, and then one of those boil water and pour set-ups that the coffee began to please me.

Papa lied, and I forgive him.

The days after her death are too clear. I can feel her loss even now when I lie down in my bed, a big old sleigh bed my second husband bought and my third husband wouldn't use. We put it in a guest room and he bought me a fancied modern bed of pale wood and simple lines. I paid no mind, the bed was active enough it didn't matter what color of wood turned his head, or what shape of leg held us up in our pleasure.

It was the animals that kept us going the first month; they didn't know the loss of my mama, they ate and shat and needed water and feed and cleaning out. The mule hollered the first morning Papa sat with me at the table and sipped that terrible coffee and his eyes told me even when his mouth kept saying how good the coffee was. He was bleeding to death inside, his heart frozen, his mind refusing further life. I can know this now, it was how I felt and he was the one to love her, hold her, mount her then forced to bury what their loving had done. I cannot guess or imagine what he felt. But that he did not remarry is no surprise.

He went out and fed the mule, the pig, gave hay to the few sheep, milked the cow although her milk would be wasted now. No babe to feed, only one small child, no woman to make butter or cheese. The entire world had been thrown into that cold grave he'd dug.

THE MULE KICKED him above the knee and Eben grunted. He looked and saw nothing, no torn cloth and flesh, no blood. But damn it hurt so he cursed at the mule and the long-eared fool humped up his back end expecting retribution. Eben grunted and laughed.

Then he clamped his mouth hard shut, the sound was wrong, he'd almost forgot. Eben stopped the mule, draped the reins on the plow handle. He didn't remember this decision, to plow the small acreage near a dry creek bed. He removed his hat and wiped the wet bald place, found his hair too long, flapping over the back of his collarless shirt. He looked down, by god the shirt was washed, not ironed but clean enough he was impressed.

His sight was cleared; he could smell a foreign scent and he wanted to see, to know if it was real. He knelt down, the mule spooked again and Eben said the words without thinking, 'Easy there ole son, it's only me back here." That brought the ears back up and the mule farted to show he wasn't scared.

His fingers seemed to know before he did, digging into the dirt, feeling that thick wet release so long gone from the land. He let out a sigh, felt his heart actually beat a decent rhythm. When the hell had it rained, why didn't he know this? Eben stood, spoke to the mule before the animal could spook or spin; "It's me again, you idiot." Words meaning against what they said; he was blessed, saved, their farm would produce again.

Then he remembered. Most of the winter had disappeared, spring had brought enough rain that he was farming again.

RUNT WENT TO school in the fall. It was only a two-mile walk but her pa drove her the first day. She was introduced to her classmates as Roberta Ellen McClary and almost immediately a boy came sideways up to her and said he didn't like Roberta, it was his pa's mule name so a little girl laughed and Runt wanted to kick her but the teacher placed her hand on Runt's shoulder and said 'let's call her Remi' and that was her name.

A month or so later, life changed again, and this time it was her pa's decision. He had to sit Remi down to explain. The two of them, in that ugly shack where the floor was dusty and tin dishes lay on the table. No cloth, just hard wood spotted and stained. He'd lost too much, he said; the wind, his wife, topsoil gone to hell, then planting too late in the spring, barely recognizing what needed to be done. There wasn't enough crop to survive another winter. He didn't know how they'd gone on last year but he knew he wasn't doing it again. Not with looking at Runt and seeing the circles under her eyes, feeling the knobs of her shoulders, the skinny legs bruised and sore. His daughter, his only family, and he knew he wasn't taking care of her right.

"Runt, we ain't gonna make it through another winter here. I got to take work and that means moving us into town. Not even Coolidge but one of those bigger towns to the north. Where they got more rain earlier than we did here." She was frightened; "We can't leave Mama and Thomas. We can't."

He looked at her as if she were a wild thing. "Runt, they aren't alive and we can't live for them no more." His voice was rough, and one of his hands reached for her shoulder; she ducked away from its weight. "I ain't leaving Thomas!"

Eben pushed back in his chair, tilted away from the table, one hand rubbed his face, mocking a good wash. Lord he was tired and he had no idea how to help his child. Runt, Roberta, naw, it was Remi now, since she started school. The baby was dead, so was Didia. He stared at the remaining family, all he had in the world, his own folks dead, Didia had no parents, there was a sister somewhere in Alabama, and two grown and married daughters who never wrote. Eben would have to move without letting them know. They hadn't been told about their ma, he didn't know how to reach them.

Now the little one was in full swing, crying and glaring at him. He slammed the table; "We're moving soon as I find me a job."

HE CAME HOME two weeks later with the news and Remi wasn't there. She'd been told to feed out the cow and clean the sheep and mule pens, her daily chore after school and the chores weren't done. A pitchfork rested outside the mule pen and she was gone.

It was easy finding her, sitting on top of the sunken hole where her ma was buried. Remi's back was to him, she didn't shiver or move when he coughed first, then called to her. "Remi, you got work needs doing." He picked her up and she squalled, kicked back and just missed his balls and he was getting mad but she wiggled and squirmed and he was losing her so he put her down and pushed her out of the hole and along towards the barn.

"I hate you I hate you" she chanted as he marched her back to the mule pen and the stench of manure, the matted filth of piss-soaked hay. "I hate you" was all she said as she forked out the wads, the first ones sailing at him until he had to duck. "I hate you" rang in his ears.

Supper was a half pound of meat he'd bartered for, ground and seasoned with the last pinch of salt. The child had no idea how close it had been. He'd starved before and vowed his children wouldn't come to that. He'd been eyeing the cow; he already knew from experience that working mules made a poor meal.

He sat Remi to the table, held her down while she muttered the chant to him. His voice was big enough to talk over her words; she was hoarse now from exhaustion but still in her rage.

"I took a job at the ranch, that Rafter H over by Roy. They need a full-time smith. We get a house of our own and they have enough kids to the ranch there's a school for you. We go there tomorrow, and we take the cow with us." He didn't tell her he'd butcher the pig tonight, and let the sheep loose. It was a waste but Eben had chewed on mutton before and their wool wasn't worth even a few pennies supposing he could find a buyer. It was kinder to turn them loose hoping some farmer would seize the chance to take them home for dinner or a new sweater before coyotes saw them as a meal.

It occurred to Eben that his child had stopped her squalling. "Are there horses, Papa, horses I can ride?" He looked at her, and had no idea how to answer. "I'm a hand there, Remi, not the boss or a farmer but someone who gets paid a few pennies and a place to sleep, food for the table. I don't know about you riding...." "But there are horses, Papa?"

He could finally smile; "There're horses child, plenty of them."

FOR ONCE HE didn't exactly lie, there were lots of horses and I was bought by the mentioning of them. Horses, those huge magical beasts who carried soldiers and cowboys and even Indians, in my dreams and in books but not in my real life.

The Rafter H ran a remuda of over forty head, none of which were suitable for a child to ride. I did learn to ride however, and a whole lot more on the eleven years we lived to the Rafter H. And yes, you can guess what I learned, all those cowboys bowlegging around, tight jeans and chaps hugging their skinny haunches. They gave me a true appreciation for the male figure. And here's a thought, any of you men bold enough to read this, if you want to advertise your prowess and possibilities, learn to ride a horse well enough you can rightfully put on chaps and swagger around. That leather on each hip, tied across low on your middle, well it cups and holds and frames what is waiting there snugged inside your jeans and calling to a receptive woman.

It's called truth in advertising, a big deal unless you put a sock where something else ought to be.

Word of warning though, don't buy fancy chaps, don't buy new ones and not ride in them for you expose your failings that way, you become a caricature instead of a real man. There's a whole lot more than your genitals hanging out when you try to be what you're not.

Any woman taken with a cowboy learns real quick they're a ghost, a declared independent man with a ready history of heading down the road. Listen to the songs, find the music behind the melody, it's Willie Nelson and Ian Tyson, Chris LeDoux and 'The Night Rider's Lament'. You ever hear that song, talking about the stars and the dark sky, camp fires and such, sounds so damned romantic even as the idiot singing it has given up a good woman and a different life.

Ladies, you can't fight this one. They might take you to bed but don't hang on when they get that look. They're gone, you're already history, a penciled name in a tally book that fades and disappears.

But oh lordy, lying next to my first cowboy, now that's a tale I'll tell with no lies, no excuses and no hesitation.

But I won't tell the tale yet.

HE MADE IT an adventure, traveling in the mule wagon with the cow bawling in their ear, walking reluctantly, Eben not willing to hurry either animal. He'd packed up what little they had, a suitcase for Remi with some of her ma's clothes, a quilt or two that wasn't stained or torn, and her school clothes and books, the Bible of course though he couldn't read it. And the slaughtered pig wrapped in old newspaper, shoved in a bucket with sawdust to cover. He hoped it would make the trip; he planned on having chops tonight over the fire.

Remi thought this was exciting, her first time camping out. She got to sleep in the wagon under that huge sky. She told her papa how much she had liked sleeping outside, so long ago. Last year, before her mama died, before Rosie left with that boy. Eben sighed, he remembered exactly the times she'd slept out of the house, her absence had given him and Didia a freedom they didn't often enjoy, until everything, the family, the night, were interrupted by Rose and…Eben stopped, no use going over that time.

They made camp in a small dip near a bent tree, shade and a spring nearby. He might even dip himself, Remi too, clean up before they entered a new way of life. He kept the calf tied to the tree near the mule, which turned out to be a mistake when the calf tried to nurse on the mule, who wasn't pleased with the demotion and kicked like a son of a bitch. Since the calf was tied, the kick didn't have the desired affect of removing the offender and for a short moment it sounded like Noah's Ark had landed near Roy, New Mexico.

She asked as he was cooking the raw pig over the fire how she would get to the school she'd started less than a month ago. He said she wouldn't be going there and when he didn't hear back, he looked up from his chore and she was smiling. "Good 'cause I didn't like the teacher and the boys picked on me." Eben thought on that and admired his child; she'd never said a word, come home from school and did her chores, excepting that one night when he found her on the grave where he'd buried her ma and the little boy. He'd been surprised by finding her there. It had been almost a year, the grieving had to be done with, getting on was what mattered.

Though he knew his life had stopped, 'cepting for taking care of Remi.

They'd packed the one picture they had of Didia and the two girls, about the age and size Remi was now, two pretty smiling children looking into the camera. Taken before the drought hit, before the horrible years of near starvation and constant fretting and worry..

Eben brought the picture 'cause he wanted Remi to have something of her mother. He wrote his name on the wall in the empty shack, about all he could write that anyone could read, and the place where they were going represented by a crude rendering of the Rafter H brand. That ought to tell anyone interested where they'd gone.

It wouldn't tell much more, though, about the two girls who'd gone to their own men, and the wife he'd lost, the mother his Remi no longer had. The life they'd dreamed on and worked for, and how the blowing winds had taken everything including Didia.

She was there, in his hand, lying across the palm as light as her dying touch. He would close his fingers and feel her, just barely, reaching for him and letting go. Her breath lay against him at night, her hand touched him when he woke in the morning. He had killed her with his loving.

The cuts of pork were done, scorched, cooked through, the smell of them brought a few coyote howls and Eben was finally grinning when he speared the pork slices and laid one on a tin plate for Remi. She stared at it, he urged her to eat. Then he realized he'd forgotten knives and forks, Didia would have remembered, she was the civilized one who kept him in line and taught the girls their manners.

He had to cut Remi's meat for her, holding one thumb on the chunk to keep it from sliding off the plate. His big dirty thumb, the old scar at its base, where he'd near to sliced the damned thing off doing just this and that time was with a fork to hold on. He cut the pieces child-sized; she was only a little girl, and then pushed the plate back to her, nodding, trying his best to encourage her.

His mouth full of tender pork, Eben thought to ask and almost spat out meat with the words. Wiped his mouth and couldn't quite look at his daughter. "That tastes right good don't it." She stared at him and her eyes were enormous, once again he was awe-struck by their color, an intense rich green like shined stones or the cottonwood leaves before they turned yellow.

She was trying to nod at him around the wadded food tucked to her cheek. Eben laughed and his only child, his whole family, tried to smile back while chewing, swallowing, taking another bite.

He did take her to the spring, carried her in his arms, her head again his collarbone, her arms around his neck. So light, so fragile for a growing child. The water was chilled yet he walked in after removing his boots, Remi still clinging to him. They ducked under, laughing and sputtering; came up into warmed night air and she hugged him closer. "Again, Papa, again."

For once they went to bed clean, wet clothes hung off the singletree, Remi in one of his shirts, himself in washed underdrawers, toes and legs to the fresh night air. He lay on the single blanket after Remi climbed into the wagon bed and he drew a quilt over her. He was hired now, on a payroll, not his own man, not a father and husband and farmer but a man paid month by month, to put food into his child, to clothe her and keep her warm, safe from blowing winds and death. Being cooled, cleaned off, finally made sleep come easier.

The stars winked, the coyotes howled, smelling that burned pig, the calf, the cow, a hated mule. No respectable coyote would come to a mule unless it was hobbled and injured and maybe half dead. So they were safe tonight. Not that he, Eben McClary, could rescue her, or provide for her, tonight it was the mule's turn to do what he never could.

PAPA TOLD ME we were going on an adventure and stuffed me full of burnt pig and I remember his eyes, so sad when we drove away from that ugly shack. I knew even then my pa was lying to me, I learned the truth early that a lie made some things better.

AN OLD WOMAN'S LIES

I was excited and scared and lonely and the oddity of lying in the wagon bed didn't make up for leaving home. Those few moments when I held my father and we ducked and snorted in the spring water made the entire journey bearable, a pleasure I'd never known before, and would try to recover in the future. Amazing isn't it, what a simple thing done with such love makes you seek it over and over.

Life's a lie in too many ways, which is the premise for this meandering essay against lies, as if we could exist without them. I won't bother with the social manifestations of lying, or what we are taught in school and church and then have our faces wiped in the morass. We all know the truth on this, we accept it quickly. "No Mama I didn't break your glass vase or the statue Papa brought you or that doodad Aunt Eleanor sent from wherever it was."

Survival is the first reason to lie. Certainly no one volunteers the fact that they ran over the dog or lost the bank deposit or added those numerous checks to their own account and then bought a swimming pool or new car. We are an absurd species when such things tempt us and we steal, and lie. The soul doesn't forget.

Papa's lie to me that this was an adventure was his sad and shameful way of offering me protection. He didn't know what to do so he lied and smiled and fed me pork and tried to pretend.

So tell me, truthfully, how is what he did called an evil lie, how could such love expressed in his actions be wrong in any sense. Except that the lies left me believing life would improve rather than become more difficult.

IT WAS A shed not a cabin. One room, tools scattered on the walls, dirt floor, a narrow bed built into the wall where a man the size of Eben McClary would hang over the edges. The shed at least had a good roof, other than the hole cut for a missing chimney. Eben was meant to work here, and sleep here, take his meals with the cowhands. There had been no thought for the new smithy having a girl child. Even though she'd been part of the original agreement.

Belinda E. Perry

Eben unhitched the mule and stuck it in a small corral, then shifted in the milk cow with her bawling calf. He figured they would stay away from the mule after the nighttime brawl. He found a roof for the wagon and harness and dragged the few boxes he had into the shed.

Remi was there, seated on the edge of the cot, legs swinging, arms folded in her lap. Her enormous eyes glowed when she turned to look at him. "Where're we going to live, Papa?

A knife wound through him, her trust lost in the dirt and cobwebs, the crawling bugs and layers of soot. He tried to force his mouth into some welcoming grin, some parody of home and hearth. "This's ours for now, child. You help me and we'll make it like. . ." He couldn't do it, couldn't say the desolate word, shape the sound through his drawn lips. It was a lie he could not birth.

He picked up a poke broom and handed it to his child. Her hands did not reach up so he laid the broom across her lap. "Remi you start sweeping everything you can find toward the door and me I'll talk to the boss man, get us a better place to live."

The ranch consisted of small cabins and sheds scattered around a central adobe barn with a locked room for gear. The grand house was distant, its red tiled roof and fancy edges foreign in a land of mud and stone and tin. He'd been told it was where a movie star lived, 'in residence' it was called. The main house from the original ranch was a low-set stone building with a long ramada shading its front from the New Mexico sun. There were a few straggly flowers in uneven beds, and a huge old cottonwood split and dying. Enough of the tree still lived that Eben knew with a bit of care he could keep it alive. It took the hand of someone who cared for plants, not just cattle out there somewhere eating grass and growing into money.

He knocked, the screen door rattled, eventually a voice told him to step inside. "Mr. Rantoul?" Eben heard his own voice waver. A bigger voice answered; "You come back here, to the office." Eben followed the sound, which took him through a large room with an enormous fireplace, and then a cramped kitchen to an open door. "You'll learn to come 'round back. In here, you want a cup a coffee?"

It was another cramped room piled with papers and a phone setting to a desk, a big rolling chair mostly covered by a small man, head bent to the desktop. "Coffee's to the cabinet, help yourself." Eben poured into a tin cup, swirled the liquid, no grounds, no eggshells. He tried a swallow, tasted a pretty decent brew. "Mr. Rantoul?"

The man grunted. Eben decided; "I can't put my child in that shed you set aside for us. When we spoke I told you I had a little girl and you said...." He lost his nerve. Rantoul looked up, eyes hidden by glasses hung to the edge of his nose. "There's no place else unless you want to try the bunkhouse. I figured well there's some lumber behind the smithy shed and I'll do what I can with a few chairs, a table or such. Meals're to the cook shack so you don't need a kitchen."

Eben found his voice; "Mr. Rantoul my child can't live to that shed. It ain't hardly decent for me nevermind a girl." Rantoul pushed the glasses up onto his bald scalp; "Mr. McClary I'm running a ranch here not a boarding school. You want the job, it's yours, a place to sleep, decent food, and a school for the child. That was our deal, you takin' it? If not, I will hire another man without your complications."

Rantoul's voice never raised or showed anger; he nodded to Eben and went back to his papers. "Door's that way." Rantoul's abrupt dismissal was directed into the desk and the work with no acknowledgment of Eben's worries. Eben left, already a failure.

He stood by the tree, ran his fingers against the bark, folded one leaf in his palm and inhaled the smell. It was still living, despite the dried branches and exposed root. An ancient tree, and Eben leaned against it, taking strength for a moment, knowing he had no choice.

When he approached the shed, he saw that behind the tilted building was a larger shed, no front to it but empty, holding the promised lumber. So here it was, he decided, with extra work he could make the small shed a home; the larger shed would become the smithy. He didn't bother to tell Rantoul his new plans. Eben went to what was meant to be their new home and looked inside.

She had swept the place bare, and the mound of trash, dirt, and dried rodents sat on the doorsill or what would have been a sill if there had been a door. "Remi, child, you in there?"

He half-jumped the dirt pile and saw her, sitting on the bunk, looking up at him. Her face was stained, her hair pulled free of his meager attempt to braid. She was struggling to breath and crying at the same time. "I want to go home." She struggled into his lap before he'd set himself down and he caught her, held her small body while she cried.

Belinda E. Perry

"I tried to clean it up so we could live here but it won't clean." Then she twisted in his arms and stared up at him and his heart broke again. "If it isn't clean Mama won't come back."

I AM NOT that little girl and I know better, we all know better, but how do you explain death to a child. I have heard all the lies, the worst being that God needed her or him more than the family. How cruel to make any god the fall guy for such pain. And it is not deceiving, the child knows instinctively, death has no value to them, no meaning beyond the loss of kind hands and warm meals, a voice to tell them, a place to cry. Denying this person to a child in a god's name is false and one of the cruelest lies.

Lies hurt, lies of omission as well as deliberate fabrication. Then again, most of life is drawn with pain, from the beginning of birth to when our spirit recedes and we await death. It comes first as infinite small dyings; loss of hearing, eyesight, speech, joy leaves us except for brief moments of contact, great-grandchildren, old friends. But their deaths can precede our own, reminding us too easily that we are on the same list.

Dying young, being killed, is removed from this terrible slow demise. But its instant relief is not a state we wish for ourselves or our families.

A dear friend and I were to go shopping one day; she forgot her purse and went back upstairs to retrieve it and did not reappear. I finally went after her and she had died sitting in her favorite chair. I stood for a moment, looking at her, seeing nothing in her face, no rictus of death, no smile of genuine pleasure. Nothing; she was dead. And her death was my loss and her relief.

We lie about death as soon as we understand its presence. Children play with death, 'killing' their dolls and then resurrecting them and killing again and again until they are bored and go find another game. But they know, as the doll is slammed backwards or falls desperately, that they are removing life from the plaything. They are in effect god, restoring what they have taken away.

Until death happens to them, a father or mother, a favored sister, a hated aunt or uncle, a loss they cannot repair by picking up the doll and giving it a new name and existence.

The lie of lies is that we can cheat this intruder. Life insurance, messages of regaining youth, can you see that woman in her seventies, painted, waxed, clothed in youth and still looking at death. Isn't it too bad that waxing doesn't remove death.

We're going to die so live now, give up pretending, don't accept the lie and do what gives you joy, survive, laugh, fuck for pleasure as well as children and know you will die and learn to not care. It happens if you obsess on your death or not, so give up the fret and worry and live your life.

I want to add 'damn it' and 'fuck' and all sorts of oaths and curses to get your attention, draw your mind to the seriousness of the situation, but I know that swearing in an old lady is more inclined to drive a reader away than draw them in. So please add the oaths and cusswords where you feel they might be appropriate. Believe me, they are there, in my mind at least.

And, hear this also, the Irish have a song in which there is sung a line of huge importance; 'The longer you live, the sooner you bloody well die.' Think on the statement and act accordingly.

SIX

A bell rang and brought Eben from the shed carrying Remi. A slow progression of men went toward a long building. Dinner he guessed and set Remi down. "Let's eat, child." She followed him so close she would trip if he stopped, he tried to haul her out from behind him but she slipped away and he stopped trying.

There were two men already at the cook shack, seated at one end of a long table. The other men sat at a distant table, hunched over the food, silent as they ate quickly. Eben sat on a bench with the two old men, Remi scooted close to him. He looked down at her, felt her trembling. A tray of sandwiches lay in the middle of the table, resting on individual bits of paper. No one said a word to him. Remi pushed herself closer. Eben gave her a sandwich.

He looked at the two men who had their heads down and were chewing into the bread and meat. Eben picked up a sandwich of his own, drawing in the odor; well-cured ham, mustard, fresh bread. He took a big bite.

Remi picked at the bread and in a small voice said she was thirsty. A pitcher shedding droplets on the plank table was within reach of the silent men. Eben cleared his throat and asked for the pitcher. The men chewed, didn't flinch or look up. He asked again, nothing.

He roared; "Give me that pitcher." Remi jumped, then pushed even closer against him. One of the men looked up slowly, mouth open, eyes barely registering Eben's presence. "What you want, boy?" The voice belonged to an old face, watering eyes, slack cheeks, white whiskers; the other man began to realize something was happening. He stared at Eben, grinned at the child, and he had no teeth at all.

Eben pointed to the pitcher, the first man shoved it, water sloshing, cold water sliding over the rim, washing the bare wood. Eben found himself licking his lips, lots of water, his first real luxury. "Papa?" His child, her eyes focused on the toothless old man. "Papa!"

Glasses were stacked on a side cupboard, Eben nudged Remi and pointed, she got up quickly, retrieved two glasses, went back and got two more glasses and slowly approached the silent diners. In her small hands the thick glass shimmered like stars. One of the men looked away

65

and Eben wanted to hit at him; the other grinned, toothless and food-spattered but it was a response to Remi's effort.

"Thank 'ee, child, that's right nice."

Remi sat down to a glass of water and the sandwich as if she'd righted a wrong. Eben bowed his head; not a man for religious rituals, he felt a thankfulness that had no place in the small room but created an opening in him. Living here would be possible.

BEING SMALL, SHE could get into places no one else could, so when the Spencer boys chased her she slid through the skinny opening into the chicken yard. The boys would stand for a time jeering at her but she only smiled and twirled around until one of the hands chased them away or they got bored.

Willard and Toby Spencer would be in the fifth and seventh grade if the school was big enough for grades. Mrs. Ravenstock taught the three ranch children in her living room. Her husband was the ranch foreman, Mr. Rantoul was the general manager, and Stan was the cook. Remi learned quickly to avoid the general manager; he would peer over his glasses at her and shake his head as if her appearance was a distraction from the true purpose of the ranch, to balance the books and be certain that the cattle reproduced.

Remi could already read better than Willard; Mama had read to her, and Betsy and Rosie always showed her their workbooks where they copied the letters. Mrs. Ravenstock told the class how advanced Remi was and the Spencer boys tried to exact their revenge. Evading them had been easy.

If they got really bad all she had to do was head toward the smithy and the boys quit chasing her. They had learned the first week her papa was no fool and no kind heart. He grabbed Toby when the boy tried to take a horseshoe and Toby's squeals kept the boys out of the smithy shed after that one attempt.

That first afternoon Papa had found a door in the lumber shed and hung it from the front frame, then he brought all their belongings in from the wagon, and took the lard tin with the wrapped pig in it to the cookhouse. He officially met Stan and the two old men who sat out front and watched whatever might happen. Milt Oppen and Pego Ortiz, who'd worked for the ranch maybe forty years and through three owners.

Remi liked to sit with them while they repaired bridles and spur straps, and Milt sometimes took long strands of the horses' tails and braided a tight, prickly rope.

They let her watch, not intending to teach her. She found her own horse hair and tried what Milt was doing, it pricked her fingers and tickled her nose and his big hands came onto hers to help her feel the tightness, the pattern of the weaving and eventually she had a rope almost two feet long that she gave to Papa and he thanked her.

Eben put down a floor using strips of boards from the bigger shed and with the new door the shed began to be livable. Remi got out the quilts Mama made and cried while she put them on the one bed. Papa had made her a mattress and he slept on a wad of hay in the far corner.

Then he got the forge set where he wanted and built up the chimney and all the time he talked to Remi like she understood what was being built. Mr. Rantoul came to inspect what Papa was doing and they went to the forge behind the shed where Remi heard loud voices and yelling but she knew her papa would win.

He came back grinning, and they went in to the supper meal with Papa telling stories and getting Remi to giggle.

NOW I SWORE when I started this that I wouldn't interfere with the story, but no one wants to hear the long drawn-out tale of a child growing up on a ranch unless it's another child and this is no book you want your children to read. Although the thoughts and opinions are invaluable to growing up, many of us are afraid to expose our children to radical ideas so we curtail their reading. Imagine banning Huckleberry Finn or Harry Potter, that's truly absurd. And yes I've read some of the Potter books, I ain't dead yet you know.

It's always there among us, the desire and need to shape and save and comfort those we love, or at least have produced. This over-solicitation can be a terrible price for being born. A friend refused to allow her daughter to read Black Beauty until she was in her teens; I read it at seven and certainly that sudden knowledge of life's cruelties did not shred my decency or create a monster.

Actually I looked at animals in a new light, having been forced to see them as living beings, not merely participants in cute stories or cartoons. This terrible blank wall of sense about animals frightens me; in recreating them as cute and cuddly foxes or magnificent lions roaring and playing with their cubs, we diminish their true nature which is to catch, kill, and eat whatever they can to sustain their lives.

I know, the argument is old, stale in fact. Boring, rehashed, with the gun-toters on one side, the animal rights bunch on the other. Neither of them are valid any more – most of us do not need to hunt to survive, which is our true nature. And for the love of everything on earth, who set these idiots loose thinking they can return all animal species to their 'real' nature and existence? Haven't they noticed that there are cities, towns, roads and dams where life used to roam free? And do they understand that most animals in the wild suffer starvation and pain as they live their shortened lives?

Have you walked the woods and found a small pile of bones, maybe a skull, so clean and delicate, barely any weight in your hands, chipped perhaps, missing a few teeth, a crack across the skull top, not hint of death but the only proof this creature did exist? It probably lived two or three years, and died either starving, injured, or eaten.

Turn horses loose, oh yes. The horses will run, and not come back – they are domesticated passively and we take advantage of this. Turned loose, they will gallop off and not return. It is a beautiful picture – one used to full advantage in a movie of maybe twenty years ago, complete in slow motioned double screen and the perfect music.

I was in Monument Valley, scene of so many westerns with our national hero John Wayne; don't get me started on him oh lordy. We were to camp in a side canyon but there was a horse stranded on a bit of grass in the middle of our designated campground.

And yes at the age of seventy-something I still went camping. Had me a great traveling futon and put a foam 'egg crate' on top and voilà, the Ritz of camping mattresses, until these aero things came along. Now that's luxury.

The stranded horse stood on three legs, one hind leg was shattered above the hock, you know, that large joint in the hind leg. Broken legs on a wild horse mean slow starvation, thirst, and inevitable death from coyote or wolf. We moved camp, no one was willing to sit outside with our portable stoves and showers and watch the horse die. The owners said the horse would live out its life and they would not interfere.

This is how the wild things die.

No lies here, no softening of reality by using careful words and euphemisms to account for a hard and terrible death. We try, we utilize our supposed superior brains and lie about the truth and it is meant to offer comfort but it creates a false hole in our lives, a fear of what we suspect leveled against what we are told.

Seems to me we started this same argument early in the writing. But it is the truth that often lies.

HE FINALLY ASKED Mrs. Ravenstock to talk with Remi. She was wild, at twelve already tall as her mother and with long dark red-blond hair and those eyes, well she scared Eben. She was almost a woman and still a girl and he knew only the barest notion of what a girl went through to become that woman, so he asked the teacher who was herself a mother with full grown daughters and two grandchildren. She was the one to tell Remi.

Mrs. Ravenstock asked Remi to stay after school when she wanted to run to the corrals 'cause they got new horses in and maybe this time there would be a horse old Milt thought would suit Remi. Pego had died last year, finally letting go and Remi had been with him and Milt, outside the cabin they shared. Quiet, nothing but a release of breath, eyes looking once at Remi and then to the door. A sigh.

Milt promised her a horse after that and even Mr. Rantoul didn't offer any objection other than a reminder to be sure the animal was suitable.

Outside the classroom window, which was nothing but the unused parlor in the Ravenstock house, Remi could watch the new horses in their corral. Whirling and kicking, even she could hear the squeals.

Mrs. Ravenstock took her into the kitchen and sat her at the table. "Dear would you like a cup of water?" The teacher's voice had disappeared; full of demand and iron, now it was sticky and Remi was suspicious of the intent. A horse whinnied and she stared out the window, she couldn't quite see the corral; the horse whinnied again and Remi jumped.

"Dear, your father asked me to speak with you. Now that you're growing up, there are things you need to know." Remi shook her head; she already knew. The woman persisted; "I had this talk with my two daughters and they are successful mothers and wives."

The words sat heavy, kind of like Stan's biscuits when he'd been drinking. Remi twirled an end of hair around her finger. "Dear, that isn't proper behavior for a young lady. Now living here to the ranch I would think, guess, that you know about, well, how we make babies, how they come out of our bodies. It is a beautiful process, giving birth and holding your newborn baby. The birth is a present for your husband as he has chosen you for his mate. You honor him with your effort."

"Mrs. Ravenstock what if I chose, does that mean the man gives birth?" The woman's eyes got huge and she stuffed her chin against her neck. "I've never heard of such a thing, child you are talking nonsense." Words answering nothing, Remi smiled innocently.

"Before you become a wife your body will change. There are delicate awakenings in your very heart which will bring a man to you. You of course will develop…well…." She vaguely passed a hand over her bosom and Remi giggled. "These are for the child's enrichment."

The woman looked at Remi with her schoolteacher glare and Remi sat quietly.

"How do I bind them, I asked Papa and he couldn't speak on the question so I guessed he asked you. They get in the way when I run, they bounce and hurt." She sat primly, studying Mrs. Ravenstock's many changes of expression. Finally the woman settled on outrage.

"This is not how a young woman speaks of her body, it is our temple of purity and value and we must take all cautions and cares to ensure we remain healthy and agreeable to our future husband's . . ." There she stopped, having gotten herself in too far, too many vivid pictures raised by her stream of words.

Remi could see her sister, up against the Voorhes boy, not lying under him like Mama and Papa but up and down on him, and she'd watched, oddly bothered by the vision, hearing their low voices, that tingle Rosie told her about, warned her against and told her what she'd done to herself in Sunday School as if the two things were the same.

The mechanics weren't quite fixed in Remi's mind but the sense had been driven into her flesh; Mama's moans, Papa's white rounded buttocks, sister Rosie going up and down. That looked the most interesting, like riding a horse Remi thought. She wanted to ride a horse.

"Young lady, listen to me. I need to explain to you about your monthlies."

THE INFORMATION WAS shocking; Remi sat frozen, hands searching for a safe place to land. That blood was expected to come out of her body every month made her angry. "Why don't the men have to do this?" That was the wrong question to ask Mrs. Ravenstock.

"Remi dear, as women we bear the pain of the world and yet it is our glory. Your husband will treasure you and work hard to provide for you and his children but you must make sacrifices for him to be so willing. Our cross to bear is our suffering, our joy is our children, and their loving father."

Remi was shown how to fold the pads and given pins, a special netted bag in which she must put the soiled linens and how to wash them out while keeping them private, not mixed in with the laundry she did for her father. This was a most precious and singular matter and it was important that Remi pay strict attention.

Remi left the net bag and the folded squares inside their cabin door and headed to the corrals. She'd ask Papa later if what this old woman told her was the truth. It made no sense to her, she wasn't convinced the woman had told her anything she needed to know. Papa of course had already left their cabin to sit with the old men.

There was a little bay horse tied off to one side in the corral and Sixto was rubbing a blanket all over the horse's body. Remi had seen this done so many times, yet the little bay horse wasn't scared. Sixto was maybe seventeen and good with the horses, even Mr. Rantoul said so. The owner wanted to raise ranch stock on the property, Mr. Rantoul said it wasn't economically feasible and the movie star protested, but the funny little man with the glasses and books simply shook his head and said no.

Remi wondered sometimes who owned the place, but Rantoul as usual had the last word. So they bought their horses down in Mexico, Sixto's father had a brother there and they sent only the best up to the famous Rafter H.

The little bay gelding was one of those broncs, and she watched Sixto go over the horse, every inch, waving and rubbing and the little horse turned his head to look at Remi while Sixto kept waving and shoving. Finally the bay stamped his hoof, flattened his ears and even Remi knew that meant he'd had enough.

Sixto came to the fence where Remi was sitting. "My uncle sent him with word that this was to be your horse." She had learned only a few months ago that Pego was Sixto's grandfather and that he had a long line of relatives who had worked the Rafter H. Pego had not gone back to Mexico when he was too old, a story no one would tell Remi. The bay horse was a thank-you.

"He's a good one, Remi. Your size and sure is quiet." Sixto was already a full hand on the ranch, and his father had been working the horses for twenty years. Since before Sixto was born. He was older yet he allowed Remi to tag along once in a while. Sixto called her his little sister and tried to show her what he could about horses. Now she had a horse of her own.

Papa had found an old child's saddle and oiled it; Milt produced two doubled woven blankets he said would keep any points in the tree from poking the bay's hide. And Sixto rode the bay first with a mild ring snaffle and the horse seemed quite content with the easy bit.

They all laughed as Sixto climbed aboard and settled himself in the smaller saddle, hugging his backside and barely enough room for his thigh to hang down. His boots didn't fit to the stirrups and he let his legs hang, toes reaching below the bay's knees. The little horse actually turned around and sniffed at Sixto's leg and the boy lightly stroked the small white star on the bay's nose. Remi found she was crying.

Sixto guided the little bay around the circular corral and then Papa opened a gate and horse and rider walked the edges of the ranch yard, stopping at the sheds and houses, the barn, a pen filled with bawling steers on their way out, a calf butting its ailing mama for more milk. The horse looked, stopped a couple of times to snort and blow at something unusual like wash on the line or the Spencer boys chasing each other, but nothing happened, no blow up or whirl or any thought of a buck. Sixto seemed to move his legs the smallest bit and the horse stepped into a lope. Remi's hands went to her mouth in fear but the bay rocked and glided and she wanted to be riding so she ran up behind the bay. The horse went sideways and spun around, stopped and looked hard at Remi who almost ran into his face.

Sixto looked down at her; "You know better'n to run up behind a horse." Remi cried in earnest and Sixto's stern expression dissolved. He swung down, the little bay put his nose out and lightly touched Remi's arm.

"Here." Sixto gave her the reins. Then put an arm around her and lifted her into the saddle. Her dress hiked up underneath her legs and her silly leather shoes and white socks fitted right into the stirrups. She rocked in the saddle, finding its support and fit, and the bay horse flipped his ears back and forth.

"Remi you be careful, this horse thinks and feels right smart so plan what you ask 'cause he'll do it quick." Sixto touched her naked knee, pressed down briefly. "That's all you need, no kicking or hauling. He's a good 'un."

Remi had been watching and listening even though she'd not ever sat on a horse's back 'cepting for that one time when Pego let her get up on his fancy vaquero rig and she even got to hold the reins while Papa led her around. That was her one time and now she was on her own horse.

She raised her legs and let them flap and the horse jumped forward, spilling her over his rump. She landed on her own backside and there was laughter behind her but Sixto knelt down and looked at her.

"You're fine, kid, don't listen to them. I told you not to kick, just breathe and think and that little son'll do whatever you want. Breathe, that's all."

He picked her up and stood at the same time and the little horse was waiting right there, reins on the ground, ears and eyes watching Remi. Sixto set her in the saddle again, patted her knee. "Now remember what I told you and think and breathe and he'll know what to do."

Sixto turned and settled the reins, patted the bay's neck then checked on the stirrups and Remi got impatient to get riding. She barely touched the horse with her legs and he walked politely across the yard, Sixto walking with them.

"Keep breathing, Remi, you're doing just fine." He stepped away, the horse took a short stride to follow Sixto and Remi held the reins to his neck, made a clicking sound with her tongue and the horse straightened out, walked forward. She was riding.

The bay circled the ranch yard, nodding now to the horses in the pens and the bawling calf, even the flapping wash. She guided him around a big tree, circled back the other way and when she leaned out of the saddle to help him make the turn, he stopped and shook, wouldn't move until she sat upright in the saddle again.

She tried trotting and bounced but saw Sixto smiling and nodding and she laughed and relaxed and didn't bounce so much. She was riding!

PAPA HAD TO take her off the horse before it was time to eat supper. He showed her how to undo the cinch and brush away the marks left by the saddle and put the saddle on a rack. To hang up the bridle correctly and everything he did, he told her why.

"Sixto said the bronc's name is Pego." Remi looked at her father, something was wrong, his voice was harsh, his movements too quick. She had learned since living here on the ranch that her father's moods and temper could be gauged by how he spoke. "What did you want to call him, Papa?" Maybe that was the wrong, maybe she could fix it.

"A dead man gave you this horse, I don't care what you call it." He left the small room crowded with saddles and gear and she had to run to catch up to him. She tried to slip her hand into his, he shook her away; "You're too old for that." Remi held back, followed slowly, aware she'd lost a place in her papa's heart when she received the horse named Pego.

That night she cried, huddled in her bed to the corner of their converted shed. It had been their home now for more than five years and she'd forgotten Mama's voice, barely remembered she had older sisters with babies and a brother who never lived. Now Papa was leaving her, only the mound of him sleeping in the small corner he'd walled off for himself was a reminder that he was there, snoring, but he wasn't hers now.

Adding what Mrs. Ravenstock said to Papa's distant voice and strange behavior, Remi was scared.

SEVEN

Papa gave up and let her wear blue jeans and boots even to school although Mrs. Ravenstock tried to object. Papa was blunt with the woman, telling her Remi had a horse to ride and he couldn't afford dresses and jeans both and it was wrong for a girl to ride in a skirt wouldn't Mrs. Ravenstock agree, not with all these cowboys working to the ranch.

Remi believed those were the most words her papa ever said at one stretch. They certainly took care of the schoolteacher's constant fussing about Remi behaving appropriately in her dress and manner.

She rode every day after school and Pego was her best friend. He always traveled with one ear listening to the world, and one ear back tending to her, her constant talking to him, singing, whistling even. She fell off on occasion and learned to stop crying and get back on. Sixto gave her a few pointers, and she rode with him when he had a fence line to check or a lost calf to search out and rescue. Papa trusted Sixto enough to let her ride with him for hours and hours over the weekend, but only after her homework was done.

She was tending to her schoolwork better. The Spencer boys were gone, their pa moved on to a different job taking most of Remi's trouble with him. Another girl had come to live on the ranch briefly, her ma a washerwoman, her pa meant to be a mechanic for the tractors and trucks but he couldn't fix any of the machines so they too left pretty quick.

Now the cowboys were leaving, all the talk of war and they were joining up. Mr. Rantoul complained to Papa that it was harder and harder to find and keep good young men with the needed skills. So he went to Sixto's family, who had relatives still in Mexico, and they sent three men of middle age and long experience.

One of them, Rogelio, was indeed expert at starting the young horses without hurting them, and even Mr. Rantoul admired his patience and skill. At first there were complaints that his methods took too much time; after a year the complaints stopped as even the rawest horse worked well on cattle. Rogelio's methods were slow and thorough, and he took the time to explain them to Remi.

"You watch, try to see what they feel. Then you make it easy for them to do what you want. Never hurt them for they will not forget." He gave her the same advice Sixto used; "Breathe with your horse and let what you want come into your bones and muscles and he will hear your desire." It sounded odd to her, too mystical, but she tried riding Pego with a softer mind and when she finally stiffened and wanted to stop, he did.

She often sat on Pego without the saddle and watched Rogelio work the young horses. She wanted to do what he was doing.

SIXTO JOINED UP in 'forty-one, three more hands left in early forty-two and Remi at fifteen ended her schooling to ride fence and check on the cattle. She had an adult saddle now, to fit her long legs and Mr. Rantoul gave her a hat out of the ranch stores so she didn't bake in the heat or freeze in the winter.

She earned only half what the men earned, and Papa took most of that but she had her own few dollars and didn't mind giving up her pay. Papa had earned the right to take in private work, easily maintaining the ranch work first, then beginning to find pleasure in creating fantasy pieces, iron men fifteen feet tall and cattle made out of old tractors, slabs of dissembled trucks. He stuck them around the ranch wherever Rantoul would allow.

Which meant that Papa hardly saw his daughter, except at a few meals or a late night working on a project. Remi worked through the war as a cowboy, hair pulled back in a single braid, jeans and chaps, face weathered at seventeen, green eyes clear and vivid against her browned skin.

Sixto Vargas came back to the ranch in the summer of nineteen forty-five and found a young woman who could rope and drag a calf, brand, inoculate, and castrate without a flinch or misstep. She was almost eighteen, and in Sixto's ruined eyes she was beautiful.

SIXTO – OH DEAR his face when he got to the ranch was enough to break any young girl's heart. He'd been in a prison camp in Germany, and he was probably forty pounds underweight, gaunt, hard, slow-moving with none of that remembered joy and exuberance he held to himself when he taught me how to ride. His hand touching my bared knee, his fingers closed over mine on the reins. Those were my memories and they allowed me access to Sixto beyond his disfigurement. I knew him, I had felt his touch; his new self was only the shell where my long-hidden desires had grown and matured. He was not frightening to me, he was Sixto Vargas, all I needed to know.

There are no lies here, no hiding of the truth, no declarations used as sidesteps to the truth. The heat of his flesh on mine as a child had initially returned those images of Rosie and that awful boy Jay Voorhes who was no longer her husband. As I matured beyond the outrage, I grew to understand what a man's touch could bring, and I invested in Sixto what I had learned from watching Rosie.

Now that's a peculiar story. Papa had written his name and then the Rafter H brand on wall of our house as we left – somewhere in the intervening years Rosie had come home and found no one but that raised and vivid brand. Papa used a stain to highlight its meaning and she came looking for us.

Jay had left her almost immediately and she had worked to take care of herself, not writing to us out of shame. She wore fancied city clothes and spoke differently than us but she was my sister. Or should I say 'we did' rather than 'us' and be grammatically correct. Those who are more educated would relieve my words of their importance by focusing on the acceptability of my grammar and punctuation. This is an easy way to escape having to listen to an opinion differing from theirs.

Rosie was saddened by the loss of her mother. Distance and time might have removed her from the family but she had always known there was home and a mother and father who waited for her. It hurt me to say the words, it hurt us both to see our papa's retreat from his own child.

I guess he lied, by saying he was glad to see Rosie and then disappearing. We knew he was in the shop working and when he came in to bed, we pretended we were asleep and almost immediately that wasn't a lie.

Belinda E. Perry

This is all very clear to me even though it was over sixty years ago. The clean snap of pain exposed by Rosie's presence and questions brought back a despair I had tried to bury in my riding fence and learning to rope. To become one of the boys, a top hand, despite being a girl and a kid, was a desired place where I could bury Mama and her loss. No matter trying to imagine what life might have been, it wasn't, therefore I must live the life I was given.

The brief reunion with Rosie brought too much with it and I was vulnerable to Sixto's return, his own private sadness and pain.

Is there valor in a young man's destruction while alive, is there any hope for a mind obliterated by suffering? These are foolish questions with no answers, no room for lies, no tolerance beyond the attempts at rescue.

Every woman knows our predisposition to bandage, bind, succor and console. And it is the wounded who need us, the bad boys who draw us with their pleading eyes and terrible stories, offering us our chance to become solace and safety for their bleeding souls.

In other words, for you youngsters who think you've invented the angst and tragedy of the teenage years, the bad boys draw us, tantalize us while the good boys, your so-called nerds and geeks, repel us with their normalcy, their pimpled features and sunken chests, their wash-and-wear pants and polyester shirts.

Aren't we the fools, for overlooking genuine distress and being taken by thick hair and long lashes, wounded eyes and torn clothes. Oh my aren't we endless fools for these boys. Although who is to say they don't need us as badly as they treat us, and that our survival skills and reasonableness are honed by the fascination and then the ultimate and always rejection.

We feel we are not good enough for these wild or feral young men as we want lives of our own and not their empty promises and eventual brutality. Fortunately for me, Sixto Vargas was not one of these boys, he was warm and sweet and very careful of me since I was considered a sister, not a female ready for the taking. Then he came home from two years in a prison camp and all was changed. I was grown, he had been imprisoned; the story tells its own tale.

Without lies, as I promised.

MR. RAVENSTOCK TOLD her to do the chore. "He's been your horse, girl, now it's you got to take care of him." Remi nodded to the boss's words and wanted to tell him she was just a kid, and a girl at that, but her pride and his treatment of her as a ranch hand and nothing else kept her mouth shut.

Mr. Ravenstock had fought against her joining the crew until fall round-up when she did the scut work and didn't cringe at cutting the male calves or notching their ears. After that, he gave her chores, which became long rides on her own looking for a one-horned cow or a mired steer, knowing she could do whatever was needed.

In the beginning she'd ridden only Pego, who was a companion and company as well as a way to get into the back canyons and hidden gullies on the ranch. Now Pego was lamed and losing weight, in his twenties, Mr. Ravenstock guessed from his teeth and eyes. She watched the foreman's hands hold the bay's mouth, cradling the muzzle, opening the lips to count the teeth as he spoke about something called a groove and a hook, cups, other terms she did not recognize.

"He's over twenty and ain't gonna come sound. He's your horse, you take him someplace pretty and shoot him, no point letting him suffer through the next winter." Remi saddled up Roy, stout and smooth buckskin, the first horse she broke to saddle and ride. He was barely six but steady and she could count on him to handle a rifle in its boot under her leg, Pego's close presence, the sound of gunfire, and the inevitable smell of death.

He would be her strength because she would cry, and her hands would shake but her friend needed this final kindness and Remi was wise enough to accept the reality.

Pego lowered his head slightly to touch soft lips against her cheek. She was already crying and he rubbed gently, erasing her tears. She stepped up onto Roy's back, settled in with quick practiced motions, picking up the reins, guiding Roy out of the yard not even considering a halter and lead but knowing Pego would follow.

He kept his head close to her, occasionally she would pat him on the neck or touch the tip of an ear and he seemed then to hurry. But the sored foot, the off front, hurt to hold his weight and his head bobbed with each step. They had tried trimming, special shoes, standing in mud, poultices; nothing had helped his expanding pain.

Twice Pego stopped and Roy stopped with him, the two horses standing close, Roy leaning over to nip Pego on the jowl. Remi heard the clack of closed teeth and Pego barely tilted his head away from the affection.

There was a rise in the land maybe two miles out, where an old road wound down through rock, passable on horseback or foot and she'd seen a few deep gouges where a fool in a truck tried to drive the hill and spun in too deep, or slid sideways and once even a Model T rolled over. It looked absurd on its back, narrow tires to the sky, a raven perched on the only tire not punctured. Squawking, cawing at her as if she'd interrupted his study of the valley below.

Pego would like it here. In the beginning they had ridden to this place and back, it held good footing and was a slow rise where she dared to lope him the first time. Before she turned cowboy, she would bring a sandwich with her, taking off Pego's bridle, putting on hobbles like Sixto had showed her so the horse wouldn't go home and leave her to walk. She ate her sandwich, sometimes sharing with Pego, more often he grazed and didn't come begging.

She rode to the bluff and its distance often the first summer. No one seemed to care if she disappeared for hours so she tied books to the saddle horn; there were books in the ranch house, dusty and some never opened. She read whatever she could borrow or take without anyone knowing.

Pego stood over her after he was done grazing, they looked to the far away places she could imagine, and he would rub his head on her shoulder in an acknowledgement of their secret voyages.

ROY HAD GONE on these journeys to the bluff, on a halter and lead alongside Pego, after Roy'd been taken off his mother as a short yearling. It was Remi's way of introducing him to the world he must know. Some of the hands laughed at her, and two of them said they'd first-ride the buckskin for her when it was time.

No one laughed when she put the saddle on Roy's back and he only sniffed it, shook slightly, then seemed to wait for her to climb up. His first few steps were awkward until she laughed and he trotted, bucked slightly and when he got reprimanded with a stern 'no', he quit bucking and flew into a bumpy lope.

Mr. Ravenstock gave her three two-year-olds to pony that year, and four the next year. They rode out real well but none of them were as good as the buckskin. Only reason Mr. Ravenstock let her keep him was her promise to work with the others, and the fact that he wasn't much more than thirteen hands. Size didn't matter much to Roy, she could rope a good yearling off him and he'd shut down, hold that steer until the doctoring got finished.

The hands never called her way foolish again and most of the broncs in her care stayed with the remuda.

Now the old horse who taught her the value of steady friendship needed one more act of compassion. The notion was ugly, the need far too obvious; Pego's walk was slowing, his head bobbed deeper with each step. It was only a mile now to the place so she reined in Roy and let Pego catch up. They stood watching three striped pronghorn graze. One head came up; the sentinel, who studied them before snorting and the trio zigzagged away.

Pego stood next to Roy, rubbing his muzzle on the buckskin's neck. Remi reached down and patted the bay skull. Pego's ears went back and forth and he raised his head, nipped at her hand; Remi laughed.

It took another half hour to make the distance. Remi climbed off Roy, tied him loosely to a scrub bush. He was pistol-broke but she needed to be sure. He might take exception to the death of a friend.

Pego wandered off to lip at a few stalks of grass. Remi pulled the rifle from its boot, jacked a shell into the chamber, walk close to her old friend. Her best friend. The weight of the rifle staggered her. Pego looked up, Remi said a silent prayer and she studied his skull, that point between the eyes her papa told her about. Draw a line, he said, from one ear across the skull to the eye, from the other ear to the diagonal eye. Where those lines cross is where you take aim. Roy turned restless, tugging at the reins, circling the bush until he got himself shortened up by tangled leather and stood nose to the low bush, pawing, nickering.

Remi put the rifle down and approached Pego, who lifted his head from the meager grass. She took a finger and touched the base of his right ear, drew the tip through his coarse hair, across the small star with its whorled white star, to the inner corner of the huge brown eye. Her fingertip left a disturbed tracery. She repeated this with the left ear to the right eye and there it was, a lethal X.

Pego pushed his nose out to bump her belly. She didn't cry. She went back for the rifle, returned to her friend who was waiting, more interested in her actions than the dried grass. She raised the barrel, touched the spot and pulled the barrel back. Pego's ears came forward as if he was trying to hear what the rifle would say.

She fired, once, again, a third time. The last shot went wild, Pego was down on his side. Bleeding out, then dying..

ROY WOULDN'T SETTLE, he kept pawing, whinnying, spinning when she went to resheath the rifle. Finally she untangled the reins and gave a good jerk on his mouth. He stopped then, mouth opened to the pain. Remi cried, holding the reins, hugging Roy's neck. He bowed his head across her back and she kept crying.

As she reined the horse around, to leave a spot she would not visit again, she heard the discovering cry of a circling raven and she leaned forward, kicked Roy and the horse almost jumped out from under her. Speed was the only blessing.

The ranch yard was empty, just two horses in the corral, no one in the cook shack so dinner was over. She had no idea of time; she was hungry, thirsty, and exhausted. Roy lay down immediately in the corral when she turned him loose. He rolled, grunted, lay on his side, sat up, shook his head, grunted again and lay down on the other side to finish the roll. Then he stood up, bucked once, then settled and nickered at Remi. She threw him a bit of hay; he'd earned the extra feed.

She went in the cook shack; dark, empty, an echo of her boot heels. She could smell frijoles and sopaipillas and her mouth watered. She leaned over the counter, observing the cook's threat if anyone stepped into his domain.

"I took enough for two, you want to share." Not a question but an offer. Spoken in a familiar voice. Remi turned around slowly and to the far corner of the shack there was a figure hunched over the table, leaning heavily on folded arms. A hand pushed a plate toward her. "Here."

She marched across the room, sat at the bench where she could eye the man who made this offer. Her mind searched for his voice and when he raised his head so she could see his eyes, she remembered. Despite the terrible scarring on his face, she knew it was Sixto.

They'd followed his erratic existence in the Army; first he'd been shipped overseas to Germany and his family read what they could from his letters. Then they were informed he had been captured; no letters for almost two years and his mama, his uncle, returned to Mexico and were told horrible stories of his captivity and inevitable death.

The right side of his face was ruined, a deeply imbedded shattering of cheekbone and brow, and matted tissue along the jaw line, twisting the lower lip into an inhuman shape.

He turned his face away from her, so only his left eye, the good side, showed. He was barely smiling. "I was hungry. Mr. Ravenstock told me to take what I wanted." His voice was lower with a raspy sound. His face was thin, tight over the cheekbones, drawn in at the eyes. The left eye was open and she could see its nervous moving; the wounded right eye was pulled almost shut. Remi wanted to cry.

Instead she reached for the offered food; tortillas, spiced meat in red chile, even soured cream, which she didn't like. She piled the tortilla with the meat and bit in deep, chewing quickly, then finding herself unable to eat a second mouthful.

"Ravenstock said you took Pego out today, that he told you to shoot him. The old boy had to have some age on him but why now, what happened?" The words wouldn't come from her; Sixto's face, the good side, actually looked sad and worried and the other side was even more fierce and that finally made her cry. She gulped and strangled and coughed and the tears flowed out like a broke water pipe until Sixto got up and came around to her side of the table and sat next to her, careful it was his left side. He put an arm around her shoulders and she buried herself against his chest, snuffling and burping and finally safe.

Belinda E. Perry

Slowly the tears stopped and yet she stayed within his arm. She was at peace for the brief time, until the men came back or her papa walked in looking for her to do chores.

She realized leaning against Sixto that he was thin. Muffled against his shirt, damp where she had wiped her tears, she began to ask what had happened. The tiniest tremor went through him and she'd never felt another human response like it, a deep tremble only she and Sixto would ever know. She lifted her head and saw straight into the left side of his face, the mouth drawn tight, the eye closed and she could imagine the rest of his wounds.

"It was a grenade near steel bars and I didn't remember who I was for a year." "We were told you'd been captured." His chest lifted in the smallest of laughs, she felt rib and muscle move, then resettle. Being held by him was a pleasure. "I was gone from the squad and no one knew who I was, a snafu." She echoed him; "Snafu?" "Situation normal, all...fouled up." She read the interrupted word and grinned, shoved against him and said it out loud. "Fucked." His whole body stiffened and she poked him lightly in the ribs. "I'm a hand here, you know. I castrate the bull calves and notch their ears and I don't cry when one of the boys swears. I had to work, we kept losing the good men like you."

"How old are you, Remi?" She spoke into his chest, bound by his forearm. "Seventeen." There it was again, that tremor or stiffening, fear or worry but whatever it was he pulled away from her. "You're too young and I'm too goddamn ugly." It hurt, his words, but even more his pulling away. She sat up and turned, straddled the bench. He looked beyond her so all she had was his neck and some scarring below the hairline on the right side under his ear.

"I'm not too young. I'll be eighteen soon." Not much of a comeback; he snorted, his back still turned to her. "Well maybe not kid but I sure as hell am too ugly for you." He spun around her on the bench, half-knocking her sideways and leering his face into her, so close she could touch the raised scarring with her tongue or even her eye lashes. She closed her eyes, felt the soft brush, then stuck out her tongue and it was his mouth she found, where the torn and restructured lip corner felt like sand paper and mud but he tasted good, her first kiss, started in anger and then he pulled her against him, wanting her this time despite the childish games.

85

She hadn't ever been kissed, not by a boy or man. Not like her sisters or her folks, only her, imagining and dreaming but not getting close enough and then there weren't any boys, they'd all gone away, becoming soldiers who didn't return.

Sixto tried to slide her mouth to his good side but she held on, knowing from pictures and movies that she was meant to kiss all of him, and she did, feeling him press lightly at first and she pressed back, then a strange moment when he echoed what she had done to start this and slid his tongue between her lips.

She jerked, he moaned, she opened her mouth and his tongue swept inside, her lower lip, then the upper, where the lightest touch sent her body shivering. She let her mouth open, tried this with her own tongue and met his, the contact sparked them both, he jumped, she drew in a quick breath but didn't let him escape.

He felt good to her mouth, when she breathed he breathed with her and she tasted sweetness, a hint of red chile, the scent of someone else's life. Finally he put a hand on her shoulders and pulled himself back, cocked his head so she was given his good eye. She wanted to cry, raised her hand to her mouth and wiped at the tang. He was sweating; she could feel the heat, smell the released salt, the familiar odor of hard work and tired muscle. Yet all they had done was kiss.

"Child you won't know what you're doing. You're too pretty to take on an ugly son of a bitch like me." She raised herself, tired of being told how she was meant to feel. "I've known you most of ten years, Sixto Vargas and what happened to your face ain't much loss, you weren't a raving beauty to begin with. If I waited to kiss you, well then damnit it was a compliment and don't you go telling me what I can and can't do, even Papa knows better, and Mr. Ravenstock, he lets me do pretty much what I please."

For good measure she grabbed Sixto's two ears and steadied his face and kissed him all over again. This time she stuck her tongue in his mouth first and heard that moan again, knew that his hands rested now on her waist, then up along her ribs to touch the beginning swell of her breasts.

I WILL INTERRUPT here, feeling that a big part of me is about to get exposed and it makes me uncomfortable, and by the way there is truly no pun meant in these words. Friends who read what you've written, any author at any time, tend to immediately identify who you was doing what with and when, who's the basis for each character. What no one wants to understand is that no character in a book is completely someone else, they are themselves, unique, owning characteristics of others but still their own being. They become valued by the author, so deep a part of the imaginative life that finishing their story becomes a pain of birth.

Now I will tell you a lie, to your face, but you won't recognize it and that's what makes lying so sweet. One of the hardest things I've done in a long and awkward life is to shoot Pego. And one of the easiest was to love Sixto, ugly face and ruined soul.

SIXTO SEPARATED HIMSELF from her, first by removing his mouth, kissing the hollow of her neck and giving her the chance to stare at his wounding. Close up it was a succession of waves, rubbery-looking, then holes, and deep caverns. She leaned her head at the right angle and kissed the top of the deepest scar, the one through his brow, above his ruined eye. His whole body shivered and his hands clutched her waist.

They rested a moment, her mouth on his forehead, his hands soft around her hips. She drew in his scent, he gently pushed her, hands strong as she remembered, that hand resting on her knee, telling her how to carry her legs around Pego, fresh in her new child's saddle. A world all her own, with Sixto as guardian and guide.

He tipped her off the bench, forcing her to stand. Then he too stood up, his hands across his chest, head down and canted away from her so only the good side was visible.

He'd had learned this new art quickly; Remi reached out and took his chin, drew his face around so they were eye to eye, ruined side, vivid scar, matted dark curls, that mouth tasting like honey and red chile.

He tried to smile and the ugly action shattered her. She jumped at him, landing close, inhaling his scent. "Remi." Her name in his mouth, like nothing she'd know. She laid her head on his chest, let her arms go around him and felt unyielding sinew where there needed to be muscle and warmth.

'Sixto'; his name breathed into his skin, through a washed blue shirt, down to fragile flesh and sweet bone. "Remi", her name called out, gentle, whispered into her hair. "Can you bear me like this?" She nodded, safe, held by the only man she knew to trust.

Then there were voices and horses and loud names, a short cheer when Sixto stepped out into sunshine, followed by absolute silence. Five men riding in, standing grouped against Sixto's appearance. Rogelio slid off his bronc, a stout roan who'd thrown maybe seven men before Rogelio worked the kinks out. The vaquero walked forward, hesitated, took another step.

"Sixto?" Remi saw the barest of nods from Sixto, his head cocked, his good eye on his cousin. Rogelio was smiling now, his voice rising in intensity; "It is you." Then he lapsed into rapid Spanish that Remi barely understood. And finally he embraced his wounded friend, his student and amigo. His family.

The four men stayed on their horses. They were new to the Rafter H, hired when the cowhands trickled off the ranch. They were old, lamed, weakened by some defectt that kept them from the fighting. As a slow group they turned and rode to the corrals, Rogelio's roan at first trailing after them, stepping on its own reins and deciding it was tied fast to the ground.

Remi went to the roan, picked up the reins, led the bronc to Rogelio and Sixto and tucked the reins into Rogelio's clenched right hand. She was shaking, her legs wobbly; she went directly to the shed where she and Papa had created their strange home, and lay down on her bed, boots and hat and sweaty hands, closed eyes. One moment of today's sadness had been overwhelming and then quickly lost in Sixto's unexpected return.

EBEN MCCLARY WAS HOME before supper and yelled when he saw Remi asleep in her clothes, boots on the bed, hat thrown across the small room. His immediate fear was her being alive; she was lax, spread out, too open and quiet for his child. His yell came out of instinct; she barely stirred but at least the movement of one hand, the shifting of a booted leg let him know she was living.

He couldn't bear another loss; his Didia still came to him in dreams, his two girls were distant, his son, his only son, was nothing more than powder and bits of melting bone. His heart had been the champion of these lives, they had deserted him to live within fading remembrance. Rosie's visit had been too much for him; too many lost faces in the fierce, unknown years.

Eben lowered himself into a chair, a heavy woven item cast out of the movie star's home as too ugly but it suited Eben, its edges were fraying, its legs bent under too much weight but it held, squatting inside the crude door he'd made so many years ago, waiting for these moments. When Eben needed to sit, when his breath was labored, his energy gone from his arms and legs.

He rested and took satisfaction from watching his child. She had become beautiful to him, with her thick braid of streaked and darkening red-blond hair and the green eyes that had deepened but never changed. She was slender now, hard-muscled from her work and Eben didn't approve of what she was doing and Ravenstock's treatment of her but there weren't many choices. Now that the men would be coming back, she could try life as a girl again.

Eben suspected his daughter would not take lightly to the change She liked the horses, riding, the hard work. He'd seen her face as she roped out a reluctant steer one of the boys had missed. Accomplishments such as that were hard-won in life, and especially for a woman.

He stood slowly, grunting with the effort, and went over to stand next to Remi's bed. Gently, seeing within her the softer face of his child, the baby he'd once held, he shook her arm, marveling at the muscle, remembering her lying in the crib next to their bed. Watching her now he could hear those baby breaths, little gasps, puffs of air that warmed and then cooled his fingers when he laid a hand in front of her mouth, just to feel her life.

Remi finally woke up and she was smiling. "Hey Papa." Then a long moment, when she turned into a true beauty; "Sixto is back."

EIGHT

Watch a man watch a woman; it's educational as well as grand amusement if you have nothing else to do that day. His eyes judge quickly, his body responds to what the woman offers; he can't help it. I would not wish ever to be a man trapped in the base concentration that they continually encounter.

The corner of the mouth, the lower lip, that hair, those hands; parts of her which induce his reverie, the motion and length of leg, the rounded hip, that small area above the buttocks, indented, sweet smelling, soft and hard, a place where he may capture her.

As women we do not contend with outward signs of arousal, and we are better adapted to being practical. A man is wholly owned by his genitals, we all accept the fact as universal.

Sit and listen, watch, as a man, married or not, encounters a prospective sexual partner; whether in reality or fantasy; he immediately tests and judges and she cannot help but toss her hair, expose her throat, push her breasts forward in subtle offerings. Of course the subtlety is not needed, the man is already in his own imaginings; her gestures are proof he is correct in his diagnosis.

I have sat in one room and listened in on two reasonably attractive men deal with a single woman. She had dressed for them, a combination of business and seduction, with a short tight skirt and high boots, a long coat, a tight brightly colored blouse. She was not beautiful, but she had the loose and fluffed hair and make-up designed to point out her best features and enhance what had been given her.

They laughed with her, she told a silly story, they commiserated and applauded her integrity; she flounced the hair, crossed the legs and I am sure that for a few minutes it was uncomfortable for both these men to be seated in a chair, feet on the floor, lap compromised by the hard leather seat. Their sexual torment is eternal and every woman's delight.

Belinda E. Perry

We have small areas of power given to us, and why not take joy and pleasure from what little we own.

Of course now in contemporary times women are on boards and become CEOs and run studios — but that certain power, that rising of a noble erection is the sweetest power we do not earn. We deserve the accolade to our charm, to that narrow place we reserve for our affections. It isn't ever given lightly, even if we have succumbed to the doctrine of easy sex, there is that moment when we can say no. Alcohol and drugs have loosened our self-preservation and esteem and this has not enhanced our value, only lessened our importance. Yes ladies, those of you young enough to know my words and feel the absence of shame. Yes we have all lost something in easy sex. Too bad, for knowing the value of what we keep safe is part of the pleasure of eventual seduction.

I do feel sorry for men though, their daily fights, their incessant rutting simply gives them to us. And they suffer badly for their weakness. Unfortunately, we suffer along with them, for their infidelity and our own, a difficulty expressing what is needed and desired. Neither side of our sexual species can tell the other what is wanted. Sad, realistic, disenchanting. It is why marriages fail, we do not explain or direct, we do not say 'here' or 'there' or some other simple command which might well bring us closer.

As an old woman I have finally learned to listen. I am tired of my own stories and suddenly those around me are brilliant and witty with their practiced retellings. Wish I'd known this earlier in my life, that the rest of the world actually might have something to say.

RAVENSTOCK HIRED SIXTO back despite his wounds. The boy was just twenty-two yet he carried with him the dignity of an older man. He spoke rarely, and took the farthest fences, the most distant pasture, welcoming the solitary ride and the hard work. He ate quickly each morning and night, disdaining the noon meal, and did not put back on any of the baby weight he'd lost. He was darkening, his black curly hair filled with grey; a man within the years of a boy like so many of the returning soldiers.

AN OLD WOMAN'S LIES

Sixto stayed hard and silent, his talent for the horses lost in some deepening fury he could not control. Twice his cousin Rogelio had to pull him off a young horse and Remi found herself frightened of whatever rode within Sixto. She had not been afraid of him in the cook shack, the wildness had not yet surfaced and she remembered his kiss, his smell, and wished that same boy could return.

Sixto took out a spooky four year old, a big sorrel colt Mr. Ravenstock thought might make a herd sire. His dam was one of the newly registered Quarter horses, and the sire was a military remount stallion, pure Thoroughbred. Remi was saddling Roy and almost spoke her mind that Sixto had no business on the colt but Mr. Ravenstock came to tell her of a cow bogged down near the Walker tanks and she best get there real quick.

Her time as a cowhand was limited; a few more of the boys come back and she would have to find a new life. So she couldn't refuse, couldn't argue against Sixto riding the sorrel colt.

Roy glided into an easy lope and Remi put out of her mind any worry about the colt. It took a half hour's travel to find the bog, near that well had itself a leak from deep underground and the well crew was due here next week. So of course a cow had to find the muck and bring herself down, this time with a calf and Remi wanted to yell at the stupid cow but knew from experience yelling did nothing but exhaust her without affecting the cow at all.

Remi roped out the calf, having learned not to tire Roy on the heavy cow first. The calf slid and bawled and cranked its tail, its tongue stuck out as its head twisted around the rope but Roy pulled back steadily, gently, no jerking, no charge, and when the calf was skidded out the youngster stood, shook, the noose slipped and she lifted it from the thinned neck. Bleating and jumping, the calf made a small circle and headed toward its ma. Remi got there first and spanked the calf with the coiled rope until the youngster galloped off.

It was much harder getting the cow out; Roy had to dig in, his hindquarters almost to the ground, his front legs braced, to help the cow's sullen escape. The little horse sat down when the cow stepped on firm ground and the calf went bouncing to his ma, tail twisted over his muddy back, mouth already sucking. Remi gently drove the pair toward the rest of the herd, and then dismounted, slipped Roy's bit and loosened the cinch. He'd earned a break.

She sat with her back to rock and watched Roy snip off the grass real close. Neat clicking bites, taking a good inch off, right to the roots and common sense said she couldn't stay here long, he'd do too much damage over what the cattle had already done.

The sorrel colt came blasting up to Roy, tail high, eyes wide, reins trailing, one broken. Remi was up and speaking to the colt before he came to a stop. Roy snorted, whickered at the colt, then went back to grazing. Despite her soothing words, the colt, she called him Jocko, kept circling Roy, ears going frantically, sidestepping entangling leather. Finally Remi went over to Roy and put his bridle on, redid the cinch, spoke to the buckskin and fiddled with the bridle until Jocko halted, blew out a great blast and put his head down to graze. Remi walked over and picked up the end of the one rein.

Jocko raised his head and nodded, Remi tugged on the single rein and he came close to her. She stroked his neck, then checked back along his ribs. And started cursing; there were spur marks, ruffled hair and dots of blood. She would beat Sixto as badly as he misused this horse. She pulled the rig off Jock, dumped it in fresh cow patties and swung up on Roy, dragging Jocko with them. Backtracking was pretty easy and she let Roy pick up into a lope. Jocko had left wherever he was in a hurry, she made the trip backwards in the same fast time.

She saw Sixto walking and slowed the horses. His ruined head came up and he stared at her, full on, no hiding or retreat. The good side of his face was bloody, he limped slightly and she had no pity for him. She reined in Roy, using his sturdy frame to block the sorrel from Sixto's approach.

"You touch another one of my horses like this and I'll whip you so hard you'll head on back to Germany begging them to take you in."

The words stopped him. His eyes got big, even the bad one, and he wiped at the blood trickling down from under matted curls. "You deserve whatever Jocko did, you son of a bitch, he's never been ridden bad, never offered to buck. Just a little spooky, his mama died in a thunderstorm and he lost confidence and he sure won't trust no man to ride him again. You miserable worm taking out your self-pity on the horses, I been holding my temper but you've gone too far. Walking home's the least you deserve for what you done."

I'M INTERRUPTING AGAIN because a story like this can't be told just with telling. There are asides, explanations, moments in our lives when if we only knew, we'd rejoice in the understanding. As a child, or young woman since I'd been working as a cowhand for several years, I had little or no knowledge of men, boys, the dating rituals of growing up in a small town with a high school and games and places to go, none of these small notions were part of my life. So my connection and attraction to Sixto was completely misunderstood.

He'd been kind to me when I was a child; back from the war he held me and kissed me, my first kiss, think on it, in a dusty empty cook shack with a half-blind wounded war veteran sitting on a splintered bench. I'd never tasted any of these things, his mouth, his hair, the strength in those hands at first threatening, then holding, endearing. It was much more than what I had known. A few goodnight kisses from my Papa, a peck on the cheek from Pego once. No uncles, no cousins, and only the vivid memories of what I saw my sister doing with that Jay Voorhes.

My feelings then, of shamed arousal, had no place in the rest of my life to that point. Mrs. Ravenstock's polite discussion of my monthlies and Papa's fumblings through male and female doings didn't offer me much of anything except more shame. I had of course discovered that using my fingers to rub gave me the most wonderful although far too brief pleasure. Not enough, not ever, and I usually cried afterwards, tears to shed an ache I couldn't comprehend.

Sixto was mad clear through, any fool knows that without hearing the rest of the story. Mad at himself, mad at the insane world that had taken him away from his life and then ruined him. His anger was a force I did not understand, yet I had the basis to feel what he was feeling. My losses too had been significant and disruptive, destroying a childhood while separating me from my remaining family.

I had only the memory of being held by my mother, and then watching her with my father. Coupled (ah ha don't you like a pun; some learned scholar says that only those who have English as a second language delight in puns. Where did he study his subject?) with seeing Rosie outside the house, sliding up and down – I've already spoken of this, how it affected me. Some memories deserve several mentions.

The most destructive nature of these visions, the damaging effects, are in my notion of what made up loving, being loved. No one was there to explain the difference from being fucked and being loved. Now that is a heavy burden for a young girl with no way to learn the truth. Here's a lie; "I love you." Hurts doesn't it.

SIXTO STOOD ABSOLUTELY motionless; his heart still raced from the battle and the spill. The sorrel colt knew how to buck no matter what little Remi told him. He tried to absorb the words, hearing her insults, inspecting each morsel of what she called him, slammed him, gave back to him.

He had felt the eagerness in the colt, tested the young mouth with a few twitches of his fingers. The colt bowed his neck, loosened his jaw and gathered energy through his back, carrying Sixto at an easy trot for several miles toward the line of broken fence. Traveling gave life back to Sixto, the barbed wire held a certain memory, he could smell the rusted metal, taste the prick of his hands on the single barbs. He'd been isolated even from his own side in the camp. He was foreign to them, a survivor from a wasted platoon, uncertain in any reference to the men imprisoned with him.

He was built to be a horseman, narrow hips, slender in the chest and shoulders, hands made of steel with silk in the fingertips, a softening in his mind to allow these colts and fillies a life of their own.

The sense, the touch, had been blown away with half his face. He could watch his fingers wrap around the braided reins, inhale the salt of sweat and leather, a heavier, thick scent of cow and mesquite, grass, and tanning solutions. The hands that scraped the flesh clean, soothed brains or urine into the hide and eased the edges, cut the length. He could feel all this in memory but it was distant, not part of him any more, not his life this time.

The reins were lead, stiff and thick, rubbing across his palm, hurting with their silence. There was little motion or life at the end of these lines, the barest sense of the colt, the eye that saw the neck bow knew what it meant but yet he could not find the feel. He rode the colt's trot easily, that he hadn't forgotten or lost. But when the sorrel spooked, only a half-exposed wagon wheel rim as Sixto discovered painfully, he laid his spurs into the colt's side and yanked on the reins.

He wasn't there with the colt, inside his head, feeling what the colt saw. He hated the fight, jerking and spurring while part of his brain yelled at him. The more the colt fought, snaking his head and neck against the harsh feel from the bit, the stronger Sixto's anger grew. Sixto couldn't breathe, he set one hand on the colt's neck and drew the other up and back hard as he could. The colt's head twisted, Sixto heard the grunt and then, with his head in the air, the colt let out a tremendous kick that flew Sixto over his head, directly onto the iron rim of the rotting wheel.

He remembered lying there watching the colt kick out again and again, stepping on the rein, tearing his mouth as the leather held, then broke, he remembered thinking that his uncle told him a horse couldn't buck if you kept his head up. No one told the sorrel colt that he couldn't toss off a rider like flicking away a mosquito.

Sixto's mind slowly processed what had happened to him. He'd been thrown high and wide by a green colt that a mere girl could ride, and who now defended the colt as being timid and scared. His head didn't hurt, he didn't feel a thing, must have been hit on the scarring padded by newly-growing hair.

When he first walked in the prison camp men had looked at him badly and he wanted to fight but nothing was in his fists or brain. No move that could defend his honor, his stature as a man. Even in the horror of war he was stared at as strange, and when he spoke men walked away. His accent defined him, and his darker skin, both proof of his vaquero heritage.

He had known the prejudice early, and then again in the military camps, but he had earned a right on the ranch, given to those who did more than they were asked. His touch with the horses raised him above the steady peon out of Mexico. He was a mounted warrior, he could ask a horse and the animal willingly bowed to Sixto's command.

Belinda E. Perry

Walking into the prison camp that first time, lame and thin, shaved head with its scarred ridges, he had become what he hated his entire life, a man less than those who surrounded him.

She sat there on the pretty buckskin and scolded him; voice shrill, words too clear and hurting. She would know the points, the secret places, she knew his weakness and hated him for it. Hated him for coming back a different man, a man he no longer recognized.

His body forced him to move, aching, hurting so deep inside he could not point and name. The wrong wounds healed, left an outward warning that most saw as finished, complete; inside the scream was a lion's roar.

A step, then a second, the push of haunch muscle, the flex of knee, tendons in the leg bunched to cover distance. The shoulders hurt, knotted high against his neck, rage built into each side, fury at old forces; his genitals, without feeling for too long, now erect, impeding his walk. A goad, a stick to his belly, a prod like the camp guards, thickened in need of release.

He grabbed for the sorrel colt, Remi swung the buckskin to shove against him and he raised his hand, saw her eyes, felt the sting of leather against his forearm and jerked her off the horse. She slammed against him and he held her warmth, his hands slid to her breasts and held on as she struggled. He remembered her taste and forced his mouth on her. She bit him, he grabbed, hands around her waist, keeping her struggles against him; he'd known nothing like this.

She pressed against him forcing him off balance; her hands got between them shoving on his chest, then gathering in a fist to dig into his belly. He could not stop the movement, his hips slammed her and she knew, she rubbed and ground until it was torture and he climaxed, more and more, head back, eyes clamped shut and hips thrusting.

Then he was spent, exhausted beyond the suffering of his wounds, the prison camp. His legs gave out, dumping him at her feet. Eyes closed from shame, he sat head bowed, smelling his release, feeling the wetness, cold now against trembling flesh. He was less than a man, unable to withhold himself, willing to use a girl...

The child sat down next to him, his eyes cleared, he could not look at her – would not look at her, she sat on his right. He was exposed again, soaking wet, bad eye running, blood on his teeth; a caricature of humiliation.

He raised a thigh, slid it over the other leg to hide his shame and she put a hand against the terrible scarring and spoke his name. "Are you all right, you're still bleeding. Stand up, let me wash out the cut." How could she offer him such salvation?

She stood, looked down to him, he lifted his face, hating her glance and then she smiled and held out her hand. She smiled while staring at the wreckage of his life, what he had become and would always be. Her hand was trembling, he reached for it, took her strength. Together they stood him up, he spread his feet wide apart and would not look at her.

His groin was sticky, he shifted weight, wanted to scratch and adjust but that would be insulting. He felt his knees shake, his belly rumbled and embarrassed him he so desperately wanted to let the gas escape but even that most basic need could not be expressed.

She smiled, so gently his eyes filled with first tears. She walked away from him to the grazing horses. Roy would not leave and the colt stayed close by. She slipped the buckskin's bridle and loosened the cinch and it registered on Sixto's tired mind that she was giving him a time of grace so he could attend to his various problems. She was rare for all her wiry prowess and skill with the words.

HER HANDS SHOOK and Roy brought his head around and touched his muzzle to her fingers, dampening them with blobs of grassy saliva. She pressed her head against his neck and let out an enormous sigh, as if pressure was competing with her heart. She had been afraid, Sixto's surprising charge, his eyes, the slam of his body and that rigid belly pole rotating across her hips. True fear added to a shocking need. She knew what he was hiding, she had seen one, in the evening's thin light, with her sister impaled, removed, impaled again in joyous rhythm.

The edge of feeling stayed with her, need she had never named, his hands, on her breasts then holding her, imprisoning her in his fury. She risked a glance, saw what he was doing and giggled, stuffing her mouth with Roy's mane until her tongue was rasped by coarse hair and she spat out, wiped her mouth. Risked that second look and Sixto had settled himself, feet set, staring to the mountains. What had happened was done.

She caught up the colt's one rein, led him to Sixto. "I dumped your gear back by the mud slough." She gave him the rein. "You ride him right this time or I'll castrate you like one of those randy bull calves. I been doing that for three years now, ain't no difference to me."

No argument, no complaint; Sixto started walking and Remi swung up on Roy, rode along side. A few minutes and the gear could be seen, a dark mound with a coyote sniffing at its edges. Sixto yelled, the colt spooked sideways and spun around Sixto, who talked soothingly and the colt cocked an ear, slowed, seemed willing to take a chance and settled in next to Sixto.

The coyote took a moment to check out his pursuers and then walked quite deliberately away, finally settling into a sideways trot, tail straight, showing neither defeat nor fear.

The spring water flowed from a pipe into a cement circle before sinking in to richer soil and creating the lethal bog. The cement circle where the cattle watered always overflowed; Mr. Ravenstock had tried but had no ability to contain or slow the water. Sixto stood and looked at the wasted swamp.

"He needs to bring in one of those water towers from the railroad, I've seen them abandoned, down near Coolidge." Remi flinched but Sixto didn't seem to notice; "If he rolled that here, we could store water." Remi interrupted, "Why don't you tell him? How do you 'roll' something that big?" Sixto had a reply; "I saw it done." He quit, snorted, Remi dropped a hand to his shoulder. She let her hand rest there as he finished his thought. "In the camp, we had to roll a tower like that, it can be done, I know how."

She squeezed, his hand came up and rested on hers. Then he handed her the single rein and walked to the cement tub, climbed the rim and threw himself into the water. He rolled over on his back, floated, started to unbutton his shirt. "Come on in, Remi."

I NEED TO explain something here. It won't take but a minute.

Growing up on a ranch I had no choice but to observe the male organ, hanging from a tired gelding, let down to urinate, swinging at the end of a bull's tasseled sheath, dogs locked together, tied by a strangled pink protuberance. Now these descriptions give the illusion that I paid close attention and focused incessantly on the exposed penis, but it was sideways always, shamed by my interest yet needing to know and certain that my father would not, and could not, tell me. Due to his vigilance, and a degree of indifference brought on by my mother's terrible dying, Papa had no further interest in females. And from my own distance, having wed three husbands, I can assume that as he got older, he no longer woke with any degree of erection other than the need to piss.

Is all this too much for you? Is the choice of subject and the words considered too unladylike for you to accept? Inside the considerable conventions and barriers we have erected to prevent understanding, there is a space where a good and curious mind can frolic, thinking and considering all manner of odd and suspect thought.

Have you noticed the walk of some old men, where their butts have given up and disappeared and their thin shanks barely support them, so at the position in their pants where there had been muscle and fat, a place for them to sit, there is only empty space. Well I notice, how could I not notice, having married the third time to a man whose butt was my singular source of pleasure and then it dissolved as he aged, the muscle seeming to shred, lean out and disappear. I would have liked to examine the area and find out exactly what happened, in fact I asked Archibald if I could do just that and the look on his face reminded me I'd married a basically shy man.

Now where is all this babble leading – it is to set the background, before and after, of what happened when Sixto threw himself into the stock tank and took off his clothes.

EACH BUTTON WAS a struggle and sometimes Sixto sank to where the water flowed over his face and yet she could see his fingers working at the fabric. He would not stand, nor would he quit the unbuttoning process and finally in a wiggle and yank he had the shirt off, waved it above his head like a victorious flag from some unrecognized battle.

Sixto rolled over and jacked his butt to the sky and his head disappeared and he came up splashing and blowing water about five feet across the tank. Remi laughed and sat down to pull her boots and socks, then she rolled over the cement wall into the pool. The water was chilly, and there were green things floating past but basically she could see clear to the bottom. She tentatively stuck down a foot, felt the sand roll under her weight and let the other foot settle. The water came up to her breasts, which immediately bobbed up close to her chin and she saw her nipples poking through the wet chambray shirt.

Horrified, she glanced over at Sixto, who seemed preoccupied with undoing his jeans while floating on his back; he kept sinking, then having to paddle wildly. He went under completely and didn't resurface and Remi started walking toward him when a hand surface. Clenched in the fist was a pair of jeans, water pouring out of empty pockets and down one leg.

Then a small white blob floated to the surface and she averted her eyes, knowing it had to be under-drawers and she wasn't allowed to see a man's under-drawers, it wasn't lady-like or so Mrs. Ravenstock had taught her. Of course Remi did her father's wash and knew all about pouches and flies and where things went. She just wasn't sure how the mechanics worked pertaining to her own anatomy.

Papa didn't keep a mirror to the house; she got used to braiding her hair by feel but as far as her body, her private places, she had no sense of what her fingers felt translated into what a man wanted, saw, or entered.

Her views of her parents and their activities had been shocking enough she did not remember details, and Rosie going up and down on that boy, it was dark, they were mostly shadows. She had an idea but still it didn't seem possible.

Remi walked and half-floated over to Sixto, who was on his back again, water halving his body, shoulders, hips, toes sticking up, ears not quite submerged. The good side of his face was fingered by dark hair, wet and glistening, sticking to his jaw and over the arch of his brow. He was grinning, she could see the lips curled up.

It occurred to her and she slapped both hands hard against the water; a small wave pulsed toward Sixto and the skip of water from her hands sprinkled his belly. He shifted weight and his face submerged, his long thighs and knobbed, bruised knees rose up. He looked funny, all white and dark lines, hair and that small muscle that bobbed and pulsed and she was giggling.

Sixto rolled over and floated on his belly, head toward her, the ruined side up, water sparkles glinting in the folds and rifts. He was still grinning but the mouth was contorted. His buttocks were startlingly rounded, two split hills, white and hairless, with the dark hair starting at the joined thigh. She was intrigued and stepped closer; the white flesh lay within reach and she grabbed on, taking a fist-full of Sixto hindquarters and giggled.

Sixto sank under the water and she went down with him, holding on until he snaked around her, legs grasping her thighs, buttocks pulled away from her by his twisting and she went underwater too, gargling a mouthful, then launching herself upward and throwing her head back, glad to breathe air again. Sixto was holding her legs, she grabbed at arm or rib and got that small white retracted muscle. Sixto snorted and sank under, his legs released her and she pushed herself toward the concrete wall.

When she was safe, steady on her feet, she turned around and Sixto was there. About a foot from her, standing this time, lank dark hair swirled around his head, eyes steady on her, even the destroyed one. His chest sparkled with water drops tangled in hair, his belly was pure white, she could tell his legs were spread.

"Do you know, Remi? What you are seeing? You have watched the stallions, you must understand." She reached out to the capped pole showing near his belly, distorted in the fractured water; still she knew what had taken place in Sixto, how he was seeing her. Her shirt still clung to her raised nipples and it was more and more difficult to breathe.

She ducked down to cover her breasts and could see Sixto's body hanging in the water, a bent and strange illusion. He arched back and his head disappeared, leaving only his white chest with the dark line of hair tracing to his groin, his long thighs merging to cradle the small penis and rounded balls.

Her hands opened and closed, she'd cut so many sacs, grabbed their skin and pinched them, snipped, threw them into a bucket for later.

This had to be the worst possible experience for a girl before seeing her first naked man.

Sixto seemed to slip away from her, his head going deeper, his belly gliding through the water as if upside down and then his feet splashed, kicked and he was gone underneath, brushing against her legs. She could stare through the water's split images and see his parted hair, his long back, the rise of his buttocks and then his legs, opened, closed, in short quick bursts to propel him through the water.

She felt him roll over on his side and curl around her knees. He tugged on her jeans, then pushed away from her and came exploding through the water to stand, shake, look at her. He was exposed, every inch of him; hair slicked back from his features, terrible damage on his face and torso. She had to stare, he invited her invasion, nodding once abruptly, then spreading his legs and folding his arms at his waist.

"Look all you want, girl, the best part of me is still in one piece." It was a dare, words not to be said to a child. She recognized his pride and answered it; "You're Sixto Vargas no matter what happened to you." She couldn't help but stare; his belly was peppered with little red marks, there were burns higher on his chest, along his neck. She had put her mouth to the burns there, and against his lips; having tasted them once made her swipe her tongue along her own mouth and Sixto seemed pleased by what she was doing.

She let herself sink, then raised her legs to comfort her own belly and sort of skipped along the bottom, head bobbing in and out of the water, seeing Sixto sawed in half, legs and hips to one side, chest and head leaning the other way. She began to giggle, then laugh as she made her way around the cement tank. Sixto seemed to be walking beside her, finally he rested a hand on her shoulder and she came up, stopped, straightened out and stood next to him.

"What in hell're you doing?" She laughed again; "I can't swim like you, never have learned, but it's fun being in the water like this." He smiled and it was sweet as it was sad, the mouth slightly twisted but she knew how he felt. "Can you teach me?" He nodded this time, and she walked over to him. "Teach me now." He shook his head; "Only to swim." "Fine, what else was I asking?"

Sixto slid backwards and she remembered, he was naked and that nakedness suggested so much more but he grinned and took her

103

hand. "First you shuck out of them clothes. Learning to float's tough enough you don't go weighing yourself down with wet clothes." She looked at him, studied his face and he smiled to her, grotesque and real; "Hell, Remi, I lost my chance needing you a while back and now, well I don't want taking you less you want me. That's where it stands."

What he was offering suited her; "Okay." With that she pulled free of her soaked shirt, mostly sliding from under it as water and air made it into a balloon, and then the jeans came quick, leaving her in soaked panties which had their own air bubble, and the restriction of the modest white bra Mrs. Ravenstock forced her to wear.

Sixto reached across the water and tugged at her panties, she jumped up and leaned back and he pulled them off. Looking down she had a glimpse of her own belly and that patch of darker curled hair, which she never had understood. She slipped into the water, sputtered while she worked on the bra clasp and then let it float away. She jumped straight out of the water, absolutely naked and wet and free.

"Feels good don't it." She nodded, slapped the water hard and it sprinkled Sixto's drying chest. He was laughing and slapped the water, putting his hand sideways to the edge and the splash was bigger, got her wetter. For a moment they played, back and forth, seeing who could wet the other one more. Remi shrieked, Sixto laughed, and finally it was time.

"You want to learn to swim?" Yes, she said, by nodding her head. "Come here." She walked to him, feeling the bounce the water gave her, conscious of her breasts floating, chilled by a soft breeze. He let her come up to him, inches from his ruined face, and she reached up, tucked a lank strand of hair off his eyelid and around his ear. "What do I do?" "Lie on your back, head in the water, let me put a hand under your shoulders and butt." She looked at him. He looked back; "I made a promise, Remi, I won't do nothing until you ask. This is how you start learning to swim, or I throw you in over your head and you nearly drown from the water till you figure it out. What's your choice?"

He'd given his word and she accepted that trust. It felt funny to rest her shoulders against his arm and let herself fall into the water. Then the other arm went under her backside, she wanted to giggle and when she did, she sank, getting a mouthful of water. "Don't, Remi. Keep still, and breathe, let yourself float, be quiet, breathe, again, and again. Like with the horses only this time it's your body you listen to." She tried, it was strange, letting her arms rest at her sides, her knees slightly bent, her head just out of the water, careful not to get too much in her ears.

His arms were steady, letting her drift, float; it was the most wonderful dreamy sensation. She closed her eyes, hardly breathed and could feel Sixto holding her, cupping her body to let it ride, let it drift and move with each small ripple of the water.

Then he dropped her and she sputtered under, fought to the surface, opened her eyes and he was grinning; "There you are girl, floating on your own now." She was, belly showing triangle of hair, two knees, skinned up and scarred, her breasts bobbing, easy to breathe if she didn't struggle.

"Damn," Remi said. Sixto threw his head back and laughed. Then he grabbed an arm and a leg and rolled her onto her belly, slapped the rise of her buttocks. "Now you keep your head up, like this." He shoved an elbow under her sinking chin and brought her head back. "You put your face in the water, you take a big bite of air first. Then you bury your face, come up again for air. Sort a roll your face in and out of the water, like this." And he grabbed her jaw. Rotated her face in and out; "Breathe when you come up, kid, not when your face's in the water. You need air, not drowning." He kept pushing and pulling her head and she found the place, took in air and let out and it began to feel like she could manage.

Then he let go of her and sank into the water close by. "I want you to watch." He began by laying himself out, face up from the water, body floating on his belly and then he grabbed for the water with his hands and kicked with his legs and stuck his head into the water and pushed himself a few feet, raised his head, grinned at her and took a deep breath, and did it again.

Remi mimicked the motions, felt herself lurch through the water, forgot to close her mouth as she rolled her head and gasped, spat, and tried to follow Sixto's lead.

When she was able to swim the perimeter of the tank, the lesson was over. Sixto climbed out of the tank and began to dress. Remi knew it was time, so she too climbed out and dressed as if swimming naked, being held by a naked man, was perfectly reasonable.

SHE STEPPED INSIDE the house and her father was raging. "What in hell do you think you're doing, swimming naked with that damned...." Here he couldn't seem to catch his breath and Remi stepped back, then steadied herself. "That what, Papa? What is he, a 'damned Mexican', is that all you see?" Her papa sat down, hung his head, she could hear the gasps, then he looked at her. "You know I don't think that way." Remi stood her ground; "Any man who's interested in me is damned, is that what you're saying, or is it his face, what's left of it. You don't want him in my bed because he's maimed!" Now she was getting mad from her own words, hearing them spoken, knowing they held a place in her nevermind what her papa was thinking.

Her father's voice was very quiet. "I don't want no man in your bed, not now. You're too young to know your mind and taking a man to bed means babies and homes and jobs. You got too much you can do, Remi, babies keep you to home."

Remi sat next to her father on the edge of the lumpy mattress. "What can I do, Papa? You know with the men coming home, Mr. Ravenstock'll begin to complain about hiring on a woman. I can't make a living here, and I certainly ain't got knowledge enough or want to go to a big city." Her papa put his hand on her knee; they both looked down, the gesture was so unfamiliar. His hand was broad, its fingers spread, the knuckles broken, small dots of scars covered the back of the hand. From sparks flying as he pounded on heated metal.

"I didn't choose us this life, you know that, child. I made mistakes and the land came up against us, and then...this was the best I could do." Her life was buried in those few words, her value diminished by his lost dreams. "Papa I don't mean to make you mad but I can read and write and that's it." He squeezed her leg; "Child you're pretty and smart and you need to live a better life'n being a cowhand on this old place. That movie star's light is fading, he'll sell up soon enough and you and me, we'll have no place to go. Now you find a good man, you'll be set for your life."

I THINK RIGHT here those of you who have actually been reading this book and paying attention can hear me screaming and jumping up and down. Even as a child I knew that what Papa was trying to preach was wrong. Despite my lack of a decent education to that point, I chose not to link my fortunes to any man's taking me on as wife and partner, which in 1945 certainly put me in the wrong place at the wrong time.

My anger at my father didn't help; I couldn't find what I needed to say and he would not have understood if I had. But our talk had a lasting effect on my life; the following morning my father stood up and walked to the door of our small house, and dropped dead. Flat against the sill of the doorway he'd built with his own hands. Head rapping hard on the unforgiving door. These are the things that shape lives, these moments when the world shifts and what you know instantly disappears. Think of coming out of your condominium and finding a sinkhole where the parking lot and your brand new Porsche had been sitting. Gone, the leather interior and the golf clubs and your fine cashmere sweater you'd forgotten in the passenger seat.

The life I had slowly accepted disappeared just as completely. Ravenstock said they would bury Papa in the ranch cemetery, and Mrs. Ravenstock took me to their ranch house and tried to hold me while I cried. I refused her of course, and went out to saddle Roy for a long gallop. Mr. Ravenstock actually approached me with the information that I was no longer employed on the ranch since I was an unaccompanied minor and as such could no longer use Roy. I pushed past him and walked right up to the buckskin and slipped the bridle on, mounted bareback and raced past the angry ranch foreman as if he did not exist.

I still cannot believe the truth of his nature revealed; that he would deny a grieving child a few hours on a horse. And from what I knew of Mrs. Ravenstock, I suspect that her husband would miss many of the private benefits of marriage for a long while. She was furious at her husband's callous words, and her anger showed me that women had strength and a moral purpose.

She kept me at their house for five days and her husband never spoke to me or even looked at me. The burial was simple; a local preacher came and I thought of my mother, and my baby brother, and heard the words through them as if now they were rightfully buried as well. I still had no faith in a god but I knew my mother's strong belief and finally she was hallowed wherever she and Thomas had landed. And now they would be with Papa.

There is no wrong in honoring another's faith, no retreat from your own beliefs to speak the words, bow the head, listen to the sermons. It is in honor of someone you loved, not a slap in the face to your private moral and spiritual choices.

Never make the mistake of drawing the hard line over minor choices; food, lovers, shoes, cars, religions. There are few things you must hold dear, honor is the strongest. But what you eat, 'I never eat there...' that's foolish, cutting yourself off from a place just because you chose another taste. I have had brief encounters with people who hold their likes and dislikes closer than their friends, refusing to go to certain places. It is about the company, not the food you idiot, food or certain standards are arbitrary, rejecting a meeting with friends in the cause of social standing negates the trueness of friendship.

I know, more of my lecturing but I have watched and listened and endured and what comes to me as small moments of wisdom deserves a place of their own. Do not allow yourself to be guided by false standards; choose always friends and lovers and compassion over respectability. I certainly did not spend much time courting respectability; my first love was a battered and maimed Mexican cowhand, my second husband was a small-minded and statured Texas boy, nevermind he was a full-growed adult. He stayed a boy, which he could afford to do. My third husband I won't talk about yet.

SIXTO FOUND HER AT the rim where the bones of her beloved Pego were stripped and scattered. She sat among the ruins while her fingers touched bone hardness, imagining her father reduced to this same pile. Knowing her mother and little brother Thomas were less than this, buried in dirt, musty, crawling with bugs and mold. She decided that on her death she would be laid out unadorned, unwrapped or mummified, left for the wind and the coyotes. Being buried in the ground was a contamination, a horror she could not accept.

Belinda E. Perry

The horse Sixto rode was the red sorrel colt, and this time the animal walked amiably up to Roy and nuzzled the little buckskin while Sixto slipped down, loosened the cinch and pulled the bridle and let the two horses graze on what little grass was left while he approached Remi's grief.

She had avoided him until now; she even thought of running but he would reach her too quickly. There was no place; she was caught. "Remi your father was a fair man, he did not look down on us who came here from Mexico to work. We grieve for him, and for you." The words were formal and rehearsed and she wanted to tell him the truth. Her father's face was behind her eyes, his drawn mouth, the bitter fury of his words telling her to stay away from the Mexicans, to marry a man who could do better for her.

His dying came too soon after their fight; she felt the responsibility, denied it even as it wove into her.

Sixto took her hand. Turned it over and they sat together, mute, both staring at the vulnerable utter whiteness of her palm. Sixto's fingers gently squeezed, then tapped her skin and when she looked, the difference in his color shocked her. She had not thought of this difference before.

"Will you marry me?" Her head came up, she pulled her hand free. His deep breath, the sense of him physically pulling away although he did not move warned her. "I did not intend to..." She wouldn't let him finish. Raising her eyes, looking at him fully, she saw the ruin, and the heart, and nodded. "Yes."

I WILL STOP here, just for now, needing time for a good cry. Having brought all the sadness in my life to surface, I crave private oblivion.

It isn't misery or pain or terrible hardship, only a personal loss of those I have loved. And a loss of wanting to love, of needing love. I can no longer bear that burden, I look at new people and choose to shift them out, to push them away. The pain of their eventual departure shreds me, tears at me through all these years. When I was younger, I suffered loss but could recover, did recover, for I hadn't known enough yet, not enough death or betrayal or simple disaffection.

AN OLD WOMAN'S LIES

Now even the memory of love is heavy, weighing down what little patience and compassion left in me. I have no source remaining, no depth of feeling – it has eroded with sequential losses, and I am naked with exhaustion.

Belinda E. Perry

NINE

Mr. Ravenstock was furious and Mrs. Ravenstock asked Remi if she really wanted to marry a, well a cowhand, when she could do so much better. Remi simply looked at the woman, then glanced down at herself, her tattered shirt, the jeans snugged tight around her waist, the boot toes needing polish. When she raised her head she felt the tag end of her braid slap her shoulder blade.

"I'm right set up to marry a lawyer or doctor, now ain't I, ma'am?" She lengthened the drawl, knowing her language was almost an insult and the woman thought she meant well but it was Remi's decision, no one else had any right now. Mrs. Ravenstock's face creased then became a frown. Lord the woman was easy.

"Child, you can't marry one of the...ranch boys. It simply isn't proper." Remi shook her head; "You already told me that bit of information. And I told you I'm already one of them boys. There ain't no other life I'm suited to."

Mrs. Ravenstock surprised her; "It isn't a question of what you do in life, but do you love Sixto? Can you love him fully, as a man? Can you live with his wounds? It is already difficult for you, so many cultural differences, but his face is, well, it's horrifying."

Remi had not expected such honesty from the woman, a first and quite rare, this bluntness which shocked Remi into silence. She looked at the wood floor, saw the toes of her boots, worn, patched on the outside where the stirrup rubbed, the leather almost white from dust and abuse. There was her life, already worn and frayed, dried out like any rank piece of leather. She rubbed her cheek with one hand, felt both the nicks and scars on her hand, and the beginning wrinkles on her face, from sun, wind, long days, poor food. Youth was gone before she recognized its arrival.

"He asked me to marry, who else'd want me? And no, that face ain't a problem, he's a good man, and I ain't scared of how he looks." Remi wasn't sure she'd told the truth.

Sixto wanted to get married in a small chapel near the ranch where his father still worked. There was a fine ranch house, several adobe barns and a small chapel on the rise of a hill, looking out toward the east, across the grasslands into the river basin. He had asked, and

111

received permission. She was the child who learned from Pego and so was welcomed into the C Bar compound.

Sixto presented this fact to her and Remi smiled. It was done, in two weeks she would be married.

Mrs. Ravenstock again pushed reality into Remi's dreams; "What will you wear to be married in, child? Do you think jeans and a checkered shirt are suitable, do you have so little care for tradition and celebration that a long braid and your hat are enough?"

It was a place Remi had not been before, considering what to wear, how to present herself in a social situation. Now she was scared.

I STARTED THIS lecture a while back and got distracted, which is what happens when you free-associate, and when you get old, take your pick. About finding yourself, your true center and core. I lied to Mrs. Ravenstock and it was my first adult lie. Yet at the time I thought it was the truth; I felt a pull toward Sixto, I always had, and to my unconstructed mind that pull equaled love. It was of course lust; where is the line between them, how could a child newly eighteen and living on a ranch miles from any large gathering place know anything about the bonds of sexual attraction between man and woman? I did not know how to differentiate between the yearning of a wounded child for a lost mother, now grieving for her father; and suddenly receiving a grown man's attention. How could that child have any sense of what such loving would demand?

A place we come to, hopefully sooner rather than later, is to know the peace of our own mind unfettered by the outside world. To know who we are, not in terms of how others see us but to honor our own voices, see our own way. It is a place of raw contemplation, painful examination, daily reminders to keep to our own truth and not allow the outside and all its power and push defeat us, undermine what we know to be true.

Does all this sound difficult, uninteresting, too complicated to bother with - it is where we become ourselves, where we find the truth behind our outward behavior. We can lie to others, we can skid around the truth and barely tell a fib to get by in our living, but to ourselves we must speak the truth.

Speaking the truth to our selves, to the very core of who we are is one of the most difficult challenges we face as human beings. It is easy to lie to others, they don't know the truth. But to be able to lie effectively to ourselves, we become so much less of who and what we are, we must not lie to that inner being. Know why you are afraid, tell the rest you aren't bothered by rushing water or bees swirling around your head, or being raped when you have already been raped. They will believe you and you can act on that belief to strengthen yourself and carry on through the fear.

But you must be honest enough to know that rushing water terrifies you. There are far more serious lies we tell ourselves, machinations we go through to avoid the painful truth and in refusing this reality we lessen ourselves, going around and around from fear and never mind how close the words come to your private nightmares. Face these truths, do not avoid seeing who you are. It is a strength we have offered us as sentient beings, and those who do not accept this gift are miserable although they think they have escaped.

And if you think you've heard enough of the subject, let me give you an example. A friend has a dog and takes in a kitten, who grows up to be a large and rather cranky cat. Instead of admitting to herself that she cannot stand this animal, (after all that might not reflect well on her self-esteem) she sets up a situation where she must get rid of the cat in order to move to a new apartment where the landlord does not allow cats. She 'sneaks' the cat into the apartment, knowing the cats are not allowed, then opens the door for the landlord with the cat in her arms. Of course she is told the animal must go and therefore she becomes the victim, 'poor me I must give my cat away or find a new apartment, oh poor me.' That is lying to oneself on a large and convoluted scale and it becomes a pattern where nothing is done to the truth, everything is given over to preserving a lie which makes us feel unable to account for our life, putting us as permanent victims thus relieving any necessity to act on our own. You can go through life this way, always being persecuted, such a sad and destructive choice.

Telling yourself the truth is where we start to be viable beings instead of pitiable victims.

SHE MET SIXTO'S mother and father who lived in a small adobe home on the ranch. The house was bare, swept dirt outside, smoothed walls that Señor Vargas placed a hand on and smiled at her. "My son knows how to build a home such as this. He will do so for you and the children."

It was the first time it occurred to Remi that she might have a child, children, babies and diapers and all that she knew nothing about; a family of her own. Mrs. Vargas put her warm hand on Remi's shoulder. "Child, what will you wear for your wedding?" Remi looked at the woman and felt tears blur her eyes. She almost wailed; "I don't know."

Sixto's mother put an arm across Remi's shoulders and drew her in to her hip and side. It was a place foreign to Remi and the softened contact let her cry. She sobbed and Sixto's father was alarmed until his wife said to hush, leave the child alone.

A white dress was pulled out, long and lacey and when it was held up to her, close to her chin, and she ran her hands over the smoothed material, the fine fabric caught on the rough edges and calluses of her skin and that made her sob even louder.

Mrs. Vargas, Señora Vargas, took the dress away and sat Remi down in a chair. "You are not suited to such finery, have you ever worn a dress? I only see you in jeans riding the ranch land." Remi opened her mouth and more tears came until Mrs. Vargas brought her a glass of water and a large white square, with pretty raised flowers along its edges. She had not ever seen such an item and it startled her enough she held it gently with her rough hands and stared.

"Dear, it is to blow your nose and wipe your eyes." "I can't do that to...this." Remi held up the perfect white square and the woman took it, wadded it in her fist as if it were rough gingham and wiped Remi's dripping face, the mucus from her chin, the moisture from around her eyes. When her face was covered with the fresh white square she was a baby child again, a mewling infant being comforted by her mother. She could almost hear Mama's voice and knew that Papa stood next to her, watching her being comforted, smiling at his wife.

Señora Vargas removed the soaked dainty; "Child, I can help you, we can make an outfit to suit you, but it will not be what others expect of a blushing bride." The words were true; Remi heard them and instantly saw what she wanted. "A riding skirt, Señora, a pale cream riding skirt and a creamy blouse, like I saw a woman on the ranch wearing." The señora nodded her head; "That was before the war. Sixto told me, she was a woman from that movie place and she rode about the ranch as if she was its new patróna. Sixto could not stop speaking of her. But she went away, like most of the women who come to your ranch."

There it sat, between them, her son and his dreamed vision, a beautiful woman on a pale horse against Remi's need to find her own version of lady-like to capture all of his heart. "We have some soft leather, child, it is a dove grey which would suit. I can make it into what you describe." Understanding, between two women, acknowledgment of needing to remake themselves into what their man wished. Remi knew this one time she would accept the tactic. Behind her closed eyes she could see Sixto running toward her, pants filled with his erection, then naked floating in the stock tank. He wanted her, now she had to learn what that want would mean.

Ravenstock gave her a few days to prepare the wedding and only on the insistence of his wife. He spoke of 'the child' taking advantage of his better nature, although Remi worked even on Sunday, under the subtle threat of losing her place of employment. When her father was alive, short months ago, she at least was allowed the one day.

Remi stared at the man, who looked away as he spoke. She already recognized this disinterest for what it was, an announcement that the speaker knew his words and intent were wrong. She accepted the days, paid no attention to his disapproval, smiled at his wife and took a few clothes with her when she rode out. On Roy of course, the little horse Ravenstock had forbidden her to ride when she was 'fired' after her father's death. For her own good of course, as it was inconceivable that a woman could continue to do a man's work.

How Sixto would feel about his wife working suddenly occurred to Remi; a wife, 'his' wife, his possession; the words had never meant anything until now. Her mama had been beloved, not owned, by Papa.

Remi touched Roy's sides and the pretty horse stepped into a lope. It was only words, the oath, her promise.

Sixto would of course belong to her.

IT FELT STRANGE to have another's hands on her flesh. Hands that were callused, frayed, scared with small cuts and even a broken knuckle where the Señora had slammed a dog who was terrorizing her chickens. The hands were tender and careful, but they were hands not belonging to Remi and she was shy with the contact.

"Don't squirm so, child, I know it tickles but we want this skirt to fit you." She took in a great gulp of air; "It is my own sister who prepares the wedding feast, and my husband who is talking to our son, but you must be quiet while I pin each bit into place." Remi stood on a low table, in her bra and panties, new panties Mrs. Vargas had bought her from the catalog and dry goods store in Las Vegas. She had even bought a long white gown of some soft cotton, which Remi was meant to wear on her wedding night.

That conversation was jumpy, between pins and Remi's twitching and Sixto's mother searching for the words, it had to be an uneasy discussion. "You know about men, how they are constructed." Remi nodded but bit down on her response, that she had already seen Señora Vargas' son naked, had seen his smoothed belly and his floating testicles, the nub of his chilled penis barely rising to the water surface, that small slit in its tip, the skin pulled back, looking silly and uninspired in the cold water.

This was not what a bride told her prospective husband's adoring mother. The venerable Señora continued, halting occasionally as she reached for the most gentle of words to convey the peculiarities of men. Even her beloved son, maimed now and spoiled to the eye, would have these needs and the girl must be warned. Genevia knew men well enough that she was certain Señor McClary had not told his daughter the impossible truth.

"Who has spoken to you of your monthlies, who has told you about becoming a woman?" A soft beginning to a most perplexing subject, and the answer was not reassuring. "Mrs. Ravenstock sat me down when I was thirteen and told me, but she made being married sound like a job."

As the Señora thought, the tight-mouthed Anglo woman would not have enjoyed her marriage bed with that vulture she wed. "The bed you take, the husband you choose, is to create children. But the act itself can strengthen love, it can bring you together and give you both comfort." Then she giggled, and the pin against Remi's hip went in sideways, creating a gap that Genevia immediately repinned. Sewing on finely tanned leather was always difficult and it was hard to keep her focus.

"If you teach your husband well, there will be much pleasure for you, a sensation for which you will not be prepared. Like magic, lights and stars and so much intensity, ah child, if you train your husband right, he will mean everything to you."

Remi wanted to ask around her curiosity and a sense of unfamiliar shame. Men did not come with directions or work from logic, that much Remi had already learned. She listened intently to Sixto's mother as she stammered and circled around the act itself.

"You've seen the animals?" Remi nodded and felt a pin stick in her belly. "The male he has that long thing." Remi could look down and see her mother-to-be actually blushing, even the backs of her hands were red. "That is to push the seed needed to make the baby in deep, where it will be nourished and grow." Remi hadn't thought of that side of the act. The words and their vivid description made sudden sense.

"Animals most often do not stay with their mates or the males care for their young." She sighed, sat back and studied Remi, who was holding her shirt tails up so the waist of the divided skirt could be properly fitted. The stilled air on Remi's belly tickled. She snorted; la Señora looked up. "Women run the family, Remi child, they make the decisions as to the fate of their children. We need men for this, to earn and protect while we stay with our niños. It is how humans raise their young."

HAVE YOU NOTICED how odd the human body is - we have arms and legs in the same places, most of us, but how differently we hang together. One hip higher, the tilt to the pelvis, the shoulder width, a concave chest. When we are young, it is all pretty; firm flesh where it is meant to be, arms that are slender and muscled, necks which rise back in being offered to a mate, firm, smooth, ah yes the touch of fingers on hidden zones, skin delicate and veined, muscle hard, firm, defining each area so the eyes do not have to see.

We do not stay this way for long, despite all the attention now on exercising and anti-aging, we change, we dissolve, our flesh weakens, our tissue shreds. We are dying, the moment of birth is the beginning of death. No secret, no famous statement there, a fact we all begin to know. Look at your arm, raise it up, stare at the rigid veins and the small waves of loosened skin, fascinate yourself with your own mortality. It is coming, remember that. Do it now, get it done. An old admonition still alive with truth.

I am watching people closer now, less inhibited in my staring; the qualities of an old woman's life allows for such rudeness. Such antisocial behavior can be ascribed to senility and ignored. Oh if they knew what I was seeing and thinking about them. One particular man I remember; high small head, long nose, a protruding chin, long neck. Now on a woman a long neck is a sign of ethereal beauty, on a man it belongs to a chicken. Then to his narrow chest and long arms, a small belly, wide hips, bowlegged and elongated scrawny limbs; an odd-looking man who was resolutely cheerful to the point where I believed his cheer and humor were the only way he could face the world. None of us are that bright all the time, yet if he gave in to the moodiness his physical attributes would engender (yes I can use fancy words and sound educated), he would instantly become a caricature, a clown of poor proportions and mismatched bones.

I admired his bravery as much as I could not bear to look at him. I wanted to laugh always, to distance myself from his unfortunate appearance.

We are cruel in our perceptions.

A well-known advocate for animals spoke once to a most absurd conceit; that we should emulate animals in their chosen sexual partners. For animals do not choose on appearance or status, they...here is where her thesis breaks down. Animals choose a mate on a flutter of plumage, a frenetic dance, and the scent of ovulation. Nothing more than animal lust - and this is admirable for what reason? Different how from what men do, choosing on a basis of sexual titillation or supposed wealth? I thought the woman mad to make such a foolish analogy.

Although we often choose on the basis of scent but we don't want to admit this. I can draw up my favored husband's odor, no, that is not gross or obscene but real. A light cinnamon tang, his hand on my shoulder, my head turning to the touch, able to taste still the ghost of his flesh.

Nothing more than a signal...a benediction of physical union, reunion, so many times I have only blurs of the smallest moment, his face, his mouth coming down to me, a finger against my pulse, walking past his back while putting toast on the table. It is still difficult to separate the simple act of making toast from that husband's presence.

It is the depth of trust we establish in a loving relationship, the offering of thoughts, impressions, worries and fears that distinguishes us, not our choosing a mate based on availability. Knowing that your thoughts and the speaking of them will not be harmed or diminished by the chosen partner. Such trust is fragile and easily broken, rarely repaired. It is where we fall down as a species. We fail, lie, cheat, then it is all gone and never reclaimed.

THE SHAME OF her ignorance disturbed Remi; the act itself was known, the trappings around it seemed to be something the Señora was trying to describe without resorting to indelicate words or demonstration. That Remi had seen some of the gestures with her own parents was a fact she did not wish to share with the older woman. It was better this time to play complete ignorance; it was too close to the truth, her mother had been dead more than ten years and what Remi held dear might well be a child's fantasy.

Yet she knew she had seen her father take Mama's hand, gentle as if the work-frayed fingers were made of glass, a newborn's breath, the most valuable of golden coins. Her blunt, reddened hands, swollen, cracked; his hands surrounding them, his mouth breathing against the worn surface of her life blood, her heart encased in each tip, their life together seen in one small gesture.

This image was spoken about by Sixto's mother, as if she knew but could not explain. Remi felt herself smile and the woman stopped her talk, looked at Remi, then tugged at the pinned waistband. "You are lovely, child, so young and steady, you and my son..." Here she faltered, and Remi felt the woman's wounding. "He is still my Sixto despite what they have done to him. Find him in there, hold him as he deserves." There was a sudden catch in the voice, the softest sob; "Love him, child. As a man deserves to be loved."

THE WEDDING CEREMONY was brief despite pressure to be married more formally in a church. Remi would not give in, she was not a believer and Señora Vargas spoke quickly to the husband, Remi wishing she could hear what the woman said. A judge from Tecolote came to the ranch and read the words. Remi listened, trembling, hearing her life assigned to another person.

She wore the divided skirt, a softened gray, and a white blouse mostly of lace and ruffles. They moved almost before she did, and their constant motion annoyed Remi. She vowed never to be at war with clothing again. The stays of the bra itched, the long divided petticoat chafed between her legs and the panties underneath pinched when she moved at all. And the hat, don't think about the hat, it was snubbed around her skull like a dallied rope and she couldn't wait to tear it off and release her hair.

All this so she could agree to become the wife of a certain man. She already didn't want to be married and looked around frantically to find just one person who would aid her escape. Instead the judge must have made another pompous statement and Sixto grabbed her shoulder and kissed her. In front of all these people; Remi started to fight him off before she remembered.

Even though most of the guests drove pick-ups and old cars to the ceremony, there was a fine matched team of grays hitched to a buckboard freshly painted and streamed with ribbon for Sixto to drive his new bride to their home. After hours of celebration, Sixto was drunk and Remi took the lines. The grays settled to an easy trot and her husband nearly pitched himself out of the buckboard.

A husband; her husband; Remi snorted and shoved Sixto until he collapsed backwards into the straw-lined bed, as if whoever harnessed the team knew the man of the family would be riding home in disgrace. Or at least too goddamned drunk to take care of his wife on their first married night.

Sixto slept in the shed, rolled onto his back so he wouldn't drown in straw, after Remi unharnessed and put away the grays, making sure they had water and some hay. She stood a moment, slightly dizzy from a glass of champagne. One glass, while she knew Sixto had swigged down tequila with his father and cousins and other returned veterans. She had liked the taste, and the slightly buzzy feeling the champagne gave her. Now she was tired, and disgusted with the sprawled shape of her husband.

Her wedding bed would be solitary, which right now suited Remi.

SHE HEARD HIM first, stumbling outside the cabin her father had turned into their home. He was cursing and there, he hit the bench where she'd sat, alone, at night after the supper meal, watching the sunset, hearing the horses, smelling the sweet air. Sixto's cursing grew in volume and Remi sat up, holding the covers to her breast, knowing for sure he would come at her, drunk or sober, fouled by his night in the shed, expecting more than she would give him.

Remi climbed out of the tangled bed and slid into familiar clothes, a work shirt, cotton briefs, jeans, thick socks to comfort her cramped toes, boots for security, her belt buckled just enough to feel steady against her stomach. She was prepared. Sixto's shadow covered the open door.

Remi cried; he was bloodied, scarred features twisted, opened, revealed in private terror. He stopped his lurching advance and stared at his new wife. She could not help the tears but she wouldn't let them defeat her. She walked to Sixto, who had leaned against the doorframe. Remi touched the wood, remember her father's hands placing each strip, letting her guide the narrow board into place, individual nails blessed in a silent promise.

She stood close to Sixto, her right fingers finding certain nails hammered into the wood; he watched fascinated, head bobbing with each stroke. She ducked her head, he smelled, of piss and vomit and congealed sweat.

"Them demons won last night, Remi girl. They won't win again, I make you that promise." Remi looked up, now his eyes were clouded wet, his mouth trying for a grin. His hands trembled against her forearm and she stepped back. His grip tightened until she swatted at him. His cry jarred her; "Don't, Remi. Don't back from me I can't bear that look, you hate the sight of me, I knowed it at the stock tank. Goddamn we're fools to be marrying."

Such brief revelation of fears calmed Remi. Sixto kept talking as she inched closer until his stink was too strong; "You need to shower, and get into clean clothes. Here, your mama and I brought everything to the cabin." She stepped aside, gently tugging on his arm and he took the first step inside the cabin, over the threshold her papa had installed, onto the scoured wood floor. He snorted, pulled from her. "This is where you live, I don't belong here."

She looked at the small space, trying to see what spooked him. The walls had been paneled and planed by her father, the floor was sanded wood, laid and hand-pegged. Each window was carefully framed, the ceiling of narrow pine that Remi herself had painted white. There was one bed now, her parents' big bed with Mama's quilts adding vivid color. A table and four chairs sat near the crude sink and narrow counters. Most of their meals had been taken at the cook shack yet it was possible to prepare a meal here, entertain a friend or two. The three windows had checked curtains, bright yellow and white - Remi had made them for her husband, sewing diligently under his own mama's teaching.

She tugged his hand; "There's a bathroom through the door, Mr. Ravenstock let Papa use what he could find and it's complete of course nothing matches but that doesn't matter, there's a sink and a shower inside the tub that Papa found in a homestead, one of those big white tubs with the feet. I liked a shower so he built a metal stand and hung a hose and shower head, you know what I'm talking about."

Where the words came from she didn't know but they seemed to work, slowly drawing Sixto across the wood floor to where she placed his hand on the white doorknob her father had found in the ruins of an abandoned log hut. About when she and Papa left their own pitiful home. She pushed at the door, led Sixto inside. White walls, the floor of fractured linoleum, a rug woven out of used shirts and dresses. The commode was complete, and it flushed, it wasn't a one-seater and its porcelain tank might be cracked so Papa put a metal brace around it but it worked and she didn't have to go outside in the dark or cold, or risk splinters and spiders.

She pushed Sixto to sit on the edge of the tub and started to unbutton his shirt. He was quiet, head hanging, barely registering that she was taking care of him. His chest was smooth, she knew that, little hair, mostly around the nipples. She looked away, suddenly overheated and uncertain. "I can't undress you, Sixto. You'll have to do this yourself." She laid two towels on the toilet seat and lightly touched his shoulder, naked now, stripped of the stinking shirt. She took the wadded mess and retreated, closing the door with a quiet thump.

Five minutes later there was still no sound of running water so she pushed the door open again and Sixto had not moved other than to shuck out of his boots and jeans. His head came up, pure pain in his ruined eyes; "I don't know how to use these damned things, I've never...." He couldn't finish, Remi's face got hot and then she shivered. Her husband had never used a simple bathroom before.

"What about the Army, what did you do...there?" "In training it was a long shower they turned on and we had three minutes. Overseas, in the..." He quit, raised his head with great effort and Remi flinched from the exposed stare. "In the hospital I was washed, in the camp we didn't...."

He looked at her, an act of faith, and raw need swept from his eyes. "I didn't want those sons knowing how country-dumb I was."

Remi was wise enough to recognize what she'd been given. His own mama's words, about the fragility of the male soul, the rare times when it was exposed. To be gentle, to take with cupped hands and treasure the barely-spoken words.

Very carefully she leaned over, brushing against his naked shoulder, aware of him as a man, not just a wounded boy, and she turned the faucets, adjusting the temperature of the water to a gentle heat. "Here." The rushing water hit against the porcelain and scattered, small droplets rising against her face, his back. She steadied herself, put her hands under her husband's arms and tugged gently; he stood into her, naked as if a babe and she felt all of him, sweat and stink and hair, the nested penis and testicles, the wrinkled scarring rough and indecent to her touch.

She could feel him smile against her shoulder, his weight drifted in her grasp and they stepped into the shower paired. She was stunned, then laughed, shirt plastered to her body, jeans suddenly heavy. Sixto released himself and edged past her into the full spray. He slid her the bar of soap and she lathered him, first only his shoulders and upper back, then his hands came around to slide her scrubbing to his behind. She froze, his back shimmered, her hands went to his waist, rubbing until the soap bar slipped from her grasp. She turned sideways, bent down, conscious of his skin, the close swell of each haunch.

He turned while she groped for the elusive bar. He was erect and waiting for her; his hands touching her drenched shirt, his head thrown back, eyes shut; smiling exactly as she first remembered him.

I TOLD YOU I would describe my first time with a cowboy - I lied.

TEN

Smart aleck ain't I, talking and promising and doing what so many men do to us, not coming through. Reality is, Sixto's emotions were entrusted to me and though he's long gone I cannot break the trust he offered. Let me tell you though, I would marry him again, and again.

The first time was briefly painful, uncertain, and hurried, as if he still feared me. Getting me out of my clothes proved the most difficult, ending up with Sixto jammed between my legs as I was hobbled by the wadded denim. This of course made the initial penetration difficult, chaffing and poking until I cried out and he pulled back. Finally we took time to remove the denim and the act itself was more successful. When I think of it now, I am amazed that Sixto's sensibilities could take my cry and still be ready for completion. He later proved an enduring lover, though infrequent, and that flaw could be ascribed to the work we both did on the ranch. Physical exhaustion at the end of a day was not uncommon, and days off, vacations, were unheard of.

This is as much as I will tell you about losing my virginity.

SHE WOKE FROM a dream to a strange noise. Sat up, cried out with the hurt and then saw her husband. He too was dreaming, and his dreams included snorts and cries. Remi wrapped her arms over her naked breasts and remembered.

Between her legs was sore, the tender skin bruised, even a place on her inner thigh had a darkening mark. Now it was her turn to snort, as if what he had done to her was that marvelous she was transformed into another person, all sighs and giggles and flutters. Hell, she thought, this sex ain't much after all.

As if her papa heard, a voice called out, "You two gettin' up and comin' to work?" That was what woke her, the bell for breakfast, not Sixto's snores and gulps. Remi shook him hard, then crawled from the bed wrapped in the sheet's edge. It was uncomfortable knowing a man's eyes might watch.

Sixto reared up like a cut bear and lunged from the bed, flashes of him as he yanked into clothes was more than Remi wanted as she raced through her own dressing, barely tugging her hair into some kind of braid. They'd gone back to sleep after the shower, after...oh hell, she thought, I can't do this.

They barged out of the cabin into sun and thunder; claps and bangs, high ringing, jeers and calls and fouled words that made Remi blush. She felt Sixto behind her and almost tried to run but his arms came around to hold her shoulders and his mouth was on her neck. "I won't let them." Whispered, unfinished but she knew.

He stepped past her, held up his hand. "You fools're fussing up the horses." And it was true, the sudden jangled noise had the corralled stock bucking, racing, kicking each other and the stout fences. The crack of broken wood stopped the chivaree cold. Remi hadn't known seven cowboys and a cook could make such a racket.

"Boy you ain't needed to work today, Ravenstock give you the day off. And you, miss, I don't know you still got a job." It was the cook of course, still the same cook who had offered sandwiches and chilled water their first day on the ranch. Stocky couldn't look at her; "The boys here had to have their say." He turned around and faced the crew, who stared at the ground. "You boys git to the shack. I god it's breakfast time for sure."

Remi backed up into Sixto. "He can't fire me, he can't make me not work." Sixto steadied her, and she could feel him breathe. "I'll talk to the man, he ain't shutting my wife out." Remi turned her head so gently and found herself against his scarred side but his hands held her and the strangest sense came inside her belly. She rested her head on his throat, her shoulders on his chest and his hands were at her hips. She belonged here, protected by him; then she pulled away. "I can fight for my own job."

WHY IS IT so difficult to trust what we feel? And how often are we wronged for that trust? I can tell you in intimate detail how his body felt, his scent even in those private places, a scent that became an instant aphrodisiac for me. I can describe for you the slightest inhale of certain places that fluttered my heart, and soaked my panties. Oh dear, how graphic for an old woman to mention such a private sensation. I wonder what others think when they speak dryly of romantic notions, do they believe that it is all chaste and clean without any physical responses?

Makes you wonder if these notionalists have ever been in love, have had wild sex, ever actually enjoyed themselves. We cannot separate sex from anything in our lives; even going to church with family is an observance of sex, the unity of the family, the bond of children, the act of 'love' that creates each life.

Yet my uncertain childhood, my early losses, and my fierce independence gave my life a ragged beginning as an adult, and a predestined despair that has never quite left. I am erratically mortal, on occasion knowing my flaws and seeing how their rubbing on my life has pushed me in certain directions. I can know these flaws and expound them to you but I cannot in the heat of any decision understand fully how they control and direct me. I am, as we all are, the sum of my experiences, from the moment of birth and before, to the exact and raw moment we live through the days. That second, already gone once spoken, shapes and forms us despite our wishes, our longings and dreams are at the mercy of outside forces.

Life certainly is not what we plan and decide but what evolves through so much we never know or realize.

All this is my excuse for not understanding my first husband, not seeing into his wounded heart past the roughened scarred flesh and hearing his cries. I simply did not know, was too young and unformed, too innocent and untutored to accept empathy as a valid tool.

SHE WAS REMOTELY aware of a shift in Sixto, a removal of his body even though he did not let her go. Then he roughly spun her and pushed her into the house. Wild calls and jeers followed them inside, until it was Stocky's voice again, harsh and brief; "You boys leave 'em be, you all git." This time they had listened; the sudden quiet forced Remi to turn around.

Sixto, her husband, impaled her; "My place to fight for you, don't you know that little girl?" She pushed at him, hands hard on that scarred chest that had lain on her, rubbed against her breasts until they were tender. "Don't you shove me around, girl. I'm your husband, you do as I say." She stepped back, giving him that much. But the words echoed and she hated them. "I ain't owned by no one damn you." He looked surprised, then oddly saddened. She heard her speech and knew it was ugly, wrong, how her mother would scold for the poor words.

"Did you think, child, did you listen to the vow you took? It says 'obey', what in hell did you think that means?" She wouldn't give her life away to a ranch hand with no reading, no extra thinking or ideas. She owned herself, not no one else.

"I didn't marry you just to bed you, I can get a woman easy." Here he rubbed his belly and grinned. "That old scar it don't keep me from being a damned good lover." She didn't know, she'd only seen flashes of the act, and he was the first man between her legs. The slight ache, the rawness she felt at each move, reminded her.

"You sure weren't much good to me last night." It was all she had; he drew back and the look to his dark eyes, a flash of brilliance and anger, almost kept her quiet. "No man's much when he's drunk. Hell girl, you ought to know that from good sense."

She rubbed her mouth, finding his taste there too, on her hands, her flesh, she could only imagine other places. Places she realized she could not see, parts of her gently described by Sixto's mother to her, their function and physical description which Remi had not quite believed. "Then why'd you get drunk?" Maybe it weren't right to slam him but she was wounded too in this beginning battle.

After that first flash of pain he had actually been inside her; she had stiffened against the advance, then lay compliant, remembering what she had seen and been told. The wrong time to think of his mother as he lay on top of her, pressing her into the mattress, shoving and jamming and it was wrong.

His face changed and she almost wanted to reach for his smile. "You didn't know, did you, your mother's been dead...how long now?" He couldn't have her, no, not this way. He turned away first and left her, shrugged into a shirt, buttoned and tucked, went into the bathroom and left the door open while he pissed into the toilet and didn't yank down on the handle. He leaned into the sink, seemed to grin at his face in the mirror as he used water to slick back his hair.

She yelled at him as he passed her; "Flush the toilet." He didn't even slow down; "What the hell're you talking 'bout?" No answer, just motion.

It was a moment or two before she figured out where he was going. Her first impulse was to rush the door, charge after him, beat him to the main house and Mr. Rantoul's desk, or to confront Ravenstock and argue with him. She sat down on the bed, wiped her face, dug bony knuckles into her eyes and unaccountably cried.

Sixto returned while she was sitting on the bed, face dry, eyes swollen. He stood over her; "We got fence to ride."

IT WAS PRETTY clear what had happened; wire broke, posts pulled flat, great gouges of prints through the fence line; a bull had got whiff of some heifer in the distance and made it his cause to break through and find her. Even a few of the barbs had hair tufts, some hide, specks of dried blood. No returned tracks.

Remi saw all this from Roy's back, Sixto got down and knelt, let his fingers tell him. He snorted as Remi spoke. "We got to go get that son, can't be leaving him in the wrong pasture." Sixto shook his head; "Damage is done, Remi, he's been at her maybe twelve hours. She's carrying, and he's in no mood to be pushed."

"It's the Block pasture, Sixto, it'll take a day trailing the brute to bring him home we fix the fence now. Mr. Ravenstock'll have a fit you leave that ole bull in the wrong place." She edged Roy through the gap, Sixto stood abruptly, spooking his own dozing roan who yanked and dragged Sixto backward.

When the dust settled, Remi had Roy headed in a lope along the tracks and behind her she could hear Sixto's feeble yells. The words were uncertain, lost in the wind but she knew what he was saying.

She had no intention of listening. It was a pleasure to rock forward as Roy's lope increased to a gallop; they were flying, up the shallow slant of the hill, to the ridge where she turned the buckskin by only looking and he traveled the path of the ridge, then turned suddenly against the ridge to follow the shallow troughs of the bull's descent. She leaned with his rush, heard his breathing, felt his balance through her hands on the leather rein and she threw back her head, cheered as they hit the flat plain and Roy bounced, squatted, leaped into the air as if the devil were chasing him.

'Goddamnit Remi' followed her, a pale shadow of thoughts and rules. The bull was ahead, snorting now, overtaking Sixto's weak voice and her own breathing. Slobber tossed over his back, a small herd of becalmed cows, a deep scent strong enough to turn Remi's head, following the flow of potent air.

The bull's massive head swung toward his serviced ladies and then he rolled into a charge at Remi. No warning, no hesitation; Roy skidded in a stop, shook his head against Remi's hand and spun over his hocks in pure retreat. Remi yelled and spurred the little horse, yanking his head sideways to turn him and he hit a small bush, tangled his legs and went down, in a slow roll that gave Remi enough time to know how bad...how wrong; terrible, no chance to hide.

The ground actually shook; she had enough time to take notice. Then Roy scrambled up and was gone, no loyalty, no sense but panic and gone. There was that moment to feel hot air, smell the stink and then a hand grabbed her shirt and shoulder, dragged her across a galloping horse and she was glad to hear Sixto's clear voice cursing and yelling. She felt the roan jump, jump again into high gear and her one hand bounced on Sixto's thigh, felt the savage motion of his legs and knew the roan was being spurred through the hide.

They rode maybe a quarter mile up to the ridge, and down again, slowed to a walk outside the ravaged fence and Sixto's voice was clear now, strong enough to be heard through her beating veins. "Damn you, Remi. Damn you."

Her face was rubbed on the roan hide, salt stung the small scratches, she began to struggle against Sixto's hand on her back, pressing her hard, his voice continuing the chant. 'Damn you."

Still she saw what he was cursing. Upside down a golden leg marked with high black hobbled toward her, its partner lifted, held from the impact of each step; blood poured out of the wreck, white bone showed clean. She felt the words dig inside; "Damn you. Damn you."

Sixto reined in the roan and was off the horse, rifle pulled clear, before Remi could struggle and slide down to go to her beloved Roy and what she'd done. "Don't bother, Remi, don't you cry and say you're sorry. You done this, you wouldn't listen. You know too damned much, damn you." He wasn't looking at her and then he fired and Roy's skull flowered into spewing red and Remi knelt on the ground, crying as he'd told her not to, disobeying again, unable to stop her grief.

It was Sixto who picked her up and held her across his chest as if she were a baby or the wounded one. Held her close, rested his face in her hair and whispered; "I'm sorry I didn't mean forgive me I wouldn't hurt you." Over and over, the sweetest words she'd heard. For her, no one else, forgiveness with redemption.

He put her down next to Roy and she unbuckled the bridle, slipped it from the shattered skull while her husband struggled with the cincha. Finally she suggested he cut the latigo, loosen it that way and no, please leave the blanket she didn't want to put it on another horse ever.

They rode back double, Remi perched on the roan's quarters, trying to keep her saddle from bumping the horse's legs or thigh. It was a sideways trip made bearable by the bull's appearance, a volunteer through the fence they repaired in back of him. At least the bull was back where he belonged.

Sixto deposited her near the main house and let her walk in the back entrance to Mr. Rantoul's office. She was the one to explain. Sixto would tell Ravenstock; tell him the truth and let Remi take the consequences.

WHEN REMI ENTERED the small cabin Sixto was not there. Nothing to tell her where he'd gone. Then again she didn't know what to expect; would he wait for her, would they go to the cookshack for the meal together and risk being hurrahed. She needed to know where he was.

She had to use the bathroom and she was appalled by what waited for her. The seat lifted - she looked for her father then remembered; her husband, a man now part of her life, including such basic needs as relieving himself in her bathroom. Uncharitable, she thought, as she stood and tried to avert her eyes, not see what floated in the clean white porcelain bowl. She never looked at what she left, yet this was someone else, a new presence and having him here meant these interruptions, intrusions of his waste, his animal smell, his nighttime noises.

131

AN OLD WOMAN'S LIES

She had to look and as she got closer, the rank scent, metallic and almost sweet, rose into her face. She gasped, put a hand to her mouth; in the deep yellow urine floated streaks of red, almost like a loose thread, too many of them. Visible reminder of his prison years. Remi looked away and flushed the toilet, let down the seat, sat and did her own business, conscious of the stream, the stench, her peculiar odor. This was being human, an animal cautious of its waste, tuned in to scent, odor, wary of anything new.

She stood up quickly, flushed and made a pretense of washing her hands, hearing Mama's voice as always, cheating on the dead as she wiped her hands dry on her filthy jeans.

I WAS IN town recently, with two friends, one quite a bit younger and doing the driving. It was meant to be a lark, an escape from the crowded residence. We sped through the downtown streets, secure in knowing we could park at the front of the restaurant, Haley being blessed with a replaced hip and a handicap-parking placket. She was always invited despite bad breath and a simple mind. Me, I'm too proud to be so labeled but I'm not above making practical use of another's misfortune.

Marian, our driver, almost hit the back end of a low-slung monster Buick from the seventies. Populated by five or six teen-aged boys who had seen something of great note and slammed on the brakes to take a closer look. Which meant, of course, that we were exposed to the same fascinating item.

It was a woman. As she stepped through traffic I am sure she stopped a lot of cars, and hearts, and gave rise to some wildly fantastical thoughts and images none of which could ever be satisfied. Now what I am going to say might not be politically correct but by god it's a truth. This woman was asking for the fantasies and the lust, by her dress and walk, no possible way to read her other than 'look at me, boys, dream about what you can't have.'

And it's wrong to make a promise, to offer it at least, and then not make good. Keep that in mind.

Belinda E. Perry

This woman was tall, about 5'10" I'd guess, and slender, and stacked. And I mean the word stacked; she must have been 38 DD and proud of it. Tight black jersey, tight black skirt with a high slit up the back - and spiked heels, damned things are back in fashion and women are buying them. Idiots all.

From her build and her shoes she was tilted forward, top heavy from the weight and the balance of her legs and feet. Swinging and bouncing and her face was non-committal as if she knew and didn't care. I can't imagine what thoughts if any were in her mind as she veered dangerously close to the stalled Buick and a hand reached out to grab her, any part of her but aiming high, for one of those globes she carried on display.

If the young man had reached his goal she would have slapped him and perhaps even been insulted at his behavior. What did she expect of the world as she showed herself, nothing subtle or fashionable at all about her clothing; if she leaned over a desk or counter, the man behind that desk or counter would have had his face almost literally smothered by her exposed flesh.

As I said, this might not be correct thinking but the woman made a choice and then expected the rest of the world to ignore what she was offering. It's almost a joke, her blatant thrust of enormous breasts into the world's view, saying all the time, oh you must take me seriously, I am a woman but I am a mind and brain also.

And just who do you think will notice clever words on a page or a suggestion that will save the company money for their male eyes will be focused on her boobs. Boobs themselves, they will react the only way their nature allows.

To dress to this flamboyance is to realize and calculatingly utilize its effect, to then say the world must not look is false and deceitful.

Had enough of my opinions yet? Don't worry, there's always more.

CLEAN CLOTHES AND combed hair oddly made her feel better and she chose to sit outside on the crude bench Papa had made from a half-sawn log and welded horseshoes. It wasn't exactly comfortable, but it held her while she waited.

As the sky darkened and she was still alone she began to worry. Where could he have gone, why would he leave her? She'd done wrong, made a bad decision, he could hate her for the buckskin's death, as she hated herself. But it didn't seem enough for a man to leave his wife. She didn't know, couldn't know, no one told her, she hadn't seen what made a man angry; her Papa got furious at a bad weld or iron broken under a blow instead of bending, not on what she did, not from her stubborn actions.

His hand on her shoulder was enough to scare the bejesus out of her; Remi jumped, stuttered, Sixto bent down and kissed her on the mouth. In full daylight, outside their cabin, not a care, no shame or manners to him. She felt his mouth turn into a smile even as he held to her lips. His breath tasted of chile.

"Missed you at supper, Remi. Boys was asking for you, I told them you had the vapors." He pulled away then and she looked up, scrubbed her mouth clean while holding on her temper.

"You don't talk 'bout me to them 'boys' you like so much. Not if you want me in your bed." She revised the statement; "If you want to sleep in my bed." Flat words to mirror hard anger. Now he could leave, she'd given him good reason. He sat next to her; "What's the matter little Remi? Did you get in trouble when you told Rantoul?"

How did he know? She swung her face around to look at him and true to his nature he was seated so she had his bad side, rough, sanded by the day's work, almost bleeding in places and her hand went out to touch the rawness. He leaned into her fingers and smiled. "What'd he say?"

She panted short breaths, her eyes hurt and all she wanted was to lean against him and find his arms holding her. She sat up straighter, looked away from his gaze and she couldn't get enough air to tell the truth. Any truth; the words sputtered out not what she wanted to say. "I told him Roy got run down by a bull and we had to shoot him." Was that enough, would he accept the words? He smiled, ruined skin moving in jerks across his cheek. "Is that what you wanted to tell him?"

He knew, he heard and judged and wanted her to speak out. "It's the truth, I just didn't tell him how...why." Her hands shook and she slid them between her knees. The vibrations were transferred, into her voice, her lower lip. All of her jangled; "It is what happened." She waited, he only breathed in and out where she couldn't get a breath and the tears flooded into her throat making her swallow hard.

"What did happen, Remi? Do you know?"

Her tears were strangling her, she gulped and he pulled her up to be leaned against him. Her face rested on his chest, she could smell his sweat, stale and harsh and she cried, sobbing as if all sections inside her broke and ran together. His hands rested on her back. "You told too little, Remi, you did not explain and so you dishonored Roy. That good horse would not panic unless he was where he could not do his job. It is wrong to leave his memory spoiled. You need to tell all of the truth."

She gulped out the only answer; "All right. Tomorrow." He pushed her away; "No, tonight."

RANTOUL ONLY GRUNTED. "His worth comes out of your pay, Mrs. Vargas." That was all he said; Remi pushed, asked the question. "How much was he worth?" Rantoul didn't look up; "Thirty dollars." "Oh."

Sixto laughed when she told him; "That little bronc was the best here and Rantoul don't knew what he's talking 'bout. That's old time worth. That pretty little horse with the manners you put on him, we won't tell ole Rantoul what he could a been sold for. Here now, come with me."

It was as if last night and this morning and the whole terrible day never happened. It was dark now, and they did not light a lantern or sit outside and watch the stars. They went deep into the bed Papa had made and Remi finally forgot about all that went before. Sixto's hands on her breasts, then his mouth, then his soft words calling her beautiful in his own language, then hers, gentle words which did not fit what she was feeling from him. Hands on her thighs, close up and inside, suddenly moving and she tensed from his touch. His mouth found her breast again, then her lips. "Let me, it is all right, let me touch you. Here. Here. Give me your hand."

135

The shape and hardness were no surprise but the tenderness of the outside skin, how it slid and moved and she could hear his quick gulps, feel his heart speed up as her fingers explored, tugged, cradled and then squeezed. Finally, grunting, breath hot on her face and neck, he pulled free of her hand and moved above her. She was quickly conscious of what he wanted, where he needed to be and it was simple to slide her legs and raise her hips so his entry was easier.

He moved a few times hard inside her and now she couldn't breathe, tried to ride with him, ahead of his moving until her head jerked back and she gave up trying, moved with him, against him. His hands grabbed her hips and each thrust became exquisite pain until he cried out and collapsed on her.

She allowed him a moment's rest, then began her own dance around him until she cried out too, unable to find anything except her belly and between her legs and fight for her breath until he lay limp against the inside of her thighs and he gasped, panted, his heart pounding to an internal beat.

THE FIRST TIME wasn't the first and the real first came again and again with startling force. As long as Sixto stayed in me, I could rest, wait, almost in meditation, and then begin squeezing muscles I'd never known about, in places I would never see and oh my oh yes. And oh my again.

I am certainly glad I had no preconceived (yes that's a pun, a rather soggy and overused pun but still valid) notions about sex, about the physical act and its sensations, those leading up to the actual penetration or insertion and the sometimes-outstanding waves of pure undefined pleasure. Of course it wasn't always the same, sometimes better, sometimes nothing at all, but even at its worst, when I was exhausted and Sixto was thinking of something else, it still was a connection between us and the smallest of each pleasure was a gift.

I learned quickly that Sixto didn't always have the stamina to finish me, so there were nights when I went undone, twitching and moaning beside him until I guess the noise and fussing kicked something over in Sixto and he began to use his fingers, then his mouth, on me. I didn't mind, in fact I loved the tongue gliding around that place I couldn't see until I went berserk, rolling and arching and Sixto had to grab me to get it all done.

No one ever told me that men had limits; their endless bragging implied that they were continual motion machines, ah yes that song Sixty Minute Man but that of course is not the truth. See, we are back to my original thesis; we lie, all of us. Even in our eagerness to seduce and impress with the truth, we lie by our own imaginations.

Sixto was pure male, arrogant, gentle, single-minded, delicate. Needing a female, willing to give over half his life to have a companion in bed. That he and I were together on horses and hard work made our partnership endurable. He wanted a partner when he wanted her, not all the time, not the same each time, not for very long each time. The isolation of the ranch, the times' morality, distances and costs of a city woman made it acceptable for him to keep me in his bed.

I think he loved me. He was moody, fragile on some level, anxious and single-minded about his work. Evenings were spent braiding and working horse tail hair to form the most beautiful and simple of headstalls and reins; I envied the concentration and the results, but it often brought him to my bed late and tired, swearing at me when my hands went seeking what was not there.

I learned too quickly to want sex and I learned far too slowly to be less demanding. There was so much to know, so many ideas that intrigued me, and Sixto's simple upbringing compromised our growing together. I had had no fetters on my imagination, and I was left with vivid pictures of my sister riding up and down, my father impaled between my mother's legs and that last horrible exposure of her as she and my brother died.

And you know what, to hell with all those images. I know they influenced me when I was much younger, oh so much younger, but they are only a small image now, known and remembered but no longer savage in their importance. Not having the time to dwell on their import, I moved on, as a child growing up on the ranch there wasn't time to think or ponder or get all moody. When I got Pego and could ride, I was gone. For hours, seeking out stray calves or desolate mothers, noting broken wire and sagging windmills. I was useful, needed, and on horseback. Life couldn't get better for me.

This does not mean I rode past what was there, what lay behind my memory. I knew my mother's death every day, I revisited Rosie's sodden actions at night, especially when I was reaching that indelicate age. But these horrors were not all and everything in my living; they were small fragments holding much importance but not preventing me from my own life.

You can note the lies, perceive their intrusion, but what you must acknowledge is that we all have a choice, and given such freedoms I chose to enjoy. Even now I miss the sense of the horse beneath me, and not in that silly sexual innuendo that boys love to rail about as they tease the girls. The horse was home, sanity, pleasure, air and sun and sweet smells, company that didn't demand anything except common sense and long drinks of cool water.

There were nights when I sobbed for my mother and Papa couldn't hear me. There were times in bed with Sixto that I saw in graphic detail the size and color of Rosie and her young man and I wanted the same loving from my own husband. Unfortunately my inventiveness did not fit in with his perceptions or his sexual drive. Such is life or some such foolishness. I wanted it all and Sixto sure as hell tried.

Eleven

The first fight was terrible; she never did recover, and it was about horses. Her horses; damn him for challenging her.

They had gone down to the corral after a two-week sort-of honeymoon where they rode out together on simple chores like checking fence and measuring the depth to the filled or half-filled stock tanks. It was Mrs. Ravenstock forcing her husband to give them that much time.

Ravenstock didn't look at Remi as he handed out the orders. 'They' was to work on the broncs, especially getting that big sorrel colt mannerly. If he was to be a herd sire he had to prove his worth. Sixto kept nodding his head and ignoring her and Remi snorted once, letting her husband know his tactics wouldn't work.

Turns out he had paid her no attention, not getting her message, not even trying to listen or maybe not remembering he had a wife. She walked beside him, letting the anger build up till they got to the corral and he dared to give her an order. "You catch up that dun, he's been started so he won't give you much trouble."

Remi came around and let her hand slap his face before she even thought through what was happening. Sixto stepped back, shaking his head. She thought there were tears in his eyes but that couldn't be true. "Why, Remi?"

She was momentarily wordless. She wiped her mouth; "You don't get to order me around." He ignored her and opened a loop to catch the big colt, Jocko. The houlihan went smooth and easy over the high neck. Jocko was spun around by the pull and the colt squalled, pawed out, and Remi got madder.

"He's mine to work, Sixto, you got no right to tell me what horse I work and you damn well get that rope off of Jocko, I started him and you're the one made a mess out of his hide with those damned spurs."

Sixto tried a grin and it twisted his face; "Doing what the man told us, Remi. He wants them broncs ridden and the dun's too small for me." She grabbed at the rope and Jocko backed up. Sixto didn't let go even as Remi shook his arm. "Girl, I started horses when you was in pigtails, you leave me be, this's a man's job."

The words stunned; she turned and ran. He yelled after her; "What about the dun?" That ground her to a full stop. She wiped her eyes, gulped for air and turned around but did not look at her husband as she fashioned up a loop and caught the dun. The rope settled clean; there, she thought, see what a nothing woman can do. Sixto grunted.

The dun had a poor eye and shallow chest but good hindquarters and he took the saddle blanket and cinch like it was old hat to him. She wondered where these few broncs had come from; they were rough string for sure. Five of them, not counting the big sorrel. Rank looking, straight legs, bench knees, two were sickle-hocked, slab sided, a poor lot she thought. Then again most of the breeders'd gone out of business with the Army no longer wanting remounts. If these were the best of the lot, not much of quality was left.

The sorrel reared without warning against Sixto's hand and knocked him down. Sixto lay still, the sorrel pulled away, rope trailing his careful steps.

Remi let the dun go and went to her husband.

IT TOOK THREE men to carry Sixto to their house, lay him on the messy bed and leave. Not one of the men looked her straight in the eye or said anything but mumbles. They were snickering when they got outside; Remi hated them all.

There wasn't a mark on him, just dust on his shirt and jeans, bits of straw in his hair, but his eyes were firmly closed and only his hands moved, clenching at the sheet, drawing it up in fistfuls. She sat with him for maybe a half hour, washing his face and touching his hands. When he showed no signs of waking, she went back to the corrals and caught up the dun, removed the gear and took it to the sorrel colt.

She spoke to him first, standing with the saddle at her feet, the folded blanket in her one hand, the bridle in the other. The men hadn't bothered with these two horses, leaving the sorrel neck-roped and liable to choke himself. She'd get them later, when Sixto was all right and the sorrel colt was rideable.

The colt's neck was raw, and he was sore on a hind leg, holding it gingerly from the ground. She could read, skin worn raw on the pastern, a swelling and some fluid. Damn. Her fingers went out, blanket on her arm, lightly touching the colt's muzzle, then she stepped to his neck, stroked him carefully, and he bowed his head, let out a huge sigh and fart and then began licking his lips.

So she slid the bit into his mouth, tugged the bridle over his ears and his eyes rolled but he held quiet for her. Only then did she loosen the rope and slide it free. The colt sighed again and dropped a huge pile of manure. She stepped him forward before laying the blanket on his back, careful over the high withers to leave room. He took the saddle steadily, barely twitched as she tugged the cinch.

There was nothing wrong with this one, it was Sixto's heavy touch, not the colt's temperament that caused trouble. She tightened the cinch and stepped up into the saddle and the colt grunted lightly, turned his head and she touched the hard bone of his skull. He had a small diamond there, she traced the outlines with her fingers and the one eye she could see was reassured.

Light leg pressure caused the colt to walk forward; she urged him into that smooth trot of his and they circled the pen easily. There was a slight hitch in his gait, then it eased out and she knew the raw burn meant nothing. Then she settled down, asked for a lope and he offered to buck against her hand. She kicked him, scolded with her voice, and his head came up. She laughed and patted his withers, scrubbing with two fingers. The colt was a delight to ride.

Ten minutes later it occurred to Remi that she needed to check on her husband. Instead she stepped off the colt and tied him, then caught up the ratty dun. This wasn't as nice a horse, all ears and thick neck and legs that looked wrong. Bench knees, short pastern, terrible angle to the hind legs but it was a horse and she and Sixto had been told to ride it into some useful manners.

The horse was saddle-broke and that was all; turning was impossible, only the head and neck gave to the rein, no sign that the body knew it was meant to follow that new direction. As for trotting, goddamn was all she could think as the dun jarred and bounced her almost out of the saddle. She hated the thought but kicked hard and the dun reluctantly went into a lope as if it knew how bad the gait was. Goddamn.

She rode the dun and led the sorrel up to the small house. She called her husband's name and there was no sound, no movement and after calling his name again she got scared. She tied the two horses at the hitch rail and didn't bother with the colt's squeal or the dun's heavy grunt as she ran into the house.

He hadn't moved, still laid out on the bed, nothing shifted or changed and that scared her even more. She crawled in beside him and started crying, soundless, wanting him to comfort her.

ISN'T THERE A there a current slang saying 'life sucks.'? Well it certainly did for me at that moment. And it wasn't too great for Sixto either. He was dead. Cold. Without life. Gone to his reward as his mother said later. Gone away from me was all I could recognize. All I felt; abandoned, worthless, my husband of twenty-three days dying alone in our marriage bed.

The mourning and the burial took longer than our marriage. All done without me, without what I wanted, how I felt - it was his mother who dominated the proceedings, his father whose stern face glowed at me whenever I looked up. I was the culprit, the bad child who took their son. It didn't matter that the sorrel colt had hammered him to the ground, I was the one responsible, the one to blame. A war hadn't gotten him, a prison camp had not held him; I had killed him in less than two months.

That Ravenstock came to these various gatherings, face stern, hat in his hands, dressed in rusted black, didn't seem hypocritical to any of Sixto's family. He was the patrón, the boss, what he said had to be done. It was my taking Sixto's mind off his work that killed him. Not Ravenstock's orders, not the colt's restless fear or Sixto's private violence. We had not spoken of his earlier encounter with the colt, or his attack against me. These were sides of their beloved son the parents did not need to know, but their anger at me was a harsh price.

All this was much later; I crawled back into the bed after they took Sixto's body and I cried until I was sick, barely making it to the bathroom and then I went back to the mangled bedclothes carrying his smell and I cried again until I slept.

Belinda E. Perry

Deep in my dreams I remembered the horses and crawled out to find that the dun had wrapped his rein around his leg and stood head almost to the ground, grunting occasionally but otherwise not making a fuss. The sorrel colt had disappeared.

Having to deal with the dun's predicament forced me to move, to take care of the horse's mute suffering and I responded by slicing the rein so he could raise his head. Then I led him back to the corral and managed to strip him of the gear and even hoist the saddle into its place, next to Sixto's rig, which told me the colt was taken care of. I vaguely wondered why no one had seen to the dun.

I won't bore you with details; funerals and gatherings and the long process of mourning is not new, lies spilled through the rooms, even to the cottonwood outside their door where the men spoke in savage drunken tones of Sixto's skills, fighter, lover, tamer of wild horses. Then their brutal speculation turned to questioning who would take me on. 'Just broke in' I heard one man say, his tongue stumbling over the delicious thought and I hated all of them immediately and forever.

The lies were terrible; hearing them repeated I hated the whole village and especially the few men from his imprisonment who came to mourn him publicly. They were whole, alive, sturdy legs and clean faces; they had no right to his memory, they spoke evil lies of his bravery and his soul, his honor held dear by those who loved him.

I hated Sixto for dying, and hated anyone who tried comforting me. Sixto had not been taken to a better place; he had been taken from me.

EVEN MR. RANTOUL took pity on the child, for she was only a child despite being a wife and widow. However, he had sent in papers on the advice of one of those few sad bastards who came to the funeral, lean and scrawny in their tired uniforms, faces the same, drawn, grey, secretive and superior as if they knew what no one else could.

Rantoul did not bother to tell them he had served in the earlier war; no one who survived this war wanted to hear other stories. Their wounds were too fresh and insolent for any returned survivors.

He was religious about calling her Mrs. Vargas and refused seeing her head jerk every time he spoke that name. She was in fact a young widow, and soon enough the Army in its wisdom sent her Sixto's pittance, what his country owed him for dying. That his death was entirely due to his injuries and his private war was not doubted, except by the living officers in Washington who tried to question and correct her claim.

Rantoul wrote a suitably angry letter when at first her marriage and Sixto's death were refused by the military, then he got in touch with the local congressman and finally the checks arrived.

He allowed Remi to stay in the house, and he gave her the horses to work with, to keep her busy. He noted that she rode out often on the sorrel colt, which was good for the colt. She was gone maybe five hours, brought the colt back leaned and crusted with dried sweat, but the colt blossomed instead of losing weight so Rantoul didn't complain.

HAVEN'T YOU EVER spoken with a person in such pain that your first urge is to hold them, nothing about sex and that is no lie, only to hold, cradle, offer comfort to ease whatever causes such devastation? It is an extraordinary sensation, completely selfless since it has no sexual motive, no greed or self-recommendation. Only the need of another that reaches in and grabs, shakes, demands resolve.

There is no distraction to the question, no clever ploy to gain your sympathy. I have received such love, in odd forms, and I have offered it with no expectations. It is how we survive, or dissolve, it is the manner in which we combine our senses and become more than we expect of ourselves.

Mr. Rantoul gave me a life and a chance for no other reason than Sixto's sad death and Rantoul's small power, which enabled him to offer me something better.

SUNLIGHT HURT HER eyes, and the rub of horsehair on her fingers hurt. She licked her lips and the dried skin peeled off; she needed water, a long drink slow down her throat, each gulp an effort of will. If she didn't drink, she would fade, erode, fall just like her husband.

The dun was proving to be a decent horse despite his shortcomings. He'd never be much at the end of a rope, too slight in the front, too easily yanked off balance but by god he could travel, and stand, wait, pull a broke fence post, a bawling calf. Just not stout or balanced enough for roping and holding.

She told Mr. Rantoul this and he offered to keep the dun for her personal use, since she seemed to get along with him. The men found him skittering and useless. She took to calling the dun just that, 'Useless' and the bronc often nodded his head to the insult as if he'd heard it before.

One Sunday after a roast dinner with the fixings, Rantoul stood up and told them. "The place's been sold, they want you to stay on but it won't be the same. Ain't gonna use horses no more, so guess it's time, boys, our world has changed."

Remi snorted; how could they not use horses to work cattle. Trucks just couldn't keep up with the ornery beasts when they decided to run. Only a good quarter horse from that new registry stood the test, trailing cattle, holding them for doctoring. She shook her head and Rantoul spoke again; "I want you boys to know it's been good working with you." With that, Mr. Rantoul left the room and the hands sat a moment, looked at each other.

Finally one of them spoke up; "Hell, there ain't no horses, there ain't no need for no one to ride 'em." He too got up and left and eventually it was only Remi seated in the dark room that smelled of stale food, grease, hot biscuits and old sweat.

Twelve

When the new crew arrived there was Remi and the cook to greet them. Most of the saddle stock were turned out but Remi had kept the sorrel colt and the five range broncs to the corrals so she had a reason to be staying on.

No one paid her much attention; there were moving vans and trailers, massive trucks like she only heard about, a low car carrying three men and a slender, dolled-up woman. Remi saddled the dun, oddly her favorite now even over the sorrel colt, and did some spins and stops in the corral to keep her head where it belonged.

On the last spin it registered that a figure leaned against the fence watching her. She reined in the dun and brought him together, headed toward the figure. A woman, in a long sleek jacket and skirt, a big hat that took the dun by surprise when the woman shook her head and spoke to Remi.

"Why you're a girl. I didn't know a girl could ride that well. He's soooo pretty..." That told Remi what she needed to know; city folk thought color was pretty, didn't or couldn't see build and soundness. Didn't know nothing about working stock. She reined the dun over his hocks, set a spin in him, then angled off in a soft lope and set the pony down hard in a stop. Patted the bronc's damp neck and studied their new admirer.

City folk all right, in a wide-brimmed hat with a red sash, a long top loose at the neck, fitted close on the hindquarters and shoes not made for nothing but attention. Couldn't walk a half mile in them, open toes and straps around the ankle and wobbling even as she stood and looked back at Remi with the same derision that Remi felt.

She could only guess what the city woman was seeing; lank hair, peeling nose, worn hands and only eighteen - a damned woman, lost a short-time husband, no folks at all. Hard to work, difficult to like. Scrawny in her man's shirt and rolled jeans, proud of the handle she put on a horse, good or bad, and not much else.

Two women staring at each and already knowing without a word being said. "My name is Anne Marie, and you must be Remi. Mr. Ravenstock and Mr. Rantoul both said we must keep you if we wanted to be known for good horses. That seems high praise for a child. But my brother believes them, and now, well, watching you and that lovely animal, I can understand why the men would make such a recommendation."

There was too much spoken and even more not said that bothered Remi. Compliments were suspicious, especially when you didn't know the speaker. She offered her hand over the top rail, the woman reached up and took it. The brief shake was peculiar; Remi's quick-callused grip was challenged by soft fingers, long nails, no cracks, no rough skin. A world Remi knew existed and thought foolish without ever talking to its inhabitants.

"Name's Remi but you know that. Remi..." Here she was stopped; her legal name was Vargas, her own name McClary. She'd never had to say them to the world. "Remi McClary Vargas to be exact." There, spoken to the wind and the curious dun whose ears kept swiveling and rolling until Remi had to pat his neck again to settle him.

Anne Marie nodded and stepped down from her uneasy perch on the bottom railings of the peeled fence. The child was merely that, a rough ranch orphan of no great beauty yet in the darkened eyes, holding a surprising green light, and the thick red-blond hair streaked and trailing underneath the battered hat, there was an elegance and grace, muscled by hard work and long hours. It wasn't easy to see into the child's face, that hat, and the tilt of her head, gave cover to her features and expression but Anne Marie could recognize good bone structure and clear eyes from a long distance. This child had possibilities, no doubt at all.

She smiled, waved gently, waited until the child waved back and then she carefully picked her path to the house. They were settling into the foreman's residence recently vacated by Mr. Ravenstock and his wife to a smaller building once the home of the top hand. There had been some grumblings but her brother chose not to listen. In this time of dwindling ranches, a foreman would be easy to hire; if Ravenstock's wife made things uncomfortable enough, then they would have to move on.

Her brother had big plans for the main house, built in the twenties and so out of date it was laughable. Even the swimming pool needed redesigning before it could be called an attractive addition. The fading Hollywood glamour held no appeal for Harry. With the Texas oil money they had inherited, rebuilding the main house would be a glorious extravagance. Then Harry would move in, and she could have fun with her new home. All to herself, no more husband to bother her, no children running through and upsetting various and precious ornaments.

She stopped, let out a deep breath; she had lost custody of the children in the divorce, hating them made no sense when it was herself she hated.

The ground rolled under her shoes, already her face felt scorched; she remembered the face of the child working those horses, lines at the eyes, a raw look to her skin. Anne Marie vowed she would not ever let herself go to that point, where no man would wish to put a hand on her, to touch her face, caress her body, rise with desire from wanting her. She put more energy and balance into her retreat toward the shabby house she would share with her brother. It would not do to let anyone think she had been defeated.

NO, DESPITE HOW it might seem I am not going to tell you the minutiae of each day, the long dragged-out story of my entire life. No one has a life that interesting - go ahead and read some of the highly detailed biographies and even worse the autobiographies where the writer could not distinguish between monumental and ordinary - they are mind-numbing in their exposure of how banal life can be.

What I remember, so far back that detail is obscured, are the highlights, and the beginning where I learned lessons that shaped and formed the rest of my life. It is the beginning, when life is tenuous and learning scarce, slow, extremely painful, those moments hold interest. As we become middle-aged and set in our life, we are no longer interesting to anyone but ourselves and often we are bored with our own routine. The same complaints, worn thin but still potent by the years, the fading memories more powerful than we wish, the fears and worries we have learned to hide.

Here are our lies; 'I don't mind' - yeah right in the current slang; 'please help yourself, we weren't going to keep it anyway', and the kids are hungry but who cares. On and on, you know the statements, small half-truths you hope the other person doesn't register and take you at face value. Be careful of what you offer, even if it is only to be polite. Don't you remember regretting that invitation, 'oh yes please stay, I can make another pot of coffee' and the person sits down, waiting for you to fulfill your promise. Damn.

I have another bone to pick, in random order of course. Now I enjoy wine but please do not describe the beverage to me in intellectual and floral terms. This is the height of snobbery, the finer wines spoken of in the fruity tones of hyperbole and condescension.

My favorite being...'this wine is ironic and lingering' oh yes with such a description I know exactly what it tastes like, don't you. Do not speak down to your audience and expect the world to applaud you for your brilliance. It is damned foolish speaking and while it might make you acceptable to a certain group of those in the know, it diminishes your humanness, makes you sound like a gibbering monkey. We do this to ourselves willingly, wishing desperately to belong to one group or another, yet we are no more special for speaking or understanding the vocabulary.

True individualism isn't bought through glamour ads and high-powered cars. One of the great sadnesses of the modern world - individualism is through character, beliefs, actions, not clothing and surgery and that gleaming high-dollar/power car you don't mind taking out a huge loan for; after all, it will prove you are among the cool.

I think I've gone over this territory before but I don't care. The best people I've known, those whose memory is a constant treasure are the ones who never tried but simply were.

Two men, both dear to me, a vision of them in their early seventies, one on a cane, one with crippled hands, peering into the innards of a new machine, a small four-wheeler now known as an ATV. They were intent on the quest, poking and pulling out panels, checking all manner of gears and workings and I had no idea what they were doing but they were friends, of mine and my husband of that time, and they were child-like in their excitement, their enjoyment of the shared wondered of this new machine. No artifice, no wondering if anyone thought them 'cool' or sophisticated. Their delight was easily shared, and even my husband joined in the inspection.

To watch these men become boys again, talking, questioning, wondering about the new technology was a pleasure simply to watch.

So do you have any idea what I am saying - there was no superficiality among these men, no posturing or words of great import, only energy and sweetness and a real curiosity as to how the new idea worked.

They remain two of the coolest men I have known, for their realness, their strength of earnest character. The rest of the world be damned; they knew what intrigued and entranced them and no advertising, no false promise to a retail god could dissuade them sideways from their discovery.

All right, one more item before I get off my soap box; by the way does anyone know why spouting your thoughts and feelings is called 'standing on a soap box'? Well, figure it out. I'm not going to bother telling you
I would like to ask one of the buxom women patrolling the streets now just why they prefer to dress like whores. That statement might be politically incorrect, another term I cannot abide but on this occasion it is the truth. To dress with large breasts clinging to tight fabric and then expect men to not notice is radically foolish. You cannot change nature and to deny a man's arousal when you are pushing your breasts into his face is like that old proverb, don't spit into the wind. Your actions will come back and smear all over you. Want me to be more graphic than that?

So enough of the ranting, but have I made myself clear? You want to be respected as a business person, don't dress like a high-class hooker. If an attractive male wore a speedo and sandals and was obviously well-endowed where it does matter, could you look away and keep your mind on business - I don't think so, so give the men a break.

Belinda E. Perry

NO ONE BOTHERED with her, none of the ranchmen spoke to her or flirted with her or even nodded their heads. She no longer existed except to ride down the broncs and get them to handle, spin on a light rein, slide to a stop, stand and hold the downed calf for doctoring or branding. At least she was good for something.

Sometimes she rolled over in the bed and threw out her hand expecting what she had barely learned to want and it wasn't there. She learned to get up then and walk outside rather than lie in bed and cry.

Sometimes she went down to the corrals and sat with the horses. That often helped, she would lean against a corral post and listen to them, feel the night air cool her face, even open her legs and let the air reach her there. Tears didn't suit or calm her; they invited desolation and despair and she hated herself when she cried. Even so, sitting against the sturdy post, feeling cooled air touch her lips and eyes, she cried until her mouth hung open and drool filled the corners. She choked on her misery and rolled her head against her drawn knees, squeezing tight with her muscled arms, digging fingernails into the whitened palms, hating herself and where she was.

Alone, miserable, and uncertain. Hell Remi thought, I'm a widow and an orphan and no family, no goddamned job, no one to talk with.

A weight pushed on her head and she closed her eyes, muttering his name even as she knew who was touching her. A horse, nothing in her life but a horse. It was the ugly dun, lower lip drooping, green slime clinging to his teeth, snot coming from his tight nostrils. Ah hell, Remi said again, a horse.

THE RANCH ACCOUNT books did not jibe with what he had been told. The easy charm of the actor and Mr. Rantoul's brusque manner glossed over the truth of high cattle numbers reproducing at low quality. Quantity was there, but not the deep muscling and hardy temperament necessary to survive harsh winters and give birth with little stress. Harry let his fingers touch the brittle paper, closed his eyes and thought on what he had done this time, making an enormous investment in land and beef that could possibly provide his family with a vindication of their belief in him. He was not his father.

Harry's inner voice was too familiar by now, unsuccessful at defeat yet always a hole, a prod to keep him from acquiescing. He would not become what they expected. His family's disdain was his goal and energy and employing the emotion thus pleased him as it was used for success.

This matter however might reduce him to their belief; damn his urge, his gamble, a reaction to the long grasslands, the bluffs and mesas, those magical distant cones of cooled fiery rock that made him forget his purpose and his educated common sense. He'd done what was financially incorrect; he'd gone with his heart.

He stood from the oppressive desk and its ugly spread of truth and walked to the window. It needed a good wash but the view was his enticement. A low sweep of varying grass, then a peeled fence on and out to a distance he craved. The grasses were higher, thin clumps of rare golden heads caught in the deepening blue. These visions took his breath and he knew exactly what he'd done.

The ranch would work, he would struggle and change and read, study and try and by god the whole dammed thing would work. Today he would find the head wrangler and assess the horses he might use for his own. He was aware enough that he did not wish to commandeer a valued cow horse for the animals' skills were partnered with the ranch's expansion. He would ask for and choose a quiet saddle horse who would not display temper or nervous irritability at being reduced to mere transport.

Finding a way to explain this to a high-intensity horse wrangler without losing pride or stature would come to him when he met the man.

HAROLD BERTRAM SEMBACH chose his name when he was five; his mother wanted to keep calling him Harold, a feminine treatment he resented, and his father preferred Hal junior which didn't suit at all, so as a boy he picked out Harry and would answer to no other calling.

In later years he heard the tone behind the use of a man's full given name; a preemptive chiding and a diminishment in the usage, that effeminate affection which some women used to deride their husbands while seeming to adore them. He would not allow a woman to chastise him by her words, he did not listen to the young ladies his mother and father picked out for him to consider. They had that look, they spoke in soft tones using verbal iron as a weapon and he would not return their interest.

Harry had no illusions about his attraction for the opposite sex; unlike his father he was not large and imposing nor was he pretty as his mother had once been. His sister, now she was beautiful in a wild, ragged manner, with too much hair differing each month in its unnatural color balanced by a figure that men always appreciated. She was a collection of tailoring and makeup and hair stylist and jewelry that appealed to basic lust - she smiled and cocked her head and touched the back of a hand, threw her head in a laugh, raising her breasts and any man's interest.

All he had was money and a wry sense of humor. He was short, no other way to describe him. Five foot seven if he was wearing shoes with a decent heel. His father had sent him to a cobbler to have 'special' shoes made; Harry refused the gesture and its intent. He was Harry, and stacked leather would not make him stronger or more successful.

As he aged into his twenties he read about a Napoleonic complex and did not like the label or its application. He was careful to question his own actions and responses and weed out those manifested by his height.

When his sister wore those stacked suede shoes she liked so much, she was at least his height if not taller. He didn't mind, what was the point in fretting.

The office where Ravenstock had kept scattered papers and a few files was reasonable enough; he had a handsome mahogany desk and a leather chair and the file cabinets were polished oak. An acceptable woven oriental rug softened the hard tile flooring and his view out the one huge window was a source of inspiration. Using his father's money he had bought a ranch, not in Texas where the oil name was connected and known but in the remote side of New Mexico and it was exactly what he wanted.

It was up to him to turn a profit, and learn the business.

YOU ALL KNOW what happens next and I'm tired so I will take a break and leave the introductions to your own imaginations. If you've been reading this with some intelligence you will remember my first mention of Harry. He was timid yet certain in knowing about himself, not allowing his short stature to be a hindrance in his work and life.

He came down to the corrals to ask about a suitable horse for him and in my youth and grief I first offered him a rogue, then changed my mind as his innate kindness touched me, and gave him the ugly dun. Harry most specifically said he did not want to take one of the better ranch horses as he was an indifferent rider and would not wish to misuse a decent animal.

I am tired, my mind is strained with what I am trying to tell you readers. About my life and its unraveling while I struggle to make some sense of my existence. And then I take off from the story, exposing you to my opinions and ignorance, the effect of so many years without education. However, I do know that in so many ways I am wiser not because of years but because I did not come to adulthood bombarded with 'buy this want that' nor did I read novels and magazines but the few books of philosophies and histories left around the cook shack and bunk rooms.

I am tired so I will tell you briefly about the next chapter so that I don't have to write it – for an unknown reason Anne Marie took me in, saw me as a project – well if you think on the discrepancies in our lives the concept is not difficult to understand. It's all about Anne Marie.

IT WAS UNDERSTOOD that his sister was delicate and far too sensitive and had to be shielded from the realities of the life she led. There was hard-drinking in the family, a long history of proud men boasting on their incredible consumptions and while Harry had been immune to this pitiful bragging, Anne Marie had grown up adoring her dissolute father and trying to emulate him. She had inherited the weakness of drunken folly that guided her to awful choices with tragic consequences.

     He would not remember the times he had rescued his beloved sister from bars and bedrooms and strangers' angry arms; he would not believe the stories her husband told, edged with cruel joy, about her treatment of their two beautiful children.

Belinda E. Perry

Harry had decided early on he did not want children, did not wish to give them the heritage of drink and pain and relentless humiliation. He hated what family did, and would not ever choose to pass this on to a child. So he ducked his head and rescued his sister and studied the indifferent and egotistical methods of his father's company until he knew he could make even more money with the oil leases and now the cattle ranch.

Anne Marie had already taken on the strangest project; it was the daughter of a long-time ranch hand. The gentleman was buried among strangers in the ranch cemetery, a lonesome beautiful place tucked in the side of an embankment. An iron fence, one rather sad piney tree and a bare spot near a cracked boulder led Harry to believe that someone or something spent a good deal of time sitting there. Under this odd rather bedraggled tree were piles of horse manure. Now Harry wasn't an outdoorsman but he could see and think and draw his own conclusions and he thought it sad that a child like Miss Remi would spend so much of her time mourning at a place where no one else came to honor the dead. She must have loved her father, an emotion Harry had yet to share. Except for the rescuing of his sister, families and their entanglements left him cold.

The girl was odd and awkward, striding about the ranch in men's jeans and ragged shirts, some bursting at the front buttons until Harry realized she was not wearing that unmentionable female support garment, which would have lessened the effect of her youthful figure. Anne Marie would have seen the same visions; altered slightly by her female sensibilities and an urge to protect her own; this child would become Anne Marie's salvation.

He met one cowboy at the corrals when he went looking for a horse to ride. He quickly became conscious of his unsuitable dress as he watched the figure standing near the fence. The denim pants were soft blue, worn thin over the thigh, covered from the knee down in tall boots of a deep brown, their only adornment fancy stitching on the shaft, and an ungainly high stacked heel which to his eye suggested difficulty walking.

As he learned about this strange breed, he grew to understand that comfort in walking was not what a cowboy's boots were intended to offer; that steep heel was protection from having a foot pressed through the stirrup and thus insuring the dragging death of its wearer.

Harry was clothed in a starched white custom-made shirt, flared English breeches of the type worn by the flamboyant Prince of Wales, the inside of the breeches legs, or breeks he'd heard a Canadian cousin call them, were covered with the finest soft calfskin, and each foot was embraced in a laced boot which came to just under his knee. As he approached the corral fences, he became aware of the dust swirling and settling on every bit of clothing he wore. He stopped and looked down at his boots, they were a pale tan, no longer the rich burnished cordovan he'd admired this morning when he wiped them to a shine with the chamois.

When the cowboy stared at him and began to laugh he realized she was female. The bounce in her blouse front was unmistakable and Harry felt his face flush – he was so easily embarrassed it had been a family joke during drunken gatherings. The uncontrolled anxiety of those terrible moments had him stop, wipe his face, and seemed to allow the young woman to see him as an individual and not some movie caricature. Then it occurred to him she most likely had never seen a movie.

He nodded his head, she grinned. "Good morning," was all he managed. She answered back in her western twang; 'Mornin'." She was obviously not overjoyed to be meeting with him. "My name is Harry." He hesitated, for her face showed no interest in the proclamation; "Uh, Harry...well I own the place now." She did nod her head in accompaniment to her abbreviated speech. "Knew that." She hesitated, rubbed a boot toe in the powdered dirt. "Mr. Sembach." She knew that too.

He was studying her closely, and when his inspection reached her eyes, a rather vivid and unsettling green that was quite uncommon, he saw the laughter hidden there, and she stared right back, unhesitating, too knowing. He began to fidget, understanding completely that her laughter was directed at him.

NOW I WOULD never say it to his face but he knew that the picture he first presented to me was totally silly. No other word for it yet I saw into his eyes and let the laughter go for he was real, human, and suffering for his terrible mistake. Later he told me it had been fate put him in front of me that day instead of one of the male hands – they would never see his true spirit or strengths if they'd taken in the foolish breeches and high boots. Those clothes were one trademark a tenderfoot could not outlive.

Harry was short, yeah so what – as an old horse trader once said when an opinion was offered about a horse up for sale, that the beast's legs were too short. 'They reach the ground don't they.' Harry stood on those muscled legs, steady and square and not easy to tip over. Or upset, fluster, confuse – except of course if you were a female. And despite my garb, I was that and more – turns out I didn't know enough about dressing myself at the time, and my bouncing exposure to all the cowboys, and to Harry, was most unsuitable.

See, if we don't know, if we are truly innocent, then our mistakes may be forgiven. I had no idea, no possible concept of the havoc my mature breasts engendered among the crew. How could I…Sixto was my only critic and he of course loved them, laid his head between them and licked and kissed and fondled until…well you know all that by now.

Harry could not look at me that first time, and me, I tried to see what I didn't like, a city boy gussied up and out of place, trying to change daily life with his foreignness. Those damn-fool breeches and boots, the white shirt sparking in the New Mexico sun, and a scarf, probably silk although I wouldn't have recognized silk at that point, tied around his neatly shaved throat. My my but he was a dandy. Too clean to my innocent eyes, unused to male vanity exhibited in cleanliness. Our cowboys, or more rightly vaqueros, mostly had large mustaches and thick hair, and their vanity lived in their gear, high boots and horse-hair hitched bridle reins, silver hat bands. They were of necessity unwashed in a desert independent of daily bathing and often smelled like rancid goats.

My few swims with Sixto in the stock ponds were an outrageous exception to our ordinary lives.

Still, Harry made an impression on me not all silly and judgmental. He was kind, I felt that despite my instinctive distrust, and I repaid his kindness by giving him a snorty, mealy-nosed half-broke bronc I wouldn't let no one ride and soon as I handed him the reins I blushed and took them back and didn't tell him why.

HE DIDN'T THINK much of the second horse she presented to him; a dun with hanging ears and a narrow, pointed chest but she smiled quickly and shook her head when he glanced past her to the handsome bay she'd taken back and put in the pen. Harry first thought she might be teasing him, setting him up for some pathetic cowboy joke on the dun, but then he stared at her until she blushed and he offered her the dun's reins in silent question

She later told him that the dun was 'lop-eared' and of all things, 'pigeon-chested' but that these faults in conformation needed to be judged against the horse's attitude and willingness. Much like people, she said, you can't always determine by looking at a man, or a woman, what kind of moral human they might be. It was his first taste of Remi's train of thought; a fact always led to a discussion or lecture or deeper questioning. It was an irritation in the beginning but what he eventually found so attractive about her. Other than her remarkable body of course.

Her reply decided him; "No, that bay's not broke well enough, you don't want to be riding him out here." He cocked his head; she blushed again. "I don't think that bay's going to do much for the ranch. Best sell him on to one of them polo places up near Miami, he's pretty enough for 'em. But don't go admiring that dark shiny coat and strong quarters, Mr. Sembach, that bay's nasty to the bone."

She was blushing again and Harry couldn't guess why, until he rethought her words and she's mentioned the hind end of the bay and that couldn't be the cause, she was too practical for such lady-like delicacy. Yet she had looked away from his face upon uttering the condemnation of that bay, and perhaps after all there was a young lady hiding behind her facade of rough hands and high boots.

He half-bowed to her and turned to study the unfamiliarity of the western rigging. However, as in most saddles he'd ridden around the world, you put your foot in a low-hanging stirrup and mounted, either right or left side, to settle in as lightly as possible and then move forward.

"Mr. Sembach, let me catch up a horse, I'll give you a tour." He expected her to show off and ride the slandered bay; instead she stepped up onto a lanky sorrel who, as she rode past Harry, showed himself to be a stallion of some prowess, at least judging by the equipment. Harry was stunned a moment, then asked the dun to move out and the awkward-looking horse stepped right close to the sorrel and took his place. She turned in the saddle, a light move of some interest to him as he enjoyed the bounce in her scenery. Then he blushed in the privacy of his thoughts.

After a few moments of watching, he decided to ask. "Why do you choose to ride a stallion, Miss McClary." "Remi." He spoke to the back of her head; "What?" "Name's Remi. And this colt's got good breeding, needs to earn a living a few years 'fore they put him to stud. Need to find out he's got enough heart for the job his babies'll be asked to do." He nodded, she let the sorrel step back beside Harry. "No good having papers and fancy breeding you can't do the job." The sorrel stallion, a colt he believed was the correct designation, seemed to hear the conversation for he flipped his tail and then half-reared so that once again his equipment was visible.

The girl simply moved her hand an inch and then patted the colt's damp neck and the sorrel went back to a quiet easy walk. Harry hated to admit it but he was quite impressed with her skills. She nodded briefly as if knowing his thoughts and said very quietly; "You want to try out his lope, ain't much better than the walk or trot but it'll get us there faster."

He had to admit she rode the sorrel colt well, sitting immobile in the saddle, her hands quiet, the colt moving up easily under her. He did find the dun's lope no better than his trot, or jog as the westerners called it but they did cover ground. He was slightly embarrassed as he bounced and slammed against the ragged gait and the hard saddle but she only smiled and kept her colt aimed toward some distant marker he could not see.

It was all the same for him, a hard bounce, a slap to the buttocks, back jammed into the high saddle behind him, thrown forward and lurched through the same torture again and again. He barely had time to watch the ground, never looked up at the horizon, conscious of his boots slipping in the wooden stirrup and he knew enough to be afraid, a slipped boot could mean a dragging death.

Finally his male ego was pained enough he called out to halt and the dun jammed on the brakes, stood nose in the sorrel colt's tail this time and she turned so easily in her saddle and looked back at him without smiling. She was pointing at something he couldn't see.

"That's the windmill for the east pasture, thought you might like to see what good water there is to the ranch. Best thing about this spread, its water. Deep enough well and all the rights to what you can pump."

They had been traveling at high speed across rock and furrows and narrow trails, with no redeemable grass for any creature to eat and she was proud of having water. All the water a man could pump – to Harry water had always been a function of money. You didn't have enough, you bought a man's rights and added them to your own.

The horses were settled now, the girl took a sip of water from her canteen and recapped the battered metal circle. Her voice was so strong and clear Harry was enchanted; "You bought up good water shares when you got this place, I wanted you to see what you'd purchased." He thought that a bit condescending, although he didn't believe the girl would ever have used that word about herself or anyone. She touched the sorrel's sides, he was barely able to see the cue, a mere flexing it seemed of her calf muscle and the colt walked on, head low, tail swinging with the extended rhythm of the gait. The dun followed in his labored amble.

The stock tank and windmill didn't appear to be any closer after five minutes of a silent passage so Harry thought to entertain himself. "Who trains the ranch horses, miss? That colt you ride seems quite well mannered for one so young." She didn't look back; "I train 'em." Harry snorted, he couldn't help himself. And the sorrel colt jumped into an easy lope whereas the dun Harry was mounted on lurched and seem to kick out then settled into what could only be described as a double-sided stampede. He snorted again, then coughed and choked at the dust thrown up in his face.

When she drew in the colt and the dun skidded to a halt, they were standing next to a thin-walled metal circle, perhaps fifteen feet across, which held a shimmering pool. Dirt pads coated its surface; in the clear sun and air almost every distinct particle of settling dust was an individual making its certain way onto the water's surface. Pitting that sheen until it undulated to accommodate the intrusion. Harry was amazed and then distracted.

"Pretty ain't it, like sparkles made out of dust." He looked around to her voice, surprised that there was another person with him. "Can swim here if you like, water's clean under that coating." There was the smallest moment, then; "It's been done before."

He would know later why her voice had that tremble. Harry in his superior innocence assumed that the girl was tired; Remi was remembering, and shocked at how a memory could hurt.

I COULD SEE him too clearly, his burned face and neck stuck up above the water, the hint of his white belly and balls floating beneath the surface. It was a haunted echo of what had been lost. Staying to myself and riding those broncs had become my protection. The boys drifted away, not wishing to stay on for the new owners and I was comforted by their desertion because they took Sixto with them. Until that one terrible moment when I saw the stock tank and heard the wrong voice.

Later Harry apologized, he was good that way, accepting his flaws and speaking out in their defense — he hadn't known, how could he. I forgave him of course. And you will not examine the above for its lies, all life with another person is a lie - we forgive when we want to hit, we smile when we would chose tears or anger, we say yes and no, of course not while meaning their opposites. It is a full life of lying without particular malice. It is the intent and the deceit accompanying many lies that marks the difference between love and caring and simply wanting your own way. I did come to love Harry, that's all you need to know. Believe what you will, that love, as long as it lasted, was a truth.

THIRTEEN

The girl slipped off the taller sorrel as if by magic and tied the colt to a metal post. From the piles of decomposing dung scattered at its base, Harry knew the post had been put there solely for that purpose. There were no trees of any height or strength within the eye's perception. A few stunted, twisted caricatures of trees lay almost sideway, growing from a stunted root – he could not designate them as any particular species.

Harry followed suit, dismounting slowly from the dun and blessing the horse's shorter stature as he had less distance within which to tumble flat on his face. He hung on to the horn as his numbed feet searched for solid ground. He hung there a moment too long to retain his dignity. When he was able to walk, he found the girl bending over the stock tank, refreshing herself in the thickened liquid. It was not what he thought of as a great source of water but she seemed delighted to be splashing her face and even, to his horror, drinking some of the horrible stuff.

"Shouldn't we water the horses first?" His naïve questions got what it deserved; "Soon as they dry off, don't want them to founder. We rode hard that last mile or two." Harry could feel every inch of the distance in his stinging buttocks and wobbling ankles. He nodded his head; "Of course." Such a poor answer was all he could manage.

He tied the dun to the metal post and staggered over to the tank. It was only when the girl had her face in the water that he dared submerse himself – once through the green slime it felt good, cool but not cold, and surprisingly clear. He could see to the bottom and even count pebbles and see small fishes swimming past his eyes. He drew in and gulped, came up fast and spat out and saw in a high arc a small golden shape fly up, then down, back into the tank with a tiny splash.

She was laughing; he wiped his mouth, conscious that his hair hung in strings over his eyes and that his wet shirt stuck to his flesh. It felt good but was unseemly in front of this child. Who, he noticed, didn't have the same sensibilities. Her wet shirt clung to her young flesh in such graphic detail that Harry had to look at some other place far distant from her womanly shape.

Belinda E. Perry

The horses squealed, or at least one of them made a high-pitched plea and it drew Harry's attention. He was mortified; the sorrel colt had let down his apparatus and now it was rigid, enormous, and the dun horse was pulling back on the reins as the colt was hopping, trying to raise himself over the dun's quarters, moving in that rapid simulation of coitus which brought a terrible sense of disbelief, frustration, and envy into Harry's startled brain.

Remi threw a rock that hit the colt on his organ and the colt came down, bouncing on his front legs. His erection wilted, the dun went back to sleeping, and Remi turned to look at her companion.

"He knows better, and the dun ain't interested but sometimes a colt gets this notion..." She was laughing at him again and in that one moment Harry knew he had a choice, and took a risk. His first such risk in years. "I was impressed by his offering, but like the dun was not much interested." His acknowledgement seemed to ease a reserve in the young woman; "You ain't seen a stud before, it can be alarming." Harry only nodded, exhausted both by the ride and the challenge of carrying on a decent conversation with the intriguing young woman while being bombarded by raw existence.

Certainly life out here was much more vivid than his polite life abandoned in Texas. For all its vaunted stories and brags, he'd met nothing there like Remi and the sorrel colt. Harry startled himself as well as the colt, and the girl, but did not bother the dun at all, when he threw back his head and laughed. Real genuine amusement; he was going to like New Mexico after all.

I TOLD A huge lie in the beginnings of my talking and now I am shamed by what I had said. It is a lie you would never recognize, for it is so close to realness and usual for any woman that its truth or falsehood comes only from my exposing what I had originally given to you.

We did not have children, not the way in which a man and a woman bear their child, hold and love it, and together raise it. I did not conceive and bear fruit as a young woman is meant to do. No, it could not be that simple. Instead I bore Sixto's child months after his death. I wasn't even aware that I was carrying his child for I was too thin and restless, and had only recently begun to notice my monthlies had changed so that their sometimes-loss seemed part of my grieving and not a sign of new life.

I brought into the world a boy child immediately named after his father and given to his grand parents to raise. It was not yet confirmed between Harry and me but I knew instinctively he would not take on another man's child, especially, and this is a hurtful truth I evaded for years but it is the terrible truth – especially the offspring of a Mexican. Harry was a great many things, most of them good and strong, but he had the thoughts and worries of his time and to a Texas boy of money, anyone of Mexican descent was less than human.

My own attitude had gone through this terrible trial, but then I had grown as a child into womanhood among the good men of our ranch and most of them were of Spanish descent. I would not ever outlive the influence of Pego or his entire family, and thus was able to love Sixto despite his disfigurement. Harry had not known my husband, would not have become a friend to me if Sixto had remained among us, but eventually Harry acquired my special fondness for the Mexican vaquero.

Sixto's family gathered around our child, my beloved son, and absorbed him into their own. It was understood without words that they would take the baby with no mention, no trying to see me, no letting me hold him. I could not bear to hold him, not even when the midwife offered him so soon after birth. He was red and squalling and shiny and so beautiful, so much like his papa with that thick dark hair and eyes that went to my heart. I would protect myself, I would not allow the feel of his skin against mine, his heart beat close to my breast, his sweet breath on my lips.

Be careful of those small quiet lies, wishes unfulfilled, dreams lost and twisted into a terrible truth. I lied about our children, I lied, and I pay still for my one terrible act.

HARRY STUCK HIS head back into the water, all he could think of to keep himself from staring at her breasts, the nipples exposed by wet cloth, her belly cupped with soaked fabric parted above the dripping waistband of her jeans. Mud rose and fell on her delicate flesh and Harry would drown himself before he allowed such thoughts and suggestions of what to do overtake him with temptation. She did not seem to recognize her own sexuality, and if Harry hadn't known of her marriage, he would have supposed the child an innocent.

He stuck his head in the water and opened his eyes and saw those small fish again and came up sputtering. She was perched sideways on the edge of the water tank at some distance. "You can swim here, mister, I done told you that already. I'll go sit with the colt, he could use the company."

He couldn't tell if she was laughing at him so he wiped his eyes and shook his head. He would not entertain the possibility of being naked, even immersed in the water. It would be shameful to behave so around a child.

Although he had to remind himself she had only recently been a married woman.

WHEN THEY RODE back into the ranch yard, Harry was overjoyed to climb off the dun and let his weary feet find ground. He made the gesture of leading the horse to its corral home, but she took the reins and smiled at him, nothing mean or patronizing in that smile, simply a kindness he appreciated. "You get yourself to the house, mister, I'll take care of the broncs. Easy for me, I done it for years."

Anne Marie met him halfway to the house; impeccably dressed, nylons and heels and a lovely silk scarf wound around her throat. As if she had just returned from Dallas with the intent to scold her brother for his disarray.

Anne Marie stopped beside him, took his hand and yet seemed to be staring past where Harry stood. "That child, she simply can not walk around our home dressed so badly." Harry wanted to intervene but knew the folly of such a discussion. Anne Marie would challenge the girl, and the two of them would butt heads. He smiled at the thought, seeing it quite literally then erasing the picture. For in it his sister was in denim and burlap, and the child was quite naked.

Harry shook his arm free of his sister and went past her into the house. He would leave the two women to their fanciful arguments, but he wished…no, he would not think about such occurrences.

165

ANNE MARIE WAS bored so taking on the child as a project was quite suitable as an antidote to the terrible endless days out here. Of course it was not Harry's idea, he would never dare suggest any such thing to his sister but he mentioned a few times how comely the girl was with her unfettered attractions and Anne Marie quickly decided to change that focus.

She would have no competition from an unwashed and unbound child, so she smiled and put on her most casual attire, low heeled shoes, more a sandal really, rayon slacks well-tailored to flatter her rather prominent rump, and a cream silk blouse done in the style of Katherine Hepburn at her most charmingly disheveled.

She knew instinctively that to appear at that cabin in a skirt or dress and high heels, well coiffed and sophisticated, would insult the child and stop any transformation before it began. So she dressed cautiously and even buttoned the top button on the blouse.

Managing the terrain from her brother's house to that terrible shack was a feat of strength, endurance, and agility, and to arrive with her hair in place and her ankles unbroken indeed made her feel like she could conquer the world. Anne Marie knocked and stepped back carefully, conscious of assorted debris underfoot that might bring her down.

NO ONE HAD EVER knocked at the door, so half-dressed and head wrapped in a soiled towel Remi staggered sideways to the door, fingers working on the buttons to her jeans. She'd bought side-zipped pants once that were fitted to a woman and the waist came up too high, almost to her armpits she said to Sixto and they both laughed. Men's jeans sat at her waist and didn't get in the way.

She pulled back the door and it was that woman from the main house, Annie Mary or some such. Remi nodded and it didn't occur to her to ask the woman in. "What you want? Ma'am?" That was all she had time for, the towel was slipping and she needed to shuck into a shirt and get to the horses.

"Young woman you put on some clothes. You're indecent." It was that woman from the main house, dolled up and smelling like a patch of wild weeds, complaining about assaulting Remi in her own home. Then she looked down and grinned then outright laughed and that made the doll-woman frown and back up.

Remi hadn't put her shirt on yet; she laughed and her breasts bobbed up and down and that seemed to make the lady even angrier

Remi stepped back, "Please, ma'am. Come in." She hesitated only a moment; "Don't want to give anyone the wrong impression of me." That was enough; if smoke could come out of a human it would surface and plume from this Annie Marie.

It was easy to guide the woman to the one chair while Remi picked up a thrown shirt and shrugged into it, slow in her movements, fingering each button as if the feel were new to her fingers. She didn't look but knew from the woman's breathing that a fresh anger was building.

She turned and looked at her guest, her first guest; her and Sixto, they never had a dinner here, never invited in a friend. They'd never had the time. Remi frowned and buttoned the last button near her throat; there, she thought, now I'm decent. And snorted; clothes didn't make her thoughts pure or filled with high moral standards.

It finally occurred to her the woman was here for a reason. "Yes, ma'am, you wanted something of me?"

The woman seemed to be muttering; Remi heard some of the words. "This is worse than I imagined. This is terrible." Then the voice grew louder. "Child, I've come to offer my guidance and knowledge, so you don't make any more mistakes…like this." She waved a brightly tipped hand in Remi's general direction but still hadn't raised her eyes to actually look at Remi. All this hurry and dressing were for nothing, the woman didn't look to see the results.

The woman lifted her head and strong blue eyes stared at her. The eyes rarely blinked as they look into Remi, first dissecting her face, then traveling down her body to the waistband of her jeans. Something distasteful entered the woman's face, a tightening at the mouth, a hard one-time blink in the heavy eyes.

"You're pregnant."

FOURTEEN

Flesh and bone know better than human thought; I had not been able to understand why my monthlies had stopped, why my breasts ached and it was difficult to button my jeans. I had not been eating well, and tried to believe that poor and erratic diet was the cause of my secret distress.

I did not want a baby. Not now, even though it was Sixto's child, his only child ever to be. Inside me, pushing, kicking, rolling over and fighting life from the very beginning.

I bolted for the bathroom barely in time. My wretchedness sounded loud in my ears and scorched my throat as I vomited up breakfast and last night's meager supper. I didn't know it then but those ugly intimate sounds reached into Anne Marie and loosened her.

The only lie in all this is the one I kept telling myself.

THE POOR CHILD, so untutored and plain, unknowing of her own life. Anne Marie looked around the terrible cabin. Its origins as some sort of shed were obvious in the crude boards nailed across the front, to make a pretend front doorway and wall. Two windows, inserted at angles, barely held out the endless dust. Standing quietly, hearing those dreadful sounds from the bathroom – at least the cabin held a bathroom – she could quite literally watch dust motes slide in past the gaping window frame and blow across the room. Some of them dropped onto the messy bedstead, its linens stained and badly rumpled, others drifted into the room's center, where they naturally were attracted by an old braided rug and a few dishes held under water in the chipped enameled sink.

She had to pull up the sheets and smooth over them a thick woolen blanket of excellent weaving. Her fingers were admiring the textures and her eyes judged the patterns when she felt rather than heard the young woman's approach.

Anne Marie turned around and before the child could stammer out what would be a dreadful utterance of abject shame, she offered her own resolution. "I have kept out of sentiment my own children's baby clothes and furniture. It will take perhaps a month for them to arrive, so please in the meantime do not purchase or ask for anything. Everything will be in those crates, I promise you."

Only after an elongated silence did it occur to Anne that the child being without a mother, as she had been told in quiet tones by the manager's wife, perhaps the child did not understand the process of pregnancy and birth. So being the only woman of experience and common sense, it was doubly important the Anne Marie teach the young woman everything she knew.

She took the child's arm at the elbow and was shocked by the muscle and harsh skin she had grabbed. "Come up to the house with me, we have a great deal to discuss." She tugged, the child pulled back.' "Oh, and please put on a clean shirt." That seemed to deflate the child who looked down and saw the evidence of her weak vomiting and actually seemed to blush.

Anne Marie turned her back, to offer what privacy was possible. By the small noises and puffs of air she believed she could track the child's actions. First another trip to the bathroom, running water to cover the sounds of a toilet being flushed, then more running water broken by being lifted to her face, perhaps small sips that were spit out. The sink being rinsed; she believed that was the odd sound at the end.

A drawer being pulled out – the clean shirt of course. Then another odd sound hard to identify until it became clear; the child was brushing her hair, now breathing hard; hmmm, oh yes of course. Braiding.

When the two faced each other again, the problem became more obvious. The shirt was much too big across the shoulders, a quite handsome plaid well matched on the pocket and front placket yet appearing to be hand-sewn.

"Did you make that shirt, dear?" A shake of the head, yes, the child had brushed and braided her wildly gleaming hair. Quite fetching now, her face almost lovely in its simplicity.

A violent shake of the head; "Sixto's ma...she tried to teach me but my hands're too clumsy...it's Sixto's shirt." Quite unexpectedly tears rolled out of those green eyes and down through an accumulation of dust and cold water, turning briefly into mud before the child swiped at her face with her sleeve. The tracks became a smear rather than a clean wipe. Anne Marie found her fingers clenched. It was evident that with manicuring and manners, this would be a lovely young woman. Truly wasted in such desolation, but with planning and careful cajoling, she was convinced she could prod her brother into hosting weekends for a few special friends. Out of those gatherings, it would be simple enough to find a man willing to overlook the child's raw manner in favor of her physical charms.

It was how a woman captured a man; a smile, a hand on an elbow, a pretty back briefly naked under a smooth silk dress. Anne Marie smiled, and the confused young woman tried to match that smile with her own. Even in such disarray, the child was quite beautiful

She realized she had a new weapon in her sibling war. Harry would melt near this child, and Anne Marie intended to be nearby when the inevitable and ultimate act occurred.

HE WAS'T BOTHERED by his sister, her intrusive presence, her nagging at him. She was saddened, he recognized her loss, and his choice had been to include her in the move to give her renewed focus.

The girl was near the corrals where he'd hoped to find her. She was brushing down the big sorrel colt. Again she was rough in appearance, face smudged, hair knotted up with a leather string but she certainly filled out the men's jeans in a manner not intended by the designer or manufacturer. In fact there were certain elements of how those items of clothing embraced her figure that told Harry more than he'd ever known about female anatomy. He was by no means a virgin in the arena of sex, but and to his surprise he was blushing from his own thoughts, he had not ever seen a woman completely naked. Especially, well, ah, between her legs. He'd been there, with several women, both professional and amateur, but had not taken a long look or done any studying while otherwise preoccupied.

Harry went into a bout of coughing that brought him up against a solid wall. He scratched the palm of his hand on the roughened surface and cursed even as he doubled over in a stronger coughing spasm. Then a slight hand rested on his arm, he could feel its strength even as he shuddered from the unexpected touch.

"Here, mister, drink this." A dented drinking cup attached to a bent handle. Water spilled over his fingers and the slightest air of cooled liquid rose into his nostrils. He gasped, caught his breath and was licking his lips when she placed the cool tin against his mouth.

Nothing had ever tasted so good. He gulped, felt water spill over his chin and drench his shirt and she laughed. He looked up right into her face and she was lovely. Mouth wide in laughter, then a small pink tongue tip showed against the lip's rosy complexion and he was stunned at the pure physicality of emotion flooding him.

He pulled back; "Thank you, miss…" He stuttered, choked again; "Thank you." Her voice was air on damp skin; he shivered. "My name is Remi McClary. Mister." Stung and reprieved in so few words.

"I remember, how could I forget, but thank you for water." That polite almost-apology seemed to placate the child, for she offered him another drink of water and then said she would saddle up the horses.

AFTER THAT SECOND ride together, she seemed to have other work to do when Harry managed to get away from the office filled with figures and the need for long-term planning. And he felt comfortable enough now to saddle and ride the dun, wearing more appropriate clothes he had purchased in the closest town of Clayton. The jeans were stiff, the boots rubbed his heels when he walked but the shirt was understated and quite handsome, and he did indeed appreciate the shade from the wide-brimmed hat.

Always when his father brought the family to their ranch, more like a retreat for the wealthy drinkers than an actual working spread, Harry had incensed his parent by wearing the English riding apparel. Now he understood the true worth of what he'd considered the outlandish garb – protection from the sun, comfort on the ground and in the saddle.

He found her once near the ranch cemetery surrounded by intricate iron fencing and a marvel of a gate that swung easily on hand-forged hinges. He had taken to visiting up here when he was tired, distraught, under stress from all the immediate decisions that rested on the workings of his mind alone.

Talking anything over with Anne Marie was unnecessary; her response was always predictable and social, an opinion and slant on what he was trying to accomplish that had absolutely no value. Sometimes she sounded so much like their parents that he expected to hear the somber weight of their father's footsteps.

The shadow alerted Harry; a month ago he would not have noticed the peculiar mirror of a human body as a black surface, strung out from the single canopy of some bizarre hunkering pine. He hadn't seen a horse up here, and his dun seemed uninterested in the surroundings, which led Harry to believe that the child must have walked the distance. As he approached the cemetery, perched as it was on what passed for a hill in this flat country, he saw the saddled bay, hobbled and nibbling at the thin grass. The bay she had first told him was no horse for a beginner.

She was stronger than he assumed, no frail flower grieving a lost husband but riding rogue horses that the ranch hands would not saddle. She said a few words and jumped his heart; "You and Dunny there do well together...I miss..." She seemed abruptly surprised by whatever she didn't say. Her mouth closed as sadness covered her face and Harry was intrigued. Usually he did not see people, even as they stood in too close and spoke to him, or more correctly at him.

The girl stayed huddled under the tree, her shaped outline changed on the dusty earth and he squatted down to be nearer. Her face was lovely, her skin washed and fresh, her mouth pouted, the darkening red-blond hair swirled freely around her neck and shoulders and he had the unmistakable need to touch her skin.

Immediately he was mortified, as his body in its unsubtle way announced incipient interest. He shifted his hips away from her gaze, almost presenting his back to her but it was the only available camouflage.

It didn't appear that the young woman noticed, her gaze was on the horizon, and he focused his attention there also. Remarkably the surrounding land was quite beautiful, a smooth undulating horizon of dusty gold matched to an intense sky whose gradients of blue went from severe to deep to a blindness of color he could not fathom.

Her voice was low and gentle and the tone soothed him; "I cannot imagine living in a city without all this...air and distance and color." Harry took in a deep breath, too pure, too clean. Then he interrupted; "When you are raised in such a place it must seem unbearably normal, even as spectacular as this is." Here he actually moved to wave an arm and in mid-gesture remembered his catastrophic condition. Again she didn't look at him but continued staring into a distance he couldn't reach.

He was shamefully grateful for her dismissal. When he was certain she had no interest in him, he stood, sighed deeply and turned away. His interest finally subsided, for that he was grateful as he walked to where his faithful dun horse was tied. Much to his embarrassment the reins were trailing and the horse kept his head to close to the ground. The reason was evident; Harry knew at least to approach quietly and not startle the horse but the dun jerked his head up, snapped one rein and stood looking at Harry almost with a lopsided grin to mimic the one broken rein.

There was a long-enough remnant to splice with the twisted end; Harry completed the repair and started to mount the dun, thought better of it and checked the cinch, drew up the latigo. See, he thought to himself, I'm learning things of great value.

He lost all gains in dignity when he settled in the saddle and had to reach forward with his right arm to gently hold the end of the knotted rein. This time she stood, and asked him if she could ride back with him. Of course, he said, he'd be delighted for the company. The expression on her face, quick though it was, told him that she chose this method of making certain he got home in one piece. It wasn't company that she wished for, but his fragile safety.

Later at the ranch, the girl suggested that in the future with such an accident, if he tied both reins together he could hold the middle in one hand and not be so off balance riding home. He said he would remember her suggestion, although he hoped the situation would not arise again. She laughed.

When he turned his back and walked away, he stopped abruptly. My lord, had she understood the unintended double entendre; his face was hot, he felt sweat drip from under his arms and he wanted to run. She had been married of course, briefly he was told, and she had grown up around the male and female of many species. She could not help but know. Then Harry turned around and called to the child; "Remi, it's always a pleasure conversing with you."

AN OLD WOMAN'S LIES

THERE ARE TIMES when I think I actually understand men. I read in a journal, or more probably an off-popular magazine, I seem to read those rather than mainstream. A new study about the sex chromosomes – we all know about x and y. Well I didn't know their names until I was in my thirties but I certainly knew about their effects.

Then I read a short paragraph that made great sense to me. The female has two x chromosomes, this we've known for quite a while. On these two chromosomes are all the needed information, about the female thought processes and memories, and sexuality.

Here's the part that tickles me still, a good belly laugh for all of us, even the few men left my age who can laugh without falling apart. And that's not a whole lot of people, which is why I prefer watching young men, there are so many more of them, and they don't creak or groan when they walk down stairs.

The male has an x and a y chromosome, we're all taught that in school. Now it seems that the x chromosome is packed with information, as is one of the female x chromosomes (I'm tired of saying that word 'chromosome'). Meanwhile, the y part of the male pairing (escaped using that word nicely didn't I) is coated with sexual information and nothing more. And since there is only so much sexual information needed to copulate and carry on, a good deal of the y is completely vacant. All other information is absent.

ANNIE MARIE SHOWED Remi how picking through each strand of hair at night and then brushing the entire mass helped it glow with health. The hair was a darker blonde now, with reddish highlights like Mama had and the slightest wave at the ends. Annie Marie kept harping on having a permanent wave, and the hair cut to more manageable and exotic lengths but Remi just laughed. This was her hair and no fashion or fool would get his hands on it.

There were times, such as that moment when she again said no that Remi truly knew Harry's sister disliked her. It wasn't pleasant, nor was it violent, more a remote loathing, a 'you're all there is so I have to put up with you' kind of feeling that Remi often felt in return. She was, however, beginning to understand the value of what Annie Marie was teaching her. Simple manners and stupid things like the correct use of a napkin and even how to delicately wipe the mouth, tapping gently at the corners and not rubbing away a dollop of tomato sauce or catching the gravy running down her chin. It was a world both fascinating and incredibly idiotic where people fretted about motions and utensils that held within them little meaning except what some bored highbrow thought to assign.

See, she was even talking like these people, and she'd gone to her first party at the ranch house, maybe thirty of Harry and Annie Marie's dear friends who drove up from someplace fancy in Texas in the kinds of cars Remi had never seen. Bright and shiny with chrome and trim and ornaments on the hoods and some even had drivers, who Remi thought were fools for letting these folk tell them what road to take.

Then again she wore a dress Annie Marie picked out, with ruffles at the bosom and a sort of crossed and loose material over her belly with a slight droop so the baby didn't much show. Remi was introduced to several attractive older men, one of whom placed a hand too familiarly on her back, where the dress didn't cover the markings of her tan. She swung around and lifted her hand to swat him but saw Annie Marie's face, eyes far too wide open in complete panic, and thought better of assaulting the guests at her first formal party.

Instead she sort of half-bowed and backed up and hit something soft, which turned out to be Harry in his finest. Remi blushed and Harry took her arm; "My dear you are beautiful, as every man in this room knows. Here, let me get you a drink." Pure instinct told her not to drink, not this stuff, mixed liquors with names she didn't understand and tastes that were too raw or sweet.

"Harry, just juice, or maybe water?" "Certainly. We have fine French water that Anne Marie has discovered and had brought in by the case. She so loves to be first in a fad." Remi had no idea what he was talking about, and realized she didn't know most of the words and even more so the ideas behind the words, the placement of emphasis, a term she had learned from Annie Marie. These folks standing with their glasses talking and laughing and sometimes arguing seemed to miss the whole point of coming into New Mexico for a visit. They was indoors, safe between indifferent walls, unknowing of the New Mexico wildness.

Remi was acutely aware of her misuse of words, mostly in her thoughts and sometimes said directly to one of these old men who eyed her like prime heifer and saw her just as juicy as that steak served up with fancied potatoes and the wine they all loved to talk about until she was bored beyond belief. Not one of these sons knew anything about horses or the land, they only enjoyed a fine tenderloin.

She laughed at her own pun; Annie Marie, oh my how the woman hated to be called that, Annie Marie explained what a pun was and Remi appreciated the fact that she'd been making, or saying, them all her life. Came from her pa who had himself a way with words.

THOSE OLD MEN needed to leave the child alone, the very disparity in their ages was obscene and Harry spoke to Anne Marie who actually laughed in his face. "That's the point, my dear brother, she needs taking care of and who better than one of these gentlemen with means. They can educate and shape her, she is quite lovely when cleaned up, and eventually they might even marry her."

Harry was shocked; his sister had passed the boundaries of decency even for her. He didn't bother to respond or to make known his thoughts but he turned away quickly, and in doing so caught sight of Remi standing between two of the bastards leering over her and one of the sons had his hand on Remi's shoulder, near her neck, and Harry wanted to strangle him.

He realized the girl was pregnant at that moment. Anne Marie's dress designed specifically for this get-together held and cupped the soft roundness of her belly, which had always been flat and hard. Harry recognized the changes; he'd stared at that belly and the junction of those legs too often, responding as any decently structured male would respond. Remi was a wild and beautiful young woman with a figure belonging to the gods. Any change would be noticed; Harry raised his eyes and yes, her bosom, her breasts, were enlarged and now he knew it wasn't from any figure-changing ladies' garment bought for the occasion by a scheming Anne Marie.

His first notion was to approach Remi and take her from the vultures, his second and more immediate notion was to put a noose around his sister's neck and slowly, delightedly, strangle her. Remi was a widow, her pregnancy was not to be exposed and exploited. She would bear her late husband's child as was proper, and more than likely live with his family to raise the infant within the confines of its history and culture.

Two things in this internal lecture disturbed Harry; Remi McClary was not of the same culture as her husband, so the child would indeed be only half – well, native was as good a word as he could find without displaying an ugly prejudice.

And Harry knew he was too attracted to the child to allow her to leave the ranch.

REMI FOUND HERSELF admiring the house. She'd been inside rarely, when the actor owned the place he never allowed the common workers indoors, except to occasionally come into the kitchen and have hot coffee or in her case cocoa, which Remi found silly but accepted the delicious drink anyway.

She remembered one extreme rainstorm when she and Sixto had pulled a cow and her calf caught in an arroyo; it had been close, only Sixto's strength and the buckskin's agility had been able to snake that mama cow loose. The calf was easier to pull, but harder to catch up because he was scared and didn't know humans from hell so he bleated and scrambled and fought until he slammed his skull again Remi's and she remembered even now the taste in her mouth and the shiny lights circling her head.

Inconveniently, the actor had been at the ranch, for one of his 'breaks' from the terrible effort and stress of his Hollywood career and he had at first pulled back when the cook ordered Sixto and a girl into the kitchen. They'd changed out of their mud-soaked clothing but had come up to report to Rantoul and Ravenstock that two mama cows had been lost; they brought up one dogie calf safe to the barn now, rubbed down with hay and they needed some of the milk and that bottle kept for the purpose, poor little thing was hungry.

This was all spoken by Sixto with Remi nodding in the right places, too awed by the actor's face until he opened his movie-star maw and said "what's a doggie calf?' and Remi gave up on him.

She could hear Sixto's uncle speak right then, talking of these damned fools buy up a ranch and don't know to recognize a cow. Or as he put it, the south end of a north-bound cow.

177

All this memory crowded in and she stared openly at the big room. It wasn't cow skulls and Navaho rugs and twisted antler furniture anymore; there was a grace to the furniture, a delicate beauty to some of the smaller tables and the lamps that entranced Remi. The room was lovely, almost too pretty to actually sit down, but she found herself surrounded by two fat men and one wife to match their girth and they were poking fingers at each other which Remi knew always led to a fight. With this group, she figured it would be matching elephants, besides, she was suddenly quite tired and a bit dizzy, her belly rumbled in the peculiar manner which she knew from being told was part of pregnancy.

The sofa, or davenport, she'd heard that word used and didn't know the difference, was comfortable. Kind of square, not like the few others she'd seen in the few real houses she'd visited. And there were none of those lacey circles on the back of the sofa or on the arms; Anne Marie, Annie; oh how that made her mad, had explained that these doilies or 'antimacassars' were for protection of the fine material from the hair oils and filth that men brought into houses. Before they were civilized and learned to wash their hands. And no one of any standing, at least no one allowed in one of her houses would be dirty enough to stain her new furniture so she had not had the upholsterer bother with arm or back guards.

Remi had to ask what upholstery was of course and got a lecture in return, more than she wanted ever to know. You made a chair, padded the seat with old rags and covered them with a nice piece of cloth and if you got fancy you padded the armrests too. Her pa was good at making furniture; her ma was always bragging on what a comfort that rocking chair was, setting in it while she nursed her babies.

Sitting at waist level to all the talkers and the few listeners was strange; bellies and hips and dresses that fluttered, legs encased in shiny silk, men's pants with their zippers and unseemly bulges, not sexual parts as outlined by chaps and softened jeans but bellies and guts and slack muscle, too many of these parties, too much of each bit of food passed around on those shiny trays by women in black uniforms with white aprons.

The women surprised her; they were uniformly younger than the men, slender, barely sipping out of a stemmed glass, laughing and taking tiny nibbles of any food before tactfully leaving the morsel wrapped in a napkin on one of the many small tables. It was a tactic Annie Marie had tried to explain and even now it made Remi want to laugh. Or gag; the thought of any food was unsettling.

She got tired of watching these people; their clothes were too tight and mostly useless, the heels high, strapped on, their nails long and painted, their mouths endlessly working, whether with sipping that liquor or talking, laughing with the head tilted to one side, eyes never leaving the man's face as he told another tiresome joke.

The table beside her end of the sofa had a small statue on it. Remi looked and then stared; it was a woman, tall and slender and she wore nothing on her top, just two small breasts with the nipples evident, even the belly button showed while folds of metal fabric clothed her hips and down past her knees. It was nothing Remi had seen before; she'd never really seen all of her own body, only flashes in the new bathroom mirror while washing or getting ready for a bath. She knew that Sixto liked her body, he would tell her with his hands and his mouth, on her skin and then words whispered into her ears, describing places on her she had never seen.

Breasts were easy, she could look down and there they were, sloping and rounded, a weight to them now, changing as she got ready to feed a child. The smile she felt also was a surprise; she would hold a child to her teat, like the cow at her father's place had nursed its youngster. But this babe would take time, she remembered her older sisters complaining about how young and spoiled and slow Remi was when she was four and still dependant upon her ma and pa.

This baby inside her would take hold of her teat and suckle and make those sounds a kitten or a foal made, of liquid food and satisfaction. To see a foal's tail flipping in pure pleasure as it drank was a delight to Remi. Now it was her foal, her kitten; her child.

She briefly touched the statue on the table and realized it was light. Electric light. She'd never been in a house where the light wasn't kerosene, it explained the different smell from where she sat, without that tang and edge of oil.

So many of the men were fat, the women thin, elegant Annie Marie called them, sophisticated, meaning they had been a lot of places and knew a lot of things. Remi wondered how much use most of their information was; could they tell a mule deer from a white-tail or know from a distance that a cow had pink-eye? That was useful; the name of whoever made your dress didn't seem to have much need to it.

Then a fat man sat down next to Remi, heavy enough she felt the sofa shift, tilt a moment and then settle. He was perspiring, and held a glass of something clear amber and iced, which soaked down into his shirt cuff. He used the damp sleeve to wipe his face and suddenly Remi's stomach made a threat and she covered her mouth, swallowed hard. The fat man smelled, like one of the pigs they brought into slaughter, of lard and shit and some sweet perfume her ma would have said belonged to the wrong kind of woman.

She leaned forward to get up, and found that her little mounded belly held her back, changing her center of balance so she would have to grab something in each hand to get up and the only thing left was the stockyard animal whose sweat continued to pour off him and made her tremble with the need to vomit.

A hand touched her; she looked and it was Harry. "Come on, child, I need some air." He simply lifted her off the sofa; "Talk with you later, Herbert." And Remi guessed he was making their apologies to the fat man, who drained the contents of his glass and barely nodded.

IN HARRY'S ESTIMATION, Herbert McMillan was a dreadful man to consider sitting next to such a young thing, drink in hand, red face turned toward her to begin some nonsensical and ugly conversation where he could prove over and over his rare intelligence and ruthless wit. Harry put his hand gently on Remi's swelling waist only to guide her through the crowd of course. The soft flesh under Anne Marie's garish choice of color and texture for the child's first store-made dress was too much, there was a baby inside, needing to be bathed in soft tones of the palest green or blue, not bright copper silk, with cream near her lovely face.

But it was the child of another man.

FIFTEEN

Anne Marie took the girl into Clayton, which seemed to be the best alternative other than the impossible drive to Santa Fe, itself doubtful, or further south to Albuquerque. She did not consider Las Vegas; its reputation was disagreeable. Clayton was more ranchers and sensible wives and hopefully there was an obstetrician there who was up to date on the modern techniques of childbirth and could convince the girl that she simply must give up riding her beloved horses.

It was showing now, and the girl's late husband's grandmother, that was a mouthful, had sewn a soft panel into the front of a divided riding skirt and that was what the child wore to ride. It was a scandal that Anne Marie harped on every day, and Harry in his mild bemused manner said he had already learned there was no possible way in which he could tell Miss Remi anything at all. If he fired her, then where would she go, pregnant as she was, and all the men the ranch depended on to do the manual labor, well obviously they would quit en masse.

So it landed on Anne Mare after that disastrous weekend she had gathered and planned, it was for her to take the disruptive young woman to the doctor in Clayton. For all of Anne Marie's chiding and instruction, Remi still looked like a ranch hand, barely female except for the obvious bulge of pregnancy. It was definitely unseemly but there was little to be done except take the long drive and hope that nothing happened to draw any more attention to the pregnancy.

Of course when she parked the car in front of the girl's shack and got out, there was Remi talking madly to a half-drunk-looking old man in baggy pants and high boots, a ragged hat, but the girl was laughing and the old man was patting her belly and the outrage was unbelievable. Remi turned to Anne Marie and the delight in her face, the beauty brought by an unimaginable pleasure in speaking to such a person made the child glow. There was what men saw, even Herbert McMillan in his drink and obesity, he spoke of the special qualities and beauty of the girl and then had the meanness, the rudeness to ask about a possible father. He saw no ring, he said, was she actually unwed?

The crudeness was intolerable but Harry stepped in and gently reminded Herbert that he was a guest in their house, as was the child, and since she was a working cowhand she did not wear her widow's ring. That seemed to shut the man down, he went back to sipping at the good southern whiskey and found another mortal to bedevil. Harry on the other hand could not be quieted and Anne Marie had that feeling, right then, in the office of the ranch house, that her training and plans were working, that her brother might well finally take himself a wife, a female over whom Anne Marie held quite a bit of power.

Dr. Buffam was tall and white-haired, with that thin face and beaky nose which in the pictures would have placed him as a character actor; Anne Marie knew enough of the Hollywood people, she'd had her try at acting but didn't photograph well she was told. Buffam stooped over to talk with his patients, which gave him the air of a benign stork. Anne Marie suspected that her charge had been told this fairy tale and she was curious as to how patient and doctor would get along.

She had to fight to get into the examining room with Remi and the doctor. The front-desk nurse of course was suspicious until Anne Marie simply grabbed Remi's arm and walked with her through the door.

The child was trembling; Anne Marie told her to sit on the examining table and still the child stood, staring, those lovely eyes wide as if an infant had taken over her woman's form. Before Anne Marie had any opportunity to explain, the doctor had taken Remi's hand, held it in his hands and finally the child looked at him.

"We need you to sit up here, miss, but first you must take off your clothes and put on this gown. I know, it seems foolish but I need to be able to look at your body, and clothes make the necessary examination more difficult." The young woman grinned at the doctor, looked at the serious metal and black table covered in some sort of white cloth and unbuttoned her loose shirt as she used one foot to push the other foot out of its boot.

Anne Marie cried out: "Wait until he leaves the room, then you can go behind that screen and undress properly." Remi laughed; "Hell, Annie Marie I know you want to tame me but he wants to see me naked, nothing wrong with a man seeing me naked, long as he's a doc or a legal husband." She had slipped out of the oversized shirt and stood there without wearing any brassiere and clad only in the soft-paneled divided skirt, her bare legs ending in thick white socks. The cowboy boots lay at angles to each other, dispensed skillfully without the child ever bending down.

Remi unbuttoned the skirt and it slid gracefully, creating a soft fawn-colored leather circle around her legs. She did at least wear panties. For that Anne Marie breathed and offered up a decency prayer.

"Well young woman, let's get on with the exam. Miss Anne Marie, you may wait outside, obviously this child does not need her hand held, despite the fact that I suspect this is her first physical examination, at least professionally." He said all this with a grin and Anne Marie wanted to punch that beaky nose or kick him – well her thoughts were not polite as he held open the door and she was dismissed.

REMI KNEW HERSELF well enough to recognize the inner trembling as fear and she did what she always did and planted her feet square, took a big breath and clenched her fists. No fool man was going to scare her. "Would you lie down on the table please; oh, first put on the gown and then remove your panties."

She'd already had the panties halfway down her thighs and there was no good sense to pulling them back up so she toed them into the mound of riding skirt and stood bare-assed naked in front of a man she didn't know and was surprised it didn't bother her. Sixto had seen to that, when he finally got to trusting her those few days with his hands all over her. This one, he was too old and not interested in such goings on, only the result of them as Annie Marie had explained.

Remi had ridden over to Sixto's cousin's family compound and asked Adolfo's grandmother what would happen, what would an Anglo doctor do to her. The woman smiled and shook her head; "He will prod inside you where the baby is waiting, and he will listen through your belly with a cold metal cup and tell you that your child's heart beats perfectly and that the child will be loved."

Some of what the grandmother said was tradition and sadness and some was pure fact. The doc put her up on that table finally, her setting there with her backside exposed while he listened to her heart and had her open her mouth and he even looked inside her ears.

"When was your last doctor's visit? And what is the father's name?" He was good at questions, at least the answers were easy. "Sixto

Vargas's the father. He died maybe seven months ago, got hit by a bronc and never came back to us." Then she hesitated, knowing the importance of the next answer that should have been the first. She had the vaguest memory of seeing a doctor once with her mother, in order to start school. But she wasn't certain of it happening or in what year. So she simplified the truth by leaving out what could be only a thought read from a book.

"I've never been in a doctor's office, ain't had one come visit me to home neither." She might be overdoing the simpleton speech but it seemed peculiarly appropriate to the situation; here she was, a full grown widow carrying a dead man's child and, well....

The doc glanced up at her, lordy but his eyebrows were white and curly; "You can't fool me with the talking, miss. Or how do you wish to be called? Your husband's name?" No one called her Mrs. Vargas; she was herself.

'Remi. Just Remi. McClary was my daddy's name and I never did get used to Vargas. Sixto...." She cried, no reason, no time before, too much to do but now setting bare butt and sticking to a leathery top on this high table, with an old man peering at her she cried and they were all the tears held in too long. Finally the old man simply moved closer to her and put his arms around her, very careful not to touch any of the best parts of a woman but her shoulder, pulling her forward until she could put her face right at his neck and she cried until she was gasping and hiccupping and he pushed her away gently.

"We'll stick to Remi for the time being" Have you had any problems, nausea or heart burn, do you exercise regularly? I'm certain that if Anne Marie has much to do with it, you are eating correctly. She can be a stickler..." And on went the voice, deep and smooth, with always the right turn to the words, no humiliation, no reminding her of her lack in education. "We need to update your childhood shots, not at the moment but right after the birth." Then he finally asked a question that distressed her; "You will use formula of course, let me write out what is needed so that you might pick up the supplies before the actual event."

She opened her mouth in protest and confusion when he suggested she lie back for the remainder of the examination. It might be uncomfortable but would only be momentary and he needed to know how well the baby was doing. She believed him, her mind still working around the thought of baby formula and bottles and the right supplies.

"What in hell're you doing to me?" She actually spoke the words as loud as she could and tried to draw her legs together but some metal contraption was holding her apart and his hand was in there wiggling around but he put his other hand on top of her rounded belly and pressed down and she gasped and then it was all done and she wanted to apologize but then thought goddamnit he was the one needed to apologize.

"Like hell that was a bit uncomfortable, then again you docs might know the mechanics but you ain't never felt the doing."

THIS IS ONE men never can understand, no matter the jokes about proctologists and any possibility of male empathy. My child was born and the male obstetrician told me not to make such a fuss and I wanted to reach up and slap him silly for his demeaning me and what I was going through. How dare any man tell a woman childbirth doesn't hurt that much. All the possible retorts have been said, as jokes on stage or now in television comedies and they're all true. It is nothing any man can appreciate, the absolute and devastating pain of having your body widened so a child, a human being can pass through an area small enough to accommodate a man's sexual pleasure.

In turn we have no right to laugh when a man can't achieve an erection, or has prostrate problems. I wouldn't want to have my sex life right there in front of me, standing up and eager, or wilted and tired and some woman laughing and pointing 'cause nothing's happening. We pick on them for their skirt-chasing, but in order for them to be ready to perform when it's necessary, they have to be self-primed most of the time. For some of them their bodies don't recognize the civilized signals to stop and are always half-way here, sort of semi-soft and anxious to rise. Bread dough, need a warm place to self-rise – oh lordy that is a terrible image but it's the truth, or a truth anyway.

Said it before, will say it again through this memoir I'm writing – I wouldn't ever want to be a man. And what a foolish obvious pronouncement to make, like what I am saying has any value or newness to my thought – women have been cursing men and their terrible penetration for centuries, probably as soon as the first baby was born and the connection between the hard penis and the later birth was made. So I say nothing new, but I resist any male trying to tell any female that giving birth 'don't hurt that much.'

THE DOCTOR PRODDED and poked and finally let her sit up, then he took a big needle and tied a bit of rubber around her forearm and took a whole lot of Remi's blood, almost enough to make her want to faint, but the nurse brought in orange juice and a crumbling cracker, both of which Remi finished off quick as she could. Then he pried in her mouth again, and pulled down the lid to each eye and she was beginning to have sympathy with a cow when she got an exam as to if or why. Although with Remi, they already knew, how and when. Just a matter of keeping that baby healthy and safe.

"Child, what do you do for activity during the day?" An odd question, she thought. And made the mistake of telling him the truth. "I saddle up 'bout eight now, too tired to get up early with the boys. Been mostly ridin' fence, 'bout all I'm good for now, can mark where the break is but don't do much fixin'. I borrowed a flat saddle from Harry – ah, Mr. Sembach so gettin' on a bronc, I pick only the real quiet ones so me and the baby're fine, gettin' on's easier with the flat saddle, that belly a mine kept hittin' the horn and damn that hurt, I was some surprised you didn't say nothin' about the bruisin' there or is it natural for a woman's skin to bruise up as the baby grows out?" She wanted to keep talking cowboy because of the look on the doc's face, the look she expected but didn't want. Her mind and talk turned more western when she worried.

"Mrs. Vargas!" Now that was a shock and she almost looked around but that was taking the use of her married name as a game and it wasn't no game, not with a baby involved. So Remi set her face in a questioning, pleasant sort of grin, maybe closer to a lady's smile that Annie Marie taught her, and looked her best right into those old eyes, rimmed some with red and at the moment angry at her.

"Mrs. Vargas, you do not ride a horse in this condition, not ever, it is unhealthy for both you and the child." She cocked her head; "And how do I make a living while I grow this child, take up sewing or cooking or setting reading to some old man. Only skill I got's on a horse and I've ridden since I come to the ranch. It's why they pay me, not to carry the child of a dead cowhand. No money coming in for me being a broodmare."

She shivered, chilled in the foolish thin coat they gave her, butt hanging out the back, no sleeves, no warmth; scared by her own words.

Buffam leaned forward and his hand on her arm was chilled too; he'd seen the same things she'd just spoke. Out of knowing too much, being beaten by events most of her life. Buffam shook his head; "I do know Anne Marie, and Harry Sembach is one of the kindest men I've ever met. They would never throw you out, child. Anne Marie brought you here out of kindness, she will do what I tell her. You are not to ride any more, you are to rest, eat well, sit in the sunshine and let that child do some of the quiet growing and developing that a baby needs. You too, child, you need to sit for a while. Looks to me, by the tests I've done and what I see, you need to rest. Being a mother is full-time you know."

The child, belly pushing at the limits of the foolish gown, took in a deep breath and let it out in gasping spurts so that the doctor grew concerned and then she seemed to settle: "I got me a sister in Illinois, I can find her, haven't even told her about our pa's dying. She needs to know, and she's got kids, a good husband. I can stay there through the beginning till I know what to do."

Dr. Buffam heard the fact slipped in past all the talk and positive images, about 'finding' the sister. He put his hand firmly on the child's arm. "You will do no such thing; you will go home to the ranch with Anne Marie and let her take care of you. Her own loss, well she needs something else to fret about instead of brooding on her own misfortunes so you let her take care of you. It's doing her a favor. There is no chance you can travel at this point in your pregnancy. It simply isn't safe for the baby."

There was a lot the doc told her he maybe didn't mean to; that he worried about the baby's health, that something was wrong with Annie Marie and all this fussing actually was good for her. And the most frightening, worrisome, was his concern about Remi's own health. She felt strong despite pains in her side at times, and a funny ache way down there, and hurts in her head and belly that went away if she got a good night's sleep.

She needed someone and this whey-faced old man and his scientific jargon and his orders wasn't the answer, neither was Annie Marie with her matching handbags and silly shoes and her fussings about the right color draperies, 'not drapes, my dear, that's much too common a word. It is draperies'.

No woman worried about calling curtains by a fancy name was going to take in a stray and have her whelp near the wood stove or in the back closet; that much Remi knew.

THESE WORDS ARE spoken only from solitude and from knowing that I will not be called accountable on this earth for my doings. There is no lie greater than the one I lived with for so many years: that I had no children. And I tried first thing to deceive you by saying that I had children and they were late in taking care of me as I advanced in years.

I had a child yet I did not raise him; I gave birth in a clean hospital due to the charity of Harry and his sister yet the crying babe was never in my arms.

There are no lies here, only a bitter truth of constant wounding. My defense, and it is a poor substitute for compassion, is that I was young, untutored in so much of the world, with no dependable skills other than riding the broncs and mending fence, and a mother could not take along a baby strapped to her back doing such work. I did what needed to be done. As for other children, you will have to wait to learn those lies.

ANNIE MARIE WAS setting in the waiting room, immovable and upright, righteous too, Remi could see it in her powdered face. The woman was intent on doing the right thing nevermind what Remi might choose. Dr. Buffam held Remi's arm lightly, as if she were fragile and not offering hard muscle and browned flesh to his pasty old man's grip. "Anne Marie, this young woman is to ride no more horses or do any chores, she is to rest and eat well and only in this manner will she bear a healthy child."

He knew, he'd known from treating Anne Marie the few times she came to his office; he'd read her files sent on by the local doctor. A tragedy really, a sadness some women never get past. She had two healthy children and lost the third, and this loss seemed to have removed her from the rest of her family, to the point where her husband had taken the two healthy children from her and refused her any rights of visitation.

It did not take a medical mind, even one skeptical of Dr. Freud and his somewhat bizarre theories, to understand that Anne Marie's grief had found its outlet in the care and dependency of this half-wild and far too-young widow and her burgeoning pregnancy. Buffam was counting on Anne Marie's private grief to do what was best for Remi McClary.

Then he sighed to himself and made the correction. Remi Vargas.

ANNIE MARIE TALKED all the way back in the car, three hours of her jabbering and Remi's stomach was rumbling and telling the truth which was those damned hills and gravel road were upsetting something inside there – the baby. A baby.

She'd never thought of abortion, only heard the word mentioned at that fancy do Annie Marie and Harry hosted. Remi had to look it up in a dictionary, a thick ole book Harry told her about and encouraged her to use. Been kind of fun standing next to him asking about a word and then flipping through the pages, thin and hard to turn over some times but all the words in the world stared back at her.

Problem is, she told him, 'I got to know how to spell before I go looking much.' Harry'd laughed and said he could remedy that and she cocked her head, he said 'look it up in the dictionary; and so she did. Fumbling at first, figuring on the letters but she found them and then what the word meant and it was sweet to her, a kindness extended by this city boy who was pretending to be a rancher but sure knew how to read and write. And to offer kindness to a hard-luck child like herself.

Felt right now that the baby might show itself anyway despite the timing and the months ahead when it would become who and what it was meant to be. "Stop the goddamn car. Now!" Remi bellowed and knew the swearing would get Annie's attention; the car skidded across the gravel and stopped, Remi got out and knelt down and spewed out juice and crackers and that bit of a sandwich she'd tried for lunch.

The rest of the drive home, to the ranch, was slow and quiet with both women thinking on unknowns and fears, past sadness and a future impossible to imagine.

HARRY SETTLED THE issue; "There is a nice bedroom with its own bath in the right wing. It's meant for guests but we will be having no more parties in the foreseeable future." Here he seemed to glare at his sister who absolutely did not look at her brother but studied the pattern of material on the arm of the over-stuffed chair she chose as her throne.

"There is no question or discussion, Miss Remi." He always hesitated at her name as if uncertain, which was not like Harry at all. There were times when she knew 'Mrs. Vargas' was almost ready to escape, then he would cough and return to Miss Remi. Which she too preferred; the memories of Sixto were private.

"Please use the kitchen whenever you choose, and join us for meals. The doctor gave express orders that you are to eat properly, and the meals from the cook shack while nourishing for a cowhand are not the preferred fare for an unborn and its mother." My goodness he was getting stuffy and Remi had to quiet a laugh.

It was agreed upon and Harry designated one of the hands to accompany Remi to the shack where with her father and then with her husband, her life had spun out on the ranch for most of her growing up. She barely remembered the home where they had buried her mother and her younger brother, where her sisters had tormented her before escaping with no looking back. The hand, one of Sixto's few cousins who had stayed to work, was silent for a while, then he turned and put a hand on Remi's shoulder, to turn her towards him.

"He will not be forgotten with the niño you carry, and I have told his papa and mama about their grandchild. They will be glad to know the new ones at the main house are taking good care of their boy's life. The life he never got belongs to his child."

Belinda E. Perry

SIXTEEN

I learned to read past the first grade. Now with all those books hovering around the enormous house and my inability to be doing what I loved, I had to find something to keep me going. Anne Marie, (I finally gave up the childishness of mis-calling her name) made selections for me, and at times when Harry would find me curled up, much as I could with that belly getting in the way more and more, and he would sit next to me, asking to see the book and helping with the difficult words. In the beginning I missed a great deal of what I was reading, in the intent of trying to pronounce and get a grasp on what each word and nuance meant. Yes I know what nuance means now, sure didn't when I was barely nineteen.

They tell a truth when they say that proximity (another word I learned, from Anne Marie who made a big fuss one day about Harry and me), that proximity can be the start of an unlikely relationship.

Although if you remember I said I was taken with Harry despite his short legs and air of arrogance, long before those few months living in his house, you know, far as we've gotten in this foolish rambling of an old woman, the lies seemed to have gone away. After a while it's easier to tell the truth, takes less energy from the brain trying to remember what's false, what's real, keeping those lies in order and then building on them.

What is undeniably true is that I was curious about Harry, not really 'taken' with him, just fascinated as if he were a different species than any I'd known before and in reality he was; successful, from money, extremely well educated, knowing his mind, willing to take on hard responsibility and make tough decisions.

Despite his outlandish clothes, which he had quickly tempered and modified to fit in with his surroundings, the hands had a sharp respect for Harry Sembach and I guess eventually and inevitably some of that respect rubbed off on me. He became an endearing friend, concerned about my well-being while asking for nothing more than my occasional

191

company. There sure wasn't much I could give him at the time; holding his hand maybe, listening to his concerns and stories, and offering some few words of thought or discussion on ranching matters where I had more knowledge.

IT AMAZED HARRY what the child had learned from sheer experience with little or no guidance to help her understand why some things worked the way they did. Nothing about machinery, although she could actually use a forge and hammer out a few of the smaller items her pa had taught her. An odd skill in a young woman. She made him a small clothes hook with the ranch brand on the top, it actually was smooth enough he nailed it in the back hallway and proudly hung his 'barn' coat there. A badge of honor, for the ranch owner to actually get dirty enough that his canvas, flannel-lined coat could not be hung up in a proper closet. One of the hands had to explain the subtlety to him.

He began to look forward to finding her in the south window of the less formal living room, where there were soft Navaho rugs on the hardwood floor and plump easy chairs where she would curl and sort of rest her bulging belly against a propped cushion and read and read until he would smile, standing in the doorway, and cough gently to have her look up at him.

It was a while until he realized that her face, such a pretty, charming face with those wonderful eyes and the strength in her clean, clear face, actually looked pleased or even delighted when he crossed the room and sat close to her. And after a few days, she chose the aptly-named loveseat, which actually Harry found embarrassing as he sat down so close to her and they immediately talked books.

It finally occurred to him that such subterfuge as choosing the love seat would not be in Miss Remi's repertoire of ways to catch a man, or a husband. From the stories he heard, she'd lit into her first husband over the treatment of that sorrel colt she was so fond of, and made him walk home.

His musings stopped abruptly, he got up and walked to the window and she barely noticed that he'd left her. Husband. She'd been widowed young, and was turning into a beautiful woman. And she had begun to show some affection and even interest in Harry. He knew she loved the ranch, the being outdoors, horses and the hard work. It might be difficult for her to understand that she had become the *patroña* and not one of the hands, but already she had begun to listen to Anne Marie. It hadn't been lost on Harry that it was Anne now.

The unborn child bothered him. Not that she wasn't a virgin, but that its father had been a ranch hand on this particular ranch. How the social ramifications of a situation like this would work was beyond him, but Harry knew well enough not to ask any advice of his sister.

And of course it was Anne Marie who asked the one question that brought the entire matter to its awful conclusion. Harry found he was enjoying life now, planning daily life at the ranch, working alongside the men at times, learning the basics of their skills and coming to admire their good sense if unlettered in most worldly aspects. It was the different life he had craved, these rough, hard-handed men who could pull a calf from its mother and then so gently held the gasping wet head and cleaned the mucus and manure from its nostrils and eyes in an instinctive gesture of humanity Harry treasured but could not speak of, not ever to his sister. But he suspected that if he opened the subject, Remi would already know his feelings.

She had done these things, and more. He listened to the stories of the niña who rode like a man and had a feel for the horse second only to Pego, the old man who gave her that first pony she named after him. It took her repeated tries to get Pego the horse saddled, but if she wanted to ride, she had to groom and saddle her own. Many times the men who passed by wanted to stop and help but they too had learned this way and knew to walk on, even when the small face was covered with tears and the light-weight child's saddle lay tumbled at her feet.

They kept watch to prevent mistakes which might put her or the horse at risk. She was so careful; each time she dropped the saddle and tugged the folded blanket off Pego's back, she spent time inspecting the densely woven wool to pull out any burrs or stickers. It was noted by these tough men that the child had the touch, the worry, which made her a true horseman even as a little girl.

As Harry dug his first fence post and helped split and peel the logs brought at great distance, his hands toughened as his mind softened and in his fantasies Remi McClary worked alongside him in these chores, listening to his dreams and laughing at his small jokes. He rarely spoke his thought as few in the family found his humor amusing. These men laughed some times, he didn't know if it was at the joke or at him, but there seemed to be no meanness to the laughter so he smiled and nodded, and eventually got up enough courage to try again.

Remi always laughed, her brilliant green eyes held such laughter and he marveled that a child so young who'd gone through such a rugged life could laugh with abandon and pure pleasure. This almost more than anything impressed Harry; Remi McClary, ah, Remi Vargas, was indeed a most unusually accomplished female. Like no one he'd ever known.

In the afternoons she was in the loveseat, curled around herself in impossible angles and directions, hand always on her growing belly, eyes looking up from whatever book Anne Marie had her reading. Her smile was genuine, and by a subtle shifting of her body she offered room for Harry on the doubled sofa. The comfort of her, a lovely enticing scent of female, not perfume, that much Anne Marie had not been able to teach Remi, but Remi herself, and the growing child, a doubled sweetness of human flesh that even now, in her condition, seduced Harry and sometimes gave him such an erection it was a good twenty minutes before he could decently uncross his legs and truly look at the mother-to-be.

Anne Marie cornered him one late afternoon when he'd just come in from more fence work; his hands were raw, his feet hurt, his arms ached and he'd missed his chance to sit with Remi, but he was not fit for any human contact at the moment. Even Harry could smell his own stench and it turned his stomach. And he was doubly surprised when Anne Marie actually placed her hand on his arm, where it wasn't too filthy. "Harry, we must talk. Now."

CAN I TALK about this, will you listen without judgment but only hear my words and thoughts, feel my anguish and have some understanding? I don't know, at this age, what I would do if a child in my life came to me with the same terrible decision.

I knew, even as young and inexperienced as I was, how could I or any female miss the signs. Harry was taken with me; he hovered around me, too joyful when I moved my ponderous flesh and allowed him room on that doubled seat. And yes I chose to sit there for the one reason, that

194

he would have to ask, and then even touch my body in a few places along my thigh, moved out of position as the baby grew.

It tantalized us both, the almost secretive feel of another human's body. Through clothing of course; Anne Marie had me in long soft fluid dresses and they covered all of me, which was a most unusual sensation. I was used to bare arms and my hair braided down my back, a hat jammed on, my eyes shaded, no one able to see into them. Pants, dungarees they were often called, what women did not wear except on ranches or farms practicality had to take precedence.

Each breath put me against Harry's leg and then away from it, and I knew enough, having seen Sixto in full arousal long before we fucked, that this breathing touch so stimulated Harry that I have no idea how he could walk in that condition. Sixto showed me the workings of a man, naked, coming out of our bathroom washed and cleaned and fully erect, and to bind all that inside drawers and pants must have been torture. Believe me I would never wish to be a man.

He wanted me, and I already knew I would bed him. But not without marriage; in this life he and his sister inhabited, a man of his social standing did not have sex with a woman of my class or married state. Especially as I was carrying another man's child, and that child was indeed what their crowd would call a half-breed, of uncertain future but most definitely not life with the likes of Harry Sembach.

It was not money, nor was it fear; it was a growing sense of trust and confidence, that this one particular man wanted me, knew me, and would willingly take me into his life. As for Sixto's child, I was less certain. Not from Harry, but for the child itself. There would be no heritage of his ancestors, no teachings from an abuela, no cousins or extended family.

And here yes I am lying, only to myself, rationalizing what I needed to do. I knew, even as the baby I was, with no mama to guide me I knew what had to be done. A month before the child's due date, I asked Harry to drive me to the compound near Roswell where Sixto's family had settled.

"HARRY, SIT ON a wooden chair, you're too filthy to sit in that armchair, it's only recently that I found the particular fabric I wanted and had it recovered. Don't be foolish, stand if you must but do not get a chair dirty. I won't have it."

He knew the signs; her vocal anger was her way of leading up to unpleasant discussions or directions and she needed to stir him up, get him angry and rattled and then she would attack. It no longer worked, these ancient tactics that had terrified him since childhood. Her own dissolving, her breakdown if you would call it, let him know that for all the bravado, his sister was just a scared child trying to pretend adulthood.

"You can't raise that child in this house. You have to find a place where Remi can live and find some sort of work that allows her to keep the child. It simply isn't possible to have another man's child, a Mexican child in our house."

There it was, what he knew and avoided each time he sat next to Remi – she was so young, so briefly married, that the irony of one sexual week producing a child begat problems that haunted Harry each night. Lying in his bed, fresh linens, ironed pajamas, cool air coming in the window, he went over and over how he felt about her and what he hated about her child. He could not be good enough for Remi if his thoughts were so uncharitable. No man could so despise an unborn as Harry did this growing, bloating, now kicking, alive, viable thing that could ruin what might be possible.

His hatred of himself was hurtful; he often woke with his fists clenched hard enough to draw blood from his palms, he would wake himself calling out, and twice found his pillow wet with tears. What he did not do, what did not happen, were any night emissions. His dreams were vivid, almost pornographic but his body's internal sense did not respond. It was Remi he wanted, not these nighttime beauties who'd always held his body captive.

His sister had done it again; straight to the throat but this time Harry was already bloodied from self-inflicted wounds. He sat down anyway, and Anne Marie said nothing, which told what he already knew.

She too had grown fond of the girl, in her own way was becoming a mother in spite of herself.

Brother and sister stared at each other, neither seeing any answer from the other, each hoping past any reality that there was a solution. Later, when Remi approached him with her request, Harry's thoughts were already prepared.

"I WANT TO visit with Sixto's family. One of the boys, he told me they've moved to the outskirts of Roswell at the Thunderhead Ranch and I want to go there. Tomorrow, and if you won't take me because it isn't 'proper' for a woman in my condition to be traveling with an unrelated male, well, I know how to drive a tractor so to hell with it a car ain't much different."

Harry could only stare at her. His response was immediate and foolish; "But you don't have a license." She was composed and serene, ignoring his foolish attempt. Her face was pale but certainly not flushed with anger or fear; it was only her reverting to her old mode of speech that told him how upset she truly was. And he believed he understood what was going on in her mind. Remi was direct and highly intuitive and the distress in Harry, the residual fury in his sister, all would come to Remi as signals and truths.

"Of course I will drive you to Roswell."

ANNE MARIE INSISTED she accompany them as it was more proper for Remi to have a chaperone but the child set her mouth and shook her head and told Anne Marie what was to be done was none of her business, between her, Remi, and Sixto's family and Harry was coming only 'cause it was his car. There was no room for no one else, not even a picnic basket Anne Marie held out as a bribe. No ma'am.

Remi wanted to leave early but Harry made her accept one condition; that they would drive at a leisurely pace and spend one night in a motel, nevermind how it 'might look' to the more proper folk, who didn't need to know about the trip in any case. There would be no argument here, he was firm and kind together and she seemed to find what she needed in his eyes and smiled at him and Harry's knees actually went weak.

Her one trip, so many years ago, had been in a cart pulled by her father's horse, and the mule and the cow had been tied together. She had slept in the wagon bed and her father slept underneath, between the wheels, and the night noises at first terrified and then comforted her. They were the sounds from home, the mule kicking up a fuss, the calf a nuisance, coyotes coming in close but respecting the mule and only howling their disgust. Her father snored, even sleeping under the wagon he snored and she giggled through her hands, reassured by the familiar sound.

A motor hotel was another thing entirely. She said nothing to Harry, who of course asked for separate rooms, but the bathroom gurgled and the room smelled of smoke and the bed sagged even more than usual under her ponderous weight. She did walk next door to Harry's room, identical to hers from what she could see, and asked if he'd get her more pillows.

He brought her four, more than enough. They went across the street and chewed listlessly on ground meat patties, which she promptly threw up back at her room. The long night was no better than the food.

Harry asked at headquarters where the Vargas family had settled and was given terse direction; 'Down past the barn to that 'dobe. Can't miss it." She saw the outline of Sixto's mother hanging clothes on a stretched line and without knowing it, Remi cried. Silent tears, which Harry reached for with a freshly ironed handkerchief and wiped away. Still Remi didn't take her eyes from the figure of the woman.

There were children chasing each other, laughter, four smaller houses and a single-towered building that probably served as church and school. The boss to the wood-sided house was Anglo; down here all the faces were Mexican. Remi stopped crying and Harry wadded up the damp handkerchief in her hand, she took it and wiped her face clean, then blew her nose and stuffed the sodden cloth in her dress pocket. It was one of those horrible 'maternity' things that were considered acceptable for a female in her condition to wear in public. A mid-length skirt with a stretchy panel across her belly, and the most godawful ugly blue and white polka dot top with a huge bow, a bow of all things, meant to be tied under her chin. She'd tangled the strands around her neck and then stuffed them between her swollen breasts. Goddamnit

Belinda E. Perry

Remi Vargas wasn't wearing no bow 'round her neck like a Christmas present.

She smiled to herself, recognizing her nervousness in the way her thoughts ran. Mrs. Vargas stopped, turned, saw the occupants of the car and ran to Remi, hands out, thickly braided hair flying. She remembered those hands teaching her how to braid her own hair without looking, to feel the strands and divide them evenly, to find the heft and weight that put the braid in the middle so by the day's end her head did not ache. This woman had once loved her.

It was a struggle to get herself out of the car yet she motioned to Harry when he attempted his usual door-opening gallantry. No men involved; this was private between these two particular women. And it was Sixto's face imposed across his mother's features, his eyes, compassion and humor; the remains of love.

They met in a sideways embrace, Remi and her husband's mother. Their braids tangled, the mother's hands rested across her grandchild, across her beloved son's only child. It was too much. Together they cried, no shame but simple relief from the months of worry filled with the constant pain of Sixto's death.

Mama Vargas took Remi to a bench set against the adobe where the sun warmed the sitter and gave hope in the colder days. There was no time wasted; "Why have you come here in your state? Travel is not good, the roads are terrible and I do not trust Señor Sembach and his fancy car."

"It took us two days and he was careful, in fact many cars went by us on the gravel road, honking their disapproval but he did not hurry." The woman looked directly at Remi, who smiled and then leaned against the woman; nothing had changed between them. She could feel the heart beat as if it were Sixto's, she could smell that air, a defined distinctness belonging to the Vargas family. She smiled into the flesh of the softened neck, and knew above her face that Mama Vargas in return was smiling too. Now was the time to ask.

She pulled away, held the roughened hands, looked into the dark eyes, tired and beginning to droop but alive, a mother still. There was no way around the question; "Would you take Sixto's baby and raise it? I am sure he is a boy and you can name him what you wish but I would ask you include my own father's name in the ceremony."

There was silence, not fearful, not resentment. Mama Vargas pulled back, keeping her hands on Remi, allowing one hand to remain on the child's mound, the other hand moving to the side of Remi's face. She was studied as Mama Vargas's head nodded up and down.

"I had hoped, I could not see you with the babe in my dreaming. But I would not ask, I could not put such a burden on you. Yes dear child we will take Sixto's boy into our life, out of love for you as well as for our dear son."

There was only sitting then, hands intertwined, words unnecessary. Until it occurred to Remi; 'My father's name was Eben." Continued silence until the older woman finally smiled: "Did you ever know my son's entire name? We called him Sixto all his life, you may not have read it on the marriage certificate."

Remi took in a deep breath and listened. "His name was Hippolito. Hippolito Valentin Cde Baca Vargas. You can see why we chose Sixto, it suited him. As did the formal names but they were too much on the forms for him to join the Army so they accepted Sixto Vargas and we did not argue. We had tried to persuade him to not join but all the boys joined, they had to, they were Americans now and their country asked for their young lives and they gave. During the war, or after, as happened to Sixto."

The old woman shook her head; "He will be Eben Hippolito C de Baca Vargas. We will love him, as will you. As you do now in your asking such a favor from us."

They rested, worn down from too much, harsh memories that would not release either of them. Remi had to finish but Sixto's mother was there ahead of her; "If it is a girl, she will be Roberta. We will share the family and we will tell the child about you."

All she could do was stare; this old woman read every concern and worry and had an answer as if the thoughts had been churned through and discussed many nights, many times. Plans and responses were carefully spoken; for this very reason, their hope of this possible future, making Remi cry. Behind her she could hear the car door open, then it was shut quietly as Genevia C de Baca Vargas put her arms around the shoulders of her daughter by marriage and let the child cry out her heart's fear and relief.

Belinda E. Perry

HARRY WITNESSED THEIR drama through the steamed windshield of the Packard. He had rolled down the windows until the biting bugs forced a choice, to be slightly, barely refreshed by a thin breeze while dying slowly from an onslaught of mosquitoes, or gasping in the closed car with only hot air to breathe.

He chose to roll the windows up reluctantly, leaving the smallest of crack at the triangular side window where he kept his face turned, inhaling the breeze while swatting at the invaders. In this manner he kept himself occupied. Until he saw Remi's body shake, her head lowered, her hands intertwined and he could not bear her unheard sorrow so he opened the car door to help her and was waved back, dismissed, ignored once he was safely back in the car. Whatever words had been exchanged, he was not wanted as a partner in the decision.

Eventually Remi came toward the car, accompanied by the older woman, whose wild grey-black hair and darkened skin gave her the appearance of a witch on the heath from his college Shakespeare. The land did not sustain his image; dry clumps of thin grasses, soft undulations of ridge, stone, dirt watering holes. A few flat-sided steers appeared in small groups, grazing lethargically, always angling toward the low, velvet-green water.

This time when he got out of the car to open a door for Remi, there was no dismissal of his efforts, only a kindly pat on the face as if he were a well-brought-up twelve year old boy doing his grandmama's bidding. He was extra gentle settling Remi in the car, even rolling the window down partially so she would have a polite breeze. Neither woman spoke, as if all words were said that had demanded this trip. Harry returned to the driver's seat and made certain that the old woman was in his view ahead of them, before he backed the car onto the crude road which took them through the ranch headquarters and out to what passed for a main road in this part of the state.

IT FELT AS if all the emotions of her whole life were in her throat; she couldn't bear to look at Harry, and the blur of life passing by as the big Packard ate the rough miles was what she needed. Nothing to see, nothing to notice or take in or worry over — it was said, done, Sixto's family would raise his child, a son she was certain, a boy to become his father and more. To not fight in a war but to grow and learn and go on to college, which Sixto had once said he wanted for all the children he and Remi would have. Four or five, he said, no more, and they would study and learn and be as smart as their mother.

Remi remembered the words, remembered the feel of his hand on her belly as he talked of family and the future. It had been the night before he died. She began to cry again and Harry must have seen it for the big car lurched across the road before he brought it back under control. She looked away when he cleared his throat before the inevitable question and Harry, for once, read her correctly and did not press on with his bullish intrusion.

The rest of the drive was silent. They stayed in the same motor court and this time Remi slept, until finally there was a banging on the door and Harry's worried voice to awaken her. She yawned, called out gently that she would be up in a moment, and felt inside that smallest sense of peace.

YOU CAN LIE without lying and you can mean a lie without meaning it – what I did to my son was all a lie except for the core of truth, that I could not raise a child, I could barely read the directions in a cookbook no matter how much 'reading' Anne Marie had forced on me during the gestation months.

I am a mother still, a woman who gave birth can be nothing else. Even if the child is stillborn she is, for that moment of unseparated birth and dying, a mother. I have always known my son lived, I knew his first years into his teens; Mama Vargas kept me informed and then she died and no one else in that vast family accepted the responsibility she felt toward me so the letters stopped. But I knew I was a mother.

The reasons became complex and then forgotten; the pain of birth stayed bright and vivid; that is the ultimate lie to me, that we forget the birthing pain, the terrible endless sorrow. I've ranted and roared on this subject before, and most likely will again. Too often in our world a thought or concept or important idea said once is not heard, so the speaker must gear up and howl and yell until a few heads turn, a few faces open up with some degree of understanding.

Belinda E. Perry

Childbirth hurts, and you don't forget.

I notice that more and more often in these lectures which some of you probably skip over are containing fewer and fewer lies. It is life itself that boldly lies, not only the humans who inhabit it. Promises are given as we stumble from childhood into becoming an adult, all that we are supposedly able to do, to try, to reach for a dream of creation and creativity. Those lies hurt the most, that we can try, we can achieve.

Ask me, ask my son who hates me, ask my two dead husbands and the third who, well, that's a story you got to work up to. I ain't got to the best of Harry yet but believe me, life lies to us as much as we lie to ourselves and to our friends. Strangers, hah, don't bothering listening to those lies.

REMI WAS WORN down by the time they got back to the ranch. Even Harry could tell that what had gone on between her and the old woman seemed to have changed the child. For a while she did little but sleep and Anne Marie kept telling Harry that it was natural toward the end of a pregnancy to want to sleep, the child was growing in huge spurts and the carrier, its mother, was being leached of vitamins and nourishment to allow this growth.

Harry found himself only one time standing over the child as she slept, and he was startled to actually see the edges of her belly move, pushed out, then collapsed, then another place close by went through the same rhythm of events and Harry knew he was watching a baby from inside its mother kick and he could almost hear the child's holler – 'let me out, now'. He would lean over gently and place a hand near where the activity was but for knowing that it was highly improper and indecent for him to touch another human in this manner. Unless of course they were married and it was his child. He could not move his sensibilities past the fact of her being a widow carrying her dead husband's offspring.

The sense of regret and sadness surprised him and he crept away from where she lay sleeping, dozing really. For her eyes were partly open and she had watched everything go across his open face. He thought no one was watching so she could actually see him. A pain in his eyes, a sadness to his mouth, which then curved upward sweetly and she saw his hand reach out, stop, hang in the air inches from her and she made sure her eyelids didn't flutter although he was still visible through that strange bar-effect of her lashes. Removed from each other, separated; she wanted to reach for his hand and bring it down to rest intimately on her belly. The baby's kicking was local now, she could tell when and where and longed to share it with Harry. Decency separated them; Remi wanted to cry out for his touch since at night she dreamed of Sixto but could not feel his hand or rest against his chest, lay her head on him, know the rise and fall as his heart beat in a slowed sleep rhythm.

To take hold of Harry Sembach's hand would be against her marriage vows and her promise to Mama Vargas, and of great comfort to Remi herself.

SEVENTEEN

The labor pains started well past midnight and she woke screaming, the bed wet around her, fire in her back.

Harry appeared at the doorway with that scream. Anne Marie lived at the other end of the house and didn't recognize the commotion until well after seven and neither Remi nor Harry wanted to disturb her. Remi insisted he call to the ranch in Roswell and tell Mama Vargas, which he did with great reluctance. His theory was to call a local hospital and Remi reminded him that there was no way she would get out of this bed and climb into a goddamn car and bounce from here to Clayton or Raton or Las Vegas or Tucumcari.

The world became defined by Harry's hand, which she gripped and terrorized during the spasms and he didn't once cry out. Her exhaustion overwhelmed her when at midnight the next night the baby still hadn't arrived. The kindly Dr. Buffam was called, and immediately said to bring her in to a hospital and she informed Harry and the doc, who hadn't learned much about Remi during their mutual examination was informed with crude finality that she was staying put and he better goddamnit get his ass out here now.

Mama Vargas arrived before the doctor and the simple motion of her hand across Remi's belly, her lifting of the sheet covering her lower regions, as neither Harry nor Anne Marie would venture into that part of a woman's anatomy, even though it was where all babies came from, Mama Vargas's touch and knowledge let Remi cry again and then relax.

What lived in her mind was the horrible bleeding she'd witnessed from her own mother, knowing that she had done this torture to her own mother's flesh and bone, made her own birthing nightmarish – her pain lost in the delirious pictures of the body pushed out, the gushing blood, the baby who died before his soul found a home.

Remi screamed and arched her back and the devil slid from between her loins, caught and held tenderly by the old woman, her expert hands knowing just how to cradle the bloodied, wiggling being.

There was a moment's brief tugging and only later did Remi realize it was the cord being cut; no feeling really, no sense of separation. Her body was deeply wrapped in receding pain and she barely noticed what had been done. Then the old woman picked a small blanket up, smiling at Remi; "I made this for the little one, it's a boy, like you said. Do you wish to hold Eben? For a while."

Her hands clenched at her sides, her mouth opened to say 'yes' of course she was its mother, it was her child she would hold it to her breast and let it know how much she loved it even though the child was not hers. It was not possible to speak that small word, 'yes' nor could she raise her hands or open her fingers so that the tiniest of head and chest, the perfection of fingers and toes could come to her to be held.

All she could do was close her eyes and roll her head on the damp, sticky pillowcase, refusing the need and right to hold her child. He would be taken from her, it was the agreement best for the child, best for everyone so holding, touching, feeling the tiniest of heart beat outside her body and to know that it had lived within her could not be accepted.

Sixto's mama placed Eben, the baby, on Remi's breast. "For him, the niño, he needs your first milk and yes you will suffer some as the milk makes itself and finally dries up. You will hurt between your legs for a while as torn and stretched muscles find their place again. You will be tired and sad but that cannot be helped. This is Sixto's child and the best must be done for him. Right now, you do not matter. You have given birth and you are not ill so do this, let it be known that you have given everything the child needs. I will stay here one day, and I will clean and wipe and wrap our child but you will feed him, he needs that first food, and only you can provide it."

There was love in the lecture, and truth, and facts Remi did not wish to hear. But there was another truth; that she had wanted Sixto's body, she had teased and touched him until he spilled himself and she lay there smiling, holding him even when he pulled out, looking down at her in amazement.

When Genevia Vargas and one of Sixto's brothers drove off in a battered, borrowed truck, taking the babe with them, wrapped much like a valuable piece of china, the smallest section of his face showing in between folds of a deep blue flannel blanket, Remi did not get up to watch. She lay in the bed, cleaned now, herself washed piece by piece by Mama Vargas who laughed and chided Remi herself for her reluctance to deal with the human body.

Belinda E. Perry

"Do you think you do not shit, or piss, or have those holes in your body like every other woman? This delicacy is not you, Remi child, I have known you too well over the years of your growing. I have seen you slide down your pants and squat and piss right there on the grasslands, with two of the vaqueros nearby. They were gentlemen and averted their eyes, as you were polite enough to turn away when they unbuttoned their pants and pulled out their limp organ to piss away from the wind. Do you shy now when a horse lifts its tail and breaks wind or a mare stops and spreads her hind legs and squirts out her sign of desire and availability? It is our animal beings inside us, this has never changed."

The words were spoken from kindness but in Remi they settled into bitter discord where she remembered who she had been but now held no sense of any being or much of herself left. Tearing out that child had taken her self.

AFTER THOSE FIRST shrieks, Anne Marie had gotten up and without asking or any warning, packed a full suitcase and left in the Packard, leaving behind a note that she would be staying at La Fonda in Santa Fe until the whole ghastly business was over and Remi and the child were into a routine which would allow some peace back into the house. She would not be inconvenienced or talked into helping; she had gone through this herself and had nothing to show for it so her help was not to be expected.

The note was pure Anne Marie and almost let Harry smile even as another cry from Remi reminded him that a baby was being born. In his home, to a young woman he believed he had come to love

That it was a boy delighted him; the old woman allowed Harry to hold the child and he was fascinated, touching the very tip of his finger to the child's face made the mouth purse and then suck. Which put heat into Harry's face and groin for he knew what the child looked for, and from whom. From birth, he thought, right from the beginning here it is in full force. The babe began to cry and Harry returned it to the old woman whose smile had a hint of ancient knowledge that he did not appreciate.

When the child was gone, had been taken away, had been delivered to its new and joyous family, Harry found himself wandering the big house, and reluctant to make that call down to Santa Fe, to the hotel where Anne Marie was more than likely terrorizing the staff and enchanting any suitable man who came within ten feet of her.

Remi's grief was palpable; Harry tended to her as if she were ill, bringing her tea and special treats and not speaking to her about anything of any importance. She remained in her bed, pale and hardly moving, complaining only once of the pain of her still-leaking breasts. Harry fled the room and did not return until the following morning.

She still lay there, pale, frail, the curtains closed, the air thick, stale, unbearable. Harry knew it was long enough and that Remi had slid into self-pity. He'd seen his own mother, and the housekeeper they'd had attend to such situations. He jerked back the heavy draperies, far too dense and formal for this ranchland house but Anne Marie had insisted.

The dramatic gesture brought a groan as sunlight entered the room and small dust motes could be seen flying from the thick layers of disturbed velvet . He laughed, and heard Remi curse him. "Get up, child, you've been there long enough." He did not know where the courage came from to give such an order. And obviously Remi wasn't going to do as she'd just been commanded.

Harry lay down beside her, facing her, head on an accompanying pillow; staring at her paled features, her tangled hair. Her lips were peeling, her eyes had a glazed look yet when he put his hand on her forehead there was no heat, no fever at all. No expression, no disgust at a strange man lying in her bed; the old Remi would have sparked and kicked and sworn at him yet she lay there, offering no resistance, no caring at all.

Above the barest lace stitched across the sheet were her breasts, lightly covered in a thin pink cotton, lace too, at the throat and around the neck yet curving down to the rise of her breasts. The material was lightly stained, dried, crackling; the shame of even looking and recognizing that this was milk, meant for the child who had left for a different family.

He did what he would never have done if the baby were in the room, if Anne Marie were in the house, if life had any normalcy and Remi McClary Vargas was once again the Remi he enjoyed. He put a hand on the mound of breast, stroked lightly, felt the slightest hint of wetness under his hand and oddly, surprisingly, a movement from Remi herself, the merest rise of her hips as if she felt more than the single touch to her breast, as if her body recently shed of its child was coming back to it own.

He stopped, his hand remained on her breast. He leaned over, her mouth so close, his head near hers on their shared pillow. He kissed her, only on the corner of her lips, where the skin was soft, where the dry cracking had not altered her taste. His fingers tightened on the flesh meant to feed an infant and Remi turned to him, smiled at him, which he could not believe. "You want me." Not a question and her breast rose and fell under his grip, her heart touched his fingers; he smiled at the feel of her mouth moving in the announcement.

"Yes. Marry me."

EIGHTEEN

There was no fancy ceremony; no one wanted a big to-do. I was shaky still from the loss of my child, humiliated and unwilling to speak of it, that I had given away my flesh. Anne Marie of course was against any type of publicity around the marriage, although she did admit later that the marriage was what she had planned and wanted for her brother. It was that a recent widow, bereft of her own infant, was not meant to be spoken of in polite or political circles. I did not understand of course, I only knew that there was a person in this world who wanted me.

I was almost twenty at the time my child came into this world and left me. Harry's offer was easy, there was little enough available for me but to become a wife again.

This time, I discovered, I had married a man with preconceptions and ideas. He was definitely not a vaquero, nor was he truly a rancher, but a businessman who had knowledge of profit and loss and paid attention to these elements, at times letting them become more important than our life together. Then again, we both had to put up with Anne Marie and her set of opinions. Thankfully she lived at the other end of the house so at least by nightfall we had earned our privacy.

Harry and my first husband were two entirely different men, which you already know. And that was true especially in bed.

HE WAS HESITANT that first night; she had been married to a most virile man, which was obvious in the fact of her conception within a week's marital time. And Harry was not terribly experienced, no virgin of course; drunken moments spent on and inside a prostitute with his friends telling him all sorts of strange practices to try, places to lick and rub and ultimately penetrate. The whole experience remained a collegiate silliness instilled by the shenanigans. Marriage must be quite different. A few of Anne Marie's married friends had approached him, used him for their own carnal purposes and left him stunned, depleted, and thoroughly confused. The marriage bed was sacred, what he had been taught by both his mother and father. Although his father's antics with the coarse women he found almost anywhere he went, and the younger men in attendance on his mother made him question their practices and preachings at an early age.

They waited six months, well after she finally got up and out of the bed, out of the bedroom and even left the living room, to go back down to the corrals and see the horses. It had been a condition of Harry's, that she ride at least once before they married. It was flattering to him that she made the effort quite soon after that pronouncement. Meaning to him that she truly did want to marry. Love, he wasn't sure yet, but marriage could be the beginning, and he knew already that he indeed loved her.

They hired a parson from one of the smaller towns, Cimarron, to drive to the ranch and perform the simple ceremony for which the poor minister was greatly rewarded, with a binding promise that he would speak to no one about what he had done. They would chose; to whom, when, in what manner, the announcement of their marriage would be made

Because of memories their bedroom was the smaller of the two in the east wing of the house. Anne Marie threatened a complete make-over as her wedding present but Harry was quick enough to say thank you but we have other plans. Remi gave him a hug, and then an amazing kiss, which left him stunned, and in such an aroused state he considered not waiting until the actual ceremony.

Remi wanted her few things in the room, a chest of drawers her father had made for her mother, some bed quilts done by her mother, a quaint rag rug which, when he first stood on it in his bare feet, proved to be a pleasing experience.

The bed he refused; it was where she and Sixto…well he could not bear the comparison within the same framework, the bed linens had to go also, here he allowed Anne Marie to spend her time and money and the sheets were of a pale cream which delighted Harry with their fine hand. Even Remi appreciated the delicate softness on her skin. She rolled in the linens before they'd been carefully tucked onto the mattress and once again Harry was inclined to simply mount her here and now and to hell with waiting…

She smiled up at him as if she knew exactly what he was thinking. One of her feet came up, bare, naked below the length of the denim jeans she insisted on wearing, that foot came up and touch his hip, then slipped innocently lower and in just the smallest bit so that he jerked back and her grin turned wicked.

He was terrified that he would not be good enough for her.

WHEN THE PARSON left, Anne Marie said she had tea waiting in the sunroom off the west side of the house. It was her special present for the newly-weds. Remi took Harry's hand and looked directly at her sister-in-law; "I already have plans for Harry, and they don't include tea.." Harry couldn't help but grin at the look on his sister's face. Shock, as if the realization that her brother was actually a married man, with the rights and privileges that entailed. And it seemed that his wife was quite eager to get started.

Remi literally threw herself naked onto the bed, rolled onto her back and spread her legs just enough, and stared up at Harry. He knew, if nothing else from reading quite a few books in which couples, well…coupled. The most satisfied of those sharing the marital bed indulged in what was called foreplay. A matter of kissing, in more or less the usual places and then a few other places which were usually guarded by women's undergarments. Remi of course had never worn such a garment, it had been one of Anne Marie's indulgences to take Remi all the way into Santa Fe where they purchased bras and pretty panties, but no girdle, no one would ever get Remi McClary…Remi Sembach to wear a girdle.

He spoke the words out loud; "You're Remi Sembach", and she smiled and raised one leg so that the bent knee and thigh exposed the reddish triangle of hair and the slightest glimpse of those lips which hugged a man's erection.

He had seen some of the more risqué magazines where such a portion of the female anatomy was spread apart by female fingers to entice and arouse the voyeuristic male, but to see that pink flesh, parted, moist along the inner edges, and know it was waiting for only him, that was an entirely different situation.

Remi put a halt on his habit of over-thinking by sitting up and leaning in toward him, his hips of course, and she began to unbutton and unzip his pants and he had to laugh. How foolish of him to be dreaming like a distraught schoolboy while his wife awaited him.

The first kiss with them both naked, lying against each other, nearly drove him to ejaculation. Remi pulled back and raised herself the slightest so those still-full breasts touched his mouth and he suckled there, first with his lips then he allowed his tongue to run across the nipple and the aureole and he felt Remi shiver and it occurred to him his touch might be a poor memory but when he pulled his head away, her hands pushed him back into place and he knew this was what his wife wanted.

The sensation was exquisite; he wanted all of her breast in his mouth and there was another one chilled and waiting. But the rest of his body wanted more also, and Remi too had her own needs. He'd been taught that a woman, a proper woman, should and would not want sex.

Remi made it simple to slide in between her legs as she raised her hips to make the insertion easier. He moved quickly, she held his hips and helped him go slower, deeper until he was ready and she stopped, made him breathe, even tickled his neck and smiled at him and then as he was less than ready she began again and this time neither of them could stop.

He truly hadn't known that this was the state of wedded bliss.

FOR OVER A month they went at each other constantly; he could not get enough of the first insertion, that glide into paradise; she wanted specific attentions and told him, showed him what parts needed his touch before that place became his. It was a perfect partnership.

During the few times they were separated, and fully clothed, they talked about plans; Remi even went over the books with Harry. Although at first she didn't understand much, he began to realize she had a good brain, clever and quick to ask difficult questions. Anne Marie often attempted interruptions with offers of tea or a drive, or even a game of cards, until it occurred to Harry that his sister was feeling left out. But they couldn't include her in most of their time spent together, and she refused to discuss ranch business.

Eventually he suggested to a wounded Anne Marie that she perhaps might wish to return to Texas, now that the ranch house was fully redecorated. Anne Marie countered with wanting to throw a party for their nuptials until Harry pointed out that the last party including a widowed and pregnant Remi and it might be awkward to attempt an explanation of what had happened to the child and just when did the marriage occur. And why hadn't 'they' been invited.

For the first time in years Harry had the satisfaction of knowing his sister had no answer to the puzzle he offered. In silence, in shock he supposed, she threw her head to one side, actually sniffed and said that living in the country, the wild west, had not turned out to be the adventure she expected, with the cowboys being mostly married vaqueros, and the open spaces filled with cactus and crawling things which were definitely not welcome in her bedroom, and certainly not in her bed.

In other words, Anne Marie had not found what she was looking for; she might indeed have found the peace she needed but Harry knew well that peace was the last thing on Anne Marie's mind. She left for Texas in the Packard loaded with boxes, suitcases, and was sent off with a hug from Harry, a short wave from his wife.

Now they had the entire house to themselves and their only restriction was what might be found the next day by the housekeeper, including themselves and where they might end up, exhausted and asleep.

One late afternoon, lying close on the elegant rug under the crudely made 'western' dining table, Harry dared ask the question that often came to him late at night but had never found daylight words.

"How'd you learn all…?" He couldn't continue, hoped, that Remi heard the unfinished ending. She sighed at first, and rested her head on his chest, which always made him feel omnipotent, a source of comfort, her strength. "Sixto, he…" What couldn't be heard must not be said; Harry twitched and her head was too painful resting on his bare flesh. She had no choice but to pull away, letting her head lie on the deeply piled rug so she was laid out, flat, her spine touching the thick rug in only a few places. Harry rose up on one arm, looked her entire length and admired the narrowness of her waist, returned to its pre-baby slender firmness. And yet there was the slightest of puffiness in her belly, although her thighs were still muscled and her hips were absolute perfection.

Those two breasts that he had loved for themselves, rounded and soft with a core that held them straight up, the nipples now relaxed, softened; this body had crawled all over him and made him feel like the king of the universe and he had been crass enough to ask how she knew and of course her answer had to be that name and how damnably foolish and prideful of him to reject her for starting to tell the truth.

DON'T YOU LOVE where lies and truth get so tangled that there is no possible way in which one may be separated from the other and each known for what they are. I did learn from Sixto although he did not teach me. I remember my sister, outside against the barn, I remember my parents too clearly, I knew early on, watching the animals, especially a stallion courting a mare, that it wasn't the simplicity of lying on your back, spreading your legs and waiting passively while the act was done to you. And that there were variations, watching my sister was that teacher. Watching a tender stallion lick and nip a reluctant mare, in places too common, too personal, for humans to do yet it made sense since we're only animals and that I had known as a truth since we buried my baby brother.

I speak a great deal of that dead child but remember I was a child myself and lost my mother at the same time. I cannot recall her features but I can see that blue, faceless child that Papa wrapped in the shreds of a blanket and buried with his wife in back of the barn. Papa told me years later, on this ranch, to keep Mama's face in mind and not see the dust and powdered remains of her and the boy. We were flesh, we rotted, but our hearts and souls remained with those who truly loved us.

After that I had nightmares and screaming sleeps because I could not see my mama's face.

SHE LOOKED STRAIGHT up at the underside of the table and spoke softly and he believed her. "Sixto taught me about being loved, about being worthy. I had him only a short time, but we both discovered, together, how much we could pleasure and it wasn't just in that one place that felt so good but all those places, even behind his knees. I can't lie about this, Harry, I thought you loved me and I trusted you enough to want to try and find what pleases you. We're each different. And it ain't just male and female different, it's our own lives."

215

Harry felt his heart pound and he could not quite swallow. He rested his hand gently on one of those breasts and let the back of his knuckles stroke the flesh, like they had discovered truly pleased her.

His mute apology was in the form of his rolling over her gently as possible and sliding down her belly as she parted her legs and he used his fingers as she directed him and then his tongue until she cried out and drew herself up and only then did he slide inside. It was her preference and he knew to enjoy the preparation.

So two weeks later when she turned away from him and would not accept any of his touches, kisses, then ultimate verbal entreaties, Harry was confused, upset, and extremely randy. His sexual fantasies had come true and then dissolved in the huge tearing eyes and sullen mouth of his beloved.

He called Anne Marie as a last resort, not to ask her to return but was there something secret in a woman's life that would bring on such a change. She asked two questions, embarrassing but pertinent.

"Have you used any protection?" Harry couldn't catch his breath. "Have you asked her if she's in the family way, or even thinks she is? She would know if she missed her monthlies. And given the horror of her last term, she might believe you will get rid of this child also."

To Harry there was a deep element of blame and distrust in his sister's practical words, as well as some process of truth he would not wish to admit into his thinking. This was a totally different situation, Remi would know that. They were married and he was alive, would remain so for years to come. So any fears she might have of giving up this child were foolish and ill-founded.

He of course was blushing and over-heated by the time Anne Marie finished the last few words. He gulped and stammered out that he would ask his beloved those two questions. Anne Marie had the last word when she warned him that if Remi were in a delicate condition, her emotions would be on the surface and he must use extra tact and care.

Harry stammered into the empty phone that he knew how to treat his wife, she didn't need to be giving him such orders, but of course Anne Marie had hung up. He went searching for Remi and discovered she wasn't anywhere in the house so he immediately knew where she was and headed to the corrals where one of the hands had the ugly dun already saddled with Harry's gear.

"Good morning, Señor, she rode out about a half hour go and did not look happy so we all guessed..." Here the man stopped and gave the reins to Harry. "The cinch is tightened, Señor, when I saw you coming down the walk I thought to myself..."

Harry climbed on the reluctant dun and stared at the overly talkative man, who had finally learned to be brief. He pointed out toward the wells and Harry nodded. "Gracias." His small attempt at local Spanish. The man barely nodded back so Harry wasn't certain his good-faith attempt was well received.

However he needed to catch up to Remi so he flailed at the dun's sides with his boot heels and slapped the dun's shoulder and the horse actually put his head down and bellowed and kicked up behind, which unbalanced Harry and got him mad. He kicked the dun harder, pulled up on the reins and yelled threats to the stubborn horse who must have understood what was behind those words for he suddenly put all his energies into running, which is what Harry wanted in the first place.

Behind him he could hear the faintest of cheers.

EMOTIONS RUN OFF wildly fluctuating hormones when you're pregnant, 'in the family way' as dear Anne Marie and her kind would put it. I was terrified; I knew that Harry loved me and wanted the child but my body seemed caught in all the births I had witnessed, my own son, my little brother. I realize I seem to be stuck on those old memories but don't put any blame on me; think on your own past, the private one you refuse to discuss with even your closest friend or lover. We all have those secrets that become lies by omission. Hidden actions or thoughts we know are intellectually wrong but our hearts tell us the opposite, and no matter how educated we think we are, our hearts almost always rule.

I knew perfectly well Harry wouldn't be upset but delighted when he knew I was carrying a baby. His baby. But I was terrified, so I went to the one place where I knew peace waited for me.

What I did not anticipate was Harry following me. Or is that a lie even now, so many years later. What else would I expect from him since I began withholding my favors or whatever you want to call 'it'. Sex.

I certainly wanted him to follow me but then again I didn't or I wouldn't have gone to the cemetery because I knew instinctively that the destination would wound a man I was learning to love with a depth that scared me. So it looked then to me that I needed to distance myself from loving Harry, and Sixto's grave was my only weapon.

The cruelty of my destination did not fully hit me until I turned at the sound of a galloping horse and when the pair drew closer and the dun slowed to a standstill, my mouth went dry and my heart pounded. I had committed a savagery I hadn't known I was capable of doing, an act in which I sought out safety while presenting only indifference to the one who truly mattered.

SHE WAS THERE! Right where he'd guessed so he hauled the dun horse around to get the hell out and away from where he wasn't wanted but the dun proved his worth by refusing to be manhandled more than once in a day's ride.

In the dun's stubborn thought process, he flat out refused to leave the sorrel colt and even Remi's voice that called out to his rider stopped the dun, made him prick his ears at her sound. He knew this voice and took a few steps toward the girl who was kind to him instead of the devil who sat on his back at the moment and was pounding on his sides but the fool had none of those pricking tortures so the dun ignored him.

Harry felt like the fool he was, kicking and cursing and slapping the reins on the dun's sweaty shoulders and the godforsaken horse ignored him to march exactly to where Harry didn't want to go.

She rested her hand lightly on the dun's neck and the horse rubbed his muzzle against her arm and when Harry calmed enough to look at her, he could see her tears, and he could also finally see that small swelling of her belly, where she unbuttoned the jean button and didn't bother to try and recover by turning away and redressing herself.

Belinda E. Perry

"I didn't mean to hurt you, Harry. I didn't think, coming here, it's away from the house and…" She was crying now and the words weren't helping; Harry's face was dark, too angry for Remi to say any more of what she was trying to explain. She sat down, startling the dun who almost unseated Harry; no grace, no preparation, as if her legs couldn't hold her. Harry leaped off the dun, who wandered over to touch noses with the sorrel colt.

"Remi my dear Remi…" He was stuck, without words or pompous formal pronouncements. He reached for her, laid the back of his hand gently on her cheek and she, surprisingly, with no hesitation, leaned into his touch. Until he felt his hand grow damp and realized the child was actually crying. So he tried to scoop her up but she pulled back and he was completely confused.

"Harry, I dishonored you, and him." She didn't point or speak a name but he knew. "I am so afraid. I can't have another child, I don't know how to take care of them and there's no one to show me. My mother…his mama…no one." "I'll help." "Not you and Anne Marie, she would drive me mad. You, you're a man, what could you know…" He interrupted, something he rarely did with Remi for her thoughts and expression of them were fragile items needing support.

"Your father raised you, and did a fine job. I am no less a man that he was, and there are two of us together this time, to stumble through the beginnings. There are books, Remi, and people who can be called. I can hire a nanny or nursemaid, any help you want." She was almost looking at him, eyes cast down but her face was brought around, and her body, so he could see the beginnings of a smile, and if he so wanted, he could touch her now. Only a slight trembling but enough that he opened his arms and she bravely let herself be carried into them. The pulse of her body surprised him, then he reorganized the tender central push of her belly, their child, resting between them; Harry had to wipe his own eyes.

IT WAS MY heart beating inside me, and another's heart, a small impulse of Harry's lust and my willingness that would push and change and grow and tear me apart coming forth and this time I would be the one responsible. This one I couldn't give away. That terrified me and being wrapped inside Harry's arms made no difference except that it helped him and let him believe but I couldn't tell him, found that the lie of believing him was impossible but all I could offer.

Here it is, those lies you need to tell. I was nineteen, I think, already widowed and giving up a baby and now I was married again and pregnant again and if a lie or all the lies I told Harry during that pregnancy and beyond it, when the baby was born, if those lies made his life bearable while mine was dissolving, then the lies were acceptable.

"How do you feel today, dear?" "Fine, in fact let's go for a walk." When I really wanted to hide in the bed and those lovely soft linens and cry because I could not bear one more minute of my life rolling out ahead of me. This was not what I wanted, what I understood. I know now that without a mother to guide me, when I was such a small child, I never was taught about patience, to accept being a woman, to want what a woman wants. I learned as a man, from a father who could barely function. He himself had lost all his life except for this one irritating child who would not go away. He loved me no doubt, and I'm certain that were times he was glad to have me. But I held him back, kept him from traveling or finding another woman, some male friends, something else to do but work all day and then try to be mother and father to me at night.

Not an especially rewarding life for him, was it? No lie here, no glossing over by saying it's the Lord's work or that I was his joy and blessing. If we all had died, he could have restarted a life. With me hanging on, life became for him a remote existence.

And if, don't you love all these ' ifs' in our lives, not just mine but yours and everyone else's. If I'd known more about sex and sexual mores, more than just that I liked it, liked everything about the male body and the act of sex, then perhaps I would not have been pregnant again at nineteen and on my second marriage. There was so much no one ever told me, and that, my dear reader, makes for a lot of mistakes.

UNEXPECTEDLY HARRY FOUND that sex with a pregnant woman, his wife in particular, was a matter of convolutions and unexpected delights. There was a built-in freedom to their acts, a knowing that she couldn't get pregnant so whatever they did was safe, as long as it didn't press on the baby.

This meant of course a use of the imagination and his Remi proved to be highly imaginative. She always smiled and kissed him when he made overtures and then she would elevate that part of her, or twist her body and glide down on him while he brought up his head and kissed the belly that grew closer each time. The process of creating and then growing a child was truly a miracle.

It delighted him even more that Remi held the same feelings. She would let him rest his head against her naked belly, in the privacy of their living room or the bedroom, and he could simply listen and hear that extra beat, feel the kick and movement and when he looked up at Remi she was smiling down at him like a Madonna. This, he knew, was the process designed to draw man and woman close together, for both to bear witness at their child's beginnings, and on occasion he would think of the poor man, Sixto something, who never knew the creation and birth of his only child.

That he, Harry Sembach, had taken another man's rightful place in life, planted a child in another man's widow, at times left him saddened and bereft; as if he had committed a sin by being alive while this other man, one who had fought for his country while Harry ran a commercial venture deemed too valuable to have him leave, this brave soul came home long enough to find and love this remarkable woman, and then die. Leaving room for Harry to take his place and obliterate his very existence.

At times these thoughts poisoned the sexual act with Remi and it was left for Harry to bring his wife to her climax without benefit of his own. He always spoke of being tired, overworked, not for her to worry but there was a ghost between them only Harry could see.

HARRY WAS OVERSENSITIVE to all the conflicts around Sixto and our marriage, his early death. And believe me his sensitivity drove me crazy; it came between us, keeping Sixto alive in the wrong places. For all the women's cries in the 70's, you people have no idea of what you get when you want a 'sensitive' man. A decent man who is male first will be sensitive, you cannot order up a man who is all over you with worries and fears for you and your psyche and have a man good in bed.

You can argue and discuss and tell me I'm wrong, politically incorrect is the wishy-washy term currently in vogue, but I have lived through three marriages, buried husbands, and I have learned, quite early on, that too 'sensitive' a man frets and worries so much he can become incapable of the act of penetration and no matter what ladies say in polite bedroom conversation, most of us want that particular act.

You may find this discussion gross or objectionable on many levels, and you may disagree with me and that's fine, just don't bother to write and tell me. I don't care, I know what I have experienced, and the disadvantage to multiple marriages is the inevitable comparison. Now that I'm speaking on the subject, I don't think the male of the species has the same problem; he wants a vessel where he may empty himself. His climax, unless he's 'too sensitive', is a forgone conclusion unless he's drunk or drugged or has already exhausted his stamina for the act.

Women, at least from my active perspective, want the prequel as well as the act and its inevitable ending. You all know about faking the climax, that movie, where the girl gives a verbal impression culminating in the climax, we've talked this one to death. For a woman, a deep climax needs either a vigorous man or a good dildo, and dildos don't hug and kiss before and after. However, they can be more effective than some live men and their moods.

It's truly depressing, and a waste of time, to lie under a man you don't know or love, and have him pump into you; from the beginning, unless he's willing to take direction and few men are, you know the outcome is not going to be in your favor.

So call me what you will, I have learned valuable lessons, being basically unafraid to try, or bull-headed as my third husband called me. I believe once in the sixties an Englishman called me a 'bloody-minded bitch', which I took as a compliment, seeing as he couldn't manage even the slightest erection and fiddling with a finger isn't much of a substitute.

Belinda E. Perry

Now that there is a drift to the Christian right, to bland message movies and directors who out-Disney Disney with their sugarcoated stories, I doubt I will find a publisher for my thoughts. Then again they may have no literary value, who knows, but I will have my say.

THE BIRTH THIS time was a week before her due date so Harry's plan to move into Clayton and be near the doctor and the hospital came to nothing. He had tried to move Remi on the matter and only that morning had she agreed that tomorrow she would make the trek into town and give up the last of her independence.

Yesterday he had found her down by the corrals, brushing the dun horse with his old flat saddle setting on the top fence rail. He took the brush from her hand and turned the dun horse loose despite her hitting him with the bridle anywhere she could reach. Her aim was thankfully poor, the baby swollen in her womb kept her off balance and unable to truly swing the lethal end, with the bit and headstall. Still she managed a few good stings to his buttocks and thighs with the pliable leather reins. He did not take it personally; she was a victim of hormones and considerable restrictions for a woman who had ridden this land as a paid cowboy.

Being pregnant twice in just over two years must have been terribly hard on her spirit; Harry gently took the bridle out of reach and it was then that she gave her word to go to the hospital, tomorrow she kept saying, not today, tomorrow. He agreed to that small point; tomorrow. It was the first time she had been willing to acknowledge the rightness of his plan.

Now she lay on their bed, sheets wadded up underneath her, a single sheet draped decorously over her belly and loins. It would not do for anyone, especially her husband, to witness those private parts and their separation, the emergence of their child. It was too personal a moment for any man's consideration, unless of course he was a physician.

This time there were no cries, no grabbed and squeezed hands; as if she had decided and therefore the baby would be born and there was no need to fuss; it hurt, it would soon be over. Harry paced outside the door, driven there by two wives of the vaqueros who worked for him. He tried once to enter the room and a woman flew at him waving hands and screaming in Spanish as he skidded backwards and let the door close. Such turmoil was disconcerting so he had to respect their knowledge and clear boundaries.

He was pleased however that Anne Marie was still in Dallas; she had wanted to be here for the birth and intended to return in a week. She would have interfered and been rebuffed and then insulted by the two ranch women. They knew, no question; Anne Marie simply thought she could know everything without any experience.

His sister's births had been attended by doctors, nurses, and drugs. Her understanding of what Remi was doing would be an incomplete connection – Harry shook his head and began his continued pacing. He checked with his watch, heard Remi's cries which shook him badly. She was tough, strong, seemingly immune to the pains that terrified other females and yet it was her voice rising to a high wail that shook the walls and entered Harry's soul. Intercourse would never be the same, not knowing that this terrible scream and obvious agony could be pleasure's unrelenting result. Now he fully understood his sister's choices, and her question about Harry using protection. There it was, he would ask Dr. Buffam where such protection might be available.

The child was born in the early morning, and the exhausted women allowed Harry to enter after he had washed his hands and straightened up his clothing to make himself more respectable. As if what his wife had gone through was simple, requiring him to act and behave as if ten hours of the worst sounds of his life could leave no mark on his soul.

He leaned down and kissed her gently, aware of his beard growth, the smell of his anxious sweat. She had been bathed lightly, her face was dried, clean, the linens covering her were freshly white, ironed, no possible speck of blood or any bodily fluid could be shown to the husband, to soil the birth of his child, a son.

His son, seven pounds and some ounces the wife of the cook told him, a fine healthy boy with his mama's red hair, his father's light eyes which would change, did Señor Sembach know that the baby's eyes would find their own color?

He was allowed to hold the small bundle, wrapped so tightly Harry could not inspect the physical parts to know the child was complete, or even that indeed it was a boy. The other woman, the foreman's wife, saw something in Harry's distress which she recognized and took the baby from him, gently unfolding corners and tucks until there lay the flesh of his child, red now, cleaned, the cut umbilical cord held to the belly with a soft cotton band which could not be removed.

A boy; a tiny spigot emerging from the child's lower belly, between those bowed and creased legs. The testicles were red also, surprisingly rough compared to the smooth texture of the rest of the body. And enormous, protruding so that the child could never have brought his legs together. The women attempted to refocus Harry's attention on the perfection of the ten toes, the fingernails, those tiny digits that would one day drive a car or dig a hole, play a round of golf

Harry resisted; he could not remove his gaze from his son's masculinity. It had to be extraordinary, unusual, no child born other than his son could be so well endowed this early in life. One of the women interrupted Harry's dreaming.

"Señor, it is natural, there is nothing wrong with your child, all little boy babies are so blessed, he will grow into himself and never feel the stigma of such weighty cojones." She had to revert to her own language, embarrassed at speaking of such intimate matters with the patron.

DESPITE WHAT WOMEN'S literature tells you, having a child hurts right from the beginning. The initial penetration is pain, the daily growth of that tiny speck sends waves throughout the entire body, of dislocation and stretching, of lonely late-night pain.

Those oft-spoken tender moments, a husband's ear rested lightly on the high swollen belly, hearing a heart beat, feeling a kick, those are a wonderful bonding experience, for the man. The woman already knows too well that the child inside her is beginning to fight, to want out, to become its own person without the confines of the womb or the directions of a mother, any mother.

We won't bother speaking, you and I, about the experience of birth itself. We've done this one enough. I had a friend who got pregnant ten years after her first child. She went to her family physician to discuss her

225

desperate need for an abortion, to remove the child who would cause her so much pain. She had a son, she already knew. Of course her doctor would do no such thing but he promised her that much had improved in the birthing process, that hospitals were better prepared and that she would feel little or nothing at all during the entire affair.

When the first labor pain hit, she sat up against the nurse and doctor and their rules, and demanded pain medication. Which was not forthcoming and instead she received that wonderful inane placebo of 'it's only a little pain, we'll take care of it when you progress farther along. It doesn't hurt that much, dear.' I think actually it was the 'dear' that got her; she exploded, cursing the doctor, the nurse and her husband, the child inside her trying to get out

They left her alone and she climbed out of the bed, walked down the hall trailing fluids and the bed sheet she had wrapped around herself. The staff got to her as she walked from the outside steps to the parking lot. There was a tussle and it took two guards to bring her back inside. Her notion was that she was going home; the doctors hadn't lived up to their promise of no pain so she simply wasn't going to continue giving birth.

Absurd I know, but not a lie, the truth. We laughed about it later, after her little girl was delivered and she'd recovered from the effects of drugs and anger. But she looked me straight in the eye and told me that the doctors had promised no pain and they'd lied to her.

She took decent care of the child but left the husband, kept her boy with her also; she faced a world she'd created for herself with a saddened expression and a futile, too-innocent loss of faith. I don't now how the children turned out; my friend eventually drank herself to death.

NINETEEN

HE WAS A pretty baby, his eyes turning from that milky blue to a greenish shade that mirrored but did not duplicate his mother. They named him Robert Emerson Sembach after Harry's elderly grandfathers and the boy thrived on his mother's milk and the attention from the two ranch women, who came in turns to bathe and change and play with the infant.

Remi was not interested; she would nurse the boy because it relieved her aching breasts, then she would catch up a horse and disappear. The women who cared for her child were at first surprised and then nodded to each other in an unspoken understanding. A mother who has once given up a child, her heart would be hard as iron. The girl who loved Sixto was now a woman who did not have either of her own sons.

Harry was confused; his wife told him every night that she was too sore to resume relations yet she rode a horse every day. She was lying to him, but in a manner and about a condition that was considered too delicate for a man to object. A decent man that is. So he lay in bed next to her, feeling the heat rise from her flesh while he was helpless.

Eventually he could not say anything to her at all; she only looked at him and the depth of whatever it was reflected back to him. Despair, sadness, feelings she would not acknowledge or allude to, nothing, no response when he was tender, asked kindly, offered his own suggestions as to how she could deal with the sadness she so obviously felt.

Her response was to wipe his hand off whatever part of her body he was trying to reach and walk away; no words, no anger, silent and gone.

Her rides lasted longer and longer until the women had to make up a formula and feed the hungry baby, clicking their mouths in disapproval yet within each was the smallest understanding, an acknowledgement of Remi's unspoken cry. The mother did nurse at night, and early in the morning, so the baby continued to thrive. The extra feedings were left to the women and Remi was gone all day, taking a canteen of water and nothing else with her, except a small pistol she wore in a holster, for a protection she had never needed before.

AN OLD WOMAN'S LIES

Harry took to drinking. A cocktail before dinner, wine with – he spent a large sum having a wine cellar put in the ranch house, and paid a gentleman from California to tell him what should be ordered. Now when he woke in the middle of the night, in full erection and wanting so badly to touch his wife, he staggered from their bedroom to the small den and sipped a glass or two of a fine Bordeaux, or a milder Chardonnay. Whatever he was told to buy, he purchased, paying his advisor a fine sum for the advice and not minding that the man received a kickback from the sellers. Each sip of wine reduced his fretting, calmed his fears.

When he sought advice from Dr. Buffam in Clayton, he was told such behavior from a new mother was more common than expected, and that hand stimulation was the current outlet for Harry's dilemma. Given time, love, and endless support, his wife would soon enough resume her duties in their bed. Harry wanted to argue, to explain, that for Remi sex was not a duty, it was a pleasure, and not always taking place within the marriage bed under the freshly ironed sheets. It was in the barn, the hay, out near a stock tank and the windmill pumping water while Harry pumped into his wife.

She would ride him like she rode the broncs, hard and fast, with guiding hands and a firm seat. How he missed that woman he'd married, she'd become an unfilled vessel turned away from him. Denying him rights and privileges ordained during their marriage ceremony. Taking the first drink, pouring it from the cut crystal decanter, one of a set with each bottle labeled as to its contents – this particular decanter held old bourbon, not in fashion at the moment but Harry retained a fondness for it, preferring the slightly sweet woods' taste to the peat of scotch, too thick for him, and the dry lingering of even the most expensive rye, from north across the border, where they preferred their local brew to the moldy whiskey from their parent island.

He settled in with the decanter close by, the stopper barely pushed into the neck, waiting for him, telling him of his own intentions. The first sip was heaven; smoothed on the tongue, easy going down, yes that typical fire in the gut, then an absence of sensation, a retreat from his worries and fretting. Numbed; exactly what he wanted. No feeling.

Wine before and with dinner; whiskey in the nighttime to soothe the woes of absence and frustration.

Belinda E. Perry

Harry picked up his hand, turned it over, looked at the white palm, creased now from his years but bearing few scars or blisters, no calluses; no use to him, no labor or work that told him his status in the world. Using his family's inheritance, money given to him as a reluctant gift; he snorted, poured another half-glass of the beautiful liquid and sipped at it, feeling again and again the flood of nothing, tasting a bitter hint waiting for release. He let his left hand rest in his lap, above his genitals, above the now-unused and useless part of him that had created the child in there, asleep and sweet, holding a scent unlike anything he'd ever known.

Picking up the boy, holding him close, hearing those tiny mews of sound, breath going in and out of his son, breaths forming bubbles on his lips that burped a sour smell and even that sourness was a joy.

He pressed down into his empty lap, feeling the contours of what could rise and harden and make him a man and there was nothing, no feeling from the touch, no sensation at all. Numb, as he had wanted when he took that first sip of the golden-red bourbon out of the expensive and antique cut-crystal decanter.

I HAVE A theory, and that must surprise you completely – an old woman like me with a theory, on a modern and constant subject like sex. No lies here, only my truth.

See all the slender, actually skinny, young women parading around, tight jerseys and those low-hanging jeans; we've talked about them endlessly.

Look at them, find one on the street and stare at her. Slender hips, 'boyish' as the fashion magazines call them, barely room for a baby to be injected, and the thought of giving birth must terrify these stick-thin women. Babies don't recognize jeans size, 2, 4 or even 6 – a mockery of what a woman is designed to do.

However, you see this pencil-women on the gloating arms of pot-bellied men, arrogant in their nod to the world, posturing their success, in dollars and hoards of pennies and driving those enormous cars and yes I believe they are a statement of male ego, with the blind believing them, the knowing nodding their heads and guessing as to the size of the mogul's organ. Most often miniscule, in obverse proportion to the size of the driven vehicle.

Nothing new in this theory, only these men never seem to read the philosophy and psychology of their purchases. The women, ah yes their women, their stick figures whose separated thighs have no flesh on them, long sinewy muscle pared close to the bone, leaving room for the male to insert himself, with little effort, no strain, and orgasm, now that's easy within these tight 'boyish' bodies, a birth canal built for a squirrel to escape, no work involved at all, no fondling and foreplay and time to seek out the woman's pleasure, only a few good pumps into that empty, constrained passage and the male release is preordained, easily reached, no fears about under or non-performance. As to the woman, dollars and prestige are better than a good orgasm. It's a fair deal for the two of them, a deal which discarded wives once put their husbands through business school or medical training; their passages stressed and enlarged by birthing out the man's children, their bodies tired from the anger of straying husbands.

It's a deal between two devils; and it mocks love, fidelity, honor, vows.

We see it daily, it is accepted in our society, these men are heroes, looked up to by lesser men, no one thinking of the judgment hanging between those stubby, hairy, white, fleshy thighs that pump once or twice, barely able to sustain such activity from the misuse of whiskey and men's clubs and no exercise except the twice-weekly obligatory fuck of the beauty on his arm. Of course he winks and lets his cronies know that, yes, the current girl is his.

We are mortal, both sides of our species, sadly lacking in good sense, pretending civilization and simply fucking our way into anyone who will have us.

HARRY WANTED ANOTHER drink and the fancy decanter was empty so he searched a cupboard, dug through old bottles, dusty and faded, finding little to tempt him. Sherry, more than likely his sister's choice, and a few bottles with plain labels, telling him it was tequila, a drink he had yet to develop any taste for – too odd for him, too reminiscent of plants, organic dirt, a rich loamy sense in the back of his mouth. He didn't like tequila.

One bottle, quite dusty, seemed to hold a fine tawny port, an engraved label indicated as much, so Harry held the bottle up to the light and it glowed with a burnished coppery red that he could almost taste.

The contents of the bottle did not disappoint; rich, fruity yet holding strength and sweetness much to his liking. It was a comfort to sit in the thick chair he'd insisted on moving to the ranch, and stare out the enormous window, which gave him a long view of what he supposedly owned, claimed ownership of, held by his checkbook and his desire to prove himself.

The port went down easily, simpler than the harsh whiskey; Harry stared at his empty glass and vowed to order more of the beverage, a succor to his wounded heart, his unappreciated masculine soul. She was in there now, her abundant hair spread across onto his pillow, where he needed to be, tasting those intertwined strands, feeling their weight against his roughed skin. He could roll his head then, see the nape of her neck, where loose hair touched bare skin, where the separation of tendons ran from her spine to the burden of her head and only there, in that fleeting section of flesh was his wife sweet and gentle and compliant. He could feel the delicacy of her neck, the swollen tendons barely contained by skin, the slightest movement of her breathing, her attempt to roll away from him, to evade his touch.

Harry jerked out of the reverie, feeling his body swollen from dwelling in his thoughts. When he licked his lips, he could taste her mouth, her breast, the secret between her thighs she had taught him, honey and wine, the beginning and the end. He stood and sat down abruptly, then stood again, a warrior vision holding him erect. He had won her, paid for her, sired her child and now she would not accept him. It was no marriage, it was bondage and temptation and denial and he, Harry Sembach, would accept his dismissal no longer. He'd been the understanding husband, he'd bathed and changed their baby, he'd held her when she cried, when her breasts sored and she couldn't nurse. He had put his hand gently on those heavy breasts, feeling a drip of milk touch his palm. When he licked the droplet, it was impossible to breathe.

AN OLD WOMAN'S LIES

The milk that gave life to his son was drying up, the boy ate from a spoon, drank from a bottle, fed by his nanny, his caretakers, while his mother rode her horses at terrible speeds across the ranch, chasing winds, eyes as swollen as her breasts, dripping tears instead of the milk meant to feed their child.

After a moment of standing, finding his weight settled on each leg carefully, he walked with extreme efficiency to the bedroom, her bedroom now; he'd been banished to a guest room when the child turned croupy and cried all night, needing his mother's hand to quiet him. He'd gone willingly, missing sleep didn't suit his constitution, but now with the boy in his own room, and her sleeping alone, he intended to reclaim his rightful place.

Next to her, in that huge carved bed with the cream linens and soft down pillows and the comfort of her warmth, her breathing that both excited and calmed him. The right to put a hand on her rounded hip, feel the muscle slide and bunch as she rolled over to him, eager and wet and wanting him, that smile turned upward for him, half-opened mouth sized for him, taunting him then taking him in as his fingers found her.

He needed her; he'd talked and cajoled and tried presents which he'd known from the beginning would not work but his sister managed to convince him that every woman wanted presents, jewels, pearls and furs. Harry'd stuttered through explaining Remi and of course Anne Marie shook her head, 'I know your wife quite well, dear boy, and she will be overjoyed with such presentations.'

Five thousand spent on diamonds and a pearl necklace and Remi had done what he knew she would; she threw the boxes and their jewels at him, her eyes furious, her beautiful mouth thinned with spewing insults. He had cringed beneath her words, harsh and demeaning, and far too accurate. "You let that bitch whore sister do this, you told her, you let her tell you…" He had shut his ears, closed his eyes, felt his whole body grow small until he envisioned his mother, his father, all of them laughing, pointing fingers.

He had tried nothing since, picking up the scattered pearls and placing them quite carefully in their perfect velvet box. He could not help but think of her then, of what he missed, what was lost to him.

Now he would take instead of give.

TWENTY

Sixto floating in the stock tank, grinning at her, naked with his maleness bobbing foolishly and he didn't care. He knew who he was, he knew his body, his heart, and his grin was for her to join him, to play in the water and feel him harden and begin to know what it was, love between a man and a woman. Not sex, not like the bull and his cows, or the stallion who could service several mares in a day and they waited their turn, tails held high and to one side, genitals winking in an unlady-like manner.

Remi was grinning now, rolled onto her back, legs pried apart by Sixto, gentle on the inside of her thighs, high, then back to her knee, then reaching above her navel to her waist, a warm kiss, inside, lightly brushing her hair, teasing her, making her raise her hips, her own hands searching, knowing suddenly it wasn't a dream, that a rigid penis was pushing into her and she cried out in fury, eyes suddenly opening into the gaping mouth and jaw, the scratch of a beard; no dream at all.

She twisted her body, used her hands to tear at his arms, his face but his bigger hands, soft and stubby but this one time they grabbed her wrists and held her, powered by the alcohol stinking on his breath. He laid his head near hers and he jammed into her, mouthing her name and kissing her jaw line, wet in her ear, tenderness disconnected to his loins, his impaling spear.

It couldn't be helped, the movement in and out and his mouth on her neck then to her breasts, holding the old memory of pain, her son suckling, chewing on the raised nipple for food and now his father's kisses soft and gentle then a grunt of pleasure, from him, his mouth covering her nipple not hurting, not tearing, a feathered tongue and she couldn't help herself but rose to him with her hips rocking, holding and then releasing until they both groaned and cried in orgasm.

He waited, still rigid inside her, remembering and again her body was a betrayal; of squeezing, opening, closing again around him until she found a second, then a third orgasm and he too seemed to loosen more seed in her, mingled liquids of hate and rage and dreamed love.

When she could move she jammed her knee in to his crotch, felt the softened organs spread under her weight and his cry was her

233

pleasure now, his pain her retreat into a different dream. She woke in the morning, smelling his sex, tasting him in her mouth, knowing that between her legs was dried semen, her sex chafed and sore; her rage began, truly monumental and engulfing, until when she saw him that evening, she walked up to him, herself stinking of clean things; horse sweat and dust, wind and the water in the stock tank at the north end of the ranch.

Remi hit him on the nose, hard enough to break bone. She enjoyed watching the blood staining his white shirt and the fancy woven rug where they stood. He the master of his house, she the woman who would not bow to his wealth. Her words were hissed; "Don't come near me again. I want a divorce."

I WAS MAD at the time. Raging. Raped by my own husband although it isn't what we called it then. He took his rights, according to most of the legal system, who were of course all male. What made my demands possible was Harry's inherently tender heart. I could see in his eyes that he was ashamed, and now I am ashamed for treating him so badly. I did not understand at the time, how could I. Having my second child so quickly tore a hole in me, physically as well as emotionally - there, I almost said spiritually but I don't believe in such a concept. Except that it wasn't emotions wounded inside but a deeper blow, a wrenching apart of what little I held onto; my life was at his mercy, my son, not my husband, my boy who looked up at me and I felt nothing for him.

It has never been resolved - I gave up a son, bore a second son to a man who loved me enough to wait, and to marry and love a woman already taken, already damaged, although I don't think either of us understood my distress. There were no lies, nothing told or explained, no one to help me. I was a child myself, married again, still in love with the first man who showed me what life and sex meant in our narrowed world. Sixto came to my dreams and he was more real than when he was alive, more real than my husband's flesh and heart. It was wrong, to stay in love with a dead man, and Harry suffered for the unknowing betrayal. His lovemaking could not match my dreams, especially after the child was born.

Belinda E. Perry

The boy must have known, must have felt my panic and fear as he looked up from my breasts and saw my face; there were times when he pushed away from me using his tiny feet, his hands pounding on my breasts, his mouth pulling at me until I cried from the physical pain while knowing it was what I deserved.

When he was old enough, three months or so, that was when I started my rides. It was all I knew to do, I had no resources, no mother to tell me, no patience to listen to the nattering women of the house who were more than willing to give me their fears and superstitions. They heated bottles of milk with sugar and water and fed my crying son until he knew they were his mother, not me.

As much as anything in the next few weeks, the sparring and screaming matches, the accusations and threats, what remained locked in me, no words possible to speak such betrayal, was that my body had given to him, had accepted Harry's cock with lubrication and friction bringing us both to orgasm while I hated him for his use of me. At the end, when I could not stop my flesh, I clamped my eyes shut and saw only Sixto, spoke his name out loud and Harry didn't care that he mounted the woman of another man, any place to put his rigid organ, any hole, any passage would do for his needs. He was not loving me, he was fucking the world's whore, the female orifice that had no face, no heart or soul.

When Harry threatened me with keeping our son, I lied. I wailed and fell to the floor in anguish yet I watched him carefully between my fingers and when he looked to be softening I stood up and called him ugly names and told him he was a mama's boy and worse until he stalked away, back rigid, a parting gesture of a raised middle finger such a surprise from my mild husband that I made the mistake of laughing. Thankfully he didn't hear me.

I lied because I knew the truth; that Harry would take care of the boy better than I ever could. And that if I made enough of my grief yet let him win, he would compensate me very well. This much I'd learned from listening to his sister before the wedding, talking of her own marriage and how her ex made certain she had enough money to keep her away from their children.

It had seemed terrible to me then, weak on Anne Marie's part, but during our own escalating battles the strategy seemed rational and obvious. I could not believe that Harry would so easily give in and settle a large monthly sum on me with the stipulation that I stay away from our child. His lawyers put it all in a trust, where I received a sum each month. The numbers awed me but I did not let these men, all men of course, all shaking their heads at the foolishness of a woman, a child really, who would deny their husband his rights and then create such a furor that the marriage dissolved, the woman lost her social standing and her child in one simple document.

After less than eighteen months I was cut loose from my life – a monthly stipend for sexual favors once received, a promise never to seek out my son, and the loss of the ranch and its freedoms. I had not been prepared to lose that much, but once set in motion, I could not stop Harry and his power.

Belinda E. Perry

Archibald Gillespie

TWENTY-ONE

It was his turn to have appointments for the freshmen in his classes. They rotated among the faculty, one week you had meetings, for three more weeks you were free, then the time came around and you accepted set hours to listen to terrible excuses and watch the young faces slide through pre-arranged emotions and lies. In fifteen years of teaching, the last five with tenure at the University, Archie knew he'd seen and heard everything. Now it was soldiers coming back from the so-called police action in Korea, using their soldiering to explain away what they hadn't done on their class work.

He was patient with these young men; it was their war, not his. He had come back to teaching from his own interruptive confrontation, as so many had done. They were hailed and rewarded while this group of young men, and some women, came back from nothing to little response. Still they were students now, not soldiers, and it was imperative they learn the difference.

His method of discipline on any laxity was to double the amount of work needing to be handed in, as a penalty and a learning experience. Very rarely did he get more than one visit from any particular student. The complaints were suggested but not spoken and Archie sighed when he read the letters to the Dean of Students and the two of them laughed. Archie was inevitably accused of being a small hitler, always without the upper case letter, an insult of immense proportions considering the students' recent history, and that of Archie and his peers.

The Dean, Archie's close friend Littleton Cross, took in these distressed young men and spoke gently to them; a reminder that they were here voluntarily and thus must meet the requirements of their classes seemed to smooth over their fury at Archie's pedagogy. He would then point a finger at them in class and call on them to explain a particularly difficult portion of whatever was being studied at the time. He could draw out of these young men more thought and perspective than they knew they owned; his way was to dig, almost insult, offer, question, cock his head and wait patiently for their humbled attempts.

On occasion he met with a brilliant mind untutored and ignorant; in these he delighted, a challenge to his methods of teaching, a wall through which he must push and prod until it crumbled before him and a new voice spoke from the expanded thoughts.

This time it was a young woman, or more perhaps she was not that young, in her mid twenties but it was difficult for Archie to estimate a woman's age. Most wore artifice as a second skin, which confounded any man's attempt at aging them, unless he dared open their mouth and judge teeth by the archaic equine method.

Archie suspected that the women so involved would not like his chosen image of them, yet this woman, of indeterminate age, paid no attention to his blank stare and his regulations and gave him her opinion. Unformed mostly, well-read but with little comprehension of what the words meant.

It began on the third day of English class for the incoming freshmen, and Archie challenged her for being in the class, saying 'Madam, I believe you need to check your schedule, and see the Bursar for another class more of your age and schooling.' She flashed back at him, not standing to deliver her comments, or asking his permission to speak but bullying her way through as his mouth opened to give out an assignment.

"Mr. Teacher, I belong here despite your judgment. First time I've been in a regular classroom since I was seven and my ma walked me to the school house almost two miles away."

He'd been given every variation on a story designed to garner his sympathy but this was an invention beyond belief. He raised his hand; "Miss, ah, madam, I do believe you are telling an enormous lie. You cannot have enrolled in college if you did not go to a high school, therefore your statement is undoubtedly false."

She would battle him in public, exposing her ignorance to her new classmates with total disregard to how they would perceive her. This Archie found exhilarating and was thus predisposed to allow the young woman her say.

"I took a test, several tests, and I kept pestering the head of this school until he allowed as I had the intelligence to at least try." Archie looked at her carefully, calculating how far he could take this battle of wills. She was an entrancing sight; among the stern male faces and the pretty blond co-eds she stood out; strong features topped by vivid eyes, a thick roll of dark red-blond hair haphazardly pinned up and already straggling loose, tendrils along her neck, one lock she kept pushing out of her eyes.

She knew exactly what he was thinking, and the manner in which her stare followed his bodily form let him know she was not a breathy, shy maiden but a woman of some experience. And this woman studied him with exactly the same arrogance he had used to sum up her physical perfections. She finally raised her hand; "Mr. Gillespie, sir, I need your class, I need to know what you're teaching. I can read, sure, and write and all that, and I'm good in my sums." Here he accepted her story about schooling, calling math 'sums' was archaic and outdated. He nodded to her, 'Yes, miss…ah?"

"You want the whole name or the shortened, current version?" Archie laughed, this was a bold adventure for him. The female students might flirt with him but there was no actual sexuality in their posing. This woman confronting him knew how to move and present herself; she was almost beautiful but not in the more traditional wife and mother role, or the young innocent; he had no reference for this woman except from the movies.

Her clothing was plain and quite expensive, belying her supposed background. A pale cream shirt of some soft fabric, and denim jeans of all things, molded to her figure from what he could see. A wide belt with garish buckle held the ensemble together, and when he chanced to look down, she wore cowboy boots. Cowboy boots, in his class, at this university.

THE END OF that one class was all she could take; the first two times she'd sat and said nothing, listened and most of the words made little or no sense. A list of books to read, a brief description of the papers they would write and Remi wrote furiously, every word, going home at night to read and reread until she absolutely knew she could not do the work. Today her restless nature stuck both of her boots in her own mouth. Confronting the teacher that way, and a man, an older and rather interesting man, not her type at all but still a specimen she'd not encountered before.

Tall, over six feet, and lean, what her pa'd call rangy, wide in the shoulders and skinny through the belly, a perfectly rounded behind of miniature proportions, made her wonder how even with a belt his britches stayed up.

She still thought in those words despite taking courses by mail and listening to records and watching lots of movies so she could talk city but her thoughts refused that direction and stayed with what she understood.

Learning to live differently was a bigger challenge; hell anyone could hear something said enough times to keep it in their mind but having no horse, no range land, no physical freedom at first was the worst punishment Remi could imagine. The money was useful but useless, feeding her body, keeping her clothed but not offering nothing of value or worth. She thought of buying a ranch, or a small place but it could not be near Harry and their ranch, where she'd mostly grown up. She couldn't ever go back to the cemetery where her pa and Sixto were buried, even that was denied her.

Her name on that piece of paper cut her out of everything she knew. The doctor in Clayton made a few suggestions when she went to him, having no one else to trust. Her world was truly the ranch, and vague memories of a small shack and a barn, nothing else and no references to any idea.

"Try a city my dear, a small one at first. Perhaps Phoenix would be a good change for you. It is small and warm, and there are art galleries and museums and yet you can still ride a horse out into the desert. Arabs are a big breed there and I'm sure your expertise with the animals will earn you many friends."

She had listened, done as she was told and moved to Phoenix where the horse people stuck their noses up and ignored her attempts, clumsy as they were. She rented a small house in Scottsdale and tried riding the Arab horses, so pretty with their huge eyes and flying tails but they went up and down instead of forward and she got frustrated with their insistence on checking out everything they passed, even if they'd gone that way only yesterday.

She dated a few times and quickly learned her lesson. She'd been married, told the men so, they usually knew she had money and it wasn't her they wanted but access to her body and her supposed wealth.

Living in Scottsdale was a mistake, but it gave her a sense that she could survive outside her old world.

The rest was mostly listings of places she'd moved to, tried out, didn't like. Even Texas, a small town near the Jefferson Davis Mountains, but that didn't work. Remi had nothing to do, no reason to get up each morning.

Horses weren't the thing now; it was big flaming cars with lots of chrome and Remi didn't want to raise those, or ride in them. Give her a truck anytime, more useful to carry something from one place to another; mostly Remi and her few belongings to a new town.

Which was how she ended up in Iowa, figuring the west knew all about her, maybe here in corn-fed towns no one would notice her odd behaviors or her unskilled language. She even found work in a feed store, where she listened and totaled up the farmer's bill and took in cash, her first real job although she'd been paid during the war as a working cowhand. No one thought much of those accomplishments in any city. Working again, getting a small paycheck, opened up her life to a few friends.

One old rancher, after she'd figured out a way he could save on his feeding out during the winter, told her she needed to go to college, get that brain buffed and polished with new learning and she'd make any rancher a dandy wife. And by gum he'd be the first in line. Remi did something she'd never done; she stepped around the counter and gave the old man a hug and he was gentleman enough to hold her briefly, then tuck his head and push her away. "Now there miss, you're too pretty to tempt an old walrus like me." They grinned at each other and Remi had herself a direction.

School proved to be baffling, each day trying to understand what the teacher, any teacher, was telling her. History class sort of made sense; it was facts and dates and the reasons why, and you could put them all together and write a paragraph or two – she was proud of being able to do just that – explaining and tying things together. History made sense to her; English classes were a garble of written words and spoken ideas that kept her silent and terrified.

Reading <u>Huckleberry Finn</u> was a waste of time; the man wrote in dialect even Remi knew was outdated and his treatment of colored folks was a shame. She said that in class one day and several of the young men turned to stare at her as she offered her opinion. "I grew up with Mexicans and you folks here seem to see them as black or something less than what they are. They's good and bad, and I don't like what this Mr. Twain does to the colored people he writes about."

The professor held up a hand when the room buzzed with peculiar gestures and uncomfortable commotion. "You have obviously touched a nerve, Miss – ah?" She turned on him; "What name do you want?

"There's enough that Remi will do." He nodded; "What disturbs you so about Mr. Twain's treatment, I assume it is about Jim?" She shook her head, more of that blond hair escaped. "No sir, it's like he's up there making jokes at everyone, poking their ribs and calling them all fools or worse, even when he writes about the boy. Like he's superior to the people he makes up, in a way felt..." Here she struggled, Archie could almost see the wheels turn and he was curious, held up a hand when a boy from the back row wanted to interrupt.

"Demeaning, that's the word. As I said, I worked with Mexes, hell I married one and he was a good man. Better'n the folks Mr. Twain describes."

There, she'd spoke up in class and other than a few giggles she hadn't died or been shot, yet.

He caught up with her after class; she was taller than he expected, her long legs making up for the slender torso and - well – the figure that was all too distinctly outlined by the lovely silk shirt she wore, for it was a true silk, not one of the newer more garish fabrics that were all the rage.

And those skirts the co-eds wore, felt with dogs and glitter on them. He took a second look at this woman standing near him and could not envision her in any type of felt skirt, poodle or diamonds or not. The jeans were her statement, and he was beginning to see the girls and boys swirl around them as they stood facing each other, and the crowd seemed dull, predictable, and far too uniform.

"Miss Remi!" She grinned and he couldn't believe the effect it had on him. "I looked up your name finally and can see why you make a contest each time of what I might choose to call you. Shall we settle on

Miss Remi? The rest seems rather mundane, especially your last legal name."

She put a hand on his arm, then removed it. "You spend a lot of time speaking a simple thing. Sembach's a hard name, I know. And it has some history in the west so I'm mostly against using it. Remi's enough, the 'miss' makes me nervous since I been married twice, which you obviously know from reading those records."

She threw her head back and a real laugh came out, not one of the more decorous titters that a young woman of proper upbringing was taught.

"Now you got me talking that way, too many words for too little to say. Professor, my name's Remi, what do I get stuck calling you? Professor in class, that much I know, but something tells me we're getting past class mighty quick." Archie struggled for some vain expression of common sense and order. But then he looked into her face, studying her clearly, seeing the fire and intelligence and the eagerness and he gave up right then.

"It's Archie to my friends and acquaintances." She touched him again, not a coy flicker but a hand gripped to his. "Which am I?" "I don't know yet, but I do think the time for being a mere acquaintance has already passed by." He bent down to her, utterly fascinated by whatever magic it was she held over him; her scent was different, no cloying blossoms, no sweet soap but more outdoor air, cool and crisp even in the fall heat.

NOW I'M TIRED, friends, and after a while courtship between man and woman takes on a certain sameness. Yes Archie was a gentleman, as unlike Sixto as possible and while Harry had the manners, he did not have the mind or the education despite what he thought. And, as it turned out, Archie had the sweetest dimpled behind I'd ever seen. Mind you I was not highly experienced despite being twice married. Having affairs after my divorce was a given to most people who knew my history but they were wrong. I was still a child in so many ways.

Here stands a huge lie, one fostered by drooling men and spiteful women; it's gone now, disintegrated by common sense and an overabundance of divorced women, but the thought at that time was a woman once bedded, then widowed, abandoned, divorced, became a raving sexual lunatic, had to have 'it'. Wild for sexual contact, couldn't live without sexual affairs.

I had one affair, with a cowboy, or more correctly a horse trainer in Iowa. He was sweet, younger, wonderful sprung hands and no, he wasn't bow-legged. Skinny butt though, and shy, as shy as I was. How we got together; a dance at the small town hall, food outside, a thick warm night, neither of us drank but we danced and found we moved together in a sweet rhythm. He was lovely, even his sweaty scent was familiar, the move and touch of a man who knew horses, but he couldn't talk, couldn't say much of anything that meant something. It was that one night, then I never saw him again.

And I was ashamed of what I'd done for far too long after he was gone.

Another one of those wishful lies; that my shyness, and that one night, was enough to keep me away from grasping hands and sexual innuendos. I was terribly hurt by my marriage with Harry, as it varied from absolute adoration to what now is considered rape and abuse. To lose both children; I won't lie here, I simply won't tell you what I felt then and how I feel now.

To bed a man out of lust was beyond my capabilities, yet the young men at this university stared at me and I could hear the whispers and laughter and it was all I could do to walk across the campus. That walk, to each of the two classrooms where I tried to learn, was far more painful and humiliating than anything else in my short life.

Now to the practicalities: Archie was almost twice my age, never married, a WWII Veteran who wouldn't speak of his war experience and after a while I understood why he would not answer my questions. Instead he gave me books to read, about war, its horrors, and let those authors relate what he could not.

And believe me Archie was rarely without the correct words. He tried that on me, correcting my speech and I finally told him he could talk any way he wanted, and I would expect the same courtesy in return. Otherwise, I told him, when his professor buddies came for drinks or a meal, and they sure did like my 'ranch' cooking, I'd correct their speech as well as his. Who was to tell one or the other which was the proper term for almost anything.

I did learn not to swear, that I understood, or to use some of the more graphic terms I'd grown up with for bodily functions. But I would not take one step beyond that compromise, and very quickly Archie learned to respect or at least abide by my position. I believe that happened after I corrected the dean of the agriculture when he spoke of the slow erosion of the small farmer and how we were about to receive a much better and more predictable supply of foodstuffs from the mega-farms. I landed down hard on that dean, asking him where he thought the lost livelihood and family ties of the small farmer would go, and what did he think all those huge tractors spilling oil onto our grain fields and the stench of the chemicals they were pouring out to destroy weeds, did he think...oh you get it, and please note, to my own credit, how far ahead I was of the then-current thinking. Rachel Carson hadn't published her book yet, but I talked with a man who'd been spraying DDT for a long time, and he said if mosquitoes landed on his bare arm and he tightened the muscles, they were stuck there, and eventually died from all the poison rotating through his system.

Yes I learned to talk, on and on even more with Archie who, for some bizarre reason, liked listening to me, he said my opinions were fresh and realistic without being bombastic. Now that's a mouthful, and some of it were a lie. What I know about Archie, and I won't bother you with, is how much he loved to simply watch me; my youth and those breasts I lugged around for years, well the combination fascinated him, which is why I ended up being married again.

Archie, for all his posturing and degrees and high-toned utterances was a man, with the cutest behind as I said, once I got him out of those high-waisted pleated pants all the rage at the time. God love them who ever thought such getup looked good on a man, hid the equipment that's for sure and I guess during the fifties and barely into the sixties, well men didn't want their masculinity defined in such a crude manner. Of course the younger male during the sixties went in for skintight jeans that cupped and exhibited, until studies came out that spoke of lower sperm count because the testicles were too warm.

Now if an observant young male watched a bull or a horse, even swine or dogs, they'd take note that the testicles ain't jammed into something warm and close but hanging out there, flapping in the breeze in some case; there's a lesson to most anything about animals that humans just don't want to listen to and see for themselves.

All this musing would indicate that after all our short time of civilizing ourselves, we're still animals. Archie loved that aspect of my discourses, and was particularly pleased with my diatribe against a college philosophy professor who spoke of the higher nature of man, and I told him that was pure bull. Archie laughed out loud, which didn't endear him to the professor but it was a good-natured laugh for Archie had little of the academic edge to him and was not trying to climb a rung. He was well regarded in his field, American literature especially of the 19th and 20th century.

Which is how I really got under his skin, for when he asked us to read a book, any book written by an American author, and write a four page essay on what made the book a particular choice, I managed to find a book he'd never read, had never heard of, and he could not bear being challenged in such a manner.

AFTER A WEEK of class, she was about to give up. Most of the students slouched in their chairs and raised their hands in a lazy motion as if to show how bored they were. The men had been to war, the women followed fashion and Remi was isolated from both camps. She learned to sit in the middle of the classroom, and not spring up waving her hand but raise it gently, not so high that she could feel the pull on her breasts. That was the ultimate embarrassment when the second time she raised her hand, she caught all the males staring at her chest.

They were given an assignment, an easy one he said, to begin their process from reading what they were assigned to making a choice and then defending that choice. Any book by an American writer, fiction or non-fiction, and about any subject. He laid down a few rules and as he did, the older males, obviously returning warriors, sniggered and poked at each other.

"No smut, no erotica, no pornography." Very simple, he said, if the book contains graphic sex then it is not appropriate for the current assignment. One brave soul raised his hand to question and Archie had the answer. "This is a mixed class as well as a freshman class. Let us give everyone a chance before presenting them with the cruder facts of life. Women are still respected in this classroom, and will remain respected while I am teaching you to think."

There wasn't much the returned heroes could say or do other than to nod in agreement.

"You will write a four-page essay briefly describing the book and why you chose it. What relevance you believe it has to the class so far. I would rather have three pages of concise writing than anything lengthier than the four pages I have assigned. There are to be no tricks, no double-spacing and writing large to create four pages from two. I want a clear and rational discussion. Class dismissed."

Remi had read most of the library at the ranch while she was pregnant that second time, and when she left, she had taken one of the dusty, unread books, hoping that no one would notice its absence. It was the only time in her life she took something didn't belong to her. It was a small book, printed at the beginning of the 20th century, written by an American, a real cowboy, so it fit into the outlines of acceptability.

Andy Adams' Log of a Cowboy. Second Edition, which she learned was different than the first edition and the third; a small book written by a real cowboy in his own particular way of speaking. It reminded her of that book the professor first assigned, Huckleberry Finn, even to the old-sounding language, but there wasn't nothing funny or meant-to-be amusing in the book.

Her writing was awkward and it took her a weekend to find what she was trying to say. But at the end she felt she'd said her piece, made her point, and thought to take the book with her when she went to class. For once the professor might not have the answer she'd found.

He returned the papers three day's later. On the top of her first page was the notation; 'see me after class' and no grade. He began class with a discussion of the wide variety of books chosen, and how much he'd enjoyed their defense of each choice. Remi held the musty copy of her choice fiercely in her left hand and raised her right hand. Slowly, allowing as much movement as possible in her upper body, she pushed away from her chair and stood. If she was going to be judged by her physical attributes, then they might as well work for her. Every male in the class turned to watch.

"Why didn't you grade my paper?" He stopped in mid-sentence, almost stopped so hard that one foot hung in the air momentarily. "You said to pick a book you'd read and make a case for its importance. I done just that and you wouldn't grade me. Why?" Remi found her hands were wet, the book slipped as she raised it, showed it to the class. "Here it is, all the foul talk and bad-mouthing the man wrote, and it was his words, not no editor from an east coast business. This is what Mr. Adams thought, and I wrote down why I read and recollected the book."

Her knees quit her then and she sat heavily, but at least she didn't fall, or stand there with her mouth gaping like the professor and half the class was doing. She would laugh but her face was frozen; she'd stood up and spoke her piece and it was a new feeling, a sense of power.

Then she waited. "Miss, ah, Mrs. Remi, I could not find the book in our library nor any mention of it as you described it in your paper. I wanted to speak with you to prevent any embarrassment, as it is obvious you misread the book itself." He tried, she gave him that, but she already had the answer. Harry had explained to her and she was armed and loaded.

She didn't try to stand again; "This here's the second edition. You never thought of that. First edition his editor took out all the bad stuff, talk about niggers and mexes and his dislike for 'most anyone wasn't like himself. Editor felt it was too rough, and when they did a second printing, well all the rough stuff got left in. Bet you anything if there's a third or fourth all that'll be gone again. Hypocritical, that's what this publishing is – Adams he wrote what he thought and no one wanted to hear anything but the romance of the West and not his peculiar truth."

She spent a good amount of time finding that one word, 'hypocritical' and making herself easy with speaking it, going around the small rented room saying it out loud until at first it sounded natural and then it began to take on the foolishness of any speech spoken too often, too long. Words took on their own life when you gave them to the air.

But she knew what the word meant, and taking out Adam's bitter references denied what intent he had in speaking them.

"Book's real all right, Mr. Professor, Andy Adams' <u>Log of a Cowboy</u>, a book no one who's not been a cowboy can understand. Told you in my paper, you got to trust the men you work with, your life and theirs depend on the bond between you. Adams didn't trust nothing but his own kind, the way he lived his life."

Her mouth got dry then and she would have choked but the professor, he was kind of cute in a grey-haired silver way, he looked at her and smiled and all of a sudden her attack seemed silly and out of place. "Remi." He sort of stuttered over her name and she was able to smile, knowing what went through his mind. Men and marriage and her age and how nice it was standing next to him.

His question was so obvious that she'd been ready for it since she came in the classroom that first day. "How do you know what a cowboy's life is like, what is your basis for this discussion and defense of Adam's remarks?"

Now that was a double question and she had to do some sorting through before her answer came up. He waited, so did the class, and it felt strong to have a room full of people waiting on what she had to say. It was full out and no holding back, yet she did not stand, guessing her knees would give out before her mouth got shut again.

"I worked as a cowboy starting when I was thirteen, on a ranch in eastern New Mexico and it wasn't just riding fence or counting cattle, I branded and castrated and roped and mended wire." She got the snigger she expected at the second word but talked right over it, glaring at the boys who'd made fools of themselves on a necessary operation.

She glared at the closest boy, his face already beet red. "You want a good hamburger or steak, you got to have a steer and by god someone's got to cut them prairie oyster off and I was the one sent to do that specific chore." That shut all the boys up, and put a smile on the professor's face.

"Andy Adams grew up in a different time and further south and he was taught to hate Mexicans. Me, I worked with them." She hesitated, wondered, said to hell with it in her mind. "I married a Mexican, name of Hippolito C de Baca Vargas and I loved him. Yet I've been shut out of places, even up in these so-called tolerant states because I carried a Mex name so I know about not being liked 'cause you're one thing when everyone else is something they think's better."

She quit, Adams hadn't said all that but it was what his words brought up in her and she could remember the ranch foreman's wife asking if she really wanted to marry Sixto, to marry, well, out of her own…class. It occurred to her then that Harry would have endured the opposite side of the same discussion from his sister, dear Annie Marie.

She was glad she hadn't tried to stand for her stomach lurched and rolled over and she almost raised her hand to leave the class room when the professor stood up from where he'd leaned against the desk to listen, and said that class was dismissed. She bolted through the barely opened door.

TWENTY-TWO

There was a note tacked to her section of the bulletin board, which each new boarder was carefully instructed to check each time they entered the house; 'Please meet Professor Gillespie at his office at 2 pm this afternoon. It is of the utmost importance.' Remi wanted to wad up the torn bit of paper and throw it down the toilet. And there was a letter addressed to her on the stairway to her second-floor room, the writing was unfamiliar and there was no return address but she could make out the faint imprint of a small town in eastern New Mexico.

A letter from Harry no doubt, taunting her with the years lost from her child, but the handwriting wasn't his so it would be a secretary sending a closely typed note. Listing the scheduled days of the boy and his father, asking perhaps a mild question about her own history so that someone, a school or a physician, had a required answer. As she entered the barren bedroom, she glanced at the clock and it was five minutes to her appointment time with the dreaded and interesting teacher.

She ran, holding the note, finding out as she climbed the stairs that she'd brought the envelope with her, wrinkled and folded, damp, stuck to her palm. Outside the closed door with that number on it, Rm 14, and his name on a peeling golden plate, Professor Archibald Gillespie, English Department.

When she raised her hand to knock, the smudged and rumpled envelope was stuck to her so she hesitated, then tore off one end and pulled out a single sheet, handwritten, brief. Attached to it was a clipping from a newspaper, dated two months ago.

"Harry Sembach of the Cross X Ranch and his son, Harry Jr., were killed at a local railroad crossing. The accident occurred at noon, and the police are investigating the circumstances." It went on, of course, listing family including his new wife and accomplishments, but the first sentence in its bare bones was imprinted inside Remi's mind.

She wasn't aware of any sound but the door opened and Archie Gillespie appeared, took her gently by the upper arm and drew her into the luxury of his office. She took notice of the thick rug, polished furniture much like Harry's collection in his office at the ranch. The professor settled her on a comfortable sofa; she knew this, could feel the soft material, the give and then hold of the padded cushions. The material was a rich dark red, burgundy she'd learned once, from Anne Marie, burgundy like the wine she'd said and Remi then had looked at her and the woman laughed, shook her head, said 'Of course you wouldn't know a Burgundy from a Riesling' and quickly went on to another subject before Remi could have her say.

He'd called the boy Harry after himself; that made sense. He wouldn't use her father's names or his own father who he detested according to Harry. A drunk. She'd thought they had settled on two names of grandfathers but she must have been mistaken. And then she had to leap through the words the professor seemed to speaking; had Harry continued the drinking that had brought out his violence toward her? He'd been drunk several times after that, it could be, it would be terrible.

"What has happened, Remi, why are you crying?" She wasn't aware of any tears but a hand brought to her face found them, a slow stream down both cheeks, filling the corners of her mouth and dripping onto her shirt. How odd that she hadn't noticed. It was there on the paper, the print smudged from being pressed and stamped and she wondered who had her address, how did they know where to find her; this wasn't from a lawyer or the physician, old Dr. Buffam.

"My child." The words were a shock; she had refused them all these years, forcing them to the very edge of consciousness and now they wouldn't leave her alone and if this man kneeling in front of her and staring would shut his lower jaw and close his eyes so they didn't hurt her so much she would even speak the child's name which she'd never done before, and then maybe she would say that her child was dead. Now she knew what to call that small wet flesh once lodge inside her, forcing itself out in great pain, to cry as hard as she cried now. Another Harry, no remnant of her at all, parented only by a man who'd wed since she left, maybe twice. A man who was with her boy when they both died.

It would be a small casket, not home-built like her family's boy's had been. Not hers, the son belonging to her father. How could he have buried his wife and his life and been forced to keep living.

She had been there, smeared with their blood, holding her mother's legs open to try and coax Thomas out, so they both could live. She had not been able to do this, not strong enough; her father's face, his digging that terrible black hole in the dirt to hide death from the living.

"My child." She held out the crumpled paper, the terrible clipping and found herself watching his face as he read, quickly, concisely for he then put the paper down and sat next to her and pulled her against him. One arm around her, to let her cry and this time she did, she cried as if she'd known the child and never left the father.

Then she became aware of a stranger next to her, holding her so gently as if she might fall apart and then what would he tell the English Department and the Dean about this wild young woman who dissolved from her own tears and what should he do with the mess and there was no immediate family to contact. Here, he would say, see. Her family, her child, is dead.

Instead he offered her a box of paper tissues and she blew her nose, wiped and needed more tissues to sop at her eyes, blow her nose again.

"I am so sorry, Remi. This is a terrible thing for you." She lifted her head, suddenly heavy and she was so tired of carrying it, but she had to look at this man and tell him the awful truth. "It's terrible for him, for them. I never knew my baby, I let his father take him and tell me I was unfit and now they're dead. Killed. By a train." She had flashes of memory; that tangled scatter of metal frame and shattered glass where her sister's young man had escaped and then taken her away.

That was what killed them, the train at the crossing. Evening sounds and smells in mid-day, a wild high call of the train, a faulty engine, a flat tire, caught in the rails, scared, hearing the rush of sound and holding your child, holding him close so he would remember his papa and nothing else when death hit them.

She stared into Archibald Gillespie's kind face and let herself fall against him. It was the only safety she would know.

I WOULD LIKE to stop here, rest again, perhaps not bother with the remainder of my life. All that is left is about Archie and me and our unconventional marriage, which got him removed from his post at the university and put him into a far better situation back East for a few years. When I could not stand the constriction, the weather, the gray faces and beige clothes, he kindly found a new situation in Colorado where I'd lived once, very briefly. And there we stayed until Archie died.

Here there is room for all kinds of lies but I'm tired of lying, or pretending to lie, there is no humor left in my story-telling, no teasing of the listener, no imaginative digressions to my opinions and point of view. Archie and I lived a good life, no children, for I would not risk that loss again and against all the conventions of the time, forced a decent physician into spaying me like we did with a few of the ranch mares, since they weren't worth the bother of their miserable heat cycles. I felt exactly like those mares, useless at motherhood and cranky because of the risk. Those two faces, looking up at me with blinded birth eyes, never to see what they became; I could not do that again. Archie was enough; he had a surprising vein of rich humor, he was kind in opening my mind to all sorts of thoughts and concepts, he was rarely demeaning about my lack of education, and used to brag to new friends about the vacant years between my one year of formal schooling as a child and my arguing and bullying my way into college. It was ordained, he would say, meant to be, the only reason I went to college.

I never returned to professional schooling after falling into his arms, and yes, indeed, underneath those loose trousers as I said earlier, there was a wonderful tight and very active behind that I would lay my head on and sigh, and feel him laugh up the length of his belly and chest to his face forced into the pillow. A sideways laugh of humor and lust, a deadly combination when you are in love.

During those years while he taught in different places, I found myself riding again. Never with the untutored abandonment of the ranch horses and that incredible freedom I possessed then as a trade for sanity and family. But I rode, in the East on those flat saddles. That first time I sat on one I had the terrible vision of Harry's flat saddle on the corral railings and my determination to use it despite being almost ready to give birth. The instructor walked up to me and asked if perhaps I would like a quieter horse and a private lesson before I joined the intermediate group that had just formed.

Belinda E. Perry

I almost laughed, then remembered my manners, and the years since I had last ridden, and said no, I was fine, just was dizzy for a moment, and the instructor promised he would watch out for me the next few times I rode. I thanked him for his concern, and asked the horse with a light heel and soft hands to walk off and we managed to get around the arena with no particular mishaps. It was a recovered joy, a heightened pleasure after the faculty teas and ladies' gatherings in which I was meant to partake with a pleasant smile.

Archie would tease me for he knew, and he appreciated the effort I did make, so the riding became my reward, my own pleasure in trade for all those hours with those women whose lives had no meaning for me, their prattle and their fears, their proscribed existence I could not and would not accept.

When he retired, we moved away from the Denver area to a small 200-acre parcel of our own land, the house built on a rise against the Front Range, the bulk of the land spread out before us for our scenery, our peace. And my horses. When Archie retired, he was seventy, and I was a vital, self-possessed and now privately-educated 51-year-old woman who had grown up with her own take on life. The horses pleased me, and terrified Archie. After a few minor injuries, that had me on crutches or my arm in a cast, I came home one day to find Archie pacing, his hands trembling, his face wet.

I was two hours late; I'd ridden a particularly nice gelding way up into the mountains and we were gone a long time. Archie's fear was right in front of me, his shaking and trembling, the effort it took for him to keep those sounds out of his voice as he carefully asked me where I'd been.

At the end of the year I'd sold all but one old mare who was a friend, no longer rideable so no longer any burden to Archie's worry.

Archie and I were married for almost forty years. Three days after our celebration, he held my hand, smiled at me and died. I was sixty-three years old, wealthy from Archie's careful policies and the steady income from Harry's estate; wealthy, and alone.

AN OLD WOMAN'S LIES

Do you want me to go on – I can't, all I can tell you now is how terrible those moments were right after Archie died, how I stayed beside his chilling flesh and held his hand, rested my face on his cold thigh and when the house turned bleak after sunset, I called the appropriate authorities and went out to feed the old mare.

SHE DROVE TO the ranch on a freshly-tarred road that allowed her car to reach speeds of over sixty. Miles of the land that was almost familiar; too many houses, extra roads, windmills that were torn apart, blades silent, stock tanks emptied, rusted. She had notice from Harry's attorney that the ranch was for sale, the main house, corrals, the small shed where she had grown up, all for $700,000 with a thousand acres of surrounding land. A deal, the real estate agent called it when she spoke with him.

She told no one of her odyssey. There were a few friends remaining from her marriage to Archie, a few ladies she rode with, or went to movies. The house where Archie had died was her home now, there was no intent to purchase the ranch, she had learned that lesson. Memories did not remain through money but through quiet times spent reliving what had happened, who had been loved.

It was wanting to see the land, to walk up to the small cemetery where so much of her young life was buried. A sign flashed as she began to slow down, a bent and faded sign of a brand once burned into weathered wood. The ranch sign, taken from the high gate over the actual entrance to be hung on a tilted post near the road. Ordinary and uninviting, not the welcoming sign she remembered.

Remi chided herself; nothing would be the same, absolutely nothing. Too many years had passed, a whole life living with Archie. Nothing would be as remembered. Still she thought she recognized certain landmarks, a particular ridge, one isolated windmill, a distant view, but the road signs said the ranch was to her right and that windmill was to the left.

The real estate broker was waiting, standing beside his dusted SUV, wearing a rancher's version of a sport coat and holding a Stetson hat. Her small car, with its years of use, obviously did not impress him for he barely remembered to step to her door and open it.

Remi climbed out, hardly breathing; it was the main house, altered some with a new arrangement of windows and what appeared to be vinyl siding with fake brick along the bottom. She gently refused his offer to enter the house for a looksee as he called it, warning her that the place was rundown but could be brought back to its former glory; "Owned by a movie actor in the thirties you know. He was famous for the parties they had here." And he proceeded to list a few names she remembered from her childhood, and she wanted to tell him she hadn't been impressed by those names at the time either.

She wanted to visit the ranch cemetery, she told him. He shook his head, "Ma'am, you passed it some miles back, a few broke stones, one tree that died down a few years back and got chopped for firewood. No more than three, maybe four stones you can read." She answered with a careful 'oh' and then asked if there any of the hands were left.

"One old man, said he grew up here." He took her down to the pens and the barn; her shed was gone, a new Morton metal barn stood square and solid over the entire area, and the pens were freshly designed. "Rancher had that Temple Grandin woman come out and help him redesign those pens, like she said in her book, make it less stressful on the cattle to be shipped and you lose less body weight. Didn't help him, though, the drop in cattle prices, and the rise in land cost, well he figured he'd sell out and retire."

The single remaining ranch hand wandered over to them and Remi didn't ask his name. He was Anglo and a drunk so she thanked him for showing her around, and walked away with the broker nattering at her. The air was the same, the distances interrupted by fence lines and a few cars, the windmills were mostly broken derricks unable to pump water. It wasn't home.

She did find the cemetery. And the fence was open near it so she felt no reserve in driving carefully across the slow ditch to park near the iron railings. Rusted, swayed where cattle had leaned in to grab a particular blade of grass, it was her place after all. The tree stump was her tree, the rise she had ridden to altered so by houses and roads that she had not seen it coming from the other direction. There were no remnants of all the times she had tied a horse to the single tree and sat on the soft hill. No desiccated remains of old manure, no gnawed tree bark; nothing.

But as she climbed over the fence, disdaining the chained gate, she knew the direction of his stone. It was there, slightly tilted, grass waving over the incised letters but his name and dates, those short years, were evident for anyone caring to look.

She didn't stay long, filled with memory but not saddened, and a strange thought began its growth; the need to find her remaining child.

I HAVEN'T LECTURED much in these last bouts of my story – I am tired, and I know that lectures and words make little impression on those who are waiting to experience life. They aren't going to listen so why should I and others who have survived a rich and awful life try to warn them. It doesn't work, we all think we are unusual, that we can escape these mistakes made by those coming before us.

There will be passages of time when it seems the universe, the world, the elements making up existence, are spiteful to us, that we are singled out for catastrophe and despair. Take heart, all who have felt this weighty burden; it isn't personal, and it isn't the forces of the universe spitting on you and your meager life. Death happens every minute, the dying dug into the ground will tell you. Pain, emotion, fear, savage warnings, dire illness, these are not punishment nor are they important – life is what happens and we all die. Don't take it to heart – don't think that the loss of three friends in a brief period of time is a statement as to your worthiness – you aren't that important except to yourself.

Let everyone grieve, let everyone suffer their woes, but remember through the process of crying that relieves you, soothes you, the world around you doesn't care.

Will anyone in the middle of such a whirling time listen to me and take heart and courage from my words – no, they will not.

Which is exactly why I have stopped talking to you, stopped trying to explain and expose. What I say is only what I perceive and feel, it has no bearing on your life since you will tell yourself you are different, you are special – didn't your mother tell you that, when you came home and put your head in her lap and cried for a slight at school, a friend's betrayal.

Belinda E. Perry

'You are special, so beautiful and full of talent.' We hear these words as a child and we refuse to abandon them, and are always disappointed as adults because somehow the rest of the world doesn't see within us that unique and special quality our mother assured us was there.

It's easy to be flip here, to shout that deafening modern command; "Get over it." To ignore that despite age and time and all external factors we are still that child needing to be stroked and loved and told a private truth that no one else owns.

I won't disgrace myself by saying 'we are all special', that's almost cheating, giving up after all the admonitions and lectures I have presented to you. The only thing we are is ourselves.

All this talking I've been doing, out loud to myself, hoping someone else is listening, all this yammering has no meaning or validity. It is my life, no one else's, I'm the one who lived with my pain, my sadness, my joys. Don't mean to keep pounding on the theory but I was here through an act between my parents, no predetermination, no set rules, only my thoughts and perceptions to keep me alive.

Now it's come to an end and I ain't sorry, ain't playing games or telling lies, gone back to speaking the way I was raised.

My son is here, I can see him if he comes in close enough, which he don't want to do. Don't blame him, not for the pain his distance causes me; I put him in someone else's arms, family yes but not his own mama. That is unforgivable unless it's understood. There are times when a mama can't raise her own, she does best to find those who can.

Wish I could explain to the child, an adult now but my child, like I still am in a small part of me where I am the baby daughter who bedeviled my folks. I am an old woman who no longer cares to lie.

AN OLD WOMAN'S LIES

SIXTO'S BOY

TWENTY-THREE

She walked up to me in the lobby of the hotel where we had agreed to meet an hour later, not at this early time. I had just finished breakfast and was contemplating other more organic matters when she shocked me by putting her hand on my arm, stopping me in my tracks. I had no immediate idea who this old woman was, but she smiled and patted and I could not move away from the touch. I am not a spiritual man, not a mystic or a believer but I knew who she was before she asked me the question. She asked in such a way that I could believe the answer already lay in her hand, her touch, her very presence directly in front of me.

I have wondered if in a crowd we would have found each other and I do believe we would have managed this connection. It is strong even now, despite her active dying and my absence all these years.

"Are you my son?" A pause and before I could answer she tormented me with our loss; "What is your name, what did they decide to call you?"

Of course I immediately knew who she was, no one else in the world would have cause to ask such a question. I was stunned; amazed that this frail-looking being was my actual physical parent. Her back was still erect, no breaking down of brittle bone; her physical life had done well by her in keeping her bones strong. But she was younger than I had imagined; my being fifty-six, I had projected her as being in her eighties. She was a young seventy-five, reddish-blond hair paled by gray strands that gave the color a varied glow. Her face was lined but the eyes were young and clear; at least I thought they were until I found out upon a more intimate conversation that her heart and her eyes were suspect, the doctors wanted her to have surgery and she had vehemently declined.

She told me that out of necessity she had given up her driving license. "I don't trust my judgment or reflexes." She cocked her head then and grinned at me and I knew why this old woman had come so close that very first time. She had to make certain that my image was the one she wanted to see. I am still amazed at the energy and independence

260

it took her to find the hotel lobby and then recognize me, for I had only given her the vaguest of description.

She answered my first question very quickly; "You walk like him, I knew it immediately. The swing to your walk, your arms and body. Even when he came back wounded and lamed, he carried himself proud." I noticed through our conversation that at times she appeared quite educated, then she would slip into an older vernacular. Even her accent changed accordingly. I was quite impressed, oddly enough; she had made the effort to find and appreciate an education. Because the ranch was so isolated, those few years were all the public education my mother had received. It bends the mind to consider either how supremely intelligent she was, or how stubborn. I can only imagine how she behaved when her mind was set on something.

She is my mother, in current terms my birth mother since I grew up within the confines and freedoms of a large family living in and around Roswell, New Mexico. I knew it wasn't truly my family through birth for all I had to do was look at my 'brothers and sisters' or any of my cousins. I had light hair, a few freckles, and green eyes that women tell me are unusual. The family I lived in was dark-haired and dark-eyed, uniform in their coloration and general description and yet each so unique. I was loved by them, much to my young surprise after I figured out the differences. I was wanted and nurtured and comforted within this family. And eventually they spoke the truth to me, although I fought and screamed against the revelation until my uncle Jose explained how sacred and precious his brother had been, how he had fought and died for his country and I was not to sully his memory by my miserable temper.

Then, for an unknown reason that eventually delighted me, Jose spoke of my mother. Sixto's first love from the day he met her when she was a child. He spoke of her father, and the terrible life they had struggled through before coming to the ranch.

And he told me of my father's death, quiet and peaceful, newly married to a child/woman, killed by his war and a horse; a proud death for a vaquero, the end of a life founded in bloody tradition.

I quieted then, and asked more questions until Jose laughed and put an arm across my shoulders. He told me I was a man now, at the tender age of twelve, and I must live up to my families' traditions and honor. I spoke my grandfather's name, and then my mother's name, ending with the familiar name of my father. Then I ran out to play with cousins who were truly mine, brothers and sisters who had the same name and were my relatives after all. The relief was enormous and then I forgot that I was different, not so different after all.

I settled into being an inquisitive boy, who knew instinctively that horses and a ranch had no place for me but I would keep my several names and remember the stories. I became enamored of Eben Hippolito Valentin C de Baca Vargas. These names bespeak my heritage and my existence and I am proud of them, although most of my friends call me Eben. I am also an eminently practical man and knew in the Anglo world Eben is a much more acceptable name. Eben Vargas is easier to say, write, explain, in the bigger world outside our small village so I stuck with those two more common denominators, pushing aside the Hippolito Valentin C de Baca – how could I explain such a sobriquet to my colleagues at college, yes I made it to college, or to any of the people with whom I worked.

It turned out I became a studious, quiet, reclusive teacher of English at the college level, finally settling in to a university in Colorado. My names were in a file somewhere deep in the bowels of the basement there, noted but unnoticed, unspoken for so many years. Even my wife had no idea of what vast distances lay between Eben and Vargas. She once, daringly, spoke the thought that I did not look like I belonged to the Vargas name. She herself was a young woman of some breeding from Philadelphia, almost a Katherine Hepburn caricature of the well-bred, blue-blood, main-line, seven sisters-educated blond female, who despite her provenance was a loving and very funny wife.

Of course she never met my true mother, the biological entity whose legs opened and whose body strained both to conceive and then deliver me to the odd life I would lead. Those moments were brief in her life; the conception a pleasure. If I know anything about my mother it is that she enjoyed the company of men. And they in turn enjoyed her. The birth I can only imagine, which is what all women say to all men; that we cannot envision under any circumstances what the pain of giving birth is like.

I can agree, yet I disagree. In my lifetime I published three novels, of some small reputation and minimal financial gain. One of them was about a young man gone to war, and the horrors he experienced. A critic raved about one particular battle scene, speaking first of its legitimacy in the writings of war, and then wondering out loud and in major print how a man who'd never even fired a rifle, or participated in hand-to-hand fighting, could understand the feelings, emotions, and cacophony of battle.

This is offered only in partial defense of the possibility that a man might understand the graphic and extreme pain of giving birth.

Of course I would never be the one to say anything more on the matter; my wife died in childbirth, along with our child. That is the sum experience I've had of marriage and attempting a family. It left me even more a recluse, and it was then that I went back to school and received a master's and a doctorate in my subject of interest, English romantic literature and its effect on the sensibilities of women.

Not a subject I ever discussed those few times I met with my mother. And later, when we'd settled her in a home near me, her mind had gone far enough away that the particulars I might entertain her with were of absolutely no interest. It was obvious upon our first encounter that she had led a physical life, despite a few years of college, which in itself surprised me as we talked.

Her second husband seemed to have allowed her substantial freedoms. There were no more children, at least none that she spoke of to me and I believe she would have told me of a living half-brother or sister somewhere in our peculiar conversations. She did mention giving birth to a child with Harry, her second husband, but the conversation then veered into her curiosity as to how I had made myself into a published author. Her reluctance to speak more of that child figured predominantly in Harry's death and I did not pursue any questions. The single fact of my minor writing career fascinated her; she wanted to tell me stories of her father, her early life, so that I might use them sometime in a book.

I actually knew her third husband, a man of some reputation in the world of English literature, but I never saw his wife, only knowing through campus gossip that he had married a woman not of his social standing and much younger. The gossip usually veered into sexual speculation which even not knowing it was about my mother usually had me walk away, leaving the spreader of trash-talk gossiping to thin air.

AN OLD WOMAN'S LIES

This intent on telling a published author how and what to write in his next book is common among people who are curious and do read but cannot ever imagine the effort of writing. Theirs is a quick, forward, non-contemplative life filled with doing, not sitting and thinking before writing a few words in which to create a story. They wish to tell a writer, any writer, what needs to be in the next book, what they consider interesting or fascinating, especially if it happened personally. Our own stories consistently engage us. And usually no one else except perhaps a younger generation in our families. My mother's stories were becoming lost in her head, mine had come to an end with the loss of wife and child.

I listen to these directors, nod in the right places, eventually set off in a different track, usually by asking a personal question that easily diverts the interrogator from my life to theirs, which is much more interesting to them. With my mother, she spoke in the beginning of a few matters, then the tellings drifted apart, becoming incomprehensible.

Unfortunately my mother fell into this category quite easily, and it helped me understand more about her. The few college courses she did take had opened her eyes and mind to wonderment, but didn't give her enough skill or energy to do more than dwell lightly on many aspects of her life. At least not in the brief times we have spoken; her words were all of a physical past, as if the potency of introspective thought had no bearing on her existence.

She has said two peculiar things to me over the months as I became her guardian and a reluctant participant in her descent. Sometimes she is dramatically alert and clear, and we can visit as two individuals having briefly shared a common thread, then continuing on our way. At other moments she speaks to people and places I have no knowledge of, beings that must float through her tired, diseased mind to destroy her few moments of clarity.

One afternoon we were seated outside; she was quiet, not at all restless, and unexpectedly she reached for my hand. Hers lay against my palm, upturned, the fingers ancient beyond her years, having never recovered from the hard work she had done as a young woman. There were scars and breaks, each one carrying a story however brief, but the moment to question her about each mark on her life had fled with the slow destruction inside her mind.

264

Belinda E. Perry

I had asked several doctors; the consensus of opinion, upon hearing the history of her life, was that the malnutrition of her childhood added to the physical stress on her body at far too young an age had limited her lifespan.

She was, in fact, dying from the very circumstances of her life. What she said to me was both a revelation, and a shock. About three months after we had settled into her living in a retirement home and with me playing the dutiful, albeit doubtful, son, she looked at me, steadily, right into my eyes but there was a shift in hers, a change I had not expected. She looked at me in this manner, resting her veined, crooked hand in mine, and told me that she had promised God she would come home soon.

My hand must have twitched or tightened for she pulled away from me, then smiled the slightest amount. I had never known her religious beliefs, I had never known her, and was now taking on the burden of her dying only because there was no one else. She spoke briefly, in the beginning, about two older sisters but they disappeared after their mother's death, and my mother barely remembered them, could describe their childhood together but had no married names, no destinations, so we did not pursue them. They had made a choice, now she, my mother, must depend on her son as an only living relative.

Please note, among this pathetic meandering description of a woman I did not know dying within my life; I cannot call her anything. I avoid specifically calling her anything for I cannot in good conscience call her Mom, that is absurd, and Mother is too formal for this half-wild ranch woman barely covered by the veneer of civilization. Some of the nurses have come to me stricken with the old woman's language and her spoken thoughts. I suspect this is why my mother is mostly quiet now; she recognizes her outrageous background does not fit within the beige-painted walls of a respectable nursing home.

This morning, before she took her nap, which often extended well into the afternoon, she sat up briefly, and once again we held hands, or rather her hand lay in mine, with little strength left to actually squeeze or hold. Her eyes were clear, which surprised me for it was obvious she was leaving, slowly and quietly without fuss but leaving.

From all that I gleaned about my mother and her extreme life, quiet and peaceful were not words normally I would use to describe her, yet that was the sensation she gave me. No tension in the brittle hand, or around the tired, almost unseeing eyes.

Her words again shocked me, then gave me an odd comfort; "I've finished the exam and handed it in to God."

MY MOTHER DIED today at seventy-seven years and two months. I was there quite by accident, and was holding her hand when she opened her eyes and smiled and spoke my father's name, Sixto. Then she smiled and actually gasped that small choking breath which I'd been told in all the fiction I've read is the last breath we take.

I was stunned, saddened, and unable to cry. Her skin felt no different, her hand was warm and sticking to mine, alive I thought, still living despite what I had seen and heard. Until I went to release myself from this obligation, this unwanted access to something I did not know or want to know. The flesh had cooled in those few moments and simply dropped away from clinging to my warm palm. The curve was stilled, those long absurdly bony fingers like a hawk's talons or so I supposed. I could not bear the sight; their empty fold was too clearly a sign. She is dead; my mother has died.

She died in the new century and I dwell on this because I do not choose to dwell on her dying. We had barely begun to know each other, and I live in those blank years of loss, knowing now it is important to remember who she was.

As of yet, I have not been able to forgive her.

Made in the USA
Charleston, SC
18 April 2013